Praise for *Strong Cold Dead*

"A terrific book! The good, the bad, and the ugly woven into a tale that leaves the reader breathless. Great fun!"
—Sandra Brown,
New York Times bestselling author of *Friction*

"Jon Land has once again crafted a winner, with a seamless blending of historical fact and pulse-pounding fiction that will leave the reader begging for more."
—Brad Taylor,
New York Times bestselling author of
Ghosts of War

"Land has surpassed himself. Not only is the plot riveting and spellbinding, but the writing, dialogue, and character development are certain to rank Land among a handful of our most talented thriller authors of this decade." —*The Strand Magazine*

"Land is a master of action scenes. . . . Caitlin is the quintessential action hero, both ruthless and unstoppable while at the same time realistic and sympathetic. Thrillers don't get better than this."
—*Booklist* (starred review)

"Whether kicking bad-guy butt or giving a commencement address, Caitlin gets the job done efficiently and with great aplomb." —*Publishers Weekly*

"With every turn of the page, the moral epicenter grows until it, like the convergence of the story lines, erupts like a volcano in a way that leaves you fist pumping the air as you turn the last page." —*Suspense Magazine*

"Another rollicking Jon Land adventure that reads like a cross between a Randolph Scott Western, a Stephen King horror story, and a Jason Bourne movie script . . . Land pulls the disparate strings of the fast-moving, action-packed yarn together in a way that is both surprising and entertaining." —Associated Press

"Superb and sensational . . . *Strong Cold Dead* opens at the speed of a machine-gun burst and never stops hitting the bulls-eye, a high-octane thriller par excellence that places this series among the very best being penned today." —*Bestsellersworld*

"Taut, tense, suspenseful, compulsively readable, action-packed and a real page-turner in the Jon Land tradition of such fast-paced yarn . . . Land's prose has never been better: it's richer, more colorful, more descriptive. . . . He gets better with every book, and this latest in the saga of Caitlin Strong is the best yet."
—*The Providence Journal*

"Like a pack of literary TNT with a long fuse that has been lit by Jon Land. The suspense is ramped up chapter by chapter to an almost unbearable level until it finally explodes in the last act." —Bookreporter

OTHER BOOKS BY JON LAND

*Published by Tom Doherty Associates

STRONG COLD DEAD

·

A CAITLIN STRONG NOVEL

Jon Land

A TOM DOHERTY ASSOCIATES BOOK · NEW YORK

STRONG COLD DEAD

Copyright © 2016 by Jon Land

A Forge Book
Published by Tom Doherty Associates
175 Fifth Avenue
New York, NY 10010

www.tor-forge.com

Forge® is a registered trademark of Macmillan Publishing Group, LLC.

ISBN 978-0-7653-7029-7

Our books may be purchased in bulk for promotional, educational, or business use. Please contact your local bookseller or the Macmillan Corporate and Premium Sales Department at 1-800-221-7945, extension 5442, or by e-mail at MacmillanSpecialMarkets@macmillan.com.

First Edition: October 2016
First Mass Market Edition: October 2017

Printed in the United States of America

0 9 8 7 6 5 4 3 2 1

For Bob Gleason
Editor, friend, and the smartest man I know

ACKNOWLEDGMENTS

Before we start, it's time to give some much deserved shout-outs to those who make it possible for me to do what I do, as well as do it better.

Stop me if you've heard this before, but let's start at the top with my publisher, Tom Doherty, and Forge's associate publisher Linda Quinton, dear friends who publish books "the way they should be published," to quote my late agent, the legendary Toni Mendez. The great Bob Gleason (see the dedication page), Karen Lovell, Elayne Becker, Phyllis Azar, Patty Garcia, Ryan Meese, my copyeditor Jessica Manzo, and especially Natalia Aponte are there for me at every turn. Natalia's a brilliant editor and friend who never ceases to amaze me with her sensitivity and genius. Editing may be a lost art, but not here thanks to both Natalia and Bob Gleason, and I think you'll enjoy all of my books, including this one, much more as a result.

My friend Mike Blakely, a terrific writer and musician, taught me Texas first-hand and helped me think like a native of that great state. And Larry Thompson, a terrific writer in his own right, has joined the team as well to make sure I do justice to his home state along now with his son-in-law, a state trooper who would make a great Texas Ranger himself, who suggested the Balcones Canyonlands as the setting for my fictional Indian reservation in these pages. And I'd be remiss if I didn't thank Jack Briggs, the real "Steeldust Jack," for letting me borrow his nickname.

Check back at www.jonlandbooks.com for updates or to drop me a line, and please follow me on Twitter @jondland. I'd be remiss if I didn't thank all of you who've already written, Tweeted, or e-mailed me your thoughts on any or all of the first seven tales in the Caitlin Strong series. And if this happens to be your first visit to the world of Caitlin, welcome and get ready for a wild ride that begins as soon as you turn the page.

P.S. For those interested in more information about the history of the Texas Rangers, I recommend *The Texas Rangers* and *Time of the Rangers,* a pair of superb books by Mike Cox, also published by Forge.

No one really knows why they are alive
until they know what they'd die for.

—MARTIN LUTHER KING, JR.

PROLOGUE

The framers of [the Ordinance Establishing a Provisional Government] clearly envisioned the Rangers as an irregular force, distinct from traditional military units or volunteer citizen soldiers. The corps would consist of three or more companies of fifty-six men each, rangers serving one-year enlistments. Rangers would furnish their own horse and tack, weapons, and powder and shot for one hundred rounds. Each company would be headed by a captain, backed up by a first and second lieutenant. The captains reported to a major. The major answered to the commander in chief of the regular army.

—Mike Cox, *The Texas Rangers: Wearing the
Cinco Peso 1821–1900*
(New York: Forge, 2008)

I

"What 'xactly you make of this, Ranger?"

Texas Ranger Steeldust Jack Strong looked up from the body he was crouched alongside of—or what was left of it. "Well, he's dead all right."

The male victim's suit coat had been shredded, much of the skin beneath it hanging off the bone. He'd worn his holster low on his hip, gunfighter style, and his pearl-handled Samuel Walker Colt was the latest model, updated from the one Jack Strong had used since joining the Texas Rangers after the Civil War.

Steeldust Jack checked what was left of the man's shirt for a darker patch where a badge, removed after he'd been killed, would have blocked out the sun, but he found none. So this was no Texas lawman, for sure, but a gunman of some sort all the same, who'd managed to get himself torn apart just outside a stretch of land set aside for the Comanche Indian reservation a half day's ride out of Austin.

Steeldust Jack rose awkwardly on his gimpy leg until he was eye to eye with Abner Denbow, the county sheriff who'd sent a rider to the state capital to bring back a Texas Ranger from the company headquartered there.

"Fought plenty of Indians myself over the years,"

Denbow told him. "I believe that makes me the wrong man to venture onto that land the government gave them for no good call I could see."

"It was Sam Houston who gave this patch to the Comanche originally," Steeldust Jack reminded.

"Yeah, well even the great ones make mistakes, I suppose."

The recently signed Medicine Lodge Treaty had deeded this parcel to the Comanche, dividing them from their brethren who were settled, along with the Apache, in southwestern Indian territory, between the Washita and Red rivers. A treaty was supposed to mean peace. With the exception of the peaceful sect that had settled on this reservation, though, the Comanche, Cheyenne, and Kiowa continued to make war, conducting raids on civilians and cavalry officers alike. It was that fact, along with the general lawlessness along Texas's increasingly populous frontier, that had led to the Rangers being officially reconstituted just a few months before.

For the first time in the state's history, Texas had a permanent Ranger force. But the ruin of his leg by Civil War shrapnel kept Steeldust Jack from joining up with the Frontier Battalion for which his gunslinging skills made him a better fit. Instead, he was assigned to one of the newly chartered Ranger companies responsible for patrolling various parts of the state to keep the law. And today keeping the law meant figuring out what the body of a well-dressed gunman was doing within spitting distance of an Indian reservation.

"Any indication there of who he might be?" Denbow asked Steeldust Jack.

"I can't find a wallet on him, Sheriff. But the boots this man's wearing are practically new, and the wear on his trousers tells me they're pretty much new too. Given there ain't much left of his face, I don't suspect anybody'll be recognizing the man anytime soon."

Denbow took off his hat and scratched at his scalp, which was marred by scaly, reddened skin. "Looks like the work of a bear to me. That was my first thought."

"You ever seen a bear kill, Sheriff?"

"No, sir, I have not."

"People normally run and the bear gets them from behind. So that's where you find the initial wounds. Only this man's got no wounds at all on his back. He also doesn't have any wounds on his hands and arms consistent with trying to ward the animal off."

"You're the Ranger who made a name for himself in the war," Denbow said suddenly, his cheeks looking plump and rosy in the harsh, hot light of the afternoon. I recognize you from the limp."

Steeldust Jack looked at him, without changing expression. "You know how I made that name for myself?"

"Not exactly."

"I came home."

Which was true enough in Jack Strong's mind. He'd proudly served the Confederacy as an infantry officer with the Texas Brigade, under General John Bell Hood. The brigade distinguished itself during the Seven Days Battles, where it routed Northern forces at Gaines's Mill, captured a battery of guns, and repulsed a cavalry counterattack. Its status was further strengthened when it spearheaded a devastating assault at the battle of Second Manassas, overrunning two Union regiments and capturing a battery of guns.

The Texas Brigade's reputation for fighting was sealed at the Battle of Sharpsburg, when it closed a gap in the Confederate line and drove back the two attacking Union corps. Of the 854 that went into battle at Sharpsburg, 550 members of the Texas Brigade were killed or wounded. Being one of the survivors allowed Steeldust Jack to fight in the Battle of Gettysburg.

"You took Devil's Den with a bullet still lodged in your leg," Denbow said.

"Lots of men took Devil's Den, and lots more died in the process. But there weren't enough of us left to take Little Round Top, and you know the rest. Anyway, unlike most that day, I made it home."

The bullet was gone now, but too much shrapnel remained in his leg to risk removal. The field docs had wanted to take his whole leg instead of bothering, but Steeldust Jack was hearing none of that. He'd earned that nickname for shooting so fast and reloading so quick that it seemed a cloud of steel dust from the bullet residue hung in the air over him. The nickname had stuck and had accompanied him back to Texas, where still having both legs allowed him to ride and fish with his boy, William Ray, who'd recently followed his father into the service of the Texas Rangers.

All the same, the wound's lingering effects made it hard to stand too long on his gangly legs. Any quick step stretched a grimace across his expression, tightening the sinewy band of muscles stitched across his arms, chest, and shoulders.

"So it wasn't a bear," Denbow was saying, eyes back on the well-dressed stranger's body.

"It wasn't a bear."

"Then what was it?"

Steeldust Jack turned his gaze in the direction of the Comanche reservation. "Think I'll see if somebody there can tell me."

Denbow scratched at his scalp again, deepening the red patches, which looked like spilled paint. "You might want to reconsider those intentions."

"Why's that?"

"I've heard stories, that's all."

"Stories?"

"About the Comanche living on this here reservation. A strange lot, for sure, gone back to living the old ways, since way back before they ever even saw a white man. I heard some of them been alive at least that long, that they got some deal with their gods that lets 'em live forever."

"Stories," Steeldust Jack repeated.

"They never leave the reservation, Ranger. Live off whatever they can fish or farm, and make do with the rest of whatever's around them. At night, when the wind's right, you can hear 'em performing all these rituals about God knows what."

"Anything else?"

"They're a dangerous lot for sure, that's all."

Steeldust Jack didn't look convinced. He lumbered all the way back upright, grimacing until he was standing straight again.

"Tell you what's dangerous, Sheriff," he said, his gaze tilted low toward the body of the unidentified man. "Whatever did this. 'Cause I got a feeling it's not finished yet."

2

NUNAVUT, CANADA; NOVEMBER 1930

Joe Labelle was dying, the freezing cold having pushed itself through his clothes and skin to numb him right to the bone. He could feel the blood slogging through his veins, turning his movements sluggish to the point that the thick snow waylaid him more with each step. All that kept him going was the certainty that an Inuit village lay ahead amid the ice mist that made him feel as if he were walking through air choked with glass fragments. Seemed much thicker than fog, and trying to breathe hurt all the way down to his lungs. Every time he came close to giving up, though, the image of one of his boys appeared before him, urging Labelle on. Their mother being lost to tuberculosis proved more than enough motivation to make him push through the numbness and avoid the temptation to stop awhile to find his breath.

I just need to rest for a few minutes. Then I'll be fine.

Winter's harshness had come early this year to Canada's Lake Anjikuni region. It would've been reasonably tolerable if the sun shined more than six hours per day, so that Labelle didn't have to keep trekking through snow mounds as high as his waist in the darkness. But he had visited this area before and he knew it to contain a bustling village perched on the lake, where gentle currents dappled the shoreline. Formed of tents, primitive huts, and ramshackle shanty structures visible under the bright spray of the full moon, sure to be inhabited by friendly locals proud of the fact that theirs was one of the few outposts in the great frontier. Labelle felt a tremor of hope pulse through him, his heart pounding anew, his skin suddenly resilient against the frigid, prickly air.

The hope faded as quickly as it came.

Labelle could see those ramshackle structures silhouetted under the full moon, but he saw no people about, nor barking sled dogs, nor any other signs of life. Labelle also noted with a chill that not a single chimney had smoke coming out of it. Then he spied a fire crackling in the narrowing distance, evidence of some life, anyway.

Labelle, his heart hammering so hard against his rib cage that his chest actually hurt, picked up his pace and headed toward the glowing embers of the dying fire in the distance, eager to find some trace of humanity. The ice crystals lacing the air felt like flecks of sand scratching at his mouth and throat, dissipating the closer the trapper drew to the flames. He was greeted there not by a friendly face but by a charred stew that had bafflingly been left to blacken above the embers.

Labelle had spent his life negotiating shadowy and inaccessible lands, no stranger to the dark legends of lore in places that could steal a man's mind. Right then and there, he wondered if this whole thing was some illusion, a twisted dream or mirage built out of snow instead of sand. What else could account for a village being abandoned in such a manner?

Maybe I'm dead, he thought as he walked past derelict, wave-battered kayaks, into the heart of the ghost village. Either he was lying in the snow somewhere back a ways, imagining all this, or the village had . . . had . . .

Had *what*?

Labelle methodically pulled back the caribou-skin flaps and checked all of the shacks, hoping to find telltale signs of a mass exodus, but much to his chagrin he discovered that all of the huts were stocked with the kinds of foodstuff and weapons that never would have been abandoned by their owners. In one shelter he found a pot of stewed caribou that had grown moldy, and a child's half-mended sealskin coat, discarded on a bunk with a bone needle still embedded in it, as if someone had deserted their effort midstitch.

He even inspected the fish storehouse and noticed that its supplies had not been depleted. Nowhere were there any signs of a struggle or pandemonium, and Labelle knew all too well that deserting a perfectly habitable community, without rifles, food, or parkas, would be utterly unthinkable, no matter what circumstances might have forced the tribe to spontaneously flee.

Labelle scanned the borders of the village, hoping to ascertain in which direction the Inuit might've gone. Even though the villagers' exit seemed to have been relatively recent, and hasty enough to leave food on the flames, he could find no trace of a single snowshoe or boot track marking their flight, no matter how hard he searched under the spill of the bright moon.

But then the wind shifted and his nose caught a scent

that froze him to the bone, even through the chill he was already feeling. A smoky, carrion stench that reminded him of coming upon the body of a trapper who'd frozen to death in winter and whose body didn't begin to thaw until spring.

Labelle followed a narrow, choppy path through the thick snow, into an overgrowth of brush and dead trees entombed in white. He saw smoke wafting up from what looked like some sort of natural depression in the ground. The smoke rose straight out of that shallow slice of ground, rooted in smoldering clumps that the fire hadn't finished with yet.

Smoldering clumps . . .

Labelle got no farther. His legs gave out and he sank into a bank of snow thick enough to reach his neck. He wasn't sure he'd ever move again, wasn't sure he wanted to, until he heard a shuffling sound coming from the thickest part of the grove. Labelle knew the sound of feet crunching over hardpack when he heard it, though the wind and crackling flames disguised just how many sets were coming.

Labelle didn't wait to find out. He pulled himself through the drifts, finally reclaiming his feet and dragging himself along.

The trapper quickly lost track of how long or how far he walked from there. He knew only that, as he made the trek, he was the whole time fearful of looking back to see what might have been coming in his wake.

He stumbled upon a remote outpost not long after dawn, sure to be rewarded for his persistence with food, warmth, and shelter.

"What are you exactly?" a ranger greeted him after

responding to Labelle's pounding on the door. He ran his eyes up and down the trapper's ice-encrusted clothes and hair, then his face which was sheathed in a thin layer of it as well. "Please say a man."

"I am that," Labelle said, exhausted and picking at the ice frozen to his beard. "But what's coming might not be."

"What's *coming*?" the ranger repeated, gazing over Labelle's shoulder. "What say we get you warmed up inside?"

Labelle followed the ranger through the door, the blast of warm air hitting him like a surge from a steam oven. He could feel the ice crystals attached to his skin, hair, and beard turning to water, the flow from his clothes leaving thin puddles in his wake as he made his way to the fire.

The trapper's gaze fixed on a telegraph machine as he peeled off his gloves. "Does that work?"

"Why?"

"Because we must get off a message to the Mounties," Labelle said through still-frozen lips.

"Sure thing, soon as we get you warmed up with blankets, and fed right."

"No!" Labelle barked, grasping the ranger's forearm so hard it seemed the cold bled into him as well. "*Now!* Before it's too late!"

The ranger yanked his hand away, stumbling backwards in the process. "Too late for what?"

Labelle peered through the closest window. The morning sun had melted away enough of the ice crust for him to see the path down which he'd come. "For us. Before whatever's coming gets here."

PART ONE

The depredations of your enemies the W. [Waco]
and T. [Tawakonis] Indians and their hostile prepa-
rations, has driven us to the necessity of taking up
arms in self-defense . . . .The frontier is menaced—
The whole colony is threatened—under these circumstances it became my duty to call the militia to
the frontier to repel the threatened attacks and to
teach our enemies to fear and respect us.

—Stephen Austin, 1826, in Mike Cox,
The Texas Rangers

I

East San Antonio, Texas

"Nobody goes beyond this point, ma'am," the tall, burly San Antonio policeman, outfitted in full riot gear, told Caitlin Strong.

"That includes Texas Rangers . . ." She hesitated long enough to read the nameplate over his badge. "Officer Salazar?"

"That's *Sergeant* Salazar, Ranger. And the answer is yes, it includes everyone. *Especially* Texas Rangers."

"Well, Sergeant, maybe we wouldn't need to be here if a couple of your patrolmen hadn't gunned down a ten-year-old boy."

Salazar looked at Caitlin, scowling as he backed away from her Explorer. A few blocks beyond the checkpoint, a grayish mist seemed to hover in the air, residue of the tear gas she expected would be unleashed again soon. That is, unless the youthful crowd currently packed into the small commercial district at the near end of Hackberry Avenue dispersed, which they were showing no signs of doing. The third night of trouble had brought the National Guard to the scene, in full battle attire that included M4 rifles and flak jackets. Caitlin could see that more floodlights had been set up to keep the street bathed in daylight brightness. They cast a strange hue that reminded her of movie kliegs, as if this were a scene concocted from fiction rather than one that had arisen out of random tragedy.

Sergeant Salazar came right up to her open window, close enough for Caitlin to smell spearmint on his breath as he worked a wad of gum from one side of his mouth to the other.

"Those patrolmen found themselves in the crossfire of a gunfight between a neighborhood watch leader and gangbangers he thought were robbing a convenience store where most pay with their EBT cards. The clerk who chased them down the street just wanted to return the change they'd left on the counter for their ice cream, but the watch leader, Alfonzo Martinez, saw the scene otherwise and ordered the bangers to stop and put their hands in the air."

Neighborhood watch leader Martinez, a lifelong resident of J Street, who'd managed to steer clear of violence all his life, started firing his heirloom Springfield 1911 model .45 as soon as the gangbangers yanked pistols from the waistbands of their droopy trousers. The only thing his shots hit was a passing San Antonio Police car. The uniformed officers inside mistook the fire as coming from the gangbangers, and the officers opened up on them so indiscriminately that the lone victim of their fire was a ten-year-old boy who'd emerged from the same convenience store.

It was almost dawn before everything got sorted out and the investigative team, comprising San Antonio police and highway patrol detectives, thought they'd managed to get control of the situation. Then, relatively peaceful protests by day gave way to an eruption of violence at night, spearheaded by rival gangs who abandoned their turf wars to join forces against an enemy both of them loathed. Violence and looting reigned, only to get worse by the second night, when eight officers ended up hospitalized—one injured by what was later identified as a bullet rather than a rock. And now, the third night found the National Guard on the scene in force, along with armored police vehicles from as far away as Houston, barricading the streets to basically shut the neighborhoods of east San Antonio's northern periphery off from the rest of the city.

"You're still here, Ranger," Sergeant Salazar noted.

"Just considering my options."

"Only option you have is to turn your vehicle around and leave the area, ma'am. You're not needed or welcome here."

"On whose orders, exactly?" Caitlin wondered aloud.

"Mine," a female voice boomed, a moment before Caitlin heard a loud pop, like a shotgun blast, crackle through the air.

2

EAST SAN ANTONIO, TEXAS

A few blocks beyond the checkpoint, one of the spotlights fizzled and died, more likely the victim of a well-thrown rock than a bullet. Caitlin was out of her Explorer by then, hand instinctively straying to her holstered SIG Sauer P-226 in anticipation of more shots to follow.

"Get back in your vehicle, Ranger," said Consuelo Alonzo, deputy chief of the San Antonio Police Department, as she strode forward, red-faced from the exertion of rushing to the scene from the police line upon learning of Caitlin's arrival.

"You got a problem with getting some more backup?" Caitlin asked her.

"I do when it comes from you."

"Why don't you catch your breath and hear me out?"

"Because there's nothing you have to say that can possibly interest me right now. In case you haven't noticed, we're sitting on a powder keg, one spark away from blowing San Antonio to hell. We don't need you providing that spark, Ranger. No way."

Instead of settling down, Alonzo's agitation continued to increase. Her face had grown redder, her words emerging through breaths that were becoming more and more rapid. She had risen quickly through the ranks of the department, the youngest woman ever to make captain, three years prior to her recent promotion to deputy chief. And she had been rumored to be in line for the job of public safety commissioner, which came with a plush Austin office and would make her, among other things, chief overseer of the Texas Rangers. Alonzo had no doubt relished that particular perk of a job certain to be hers—until the death of a Chinese diplomat, exacerbated by Caitlin's solving of the murder while Alonzo was dealing with more politically oriented ramifications, led to her being passed over.

Alonzo had overcome an appearance that was often referred to as "masculine," even by her supporters, and much worse than that by her detractors, who seemed to put no stock in the fact that she was happily raising three young children with her husband, who was a professional boxing referee. This was Texas, after all, where a woman needed to work twice as hard, and be twice as good, in a profession ruggedly and stubbornly perceived to be for men only. Caitlin and Alonzo had had their differences over the years but had mostly maintained a mutual respect defined by their professionalism and the sense that their own squabbles only further emboldened those who sought their demise.

At least until Alonzo assigned Caitlin all the blame for Alonzo losing out on a job that was likely never going to be hers now. Since then, Alonzo had used her position as deputy chief to wage subtle war on the Rangers' San Antonio-based Company F whenever possible, seizing upon any bureaucratic conflict or jurisdictional dispute she could in a hapless attempt to make Caitlin's life miserable.

Alonzo ran a hand through her spiky hair. She was heavyset and had once set the women's record for the bench press in her weight class. She'd also done some boxing and was reputed to be the best target shooter with a pistol in the entire department. But Caitlin had beaten her three times running when they'd gone up against each other in state-sponsored contests, winning the overall title in two of those, instead of just the women's division. Caitlin had stopped entering after her most recent victory, figuring the last thing she needed was to draw more attention to herself than her exploits already had.

"You're not moving, Ranger," Alonzo told her.

Caitlin gestured toward a figure pressed tightly against the waist-high concrete barrier erected to close off the street to unauthorized vehicles. "See that woman there? That's the mother of the boy who was killed by the fire of those SAPD officers. She's the one who called me, asked me to see what I could do about the violence being done in her boy's name. She doesn't want the city to burn on his account. She wants this resolved peacefully."

"And you think I don't?"

"No, ma'am. It's a question about how you're going about things."

"And how's that?" Alonso asked, not sounding as if she was really interested in Caitlin's answer. "We got a full-scale riot brewing back there. What exactly do you think you can do about it that we can't?"

"I've got an idea or two."

"Care to share them?"

"Ever hear of Diego Ramon Alcantara?"

"Can't say that I have."

"He goes by the nickname Diablo. Leader of a gang running drugs for a Mexican cartel that sees the riots as their opportunity to solidify their hold on the business throughout the state. And Diablo Alcantara has united the city's normally warring gangs toward that purpose, on the cartel's behalf. I take him off the board, all this goes away."

Alonzo shook her head, her expression a mix of resentment and disbelief. "You alone?"

"That's right. Just give me a chance. What have you got to lose, Deputy Chief?"

"How about this city?"

Caitlin turned her gaze in the direction of the rioting. "Seems to me it's already lost. Thing at this point is to get it back."

Alonzo's lower lip crawled over her upper one, her cheeks puckering, until she blew out some breath that hit Caitlin like a blast from a just-opened oven. "We've got five hundred personnel on scene who haven't been able to manage that."

"Would it really hurt to listen to what I've got to say?"

"It hurts me, standing here right now instead of commanding the front line. The governor just approved an assault. We move inside the next hour, if the crowd doesn't disperse as ordered."

"Just give me a chance."

Alonzo shook her head again. "You know the saying 'stone cold dead,' Ranger?"

"I do."

"Maybe you haven't heard that among Texas law enforcement types it's called '*strong* cold dead' now."

Caitlin smiled slightly. "Is that a fact?"

Alonzo was left shaking her head. "Tell me, when you look in the mirror, how big's the army that looks back?"

"Well, you know how the saying goes, Deputy Chief," Caitlin said, backpedaling toward her SUV. "'One riot, one Ranger.'"

3

Caitlin skulked about the outskirts of the neighborhoods just outside the riot zone. Through windows not boarded up or covered in grates, she spied more than one family following the simmering violence just a few blocks away on their televisions while they huddled against a wall.

According to the information she'd obtained from a trio of informants, Diablo Alcantara was running the show from his sister's home, near J Street, two blocks from the brewing riot's front lines. The cartels had trained Alcantara well, had taught him the tricks of their own trade, to inspire everyday people to turn to violence to the point that it came to define them. By the time a person found himself on this road, he was too far down it to turn back. So here, in east San Antonio, closing the schools for the day had turned hundreds of teenagers into virtual anarchists, looting and destroying for its own sake. Right now, Caitlin could still smell the smoke from a Laundromat that had burned to the ground after local firefighters and their trucks had been chased back by crowds hurling bottles and rocks. Three firefighters had been hospitalized, and one of the engines had been abandoned at the head of the street, where it too had been set ablaze.

The chemicals and detergents stored in a back room of the Laundromat had turned the air noxious for a time, the strange combination of lavender soap powder mixing with the corrosive bleaches to form the perfect metaphor for the city of San Antonio. Watching those white curtains of mist wafting through the flames to chase the rioters away—more effective than any efforts the authorities had mounted—had given Caitlin the idea to which Deputy Chief Alonzo had refused to listen.

Holding her position against a house, in view of the main drag, Caitlin checked her watch, then the sky, and finally her cell phone, to make sure she had a strong signal. Because word was the gangs were communicating via text message, there had been talk of shutting down the grid, but nobody could figure out a way to do it quickly—something Caitlin was glad for now.

Above the fire smoke and tear gas residue staining the air in patches, the night sky was clear, and she made out a collection of news choppers, their navigation lights flashing like the stars millions of miles beyond them. Creeping closer to J Street and the home of Diablo Alcantara's sister, Caitlin froze. She was just beyond the spray of a streetlight, which showcased a block packed with gang members proudly and openly displaying their colors.

Amid the gangbangers unified in this unholy alliance was a stocky figure, more bulk than muscle, holding court near the rear. Diablo Alcantara had gotten into a knife fight while in high school and had ended up losing an eye to a slice that split the left side of his face right down the middle. Even in pictures, it was hard for Caitlin to look at the jagged scar, and the translucent orb visible through the narrow slit Alcantara had for an eye socket, without feeling a flutter in her stomach.

Caitlin knew that the stocky figure was Alcantara the moment he turned enough toward the streetlight for its spray to reflect off the marble-like thing wedged into his skull in place of an eye. She counted fifty bangers in the vicinity, armed with assault rifles and submachine guns no intelligence report had made mention of, meaning such firepower must have only just reached the scene, courtesy of the cartels.

The bangers, under Diablo Alcantara's leadership, looked ready to launch the assault that would push the rioting from this neighborhood into the city proper. They were intent on turning San Antonio into Juarez. Caitlin's plan hadn't accounted for going up against heavy weaponry, but the reality made the plan's implementation all the more necessary. Giving the matter no further consideration, she lifted the cell phone closer and pressed out three words in a text message: *Come on in.*

Caitlin figured she had three, maybe four minutes to wait. She spent the first of them following the gang members' antics in preparation for what was to come. Some of them wore military-grade flak jackets, in odd counterpoint to the pungent scent of marijuana smoke gradually claiming the air. She watched beer bottles drained and smashed, a few stray shots fired into the air to the cheering of the most chemically altered in the bunch.

Caitlin checked her watch one last time before she stepped out from the darkness and into the street, light glinting off her badge, holstered pistol in plain view as she continued toward the center of the block.

"I'm a Texas Ranger," she called out to the gang members, whose gazes fixed on her in disbelief. "All of you, stay right where you are."

4

East San Antonio, Texas

Caitlin stopped thirty feet from Diablo Alcantara and swept her gaze across the other fifty or so gang members, who were armed to fight a small war.

"Diego Alcantara?" she called, breaking the silence that had settled over the block.

"Who wants to know?" Alcantara asked, emboldened by having a veritable army to back him up.

"Texas Rangers, sir. You're under arrest."

The silence returned, until it was broken anew by laughter. Just a ripple at first but quickly spreading, some of the gang members literally doubling over, slapping their knees, their assault weapons all but forgotten.

Alcantara joined in, clapping. Closer up, Caitlin saw he had a bullet-shaped head to go with the horribly scarred face, which seemed to come to a point at the top, where his black hair was bunched together with dried gel. Caitlin thought she could actually smell the oily pomade from this far away, the aroma not unlike the Brylcreem her grandfather Earl Strong had used every day until his last.

Alcantara's eyes, both the good one and the bad,

were set too far back in his head, as if some cosmic force had realigned the sockets while he was still in the womb. Caitlin watched the good one narrow.

"Hey, you're that famous bitch Ranger," Alcantara said in recognition. "The one put a whole bunch of men in the ground."

Caitlin's mental clock continued to click down. The gang members started to encircle her, still giggling and chortling, seeing no threat whatsoever in her presence. The dueling aromas of weed smoke and stale sweat intensified as they drew closer.

Alcantara approached through the crowd, his misshapen features tightening and one eye narrowed, like a dog trying to figure out what it was seeing.

"You're a bitch with balls, I'll give you that, and now you're gonna have to—" He stopped midthought, puzzlement sprouting on his features. "Hey, anybody else hear that?"

The gang members exchanged glances, shaking their heads uniformly, providing no relief for Alcantara, who swept his eyes about the night sky.

"What the fuck, man. What the fuck . . ."

The faint buzzing Caitlin too had detected on the air had now grown to a whine, and finally a screech. Only then did the gang members swing around from both Caitlin and Alcantara to look farther east, toward the sky. Still unable to see anything, because the crop duster was flying without any lights. It was, for all practical purposes, invisible, until it opened its dual tanks to send the first wave of a thick, white, paste-like cloud dropping toward the ground.

By the time Alcantara had swung back toward Caitlin, she'd pulled a plaid kerchief soaked in her dad's old cologne up over her nose and mouth. And two, maybe three seconds later, the dense white cloud unleashed by the crop duster settled over the area like a blanket, spreading straight down the street toward riot central, at the head of the neighborhood's commercial center.

Of course, it wasn't called crop dusting anymore, Caitlin knew. The new term was "aerial application," and the plane that had just soared overhead, not more than fifty feet off the ground, cost more than a million dollars and was outfitted with an advanced turbine engine and sophisticated GPS system to allow for just this kind of flight. The pilot was a former Texas Ranger who'd taken up the practice to supplement his pension. He also had come up with an especially noxious formula that mixed corn starch and soap powder with a scent most closely resembling skunk oil. He'd used a version of it to repel a riot of his own, back in the day, and was more than happy to come out of retirement to return favors done for him by both Earl and Jim Strong, Caitlin's grandfather and father.

"Hell," he'd told her, "they saved my life more times than I care to remember. Just tell me where and when, Ranger."

He didn't own a cell phone, so Caitlin had provided him with one, to ensure he could receive her signal via text message.

Caitlin made her way through the vapor, which was thicker than any fog, brush fire, or West Texas dust storm she'd ever seen, dodging bodies, to Diablo Alcantara's last position. The gang members were desperately fleeing the street all around her, grunting and gasping, some doubled over with nausea from the stench. Those sounds drowned out the last of the crop duster soaring overhead, the fading drone of its turbine engine matching the cadence of its arrival on the scene.

She reached Alcantara just as he managed to unsling the assault rifle shouldered behind him. Caitlin clocked him on the side of the skull with the butt of her SIG Sauer and watched his grasp go limp as his knees buckled. She caught his dazed form halfway to the roadbed and dragged him from the street with one arm, the whole time keeping her SIG ready in her free hand.

The soupy, stink-riddled mist had dissipated enough for a few of the gang members to clear their watering eyes and follow the trail Caitlin blazed toward the thick congestion of houses and yards. She shot two, and then a third, in rapid succession, all shots aimed low, for the legs, since incapacitating the bangers was as good as killing them, under the circumstances. More followed those three, and then still more, until Caitlin felt she'd entered some crazed video game, she was clacking off so many shots.

Everything was going just fine until a police helicopter sweeping overhead blazed its spotlight down over the scene. The beam pierced what was left of the thick, soupy vapor and exposed her for all to see. A dozen bangers, maybe, left to give chase. More bullets needed than she had left in the magazine, Caitlin thought, as they struggled against their own retching to sweep their weapons around.

The police chopper was hovering directly over them,

its spot as big as an oversize truck tire, carving a cone-shaped ribbon of light into the night. Caitlin aimed her SIG up toward it, instead, and clacked off three shots. A *poof* sounded, as the big bulb exploded and a shower of glass rained down onto the remaining gang members, slowing them up enough for Caitlin to continue dragging Diablo Alcantara into the dark cover of a yard adjoining a pair of multifamily houses.

Her back slammed into the frame of an aboveground swimming pool sturdy enough to steal her breath, just as Alcantara regained enough of his senses to try to wrench himself free of her grasp and then to launch an elbow backwards. It struck Caitlin in her left cheek, rattling her jaw and smacking her teeth against each other.

Alcantara managed to tear free, but instead of running, he launched himself at her, so enraged that his one functioning eye looked ready to bulge out of his head. Caitlin tried to bring her gun back around, only to have him knock it from her grasp. She tried to snatch it out of the air, then heard a plop as it smacked the pool water, which looked like a pocket of refined oil shining in the night.

Alcantara came at her again, and Caitlin realized he'd never gone anywhere at all—he was latched to her by a watchband that had become ensnared in her denim shirt. The shirt was soaked with perspiration and dappled with vapor spots that dragged the rancid stench with them. Alcantara fired a jab-like blow, which she managed to deflect. But his next strike landed in the side of her neck.

Caitlin shrugged off the stinging pain just in time

to duck under the next blow and shoulder him hard into the aboveground pool. Her intention was to spill Alcantara over into the water, but the impact buckled the framing and, instead, unleashed a torrent of water from a tear she'd cut in the liner. Its force separated and pushed both of them backwards, Caitlin feinting one way and then launching a palm strike from the blind spot created by the marble-sized fake eye wedged into his eye socket, straight into his nose.

Bellowing in pain and blowing out a torrent of blood from his nose to match the water still cascading around him, Alcantara barreled in toward her, his one working eye as big as an eight ball. Caitlin let him get close—close enough that he practically rammed that big eye straight into the thumb she plunged forward and twisted.

Caitlin had never heard a scream as deep and as shrill as Alcantara's. She grabbed hold of both his shoulders when he sank to his knees, and began dragging him toward the side street parallel to J Street, where the bangers had gathered. The fight had stripped her cologne-soaked bandanna free. The stench and bite of the old Ranger's skunk-stench concoction pushed tears from her eyes.

Caitlin could barely see when she reached the side street. Sirens were screaming everywhere, and bright lights poured through the haze that had settled before her vision.

"Stop right there!" an SAPD uniformed officer screamed at her, pistol trembling in his hand instead of steadying on her. "Stop, or I'll shoot you dead!"

5

"I'm sure you understand my position, Mr. Masters," Julia De Cantis, head of the Village School, said, from behind a desk that seemed much too large for her.

"I don't think I do, ma'am," Cort Wesley told her, fidgeting anxiously in the easy chair. The color of its leather had apparently been selected to match the wood tones of both the desk and the impressive array of bookshelves, which looked ready to swallow the room.

"Call me Julia, please. Everyone does, even the students."

"I still don't understand your position, Julia."

De Cantis started to lean forward, then stopped suddenly, as if hit by a force field separating Cort Wesley's space from hers. Outside, the early morning sun seemed to twinkle off the dew-rich grass of the school's spacious twenty-eight-acre grounds. There was no one about yet, except a few of the boarding students out jogging. Fortunately, Cort Wesley's son Luke wasn't among them; he had no idea of his father's presence here, and would have forbidden it if he had known.

"While it is customary for rising junior students to select their own roommates, the issue of your son boarding with Zachary Russo presents the school with several issues."

"Keep talking, Julia," Cort Wesley prodded, after De Cantis had stopped, as if that were the end of things.

"Well," she started, stopping again just as fast. She was the one doing the fidgeting now.

The discomfort didn't seem to suit her. It was like a set of clothes that didn't fit right, Cort Wesley figured. Julia De Cantis had a sheen to her, a kind of persona that she slapped on for meetings with board members, alumni, fund-raisers—and parents too, to some extent. She appeared to him to be cut from a more natural cloth, stitched in the classroom, absent of political or financial pressures. The freedom to mold young minds was what she'd signed up for. In the natural order of things, Cort Wesley guessed, she'd likely become a victim of her own success and popularity in that venue, fueling her rise to the administrative level.

"Rule seems plain and simple to me," Cort Wesley said matter-of-factly.

"There is nothing either plain or simple about the relationship between these two boys."

"The relationship, as you call it, is over, ma'am. They're just friends now," Cort Wesley corrected, even though he wasn't so sure himself.

Nearly a year before, Luke had come out about himself, and then about his relationship with Zach.

Came out.

How Cort Wesley despised that term, though he supposed there was no easy way to classify the experience of learning that his youngest son was gay. That revelation had been sprung on him at the same time that he had learned an equally difficult truth about his own father, who, it turned out, wasn't nearly the bastard Cort Wesley had figured him for. Not even close. More a hero, during his final days, in fact.

Realizing he'd had both his dad and his youngest son all wrong filled him with a new respect for the truth. Now he welcomed it, in spite of the anxiety and tension it had wrought initially. Hell, he was about Luke's age when he started boosting major appliances with Boone Masters.

"All the same," Julia De Cantis was saying, "we are dealing with precedent here, more than appearances."

"So what you're saying is that a boy and a girl can't room together for obvious reasons."

"Of course."

"And my son can't room with his best friend for what you'd label equally obvious reasons."

"I didn't say that."

"But it's what you meant," Cort Wesley said, leaning forward closer to her desk. "And it implies, from your way of thinking, that Luke can't room with any other male student. So tell me, ma'am, what if he wanted to room with a girl?"

De Cantis drummed her fingers against the uncovered wood of her desk and then tightened her fingers so stiffly her knuckles cracked. "Mr. Masters—"

"I've got a confession to make, Julia," Cort Wesley said, instead of letting her continue. "I didn't take this news so well myself, and it took me some time to come around. So I've been looking for an opportunity to prove myself to my son, to show him my support isn't just window dressing. So the fact that rooming with Zach is very important to him makes it even more important to me. You hearing me on this?"

"I believe a single room would be in his, and the school's, best interests."

"I guess you're not hearing me, then. You know about Luke's mother, I suppose."

De Cantis nodded slowly, the compassion returning to her expression. "Yes, and I'm sorry."

"But not so sorry that you have a mind to do right by a boy who deserves at least that much. He loves your school. It's the best in the state, and you should be proud of your work."

"So should your son. He's been a stellar student, a credit to the Village School in all ways. He's unquestionably earned all the boarding privileges we can afford him."

De Cantis stopped, collecting her thoughts. Outside the window, Cort Wesley could see a trio of riding mowers working at trimming the grass, which was moistened by the morning dew and by underground sprinklers that he now recalled had been on when he'd driven on campus.

"Zachary Russo's academic record, on the other hand," De Cantis continued, "requires no such privilege be extended."

"That's the way you want to play this?"

"Excuse me, Mr. Masters?"

"Drawing this line in the sand. Fine strategy. But in my experience people aren't prepared to deal with what happens when somebody crosses it."

"Is that a threat?"

"Just a statement. And I could just as soon ask you the same question when you brought up Zach's—what'd you call it, 'academic record'?"

The engines of the three riding mowers grew louder as they drew closer to the window. De Cantis paused so she wouldn't have to talk over the roar. The blades churned up stray acorns and discarded twigs, grinding them with a crunching sound that made Cort Wesley think of trying to chew ground glass.

"You have quite a reputation yourself, Mr. Masters," the head of the Village School said, after the sound had abated.

"Thank you, ma'am."

"I didn't mean it as a compliment."

"That's the way I took it, all the same."

De Cantis leaned forward over her desk, hands clasped before her and elbows resting on the desk wood. "You worked for the biggest crime family in the South. You did time in prison. Before that, you were a decorated war hero. Now you work unofficially for the Texas Rangers."

"Just one Texas Ranger, ma'am," Cort Wesley corrected.

De Cantis started to nod, then stopped. "That would be Caitlin Strong. Maybe we can find a solution to this, after all."

"I'm listening, Julia," Cort Wesley said, over the sound of the riding mowers retracing their path over the grounds.

"This situation with your son is a difficult sell to the board, but one I believe I could make, if the circumstances were right."

"And how do we make them right?"

"I'm glad you asked, Mr. Masters," she said, stopping again to let the engine sounds pass. "Since you're well acquainted with Caitlin Strong—"

Cort Wesley felt his phone vibrate with an incoming

call and eased the phone from his pocket. "You mind excusing me while I check this?"

De Cantis looked a bit perturbed, but she nodded anyway.

Cort Wesley recognized the number as a Brown University exchange. "It's my oldest son's college calling, Julia. Would you mind if I . . ."

"Please, Mr. Masters."

The caller identified himself as being from the registrar's office, said he just needed to confirm some details on the paperwork recently filed by Dylan.

"Wait a minute," Cort Wesley said, interrupting him a moment later, "say that again."

6

SAN ANTONIO, TEXAS

"You made one hell of a mess for yourself this time, Ranger," Captain D. W. Tepper told Caitlin, after the San Antonio police were finally done with her that morning.

"Seems to me the mess was already made, and the way the powers that be intended to clean it up would've only made things worse."

"Seemed to you."

"That's what I said."

"The problem is nobody appointed you judge in the matter, and now they're calling for your head."

"You going to give it to them?" Caitlin asked, standing before Tepper's desk, in a shady corner on the second floor of Texas Ranger Company F headquarters in San Antonio.

"It's out of my hands, Caitlin. This is too big a pile of shit to sweep under the rug. You might have thought you saved the day, when what you really did was embarrass a whole lot of folks seated behind big fancy desks, who couldn't save their own ass from a hemorrhoid."

"I tried to explain it to Consuelo Alonzo, Captain. But she was too busy getting even with me to listen. What was I supposed to do?"

"How about nothing, like Alonzo ordered?"

"And what shape might the city be in right now if I'd done that?"

"I don't believe those folks behind those big desks care about the *might,* only the *is.* And right now they're trying to cover their collective asses, along with the truth."

Tepper was old enough to have partnered with both Caitlin's legendary grandfather and her father, stitching multiple generations of Texas Rangers together. Unlike many, he had proven adept at both relinquishing the old ways and methods and adapting to the new. He wore his experience on his gaunt face. Caitlin imagined there was a story behind each of the deep furrows lining his cheeks and brow. His thin gray hair looked glued to his scalp, dry patches evident amid all the sheen. He had youthful eyes that belied the smoking habit that had left him with sallow coloring and stained fingernails. Caitlin's efforts to force him to cut back on his smoking had also cut back on the wet, hacking cough that one doctor said made Tepper a poster child for emphysema.

"What truth would that be, exactly?" she asked him.

"Let's see, where would you like me to start?" Tepper said, tapping a Marlboro Red from its box but stopping short of lifting it out. "How about sticking your nose in somebody else's jurisdiction? How about taking on the entire gang population of San Antonio, with a riot brewing a few blocks away? How about shooting at a police helicopter?"

"I was shooting at the spotlight."

"Last time I checked, the two were connected. There's also trespassing, damage to civilian property, and arresting a suspect without a warrant."

"I had probable cause on Diablo Alcantara."

"That probable cause entitle you to shoot four other men while dragging him off?"

"All in the leg. I thought you'd be happy."

"Sure, jumping for joy," Tepper said, forgetting he already had a cigarette out, launching it airborne when he tapped the pack again.

Caitlin crushed the cigarette with her boot before he could retrieve it from the floor, and he set about tapping out a fresh one in its place.

"As I was saying . . ." Tepper continued.

"As you were saying . . ."

"Hell, I don't even remember what I was saying, you get me so ramshackled."

"You were jumping for joy."

"Oh, yeah. Turns out you nicked an artery in the leg of one of those gang members. They got him to the hospital just before he would've bled out. Somebody had tried to stitch the wound with a sewing needle."

"And that's my fault?"

"Was it your bullet? Anyway, forget that. We got bigger fish to fry. Feds are thinking about charging you with use of a weapon of mass destruction."

"Are you serious?"

"Ranger, you poisoned a whole section of the city with whatever spewed out of that crop duster."

"I dropped a stink bomb."

"That's your defense?"

"How about the fact that it worked? Locals and Feds who spent the rest of the night interrogating me have reclaimed the neighborhood. You know what's going on here as well as I do, D.W."

Tepper continued to simmer, doing his best not to seem to see her point. "Oh yeah? What's that?"

"I got it done when they couldn't. And since when is skunk oil a weapon of mass destruction?"

"Since you dropped it on the city of San Antonio, Ranger."

"I tried to play ball here, Captain. Took my intentions to Deputy Chief Alonzo, who practically spit in my face."

"Speaking of which, you've looked better."

Caitlin touched the bruises on her face, left by her fight with Diablo Alcantara, and tried to move the jaw he'd cracked with an elbow. Paramedics were pretty certain it wasn't broken, but she was supposed to go for precautionary X-rays just to make sure. Her hands, too, were badly scuffed and bruised, knuckles swollen like those of the ex-boxer her father, Jim Strong, had busted, as peacefully as he could, when the retired fighter was having what he called one of his "episodes."

"Good thing SAPD let me take a shower and change clothes," Caitlin told him. "Otherwise, you wouldn't be able to stand the smell of me, never mind the sight, thanks to that weapon of mass destruction."

Tepper shook his head, easing into his mouth the second cigarette he'd tapped out. "You mean stink bomb?"

"Camouflaged the scene, to boot."

"I'm sure you had the whole thing thought out."

"As much as I could, under the circumstances."

Tepper held up a cigarette lighter that looked more like a soda can, jerry-rigged with a computer lock to the top of his desk. He watched Caitlin shaking her head as he lit up.

"What, you need me to explain why I gotta keep a lighter so heavy it gave me tendonitis chained to my desk? Do you really?"

Caitlin settled back in her chair. "You want to kill yourself, D.W., that's your business."

"Then why do you keep stealing my cigarette lighters? You know what's worse for my health than Marlboros? You. You and this Lone Ranger role you've fallen into. Problem being that every time your trusty horse, Silver, leaves shit in the streets, it tracks right back here."

"No pun intended."

"Huh?"

"Never mind."

Tepper nodded, puffing away and making sure Caitlin could see the smoke. "That's what I told the chief of police and the commissioner for public safety: Never mind. Never mind that Caitlin Strong had a crop duster buzz east San Antonio, contaminated a quarter of the city, and shot up a street. Never mind all that. She's old school. One riot, one Ranger, just like she told Deputy Chief Alonzo. Right or wrong?"

"Wrong. Because there was no riot. That's why I did what I did."

"What you always do, Ranger," Tepper said, with the cigarette holding to the side of his mouth. "Last night took Hurricane Caitlin to a whole new level. Forget hurricane, you're a full-fledged tsunami now. They don't name tsunamis, do they?"

"Guess there aren't enough of them."

"Lucky me, having one all to myself, then. You know that desk downstairs I refinished a couple weekends back?"

"The one where the varnish never quite dried?"

Tepper frowned. "It's all yours, Ranger. Catch up on your paperwork until we get the mess you caused last night sorted out."

"I don't have any paperwork to catch up on."

"Then catch up on mine—fitting, given that most of it is about you. Department of Public Safety wanted your head on a platter this time, but they ended up settling for your ass in a chair."

"How nice of them."

"Don't worry. You can keep your gun. Just in case the office gets attacked by somebody likely gunning for you anyway."

"Should I keep another weapon of mass destruction at the ready, too?"

"Long as it doesn't stink up the place."

Downstairs, Caitlin was still staring at the empty desk, which was chipped and sticky with undried varnish and set in a darkened corner of the first floor, when her cell phone rang. She leaned against the desk chair, listening to it squeak, as she answered the call.

"Hello."

"Caitlin Strong?" a muffled male voice greeted her.

"Who is this?"

"Just thought you'd want to know a friend of yours is about to get himself in some trouble."

"And who might that be?"

"Oldest son of Cort Wesley Masters. Named Dylan, I believe. I'd hurry if I were you."

7

BOERNE, TEXAS

"New game," Guillermo Paz said into the microphone, from the table set atop a small portable stage at the front of the dining room in Morningstar Ministries at Menger Springs Senior Living Community.

At seven feet tall, Paz hardly needed to be standing on even a meager platform. But the placement was easier on the fading eyesight of the elderly residents, who sat with varying numbers of bingo cards assembled before them, patiently waiting for him to call each number.

After all, Paz reasoned, they weren't going anywhere except back to their rooms in the assisted living portion of the facility. The priest he'd been visiting at San Antonio's historic San Fernando Cathedral for more than seven years was now living in the nursing center section, after suffering a stroke. Paz had been the one who found him, the man's body canted outside the confessional, blood dribbling out one of his ears and staining his white hair red on that side. Paz had wanted to pray for him while he waited for the paramedics to arrive, but he wasn't much for prayer. He figured God's tolerance for his murderous actions hardly entitled him to heavenly favors. Although Paz had long ago lost track of the number of people he'd killed, the Almighty certainly hadn't.

"First number," Paz said into the microphone. "Under the *B*, seven. That's *B* seven. *B* for *Boylston*. That's the name of my priest. He lives in this place now but isn't in shape to play bingo. Want to hear something? I didn't even know his name until I came to visit him here for the first time. The receptionist asked who I came here to see and all I could tell her was, 'My priest.' She nodded and said, 'You must mean Father Boylston.' And that's how I learned his name."

The residents of Menger Springs's Boerne campus continued to look up at him, seeming to hang on Paz's every word, eagerly awaiting his call of the next number, bingo dabbers held like guns. Visiting his priest almost every day had left Paz with a fondness for the entire facility, for its peace and pleasantness, in spite of the stale fart smell in the hallways and the general hopelessness that characterized the nursing center section. He thought Father Boylston would be proud of him for volunteering, playing a role, making a difference. Each number he called was a small homage to the priest who'd helped him define his ongoing transformational period.

"See, a man is more than the measure of his name," Paz continued. "Aristotle is Father Boylston's favorite philosopher. Personally, I prefer the Germans, but since my priest cottons to Aristotle, I'll tell you that Aristotle believed the body and soul were prime parts of what creates our nature, that a man's identity belongs to a holy trinity of the mind, body, and spirit. The first time I visited Father Boylston I told him the first man I killed had murdered my first priest, back home in the slums of Venezuela, for daring to stand up to the gangs. He bled to death in my arms, the food he'd bought to feed the poor scattered in the street. I watched the life fade from his eyes and knew what I had to do. And I've been doing it ever since."

Paz churned the wire cage holding the numbered bingo balls, then grasped the one that had found its way to the top.

"Under the G, fifty-four. That's G fifty-four. G for *goodness,* something I look for in my eyes every day. I came here all those years ago to kill a woman, a Texas Ranger. But when I looked in her eyes I saw something I didn't recognize. I didn't know what it was, only that I wanted to see it in my eyes too. All of you have lived a long time and done a lot of things, both good and bad. But how many of you ever thought that life could change in a single moment, a single glance? I mean, isn't that something?"

Most of the elderly bingo players looked at Paz blankly, but a decent number, women mostly, were nodding up a storm.

"Ever since that moment, I've wanted nothing more than to see the same thing in my eyes. Was it bravery? Determination? Conviction? Belief? Only recently did I realize it was goodness, *G* for *goodness*. In the course of my transformation, I've done a lot of good. But my eyes haven't changed yet, so I keep trying."

Sensing the crowd's impatience, the eager residents of Menger Springs ready with their dabbers once more, Paz spun the cage again, so hard the balls inside rattled up against each other, clacking like hailstones against glass. He grasped the ball that emerged out the top, but he stopped short of reading it because he spotted the figure of a V-shaped man with a military-style haircut standing in the back of the room, smirking as he nodded Paz's way.

Paz looked down toward the first row and at a man with a John D. MacDonald paperback stuffed in the pocket of a button-down sweater that fit him like a smock.

"You mind taking my place, Francis?"

The man started to stand up, then stopped. "How'd you know my name?"

"We must have met."

"My name's Frank. Only my mother ever called me Francis."

"You must've told me."

"I did?"

"Must have," Paz said, stepping down off the slight stage and handing the ball he'd yet to call to the rail-thin man, who looked like a broomstick with limbs.

Paz walked straight out of the dining room that doubled as the bingo hall, ignoring the man who'd just arrived, until he fell into pace alongside him.

"You're a piece of work, Colonel, I'll give you that," the man said, smirking again as he shook his head.

"What is it this time, Jones?" Paz asked the man from Homeland Security, for whom he worked when the need arose. "It better be good, for you to interrupt my bingo game. Those old people depend on me."

"ISIS in Texas," the big man he towered over told him. "Is that good enough for you?"

8

BALCONES CANYONLANDS, TEXAS

The call she'd received sent Caitlin to the Comanche Indian reservation, located on the outskirts of the Balcones Canyonlands National Wildlife Refuge.

"I can't believe you're calling me," Conseulo Alonzo said, when Caitlin reached her on her cell phone.

"I wanted to apologize for last night, Deputy Chief."

"Save it for your hearing before the Department of Public Safety's oversight committee."

"I'm heading up to the Comanche Indian reservation near Austin."

"Why am I not surprised, you and trouble being joined at the hip the way you are?"

"What kind of trouble, ma'am?"

"Oil drilling crew being blocked from entering the rez by some young protesters who want to turn the Balcones into Wounded Knee. From what I hear, they just might get their wish."

"Thanks for your time, Deputy Chief."

If Caitlin had her history straight, Spanish explorers had named the land northwest of what is now Austin "Balcones" because of its rolling, terraced hills. Those limestone hills and spring-fed canyons made up most of the sprawling, twenty-five-thousand-acre refuge, which had been formed in the early 1990s to protect some endangered bird species. But one hundred thirty years or so before that, a portion of the deeply bisected Edwards Plateau on its outskirts had been deeded to the Comanche as their rightful land, first under the auspices of Sam Houston and then confirmed by the U.S. government itself in the Medicine Lodge Treaty.

The refuge, located off Route 183 through Lago Vista, was a majestically beautiful enclave of oak, elm, and cedar trees shading a lush countryside similarly rich in ground flora. All thanks to the waters of the massive Edwards Aquifer, which leached upward to keep the vegetation nourished, in stark contrast to the more barren, erosion-prone areas of the hill country. That same aquifer provided drinking water to a large number of Texans through springs that fed rivers flowing into the marshes, estuaries, and bays for miles and miles.

The Comanche reservation had been carved out of the most fertile portion of the basin before the preserve itself was a thought in anyone's mind. A large patch of prime land as lush and pretty as any that Texas had to offer, and upon which the Strong legend was born. Approaching the entrance to the reservation, Caitlin found herself searching her memory for the tale her grandfather had told her about his own grandfather, Steeldust Jack Strong, a Civil War hero who made his bones as a Texas Ranger on these very grounds.

The actual entrance to the reservation was a wrought iron gate fastened to a high stone wall layered with what looked like mosaic tile. That wall and gate, rimmed by wildflowers and accessible only via a single flat but unpaved road off of RM 1431, had been erected a mere generation before. The twin sections of gate, which had settled into a permanently open position, were today replaced by a tight line of young-looking Comanche lined up arm-in-arm to block access to the reservation by a number of trucks. Those trucks were currently parked amid the tall grass bordering the road, lugging both light and heavy construction equipment. An equally long, straight line of sheriff's deputies, Austin city cops, tribal policemen, and members of the highway patrol stood between the protesters and construction workers currently milling about, doing their best to keep the peace, while a grouping of spectators and media types watched from a makeshift gallery further back.

Caitlin left her SUV in a makeshift lot of vehicles parked in no particular pattern and approached, figuring Dylan's father, Cort Wesley Masters, wasn't far behind after receiving her text message. More than one hundred forty years ago, Jack Strong had probably been one of the few white men to set foot on the land beyond, which was rich with oak-juniper woodlands, mesquite savannas, and riparian brush that rare bird species shared with gray foxes and white-tailed deer. The preserve stood pretty much unchanged and unspoiled from that day, a swath frozen in time, which seemed appropriate given that many of the young Comanche blocking the entrance were dressed in garb better fit for the nineteenth century.

Caitlin could feel the building heat, the closer she got to the fracas, and not from either the sun or the camera lights. The bevy of construction workers looked none too happy about being denied entrance to the land on which their jobs rested, while what looked to be between fifty and sixty protesters, dominated by a dozen or so with painted faces and matching headbands, stood arm-in-arm before them.

Caitlin spotted Dylan Torres smack-dab in the center. His left arm was laced through the arm of one of the painted young Comanche men and his right arm was linked to a young, dark-featured woman whose beauty radiated even in a scene like this. She had long black hair and the darkest eyes Caitlin had ever seen, so full and shiny they seemed more liquid than solid. She boasted athletic lines and was wearing a sleeveless shirt that showed off the muscle layering her arms, her biceps strung with veins and all three heads of her triceps easily definable. Drawing closer, Caitlin noticed that the Comanche protesters, in their early to midtwenties, wore trousers that looked woven from animal skins, and open vests exposing what looked like blood streaks on their chests.

Now a junior at Brown University, Dylan wore the tapered jeans Cort Wesley hated, stretched over the boots Caitlin had bought him for a birthday that seemed a hundred years ago. He'd let his hair grow out, and it hung in loose waves and ringlets, past his shoulders, the same way it had back when Caitlin had bought him the boots, when he was often mistaken for some rock star whose name she couldn't remember. His gaze was fixed on the workers congested before the protesters, and Caitlin thought he was the only non–Native American manning the line that those workers looked ready to storm at any moment. Knowing Dylan as well as she did, his proximity to the beautiful Comanche girl made the reason for his presence here obvious.

Oh, man, she thought. *Not again . . .*

The boy was no stranger to trouble, almost all of it related to one girl or another. But the dark-haired Native American with whom he'd laced arms was the most beautiful of the lot, features and frame so perfect that she seemed painted onto the equally striking backdrop of the Balcones. Caitlin had intended to wait for Dylan's father, Cort Wesley, to arrive before she tried to sort things out. But a sudden forward thrust of construction workers, forcing the police closer to Dylan and the other protesters, changed that plan in a hurry.

The officers were barely managing to hold the line when Caitlin circled out behind them and in front of the Native Americans, even with the center, where Dylan and the beautiful Comanche girl stood.

"We're not looking for trouble, Ranger!" a big man

with a scruffy beard, whom she took to be the work foreman, shouted from the other side of the cops.

"Well, sir," she said, hands planted squarely on her hips, "it looks like you found it, all the same."

9

BALCONES CANYONLANDS, TEXAS

Caitlin's Texas Ranger badge glinted in a shaft of sunlight slicing through the shade trees, bouncing the light weakly back toward the workers.

"The trouble's standing right behind you, Ranger," the foreman resumed, thrusting a thick, calloused finger toward the neat line of protesters. "I got the permits and copies of the signed contracts in my truck, if you want to see them. And these Injuns got no call to prevent us from doing the job we were hired to do by their mommies and daddies."

"Did he just call us 'Injuns'?" asked the Comanche girl standing next to Dylan.

Caitlin turned, ignoring Dylan while fixing her gaze on her. "Let me handle this please." She turned again toward the foreman. "I'd ask, sir, that you and your people take a few steps back while we get this all sorted out. Nobody wants trouble, but if it comes, it'll be sure to delay the work you came to do even longer. I don't think that's in anyone's best interests. We on the same page here?"

The foreman scowled but then nodded slowly.

"You've got your chance, Ranger. It doesn't work, don't blame me for what happens next."

Then he backpedaled, along with the rest of his men, dispersing into smaller groups to continue waiting out the situation.

Caitlin turned back around to face Dylan. "Let's talk."

"I'm taking some time off from school," Dylan started, after they'd moved into a shady grove off to the side of the entrance to the reservation.

"Like a few days? A week?"

Dylan hedged. "More like a semester."

"I don't recall your dad mentioning anything about that."

"That's because I didn't tell him."

Caitlin gazed back toward the line of protesters.

"Her name's Ela Nocona," Dylan resumed. "We met in Native American studies class back at Brown."

"Then I guess this would qualify as primary research."

"I'm trying to do something important here."

"Let's hope your father sees it that way," Caitlin told him, as Ela Nocona joined them in the grove.

She was grinning wide enough to dapple her cheeks. "I didn't think Dylan was telling the truth," she said to Caitlin, clearly impressed, her tone suggesting they were old friends.

"About what, Ela?"

"About you. I told him I had to see it with my own

eyes." She continued to smile, seemingly in admiration. "And now I have."

"Peta Nocona was a great Comanche chief who fathered an even greater one in Quanah Parker. Any relation?"

Ela Nocona tried hard not to look impressed. "I believe I'm Quanah Parker's grandniece," she said.

"And you go to Brown, too."

"I'm a senior," she told Caitlin. "Summa cum laude."

"So are you taking some time off from school too, Ela?"

"The tribal school was short a teacher," she said, without hesitation.

"She works with disabled kids," Dylan chimed in.

"Far too many here, unfortunately. Ten times the number found among Caucasian children," Ela explained, not bothering to elaborate.

"A noble pursuit for sure," Caitlin nodded, "as long as those construction workers don't plow you over with backhoes and front loaders."

"I didn't come back here to man a protest line, Ranger," Ela said, her broad shoulders stiffening noticeably. "But this is our land. No one has a right to spoil it."

"Including your tribal elders, who sold off the mineral rights?"

"That shouldn't have been their decision. They should've put it to a vote."

"I heard they did," Caitlin noted, "and that an overwhelming majority supported opening up these lands to drilling."

Ela stiffened. "That vote wasn't legitimate. I made the elders let me address the crowd at the meeting, but they wouldn't let me introduce all of my research on the Bakken field up in North Dakota and what oil did to the Indian lands there."

"Sounds like their call, to me."

"Dylan told me you were there when his mother was killed," Ela said suddenly. "He said you shot it out with the man who did it."

"Close enough, I suppose," Caitlin said, looking at Dylan again. "Did I mention your dad's on the way?"

Dylan swallowed hard. "You told him?"

"Left him a message as soon as I got word myself, via an anonymous phone call to my cell number. You wouldn't know anything about that, would you, ma'am?" she asked Ela.

"Me?"

"Because the caller specifically mentioned Dylan Torres being on the scene. Not something a random person would make note of. Like they were doing me a favor. Or maybe that person wanted me involved in whatever's going on here."

Some of Ela Nocona's long black hair strayed into her face and she whisked it off, only to have the breeze blow it back. "There's a story my people tell about their first encounter with a Texas Ranger on this land."

"That Ranger was my great-great-grandfather," Caitlin started. "His name was Steeldust Jack Strong, and he was also a hero in the Civil War."

"The stories passed down through the years speak well of him, but the truth about what happened the day he rode onto the reservation's become muddled. Might you know it?"

Caitlin cocked her gaze across the road to where the workmen had broken out the lunch boxes and coolers they'd intended to open at a break in their labors. That had yet to commence, though things had simmered down for now.

"As a matter of fact," Caitlin told Ela, as a sliver of sunlight broke through the tree line above, "I do."

10

BALCONES CANYONLANDS, TEXAS; 1874

Jack Strong rode straight through the center of the reservation, past the pastures and farmlands, until a trio of arrows pierced the ground directly in his path.

Steeldust Jack dismounted stiffly, careful not to put too much weight on his bad leg, and held his hands in the air, watching a half dozen Comanche warriors, their faces streaked with traditional war paint, emerge from the nearby forest line, where a cluster of small log homes dotted a landscape shaded by sprawling maple and evergreen trees. Only a few tepees, likely for ceremonial purposes, were in evidence, placed not far from a series of large cooking pits, from which gray smoke rose in preparation for the tribe's next meal.

Steeldust Jack noted that the youngest Comanche warrior wasn't wearing any war paint or carrying a bow like the others. He walked ahead of them, his muscular shoulders seeming to sway with the wind, heading straight for the Ranger as if they were the only two men here.

"You are not welcome on this land," the young brave said, stopping a few yards before Steeldust Jack. "You must leave."

Steeldust Jack shielded his eyes from the sun. "You the chief?"

"The chief has no call to speak with the white man. I am Isa-tai, White Eagle in your language."

"Well, I'm Jack Strong, Texas Ranger in your language."

Isa-tai bristled at that. He didn't look all that much older than Steeldust Jack's son, William Ray, who'd just joined the Rangers himself, at seventeen, and had been assigned to the newly formed Frontier Battalion. Strange for a father to be jealous of his son, but that's the way Jack Strong felt, and he couldn't help it. The truth was, he'd have been much happier fighting Indians than investigating a killing that might have taken place on their land. But duty was duty.

"You have no business here, Ranger."

Isa-tai had eyes so dark that the Ranger was pretty sure they were black, with hardly any white mixed in. His bronzed face was angular, with ridged cheekbones and smooth skin that was free of the scars Steeldust Jack was used to seeing on the Comanche he'd done battle with over the years. Isa-tai's raven hair was clubbed back, the way all braves wore it, with what looked like a bone looping through it and poking out from the top.

"And authority here, either," Isa-tai continued.

"Is what I heard true? That you folks here are im-
mortal, that you're gonna live forever?"

"Not if the white man can help it. This land was
given to us in peace and we have kept it in peace. We
ask only to be left alone, and for the white man to keep
to himself, just as we do."

"All the same, I was hoping you could help me with
something."

"I'm a medicine man. But if you've come for healing, you've come to the wrong place."

"I come about a man just outside your land here
who's way beyond healing."

"A white man?"

"Yes, sir. Got himself killed in an especially bad
way."

Isa-tai flirted with a smile. "There's no bad enough
way for a white man to die."

Steeldust Jack felt the other braves closing in on him
from the rear. Their steps were too soft to discern
through the breeze, but the cast of their shadows betrayed their motion. He made sure to hang his right
hand well off his Colt, so as not to spook them.

"I was wondering if there were any bear in these
parts."

"A bear didn't do it. You already know that," said
Isa-tai.

"You telling me what I know now? Are we having
a language problem here?"

The braves behind Jack Strong fanned out, enclosing him in a circle, with Isa-tai still directly before him,
looking up.

"You don't know what you're looking for, *taibo*."

"Why don't you tell me?"

Isa-tai looked about, seeming to sniff the air. "You should go. It'll be dark before you know it."

"I ain't afraid of the dark."

"It's what the dark breeds that you should be afraid of."

"This all have anything to do with those rituals I heard about? None of my business, I know, and none of that dead fella's business, either. But if, by some chance, he trespassed with an intent to do harm and got clipped before he could do so, that's a case I can make on your behalf."

"We don't need you to do anything on our behalf, Ranger. We do for ourselves here, in harmony with nature and the Great Spirit. If you suspect this dead man's fate involved his trespass, I suggest you take it up with him."

"Maybe you could introduce me to this Great Spirit of yours. I haven't exactly seen him about lately.

If Isa-tai was amused at all by Steeldust Jack's attempt at levity, he didn't show it. "That is because you see only the world before you, not around you."

Steeldust Jack swept his gaze about the braves encircling him. "You trying to tell me something?"

"A warning."

The Ranger's hand edged closer to his Colt. "Don't test me."

"Not from us. You have nothing to fear here, other than your own ignorance."

"Pretty smug talk."

"Heed the lesson of the *taibo* who lies dead."

Steeldust Jack resisted the temptation to get right up

in Isa-tai's face. "You want to give me that again in English I can understand?"

"This is our land," Isa-tai said, his spine stiffening.

"Understood."

"All that lies on and beneath it belongs to us."

"Now you've lost me again."

"After my people lost our land to your kind. Forced to fight for what is ours, then presented with tiny patches like this, only to have it threatened, too."

Steeldust Jack mopped the heat from his brow with a sleeve already mired in perspiration, swabbing it under the brim of his hat. "I don't know what you're talking about. Did that man whose body got chopped up like a side of beef *threaten* you?"

Isa-tai's spine relaxed. "Time for you to go."

"What was he doing here, in these parts?"

"Ask him."

"He's in no condition to tell me."

"His spirit then. And have that spirit take a message back to whoever sent him, that the same fate awaits whoever follows." White Eagle turned his gaze on the sky. "But hurry. Night is coming."

And that was when Steeldust Jack heard the scream.

II

Balcones Canyonlands, Texas

What sounded like a gunshot ended Caitlin's tale midthought, and the next moments unfolded in what felt like slow motion. First the police officers manning the line separating the two camps whipped out their guns. Then the construction workers mounted a fresh charge, with the young protesters not giving an inch.

Caitlin resisted the temptation to draw her own pistol. The blast sounded more like a car or truck backfiring, in retrospect, but it was enough to push already frayed nerves over the edge. She planted herself before Dylan and Ela so they couldn't rush back to the entrance. She spotted Cort Wesley Masters storming across the scene, heading straight for them, red-faced and breathing so hard she could see his big chest contracting under his shirt. His focus was entirely on Dylan, as if Caitlin and Ela Nocona weren't even there.

"When did you plan on telling me you dropped out of school, son?"

"I didn't drop out," Dylan said, looking up at Cort Wesley and trying to return his glare. "I'm just taking a semester off."

"Well, I got a call from the registrar. Apparently, there were a bunch of forms you neglected to fill out, to the point where Brown isn't sure you're returning at all."

Cort Wesley's face was so red it seemed sunburned, and his breath was so hot it looked like smoke when it hit the moisture-soaked air. Caitlin could see the tension in the muscles beneath his shirt, his traps so pronounced they stretched the fabric of the T-shirt she'd bought him for his last birthday. Sweat dappled the fabric in splotches, and Caitlin figured that even the truck's air-conditioning hadn't been able to cool him off on the drive down here from Houston, where he'd been meeting with the principal of his younger son's school.

Dylan slid closer to Ela Nocona. "We're doing something important here."

"*We,*" Cort Wesley repeated, seeming to notice Ela Nocona for the first time and, no doubt, coming to the same conclusion Caitlin already had. "So is it important enough to give up your future for?"

"Have you even heard what's going on in North Dakota, on that Bakken oil field that straddles Indian land?" Dylan asked him.

"No, son, I haven't."

"It's a repeat of how the nineteenth century went down for them. And now it's happening here in Texas. Somebody's got to do something."

"That somebody being you," Cort Wesley said. "Maybe I should haul you out of here. Tie you to the bed of my truck and drive you all the way back to Providence."

Dylan shook his head and blew the hair from his face, then swiped at it again with a hand. Caitlin felt the air thicken between father and son. Dylan was still nearly half a foot shorter than Cort Wesley, at five foot nine, but he was not about to give an inch, no more than he did while playing running back for the Brown University football team, under famed coach Phil Estes. Caitlin let her gaze stray off them and found it fixing on an area where the press and spectators had been cordoned, toward a rail-thin figure who didn't look much older than Dylan. Caitlin couldn't place the kid, but something about him looked familiar enough to unsettle her in what her grandfather Earl Strong had

called the "quiet parts." She knew the kid from someplace, and wherever that was, clearly it wasn't good,
given her response to his presence.

"So you and the rest of these kids are trying to save
the tribe from itself," she heard Cort Wesley saying to
Dylan, and she turned back toward them. "Is that it?"

"The elders are lying to them, Dad."

"That's none of your business."

"But it's mine, Mr. Torres. It's my business," Ela said,
standing side by side with Dylan, addressing Cort Wesley respectfully. "This is a protected refuge. The oil
company can't touch any of it, except here on the reservation, since my people were deeded this part of the
land. So that's where they came, bringing promises to
build new schools, new housing, new jobs. My people
kept voting down a casino, but they accepted the company's promises because the elders sold them a bill of
goods. Carbon copy of North Dakota, but nobody's
paying any attention." Ela squeezed Dylan's arm.
"Maybe this will change that."

"First, my name's Masters, not Torres. Second, the
only thing that's gonna change is what happens when
heads start getting busted," Cort Wesley told her.

Caitlin held her gaze on Ela. "Are you accusing anybody of breaking the law here?"

"The laws of nature, of history, yes."

"Those aren't the laws I was talking about."

Ela shrugged.

Caitlin felt a chill run through her, and she scanned
the spectators again for the tall young man, so rail thin
that he seemed to have no waist at all. But she turned
back toward Dylan and Ela before she could find him.

"Tell you what I can do. I can speak with the right folks at this minerals company to determine if their intentions are just. I can't make any promises, but in my experience, people real good at hiding behind intentions don't talk such a good game when you pull back the curtain."

Ela looked over Caitlin's shoulder toward the congestion of construction workers milling about, just beyond the police line. Anger was squeezing their expressions taut, and they seemed ready to erupt again at any moment. Caitlin's gaze, meanwhile, drifted yet again toward the gallery of spectators, fixing on the precise spot where the tall kid with the pants sagging past his hips had been standing. She was still trying to place how she recognized him, the answer flitting along the outskirts of her consciousness like a bad dream she couldn't quite keep ahold of.

"You don't know what you're dealing with here, Ranger, not with these people," Ela told her.

"Well," said Caitlin, still trying to spot the tall kid she couldn't chase from her mind, "they don't know what they're dealing with, either."

PART TWO

They were . . . one of the most colorful, efficient, and deadly band of irregular partisans on the side of law and order the world has seen.

—T. R. Fehrenbach, *Lone Star: A History of Texas and the Texans* (Boston: Da Capo Press, 2000)

12

"You risked compromising this mission. You risked *everything*."

Daniel Cross stretched his long legs under the table in Hoover's Cooking and looked up from the chicken-fried steak the waitress had just set down on his place mat. "How'd I do that, just hanging around the reservation for a few minutes?" he asked the two men seated across from him in the booth.

"You must learn to follow the rules, exercise caution," Razin Saflin said. "There's so much at stake here, and your presence at that Indian reservation could have harmed our plans."

The two men on the other side of the booth were uniformly flat faced, their gazes caustic. Both were average looking, nondescript, just like him, except they had neatly trimmed beards and he barely needed to shave at all. Cross was tall and thin, with a waist that hadn't changed much since middle school and still struggled to hold pants up, even with a belt. His brown, stringy hair was almost as oily as it had been back then, his skin, too, and his acne was just as bad—lately to the point that he had to go back to using the medication that made him smell like antiseptic.

"What do you think you were achieving?" the second man, Ghazi Zurif, asked him, gazing about the restaurant again.

Cross tried to smirk, to be the guy in control, which was what they'd made him feel like, until now. It was what he'd enjoyed most about this whole experience: being the one in charge, calling the shots for a change. Now it seemed like he was back to being no different from "Diaper Dan," the nickname given to him in second grade, when he'd wet himself in class after the teacher refused to let him go to the lav. The nickname had stuck all the way through high school.

"Nothing," Cross told the two men who'd made him feel like Diaper Dan again. "I was just hanging around, watching. What's the big deal?"

"You were warned to be careful in your movements," said Saflin, who had a drooping eye. "*That's* the big deal."

"And you weren't supposed to leave the apartment without informing us," Zurif added.

"Am I supposed to ask permission before I take a shit, too?"

Saflin shot a hand across the table, brushing against Cross's iced tea and nearly spilling it. The hand clamped onto the hand in which Cross was holding the steak knife and squeezed the wrist so hard that Cross felt his fingers go numb, the nerve held in a way that sent pain shooting up his forearm, all the way to his elbow. The steak knife slipped from his grasp and rattled against the floor.

"You think this is a game?" Daniel Cross felt Saflin's hot breath blow into him like air from a sauna, his droopy eye bulging wide now, the angle of his glare making one side of his beard look longer than the other. "What did you think was going to happen when you left those posts all over social media, enough to command even the attention of Allah?"

"You are performing His will," said Zurif. "Today you risked the plan He has set into motion."

"Come on, man," Cross rasped, the agony knifelike now, until Saflin let go. Cross tried to shake the life back into his hand. "I thought we were in this together."

"You're in it with us," Saflin corrected. "But not together."

"I'm not a Muslim," Cross reminded. "I just hate this damn country, want to see it get what it deserves."

"Muslim or not, you are following the will of Allah, as we were when we answered your call."

"We've been granted operational authority," Zurif added.

Cross was about to poke fun at the term, then thought better of it. "What's that mean?"

"It means you need to prove yourself before us," Saflin explained, "this theory of yours, so Allah may bless the plan."

"It's not just a theory," Cross said, rotating his gaze between the two of them. "You want to kill a whole lot of people at once. I've come up with the weapon that can do it."

"That's what we need proof of before Allah," Zurif picked up. "A demonstration to show you're not full of shit. Before we get the okay to move to the next stage."

"A demonstration," Cross repeated.

"And there's something else," said Saflin. "Someone was watching your apartment building."

Cross felt a tremor slip through him, starting in his stomach and spreading upward. "What's that mean, exactly?"

"It means Allah saved you by guiding you away, proof of His blessing over our holy mission."

Zurif leaned across the booth, too, close to Cross's now forgotten plate of food. "And it means you made somebody's list, triggered an alarm somewhere. Not to worry. That's what Allah has placed us here for."

"To keep you safe, so you can make good on your promises before the eyes of God," Saflin added. "Now, about that demonstration . . ."

13

AUSTIN, TEXAS

Jones parked the van up the street from the rundown apartment building off East Saint Johns Avenue, shielded from view by leaking bags of trash piled high on the sidewalk. Guillermo Paz had counted a half dozen cars propped up on blocks since they'd hit this part of town, hopelessness riding the air as plainly as the stench of uncollected garbage.

"You know the drill, Colonel," Jones told him. "The target's a lone wolf as far as we can tell. Can't be sure, of course. That's why you're here."

"Lone wolf," Paz repeated, glancing into the rear of

the van, where the team members he'd chosen for this operation were gearing up.

Like him, they were veterans of the Venezuelan secret police, better known as the National Directorate of Intelligence and Prevention Services, or DISIP. Part of a never-ending and self-replenishing supply of soldiers, culled from the best and most ruthless that American dollars could buy. In return, they offered plausible deniability for Jones's black flag operations, undertaken on behalf of a shadowy subdivision of Homeland Security. As far as Washington knew, the colonel and his men didn't exist, and that suited Paz just fine.

"The target made overtures to ISIS via social media, but we lost the trail when he started pinging them via the Deep Web."

"But that's not why you required my services, is it?" Paz asked him.

"Nope. You got the job, Colonel, because something finally pinged back."

14

AUSTIN, TEXAS

Paz and his men were dressed like civilians, locals, secure in the knowledge that this wasn't the kind of neighborhood where residents were likely to call the police to report suspicious behavior. The apartment to which he and his three men were headed overlooked a rat-infested alley at the back of a building. This particular slum seemed to have a nondiscrimination policy, drawing its hapless from among various ethnicities and backgrounds. According to the intelligence gathered by Jones, Daniel Cross was the product of a rape, his mother having been a prostitute at the time of his conception.

Paz hadn't read any more of the file because he didn't need to. Half of Cross's genes belonged to a rapist, which in Paz's mind was as low as life could get. He'd come to realize that everyone is a prisoner of their own birth. Just as Paz had inherited psychic abilities, *brujería* as he called it, from his mother, Cross clearly carried the crazy, violent gene from his father's side.

According to visual surveillance, Daniel Cross was presently hunkered down in the apartment, working behind a computer. The lock on the building's front security door was broken, and Paz led his men through, submachine guns whipped out from beneath their coats. They shoved a kid zooming toward the door on a skateboard out of the way and stepped over a drunk passed out on the stairs, en route to Cross's third-floor apartment.

Paz stood before the door, his men taking their flanking positions. An electronic sweep before he'd been given the go signal revealed no trip wires or any other defense against intrusion. Not that Paz required such intelligence. He trusted his own instincts and the *brujeria* he'd inherited from his mother more than any machine, and right now that *brujeria* told him he had nothing to fear. But he also was struck by an odd feeling he couldn't quite identify, that left him distinctly unsettled.

Shaking the sensation off, Paz lifted his right leg off the floor and aimed the heel of his boot straight for the flimsy latch. The door shattered on impact, the hinges themselves as well as the latch, sending the splintered remnants rocketing inward.

A shaft of light illuminated a shape in a desk chair, swinging toward him, silhouetted by the flimsy, drawn blinds, something dark and shiny held in his hand. Sound-suppressed fire from his men tore the figure apart. The whole chair wheeled backwards and slammed into the blinds, which dropped from their mounts and folded over what was left of what had been sitting there.

"*Madre de Dios*," one of Paz's men muttered.

"A dummy?" Jones repeated, wondering what Guillermo Paz had tucked in his hand, when he returned to the van.

"Stuffed animal, actually, dressed in clothes and a baseball cap."

"Don't tell me, Colonel: facing away from the window so my surveillance team wouldn't figure things out."

"The blinds cracked enough to let them see what they expected to."

"Yeah, there's a post in Alaska waiting for them, as of tomorrow."

"I left my men in the apartment to make sure it was

secured for your tech team. Tell them to watch out for the candy wrappers."

"Candy wrappers?"

"They're crumpled up everywhere. Hershey bars, I think."

"You could have told me that much over the radio, Colonel," Jones said.

"But there was something you needed to see," Paz told him, showing Jones what he'd been holding. "Right away."

Jones looked at the framed picture, shaking his head. "Oh, *shit* . . ."

15

WEST HOUSTON, TEXAS

"Well, poke me with a stick!" Sam Bob Jackson said, entering the reception area of his office with a wide grin, hands clasped before him as if he were praying. "If it ain't Texas Ranger Caitlin Strong, in the flesh!"

Caitlin popped up from her chair and extended her hand. "Nice to meet you, Mr. Jackson."

The owner of Jackson Whole Mineral clasped the hand in both of his. "I am so sorry to keep you waiting. I knew a Texas Ranger would be coming, but I didn't know it'd be you, by God." His eyes narrowed, head canting slightly to the side, as he pulled his hands back. "You don't remember me, do you?"

"I'm afraid I don't, sir."

"Why, I'm the one who presented you that commendation on behalf of the Texas Chamber of Commerce after you plum near saved the state from those Russian fellas fixing to do us harm, just like your daddy did back in his time. Hell of a thing, wasn't it?"

"I'm not allowed to comment, Mr. Jackson, though I am curious about how you came by the information you did."

Jackson winked. He was a big man, with a triple chin dangling over a string tie that made him look like a fake cowboy. His belly hung well over his belt, which looked to be stitched from the same leather as his boots.

"Well, Ranger," he winked, "I suppose we both got our sources."

Caitlin nodded, figuring it was best to leave things at that.

"Now, let's go down the hall to my office so I can help you out in whatever it is that brought you here."

Jackson Whole Mineral occupied a floor of a gleaming new office tower located, appropriately enough, in west Houston's Energy Corridor, with a clear view of the Katy Freeway out one of Sam Bob Jackson's office windows. Caitlin took a seat in front of his desk and watched Jackson struggle to adjust the designer blinds just enough to keep the sun from her eyes.

"There we go," Jackson said, finally. "You comfortable?"

"I am, sir."

"How about something to drink?"

"Your assistant already offered."

"Yeah, Muriel's a peach, ain't she?"

Jackson Whole Mineral advertised itself as an

experienced and trusted purchaser of oil and gas mineral and royalty interests throughout Texas, Louisiana, and, most recently, the Dakotas, thanks to the Bakken oil field up there. As a third-party consolidator, the company's role was to generate the best possible offers for clients who, like the Comanche, were looking to sell off interests in their land. Toward that end, the company maintained a staff of geologists, engineers, and economic analysts whose job was to get their clients the highest possible return for either leasing or selling their oil and gas interests.

Still giddy, Sam Bob Jackson reclined comfortably in his leather desk chair, propped his boots atop his desk, and laced his fingers behind gelled hair that smelled like something out of a bakery. He looked like a caricature more than a man, but the persona seemed just genuine enough to leave clients with a comfort level bred by an old-school Texas oilman who seemed fit for an episode of *Dallas*.

"So, what can I do for you, Ranger? You didn't specify the reason for your visit."

"That's because my visit isn't part of an active investigation, nothing like that," Caitlin told him. "I'm just here for some background on the Comanche Indian reservation outside Austin."

Jackson nodded, poking at the air with a finger that looked as thick as a cigar. "Where those young folk are staging a protest."

"That's the one, sir."

"You mind calling me Sam Bob, Ranger?"

"Not at all."

"On account of we got history between us and all,

and I'm not just talking about that award the Chamber gave you."

"No?"

"Your daddy got mine out of a whole mess of scrapes. He was a good man, my daddy, kind and generous to a fault. But he couldn't hold his liquor, and Jim Strong was always there when a bender got the better of him." Jackson pulled his boots off the desk and rocked his chair back forward. "Be glad to return that favor any way I can."

"Well, sir—"

"Sam Bob."

"The truth is, I understand you were hired by the Blackfoot up on the Fort Berthold reservation in North Dakota. And I understand there was some trouble up that way, as well, in the course of more than thirteen hundred wells being dug."

"There was indeed, Ranger, regrettably."

"I believe the tribal chief who pushed the whole deal through, Tex G. Hall, ended up establishing his own energy consortium, with a shell company established by you, according to the paper trail. Hall's currently facing a slew of indictments and has been implicated in a pair of murders."

Sam Bob Jackson forced a smile, trying to look casual and undaunted but unable to disguise the edge that settled in his voice. "Does your jurisdiction extend to North Dakota, Ranger?"

"No, sir, but it does to the Balcones, and some of the Comanche have expressed concern over your involvement there, as well."

"You're speaking of those protesters, I assume."

"There were protesters up in North Dakota, too, Sam Bob, who got it in their mind to draw attention to what fracking would do to their land. From what I've heard, they were pretty much right."

The giddiness fled Jackson's expression like air from a balloon. His face suddenly looked smaller, his gelled hair not as shiny.

"That's something you'd have to take up with the oil companies Jackson Whole sold off the mineral rights to."

"Well, Sam Bob, the protests I'm talking about happened before the drilling operation began, when your company was still running the show. And one of the leaders of the Blackfoot protest ended up in a coma after a serious car accident. Another disappeared and turned up drowned, after falling out of his skiff while fishing the Snake River. Another of the leaders had a change of heart and ended up with a brand-new home for his whole family."

Jackson interlaced his fingers again, this time with elbows laid atop his dark wooden desk. "What exactly are you getting at, Ranger?"

"Who would have the most to lose by a protest like that gumming up the works?"

"The Natives, for sure. And the oil companies who'd bought the leases, of course."

"And if they'd decided not to drill and pulled up stakes within a specified period, on account of not wanting to push their way past a bunch of kids standing in their way? That would leave Jackson Whole holding the bag, wouldn't it? On the hook for the non-refundable advance you paid the Blackfoot, and the

Comanche in this case, for the rights to sell or lease mineral rights to their land."

"You still haven't answered my question, Ranger."

"What question was that?"

"How I can be of service to you."

"That's because I came here to be of service to *you*. I believe it's in everyone's best interests here to make sure that no harm comes to those young Comanche standing their ground, 'cause we both know this'll pass soon enough. Time and money getting lost are nothing compared to lives. And it's in those same mutual best interests for you to tell me who might be capable of something like that—which both of us would regret. I just figured that a civic-minded man like yourself would want to do right. Make sure nobody gets hurt in a way that would reflect badly on everyone involved. Would I be correct in that regard?"

"I couldn't agree more," Jackson said, sounding as if he meant it.

"That's good, sir, because Texas has one thing North Dakota doesn't, Sam Bob."

"What's that?"

"Rangers," Caitlin told him.

Once back on the road, Caitlin finally checked her phone for messages and saw three labeled CAPTAIN TEPPER, along with five additional missed calls from Tepper. She was ready to pocket her phone without returning them, when he called for the ninth time.

"Glad you decided to answer this time, Ranger," Tepper greeted her.

"I couldn't read the caller ID, Captain."

"You think I'm stupid?"

"Yes, sir, for killing your lungs with those damn Marlboros."

"Turns out the chair I assigned you hasn't been sat in. Turns out you showed up where local cops are trying to prevent a riot, outside an Indian reservation, and then paid an unauthorized visit to some mineral company for no good reason at all, other than to piss somebody new off."

"I'm guessing Sam Bob Jackson called you."

"Yes, he did. We had a very congenial talk after I explained that I was revoking your day passes off the grounds of the lunatic asylum you belong in."

"You mean the one called Texas?"

"Give it a rest, Caitlin. You pay the man a visit without even a clue of what it is you were investigating, without any authorization whatsoever, concerning something you don't even have any jurisdiction over. Is that about right? Oh, hold on. I left out the part about putting you behind a desk until things quieted down at Department of Public Safety headquarters in Austin. Well, Ranger, the volume has now been officially turned up even louder."

"I got a call Dylan Torres was involved in the protest, Captain."

"Yes, ma'am, I heard that too," Tepper told her, a grim undercurrent lacing his voice. "And you should know there's been some more trouble up at that reservation. That's why I'm calling."

"Dylan again?"

"No, Ranger, it's his father this time."

16

Cort Wesley had been hanging back, in a shady spot that cloaked him from the view of both the protesters and construction workers, when he saw the trouble coming. The kind of trouble he'd learned to sense a whole bunch of years ago, when he'd served in Special Ops during the Gulf War.

The *real* Gulf War, as he liked to call it now, where they'd had a plan for getting in as well as out and had executed it to perfection. Cort Wesley had been part of the team sent in early, through Kuwait, to act as spotters for the initial strafing runs and, later, close air support aimed at more strategic targets. It was the highlight of his military career, which had ended less than auspiciously and had left him in the service of the Branca crime family out of New Orleans, an enforcer for their San Antonio–based drug business. Only men with a security clearance at Jones's level could even access the files detailing his military exploits, because, according to one especially frank Special Ops colonel way up the chain of command, "If they ever learned what we did, they'd never let us do it again."

Cort Wesley had come to realize that combat was an apt metaphor for pretty much everything he'd experienced since then. Raising kids might not be as dramatic, but it was every bit as challenging. You think taking down a half dozen Iraqi soldiers is tough? Try dealing with a pair of teenage boys—especially the oldest, now in college, for whom no cause was too small to make a stand. Dylan had spent his early years nursing sick animals back to health and holding actual funerals when his efforts failed. The boys' mother—Cort Wesley's girlfriend, Maura Torres—had sent him pictures of those rescue efforts during the early days of Cort Wesley's four-year stretch behind bars at Huntsville's infamous Walls penitentiary. Cort Wesley had papered the walls of his cell with them, focusing on a different shot every day, long after his oldest had outgrown the practice and the photos stopped coming.

Right now, the picture he saw forming was of the police line starting to buckle under a concerted shove forward by the construction workers pressed up against it. Cort Wesley saw the line giving.

Saw the protesters, led by Dylan and Ela Nocona, holding their ground.

Saw hammers, ax handles, heavy lug wrenches, and even chains brandished by the construction workers, to be used as weapons instead of tools.

The violence was inevitable now.

Cort Wesley pictured flesh and bone split by wood and steel, an endless parade of rescue vehicles and ambulances that would follow. And then he was in motion, one with the air, as if he'd joined up with the breeze, that hundred feet passing in what seemed little more than the length of a breath. He cut through an opening and took a pair of workers as big as him, who were closing on Dylan and Ela, by the shirt collars, from behind, slamming the men's heads together so hard their hard hats went flying. He kicked the legs out from under their dazed forms and jammed a boot heel into the solar plexus of each, for good measure.

Cort Wesley would have heard them utter crackling, guttural gasps, if he could hear anything at all. Before he could record his next thought, he'd scooped up one of the discarded hard hats and used it to intercept a punch aimed straight for Dylan's face. He felt the wielder's hand shatter on impact. Cort Wesley slammed him in the mouth with the brim of the hard hat, the worker spitting out teeth as he collapsed to his knees.

At that, three big men turned their attention from their assault on the protest line and toward him. Cort Wesley glimpsed a hammer, a crowbar, and an ax handle, fixing his focus on all three at once as if the world before him was divided into a trio of screens. He still had the now dented hard hat in hand and used it both to block and to retaliate, ducking, twisting, and turning away from blows launched by would-be weapons that ought to be hanging from garage hooks.

The hand holding the hat stung from all the impacts, and Cort Wesley unleashed his free hand in concert with it. The world turned to slow motion around him while he remained at regular speed, the ease with which he moved feeling like catching a stiff wind in a sailboat, right up to the point when he swept the legs of a bearded man he recognized as the crew foreman and dropped the man at his feet with a blow from the smashed hard hat he was still holding.

Then he was alone between the two camps, the construction workers finally backing off, while the cops advanced on him.

"Drop it! Drop it!" one cop ordered, gun drawn.

Cort Wesley let the now shapeless hard hat drop to the ground.

"Stay where you are, son!" he yelled to Dylan, as the boy started to move toward him.

Then Cort Wesley felt himself shoved to the ground, too, close enough to the busted-up hard hat to see it wobbling like a top, until another cop kicked it aside.

"You boys are real good at keeping the peace," he spat at them, feeling a pair of handcuffs clamped in place. "I'm feeling safer already."

17

RALEIGH, NORTH CAROLINA

"Another, friend?" the bartender asked Cray Rawls.

"Sure thing," Rawls told him. "And one for the lady here, too," he added, gesturing toward the woman two stools down, who was futilely working her Bic to light a cigarette, in violation of the city's nonsmoking ordinance.

He caught his reflection in the mirrored back bar, a thin crack distorting his features and seeming to split his face in two, the halves separated by a jagged gap. His hair was brown and thick, same as it had been in high school, except Rawls brushed it straight back now. The murky lighting cast his ruddy, pockmarked features in shadows that darkened the acne scar depressions marring his complexion. The mirror's distortion broadened his shoulders beyond even the breadth wrought by the obsessive gym training he had forgone tonight, in need of a different kind of workout. He'd broken his nose in a boxing mishap recently and, from this distance, it looked like a lump of mottled flesh stuck to his face beneath eyes that seemed to glow like a cat's.

Rawls slid onto the stool next to the woman and fired up his lighter, feeling the bite of arthritis that had begun to plague his fingers and knuckles. "You know that's illegal."

"If that bothers you, why give me a light?"

"Who said it bothered me?"

The woman tilted the pack resting on the bar top his way.

"Don't mind if I do," Rawls said, tapping a cigarette out and firing up his lighter anew.

The bartender refilled his glass and poured the woman a fresh one. Cheap, warm, and poured from a gaffed bottle of Johnnie Walker. Rawls had a massive collection of single malts, maybe the biggest in the country, a fact nobody in this dive bar called the Relay cared two shits about.

And that suited Rawls just fine, as did sitting here, just a short distance from where he'd been born, without needing to impress anybody with his charm or his liquor selection. The woman seated on the stool next to him sipped her drink and then tapped her ashes onto the bar's plank floor, for want of an ashtray.

"That all you got to say?" she asked, puffing again.

"I don't recall saying anything."

"You must've forgot to ask me my name. It's Candy."

Rawls took her extended hand, which felt cold and waxy, like shaking hands with a mannequin. Unlike a mannequin, though, the woman wore too much makeup and smelled of too much perfume, having maybe come here from someplace else without stopping for a shower in the middle.

Candy seemed a fitting match for the surroundings, which weren't made up at all. The bar's dome lights had lost their radiance to untouched dust caked up around the bulbs. The wooden walls were sun-faded in some places and stained by cigarette smoke in others. All entertainment was provided by an old-fashioned jukebox in the corner, which still played three songs for a quarter. "Cat's in the Cradle," by Harry Chapin, was into its final bars.

"That's a stupid song," Candy noted, blowing smoke out her nose.

"You ever listen to the words?"

"Not particularly."

"Great meaning in them if you listen close enough. I should know."

"Know what?" Candy asked him, resting her face in her palm.

"Cat's in the Cradle" ended and "Sweet Home Alabama" started up.

"That's more like it," noted Candy. "So, what is it you know?"

"These songs. They were both released in 1974, the year I was born."

Candy pressed what was left of her cigarette out on the bar top. "You from around here, sweetie?"

"Close enough. Matter of fact, you remind me of my mother, back when she was still young and pretty."

"Oh, that's nice."

"Yes, it is."

"So you in town visiting relatives, something like that?"

"Nothing like that," Rawls told her. "Got an important verdict coming down tomorrow morning at the Wake County courthouse."

"You a lawyer?" Candy asked him.

"Defendant."

"What'd you do?" She smirked. "Kill somebody or something?"

"A whole bunch of people, according to the prosecution. Dozens, even hundreds. Candy," Rawls said, pressing out his own cigarette in the charred outline of hers, "you are looking at what some would have you believe is a genuine mass murderer."

"I guess I should be scared then."

"You're not?"

She shrugged a pair of shoulders that looked trim to the bone, her leatherlike pants struggling to shine in the Relay's naked light as she laid a hand atop his. "Of a local boy? Not even one little bit."

"Maybe you should be."

Her hand left his and dropped to his leg, fingers easing up the inside of his thigh. "Why's that? 'Cause of all those people you supposedly killed?"

"Nope. Of that, I'm an innocent. Never even met a single one of them."

"Then what are you guilty of?"

Rawls gulped down the rest of his cheap scotch, and then Candy's as well. "Why don't I tell you about it somewhere else?"

Rawls took off his sock in the bathroom of the motel room and stuffed it with all four mini soap bars, twisting the top to catch all of them snugly. Then he walked back into the room, which was lit only by the letters of the flashing marquee shining through the flimsy shades and splaying off the walls.

Candy was naked from the waist up, seated atop the bed covers, starting to peel her pants off.

"Don't bother," Rawls told her, holding his weighted, balled-up sock low by his hip, where she wouldn't see it. "I meant what I said about you reminding me of my mother."

"I can be anybody you want me to be, sweetie," she said, smiling up at him with bleached teeth.

"Then be my mother," he said, starting forward. "Be my mother the night I was conceived in a room a lot like this."

The smile slid from Candy's face. Rawls's frame now blocked the light of the flashing letters, so her features were lost to shadow.

"Hey, sweetie, why don't we—"

Rawls hit her with the sock, not realizing his own intention until his arm was already in motion, feeling the miniature bars fracture on impact with Candy's face. She was on the bed and then she was off it, staring up at him from the floor.

"That's it," he said down to her. "Be scared, be helpless, be a worthless sack of shit, just like my mother and all the rest of them."

Candy held the bruised side of her face protectively, back-crawling until the wall stopped her motion.

"You said you could be anybody, so I took you at your word. And goddammit if you didn't deliver."

"Pleas-s-sh," Candy said, through the side of her mouth that still worked.

"Please *what*? Come on, tell me, because I really want to know. I really want to know what my mother was feeling, the nights she came back home the way you're going home tonight. See, I was still too young to understand all that, when she died, and this is as close as I can come to knowing. So tell me."

Rawls drew the soap-stuffed sock back overhead when Candy kept whimpering, tightening herself into a protective ball. He felt the rage over her refusal to respond simmering inside him, the sock in motion again before he even realized what he was doing.

Whop!

It impacted with a sound like a shovel digging deep into a hard-packed pile of dirt. Cray Rawls smelled lavender from the broken pieces of the stale soap, his mind taking him back to the sweet scent of pecan trees in the summer, when he'd spend the night outside while his mother's "regulars" paid a visit.

"I grew up not far from here," Rawls heard himself tell Candy. "I did my best to erase it from my memory, did my best to make some good of it. But now I'm back, my life in the hands of some pissant jury. And you know what, Candy?"

Whop!

He struck her again when she refused to acknowledge him, the broken soap bars splintering into smaller chunks.

"I don't care if they find me guilty. Let the system take its best shot, throw everything it's got at me. 'Cause you know the ultimate power in the universe? Not giving a shit. When you don't give a shit, nobody can scare you, nobody can hurt you. Do you give a shit, Candy?"

When she failed to answer him, Rawls hit her again, twice. Her breathing had gone shallow and raspy, coming so fast it mostly swallowed her whimpers and sobs.

"What's it feel like?" he demanded, glowering over her. "Tell me, so I know. Tell me, so I can know my mother."

Whop!

Rawls's thin sock exploded on impact this time, shedding soap fragments that clacked against the nearest wall. He almost told Candy how he'd taken up boxing, only to find he had no talent for the sport other than to be everyone else's punching bag. Which suited him just fine. He liked getting hurt, battered, pummeled into oblivion until he hit the mat and surrendered to the world, the same way sleep had come to him as a little boy, to spare him the grunts and groans coming from his mother's bedroom. And when he couldn't sleep, he'd scratch at his skin with a fingernail, and later a roofing nail, to make himself hurt, because somehow that deadened the real pain.

Rawls reached down to grab hold of Candy, but he found himself crouching over her and then lowering his knees to the cheap, mite-infested rug before he could find purchase. Felt himself yanking her pants down past her hips, just enough, and then pushing himself inside her.

Candy gasped, something that started as a scream blowing hot, moist breath up onto Rawls as he thrust himself in and out, in and out, in and out . . . knowing the muffled sounds that came out of her, all too well.

The sounds of his mother, coming from the next room.

But beneath him now.

"What does it feel like?" Rawls heard himself demand. "Tell me what it feels like!"

Candy didn't, so he kept up with his thrusting, her head ping-ponging lightly against the wall with each entry. She'd gone slack, limp, resignation and shock claiming her features, making Rawls think she really was a department store mannequin that his mind had turned real. He imagined she smelled like plastic instead of musty clothes and stale perfume. Imagined taking a match to her and smelling burning plastic as she melted beneath him.

Then Candy's face morphed into his mother's, and Cray Rawls kept thrusting anyway, hurting her as all those men had, the two of them sharing all that pain.

"How does it feel?" he heard himself ask. "How does it feel?"

Tomorrow a jury thought it would be deciding Rawls's fate, with no idea what he had going a thousand miles away. What he'd lucked into that would make him richer than all the sons of bitches whose asses he'd had to kiss, who had left him with the same feeling that getting pummeled in the ring did. Leaving their offices or private dining rooms as dazed as he was when somebody had to help him up from the mat.

He welcomed that direct form of combat, as opposed to the more subtle brand practiced in the boardroom, even though he'd never left a conference table with his nose busted.

But all that was about to change, regardless of the verdict that came down tomorrow. He was about to be the force doing the pummeling, shooting the bird to his wretched past, his mother, and everything else.

"How does it feel?" he asked Candy again, pulling out of her for the last time.

Rawls stood up, yanking up his pants and peeling hundred-dollar bills from the wad in his pocket.

"Because it feels great to me."

18

SAN ANTONIO, TEXAS

"That all you have to say, Cort Wesley?" Caitlin asked him.

Cort Wesley pressed the phone against his ear, his truck's headlights digging through the first of the night. "No, besides thanks for keeping me out of jail."

"You've got Captain Tepper to thank for that."

"I don't know, maybe I should've let things be. Maybe getting hit by an ax handle would knock some sense into Dylan."

"How many of the workers you take down?"

"I didn't keep count. However many it was won't be working anytime soon. Likely be filing for workman's comp tomorrow."

"They're probably not eligible."

"You're breaking my heart."

"What'd you break of theirs?"

An uneasy silence settled between them, but Cort Wesley felt a smile push itself through it. He pulled a hand from the steering wheel to feel around the bruise left by one of the cops pushing his face into the ground. But he had trouble driving the truck with the hand left to that task. It was tough to close the fingers that had swelled up at the knuckles from the blows he'd struck against the workmen.

"The attack was planned, Ranger, not random. Like those construction workers got word from somebody to take the offensive."

"What's your point?"

Cort Wesley started to take a deep breath but stopped. "What time did your meeting wrap up in Houston?"

"Five o'clock. What makes you ask?"

"Because fifteen minutes later, the trouble here all started. You think that was a coincidence, Ranger, or somebody sending a message?"

Cort Wesley wished he had some ice to wrap around his swollen hand. Funny how he never remembered them hurting after he got into scrapes years back; they probably did, just not as much—or maybe he was just too young and stupid to pay attention. Like his sons, who were young and not stupid at all, although you wouldn't know it sometimes.

Looks like I'm not going to win father of the year . . .

Not with Luke ready to quit his fancy prep school because he couldn't room with his ex-boyfriend, while Dylan had dropped out of Brown University to protest oil drilling on his Indian girlfriend's reservation.

"*That's 'Native American' these days, bubba,*" the spectral shape of Leroy Epps said from the passenger seat, tipping the neck of a root beer bottle back against his lips.

19

BOERNE, TEXAS

"Was I talking to you, champ?"

"*Think, talk—same thing from where I be. I heard you thinking that, just like I heard you wishing you could ice your sore hand.*" Leroy flashed the root beer bottle. Cort Wesley was able to see through him in parts, as clear as through the glass. "*Guess you forgot about your cooler. Hope you don't mind me taking your last one.*"

"I've developed a taste for the stuff, thanks to you."

"*Notice you only buy real Hires, flavored with genuine sarsaparilla. I'd take my hat off to you if I wore one.*" The ghost of his old friend watched Cort Wesley trying to flex the life back into his swollen fingers. "*In my day, we had to box once a month instead of a year. Know how I'd heal my hands fast? Go out and catch as many bees as I could hold and squeeze until they stung me.*"

"I'll give it a try."

"Don't crack wise with me, bubba."

Cort Wesley found himself thinking about old Leroy's funeral, which prison officials had let Cort attend, in a potter's field for inmates who didn't have any relatives left to claim the body. He'd been the only one standing at the graveside, besides the prison chaplain, when Mexican laborers had lowered the plank coffin into the ground. Cort Wesley tried to remember what he'd been thinking that day, but it was hard because he'd done his best to erase those years not just from his memory but also from his very being. One thing he did remember was that the service was the first time he'd smelled the talcum powder Leroy Epps had used to hide the stench of the festering sores caused by the diabetes that ultimately killed him.

Cort Wesley looked back toward the passenger seat, half expecting Leroy to be gone. But he was still there, sipping from the bottle of root beer clasped in a thin, liver-spotted hand. His lips were pale pink and crinkled with dryness. The thin light radiating from the truck's dashboard cast his brown skin in a yellowish tint. The diabetes that had planted him in the ground had turned Leroy's eyes bloodshot and had numbed his limbs years before the sores and infections set in. As a boxer, Leroy had fought for the middleweight crown on three different occasions. He'd been knocked out once and had the belt stolen from him through paid-off judges' scorecards two other times. He'd been busted for killing a white man in self-defense and had died three years into Cort Wesley's four-year incarceration, but ever since he always seemed to show up when he was needed the most. Whether a ghostly specter or a figment of Cort Wesley's imagination, Cort Wesley had given up trying to figure out. He just accepted the fact of Leroy's presence and was grateful that Leroy kept coming around to help him out of one scrape after another.

"*As I was saying,*" old Leroy resumed, "*you sure know how to pick 'em.*"

"As in . . ."

"*Fights, bubba. I don't know what was more fun, watching you mix it up with that principal lady at your youngest's school or frying the grits of those side busters fixing to turn your oldest into mashed potatoes.*"

"You sure have a way with words, champ."

"*What do you expect, you being the only live person I'm on a speaking basis with and all? No different now than it was back in the Walls, I suppose, the thing being a man's gotta know when it's time to choose his words carefully.*"

"There a message in there somewhere meant for me?"

Cort Wesley watched old Leroy swirl the remnants of his root beer about the bottom of the bottle, wanting to savor the last sips. "*Not of my making, bubba. But now that you mention it . . .*"

"Oh boy . . ."

"*I find myself agreeing with you.*"

"About what?"

"*What you told the Ranger lady, about something spurring those workmen to action when it did. Men like that don't do nothing unless somebody's telling them to do it.*"

"Any more pearls of wisdom to cover the price of the Hires, champ?"

"*I apologize for drinking your last one, bubba,*" Epps said, swirling the last of the root beer about the bottle again as he fixed his gaze out the windshield. "*Always darkest where the road bends, like it's hiding what's around the next curve. What do you think it'd be like for a man if he could see around those curves instead of just straight ahead?*"

"I imagine he'd be prepared for anything."

"*'Cepting that goes against the grain of nature on both sides of the plane, bubba. See, I can tell you where it's darkest, but I can't see through the paint no better than you can.*"

"Is there a point in there somewhere?"

"*Just this: what happens when you shine your high beams into a Texas fog bank?*"

"The light bounces back at you."

"*Meaning . . . ?*"

"You've got to make do with whatever path your headlights can carve."

"*There you go, then.*"

"I do?"

Leroy Epps drained the rest of the Hires and blew air into the bottle to make a wind sound. "*You wanna know what's coming, when the best you can do is slow down and be ready when it gets here.*"

"You talking about my boys, champ?"

"*We travel a winding road, bubba, not a straight-away,*" he resumed. "*Best we can do is keep those we love from straying onto the pavement and getting turned into roadkill.*"

Cort Wesley took his eyes off the ghost to refocus on the road. When he looked back, Leroy was gone.

Cort Wesley realized that watching his old friend enjoying his root beer had worked up his own thirst. He reached behind him to the backseat floor, popped open his cooler, and felt about for the third of the root beer bottles he thought he'd stored for the ride up to Houston and the Village School. His fingers came up empty.

"Damn," Cort Wesley uttered, shaking his head. "Son of a bitch really did drink my last one."

20

Balcones Canyonlands, Texas

"Who'd you say we're meeting?" Dylan asked Ela Nocona, as they made their way to the back end of the Comanche reservation, nestled against the edge of the nature preserve, where the flatter lands gave way to sloping hills.

"My grandfather. Sort of," she told him.

"What do you mean, 'sort of'?"

"Long story."

"You say that a lot."

"What?"

"'Long story.' Give me the short version. Either he's your grandfather or he's not."

She flashed Dylan the look she used when she was playing around, soft and tough at the same time. It set something deep inside him fluttering and briefly stole his breath. Brought him back to the first time he'd seen her, when she squeezed by and took the seat next to him in Brown University's Salomon Center. Her hair smelled like jasmine and the rest of her like the outdoors itself.

"It's what I call him," Ela said finally, hoping that would be the end of it.

"That doesn't answer my question."

"He claims he's my *father's* grandfather—great-grandfather, actually. How's that?"

"Besides the fact it would make him, like, over a hundred and fifty years old?"

Ela shrugged. "Everyone calls him White Eagle, Isatai in our language. You want to know if I believe he's really that old somehow? He's supposed to be a shaman, and they're only born once a century."

"What happened to whoever was supposed to replace him in the twentieth century?"

"That would be my real grandfather. The bottle got him. I'll show you his grave sometime. Guess fulfilling the tradition was too much for him."

"Yeah, living forever takes its toll."

Ela gave him that look again. "Are you making fun of me?"

"Who's next in line?" Dylan asked, instead of responding. "As in, in the twenty-*first* century."

"You're looking at her."

Ela's grandfather, as she called him, lived on a ridge up a steep slope near the reservation's northwest boundary, where it joined the bulk of the protected wildlife refuge. The Comanche had been deeded their parcel of land long before anyone had thought of these lands that way. Back then, people tended to take the land for granted, unspoiled by the specters of oil and gas rigs pluming the ground. If Dylan had his bearings right, continuing for a brief stretch along one of the nature paths he spotted cut through the woods would have taken them to the challenging switchbacks off the refuge's Rimrock trail. But the clearing up ahead pushed aside thoughts of that or anything else.

The first thing he saw was a waterfall, its suds sweeping down a mansion-sized husk of jagged stone that looked like an appendage of the land. The waterfall flowed into a pond lapped with light currents that glistened in the moonlight. It was a true Texas moment for him, one of those times when he happened upon something that reminded him of the state's prehistoric beauty. It was what he missed most about going to college in the big, bad Northeast, where normally the only sights were people, and no journey to another destination brought any surprises with it. Dylan knew people around his age who were proud of the fact that they'd never left Texas, and moments like this made him wonder if they had things right.

White Eagle's room-sized log cabin sat perched at the edge of the pond. Outside, in an elegant circular assemblage of stones and rocks, he'd built a fire, which was crackling and sending embers wafting off into the night. The breeze carried those embers out over the pond, where they cut slivers out of the moonlight's shine for a moment, until the surface of the still water claimed them.

Dylan felt Ela take his hand, more a practical gesture than a romantic one, since the ridge trail was uneven and strewn with loose stone that could cause a bad misstep in the darkness. She tried to let go when the spray of the firelight reached them, but Dylan held on because he liked the feel of her grip, as soft as it was strong. He knew both Caitlin and his dad had their doubts about her, but they'd never seen her working with the kids born autistic or learning disabled, thanks to fetal alcohol syndrome. They didn't appreciate the fact that a girl this close to graduating and getting to live her own life would put it all on hold because those kids needed somebody to give them the same chance Ela herself had gotten.

Dylan squeezed her hand tighter, spotted what looked like a cave high up in the rock face, just out of the waterfall's reach, a doorway-sized opening accessible by a ledge wide enough to accommodate a man willing to walk with the stone face bracing his shoulder. He thought he spied a flickering, shadowy shape inside the mouth of one of the caves, until the moon slipped behind a cloud and it was gone.

Then a second structure in the clearing claimed his attention. He took it for an old-fashioned outhouse, except it was built of logs heavier and thicker than those forming the cabin. He spied what looked like a door latch brightening in view in the firelight, making him think it was more likely a storage shed. Except he thought he heard something clanging inside it, followed by the muffled exchange of voices. Before he could discern any words, a shape stepped out before Ela and him, seeming to take its form from the night.

"Welcome, Granddaughter," greeted White Eagle.

Judging by his face, maybe he really had been born

in the nineteenth century. It was not skin so much as a dried patchwork assemblage of wrinkles and furrows, crisscrossing each other in a battle for space across his parchment-like flesh. His coarse, gray-white hair was clubbed back in a ponytail. He stood eye to eye with Dylan, his hunched spine and bent knees having stolen at least six inches from the height of his youth. He smelled of mesquite and pine smoke from the fire and boasted the whitest teeth Dylan had ever seen in a man.

"And this would be the young man you've spoken of to me," White Eagle said, staring more *through* Dylan than at him. "You told me he was white." The old man worked a finger through the night, in front of Dylan, as if he were tracing Dylan's face in the firelit air. "You look Comanche. You have any Comanche blood?"

"Not that I know of."

"You look Comanche, because you have the warrior's glow about you. No stranger to death already, are you?"

"I've seen my share of it," Dylan admitted.

"Your mother?"

"How'd you know?"

The old man did that thing with his finger in the air again. "It's written on your face, plain as day for those who can read it. Looks clear as the words in a book to my old eyes."

"We need your advice, Grandfather," Ela broke in.

White Eagle turned his whole head toward her. "I've been watching you stand against the *posah-tai-vo*," he said, looking briefly back at Dylan. "Means 'crazy white man.' Warrior's blood runs through you as well,

Granddaughter. The spirits have chosen well for my successor."

"We can't beat them, Grandfather. Everyone's against us, even my father. He says our people deserve to enjoy the spoils of our land, that we made a mistake not building a casino or making cigarettes, like other tribes, when we had the opportunity. He says this may be our last chance to right this wrong."

"And you don't agree with him, Granddaughter?"

"I've studied what such deals have done to other tribes. Made them richer, but not better, while poisoning their land. The White man's money is the devil, but the elders don't see it that way. The elders believe we've suffered long enough."

Dylan watched the old man nodding along with Ela, as if her words were a recording he'd heard already.

"This happened once before, you know," White Eagle told them both.

"We heard a little about that today," said Dylan.

White Eagle started forward, his feet sheathed in ancient moccasins shuffling atop the ground. "Then let us sit by the fire so I can tell you some more."

21

BALCONES CANYONLANDS, TEXAS; 1874

When Steeldust Jack rode to where the scream had come from, with White Eagle and the other braves just behind him, he found a man holding a Comanche girl by the hair. She struggled against the man, and he yanked her head farther back until her eyes were facing the sky.

"Whatcha all think?" he said to five other men, who had their pistols out by then. "Should I scalp her or what?"

The man grinned and held his bowie knife up to catch the sun. Dismounting, Steeldust Jack's mind worked fast, matching the clothes and holsters of these men to that of the body found just outside the reservation. And matching their demeanors to the kind of gunmen placed in long supply by the destruction wrought by the Civil War, bitter and hardened men turned into nomads. Many had become bushwhackers and criminals, offering their well-seasoned and practiced gun hands to anyone who had need and could pay.

But there was something different and unsettling about this lot, starting with the quality of their clothes and the fact that their Colts were shiny and new—practiced with on the range rather than in the genuine battles they'd left behind in their pasts, but not their souls.

Steeldust Jack took a step forward, careful not to place much weight on his bad leg, and peeled his coat back to reveal his own more weathered Colt, making no move to draw it yet. "You can let the girl go now," he said calmly, feeling the braves take up position behind him, holding in place reluctantly with bows and arrows held at the ready which didn't seem to bother the gunmen at all.

The head gunman yanked the young Comanche woman in closer. "Who says?"

"The Texas Rangers."

"Oh, so you're a lawman."

"Nope. Told ya, I'm a Texas Ranger."

"What's the difference?" another of the gunmen asked, a trail of tobacco juice following the words out of his mouth.

Steeldust Jack rotated his gaze among all six of them. The way they held their pistols already cocked told him they were hardened gunmen, no stranger to triggers, with the exception of one who looked no more than fifteen. Steeldust Jack's biggest fear at that point was that the Comanche behind him would let loose with their arrows, thereby catching him in the certain crossfire to follow.

"Well, a lawman, by nature, is answerable to the law. A Ranger's answerable only to Texas. But this ain't Texas here. Not really."

"Coulda fooled us," said the second speaker. "Then what is it?"

"Indian land by the law, as provided by the United States government."

"Thought you weren't answerable to the law, Ranger."

"I'm not. But I am answerable to the government of both the country and the state. And the word of both says you've got no place upon the land on which you're currently standing."

"Somebody should've told that to our dead friend, who looks like someone put him through a meat grinder," said a third gunman.

"And we ain't leaving," added the man with knife in one hand and girl's hair in the other, " 'til these

Injuns give up the one of their stinking kind that done it."

"It's my job to find the man who done it, whether that's here or somewheres else," Steeldust Jack told them all. "So why don't you boys get yourself gone and let me go about my business and find out who killed your friend?"

"'Cause it's our business too, Ranger," the knife wielder said, touching the tip of his blade to the young woman's throat firmly enough to make her wince.

Steeldust Jack saw a trickle of blood running down her neck. He realized she was far more girl than woman, probably no more than thirteen. Her dark eyes, leveled on him once more, were filled with fear and a desperate plea for help. It made him think of someone holding his own daughter in a similar spot.

"Maybe you should tell me exactly what business it is brought you here in the first place," he said.

The man who'd done the most talking, the one Jack Strong now took to be the leader, took a few steps ahead of the rest. "Tell you what. Why don't you ride yourself out of here and let us serve as your deputies?"

"Fine by me, so long as you boys go first. I'll be right behind."

The leader made a show of poking a finger in the air five times, one for each of his men. "Seems there's six men here standing against you and them Injuns who won't be standing long once the lead starts flying."

"Five men," Steeldust Jack corrected, gesturing with his eyes toward the kid. "One of you looks like he still wears his diapers."

The kid stepped forward, hand ready on his gun. "You wanna see how fast I am?"

"In my experience, son, any man needs to say that ain't nearly as fast as he thinks he is."

"I already killed tougher men than you."

"You shut your hole, Jimmy Miller," the leader said, angling himself in front of the kid. "Boy spoke out of turn, Ranger. I smack him upside his head or shoot him myself, it's still five against one."

"You as good with measuring as you are with counting, friend?"

"Huh?"

"Fifty-two feet."

"What?"

"Fifty-two feet—the distance between us when I stopped. I know it real well, 'cause it's how far I was away when the Texas Brigade took Devil's Den. Had a bullet in my leg, so that's where I stayed for the charge. Down to the last of my ammo, so I didn't dare miss. And know what? I didn't." Steeldust Jack squared his shoulders to face all six figures at once. "Fifty-two feet. Same distance I am to you."

"Six of us, Ranger. Means you don't get to miss even once."

Steeldust Jack didn't flinch, blink, or breathe. "Did I mention how many times I reloaded at Devil's Den? You boys wanna have at it, let's do this. But I was sent here to do my job, without call for who's involved. And it's my job to find who killed your friend, whether they reside on this reservation or not."

"Well," another of the gunmen started, "we're here

to do a job too, and these damn Injuns are in the way. That's the whole of it."

"And what job would that be, exactly?"

"Keep your mouth shut, Elmer, or I'll shit down your throat." The leader holstered his pistol and took off his hat. "Name's William Brocius. But folks know me better as Curly Bill. Maybe you've heard of me."

"I've heard of a gunfighter by that name," said Steeldust Jack. "Heard he can shoot jackrabbits blindfolded and can snuff out a candle with a perfectly aimed shot."

Curly Bill bowed his head slightly, never taking his eyes off Jack Strong. "That'd be me, Ranger."

"Maybe you'd like to tell me who you're working for, so I can have a conversation with him instead, since you're here to do this job and all. Get a notion of what might bring six gunfighters like yourselves to these parts."

"Seven," Curly Bill corrected. "You're forgetting the one in our number who came to a real bad end at the hands of these Injuns."

"You didn't answer my question about what brought you here in the first place."

"Because it was a statement, as I recall. And maybe we're just passing through."

"Comanche don't cotton well to that, Curly Bill. So I'd be of a mind, if I was you, to respect their wishes and get yourself gone someplace else. And if your boss, whoever he is, wants to discuss the matter further, I'm all ears."

Curly Bill moved his mouth about as if he were gnawing at the insides of his cheeks. His eyes stayed locked on Steeldust Jack in what men of their kind referred to as a gunfighter's glare. The Ranger waited for him to break the stare, watched Curly Bill grin broadly.

"Me being from Arizona, you're the first Texas Ranger I ever met."

"I hope you're not disappointed."

"Still deciding."

"Fine by me, Curly Bill, long as you do it somewhere other than here."

Curly Bill backpedaled, the rest of the gunmen falling into step with him, toward a nearby shaded area, where they'd hitched their horses.

"This ain't over, Ranger," he said, before turning around. "Not even close."

"That's entirely up to you, friend."

Steeldust Jack didn't take his eyes off the gunmen until they rode thunderously out, spraying a curtain of dust and dirt behind them.

"They'll be back," he told Isa-tai, once the riders were out of sight.

"They're not your problem," Isa-tai said, standing board straight and gazing off in the direction in which the gunmen had disappeared, as if he could still see them.

"Yes, they are. The body of their friend was found off the reservation, and I was witness to them threatening you on sovereign land the United States government has deeded to the Comanche. That don't sit well with me under any circumstances."

"They will be dealt with," said Isa-tai, still staring out into the distance.

"What's that mean?"

White Eagle fixed his gaze on Steeldust Jack. "They will be dealt with."

"Then answer me this, Isa-tai," the Ranger said. "What is it they came here after? What is it they want from your people?"

"Not our people; our land."

Steeldust Jack thought of the rows of cornstalks he'd passed when he rode in. Nothing about the reservation that particularly stood out besides that.

"Which brings us back to who those boys are working for," he said. "Think I'll have a talk with him, make sure none of these other fellas end up like the one got himself torn to bits."

Isa-tai's expression tightened, his gaze suddenly so cold and resolute that Steeldust Jack could feel the chill all the way to his bones.

"There are some things, Ranger, that no one can control."

22

BALCONES CANYONLANDS, TEXAS

"I've heard of Curly Bill Brocius," Dylan said, when the present-day White Eagle stopped his tale there. "He shot Tombstone's town marshal in 1880 and was involved in the killing of Morgan Earp. Wyatt himself returned the favor, a couple years after the infamous gunfight at the OK Corral."

"You know your history," the old man said, as if he wasn't impressed at all.

"I know my gunmen." Dylan realized Ela was holding his hand, but he couldn't recall exactly when she'd taken it again. "And that boy named Jimmy, who threatened Steeldust Jack, could've been James 'Killing Jim' Miller. He earned that nickname for good reason, since he supposedly murdered his own grandparents and shot his sister's husband in the face with a shotgun."

"I've heard of him, too," Ela chimed in. "I believe he went on to become a Texas Ranger."

"A man dies as he lives, boy," White Eagle said, before Dylan could respond. "Even I will die someday, once my granddaughter here is ready to assume her rightful place—two centuries is enough for any man. But there is one more battle to fight first."

"So, who did send those gunmen in 1874?" Dylan asked him. "Who were they really working for?"

The old man lumbered to his feet, pushing off Dylan's shoulder and accepting Ela's help.

"Time for you to leave," White Eagle told both of them. "The night has given all it has to give."

"What happens now?" Dylan asked, rising and brushing the dirt and brush off his jeans, glancing toward the shed, where he was sure he'd heard something again. That made him think of the flickering shadow he'd spotted in the mouth of one of the caves overlooking White Eagle's property, but when he looked back it was gone.

"Nature has a way of setting things right. Like it did here, all those years ago." The old man hesitated, seeming to sniff the air. "Like it will again today. Nature knows no time. Go now, boy, and don't come back until someone smarter wears your shoes." White Eagle's eyes locked on Ela, piercing in their intensity, as she finally succeeded in dragging Dylan away. "Make sure he doesn't trip in the woods."

23

AUSTIN, TEXAS

Daniel Cross sat on a bench in the grassy courtyard section of the Domain, a mall in north Austin, feeling the heat bleed out of the air as night settled in. He was hungry, but all the food places he could afford were still too crowded to risk standing in line. Since he couldn't return to his apartment, Saflin and Zurif had given him money for some clothes and a motel room. He'd found some jeans and shirts on sale in one of the clothing stores and sat now with a pair of bags on either side of him so nobody could share the bench, while he watched the crowd some more before checking into the motel. It wasn't like he had anything better to do right now, and he kind of enjoyed watching people coming and going from the more upscale stores he'd never set foot in.

If only they knew . . .

Cross was particularly enjoying himself tonight, given that this snippet of humanity reminded him so much of the kids who'd made his youth a living hell, all grown up. The kids who'd giggled and whispered as he passed, or pulled his shorts down in gym, or drew caricatures of him on the blackboard, with blotches dotting his long, narrow, cartoonish face. The kids who'd christened him Diaper Dan.

He'd have his revenge on each and every one of them now. Make their lives a living hell, just like they'd made his.

Because what they didn't know was that Daniel Cross had an IQ pushing one hundred sixty. That he was smarter than any of his science teachers by the time he hit tenth grade, already bored out of his mind. That reality instilled in Cross a smug self-assurance that made him feel superior to the faceless trolls who came and went through the doors of the assorted stores around him. His tormenters all grown up, with no conception of the power he held over them.

"Eenie, meenie, miney, mo," he said to himself, pointing to a few shoppers exiting Neiman Marcus. "Oh, that's right, you're all gonna go."

The accidental rhyme brought a smile to his face. Making the drive out to the Comanche Indian reservation had actually saved him from the men who'd showed up at his apartment. That made him think back a few weeks to the first time he'd met Razin Saflin and Ghazi Zurif, when he responded to a knock on his apartment door.

"We'd like to talk to you."

"About what?"

"The posts you've been leaving on certain message boards, Twitter, Facebook, and Instagram."

"Are you following me?"

Zurif and Saflin looked at each other.

"Because I've only got, like, fourteen followers."

"We know who you follow," Zurif said.

"That's why we're here," Saflin added. "Because we follow Allah and nothing else."

"He sees your message as divine providence in pursuit of His will."

"You guys aren't cops, are you? If you are, you'd have to tell me."

They looked at each other again.

"One of your messages said you could serve Allah," Saflin started this time. "We'd like to know how."

"I never mentioned Allah."

"Our cause is His cause. Serve us, and our movement, and you serve Him."

"Do I need to convert to Islam or something?"

"Your service is testament to your faith," Zurif said. "Your actions before Allah are an acceptance of His grace."

"Now explain what you wish to place before Him to fulfill His word," Saflin added, in what sounded like an order. "How you think you can help us."

Cross had told them, holding nothing back. Let it all spill out behind the pressure released from a lifetime of pent-up frustration, the only way to escape the shadow of Diaper Dan. How his expertise in chemical engineering had landed him a freelance job on the Comanche reservation. How he'd uncovered a blight of dead animals in the course of his analytical work. With his curiosity piqued, how he'd conducted his own methodological study of the land to ascertain what was killing wildlife that included birds and small game. He had been amazed by what he found, and not about to share it with a soul until he was sure—amazed to the point of giddiness when his own experiments provided confirmation that he had found an ancient, deadly, and unstoppable weapon.

Diaper Dan no more.

Let the real losers shoot up their school, take a few lives, and eat a pistol barrel when SWAT closed in. Daniel Cross set his sights on the whole country, wanted to take thousands of lives. Millions maybe. He hated them all, no exceptions. Because if they didn't hate him, they ignored him or frowned when he passed, which was even worse. Now he'd be able to show them all, each and every one, thanks to what he'd found on that Indian reservation.

Zurif and Saflin said they needed a demonstration to prove he wasn't full of shit and that he really could pull this off.

No problem.

Cross would give them a demonstration, all right. Tomorrow.

He couldn't wait.

PART THREE

Four newly raised ranging companies, have all been organized, and taken their several stations on our frontier. We know they are true men, and they know exactly what they are about. With many of them Indian and Mexican fighting has been their trade for years. That they may be permanently retained in the service on our frontier is extremely desirable.

—*Victoria Advocate*, November 16, 1848

24

"Since when do you drink Hires?" Caitlin asked, rolling around in her hand the frosty bottle Cort Wesley had just given her, fresh from the fridge.

He took a seat next to her on the porch swing of his house in Shavano Park. "I've kind of developed a taste for it."

It was the kind of place he never expected to live. His girlfriend Maura Torres's house, actually, inherited by his boys after they'd witnessed her murder. He could have moved them elsewhere, but Cort Wesley wanted Dylan and Luke never to forget what had happened here, or the impression that violence seen up close and personal can leave on a person. In his experience, those who disagreed with that thinking had never experienced violence firsthand.

"You ever do any personal appearances?" he asked Caitlin suddenly.

"Like what?"

"Like at a prestigious prep school, maybe as the graduation speaker, come May."

"Graduation speaker?"

"Part of the deal I cut with the principal of Luke's school."

"Do I want to know the details?"

"Luke gets to room with Zach next year. That enough?"

"What's the date of this graduation?" Caitlin asked him, and sipped her root beer.

She hadn't had root beer since she was a little girl, at a local soda fountain with her granddad. A scoop of vanilla ice cream floated amid the suds on top, on Earl Strong's recommendation.

"You got that look, Ranger," Cort Wesley said to her.

"What look might that be?"

"The one that says something's grabbed hold and won't let go."

"Sam Bob Jackson."

"Is that a real person?"

"The minerals broker I went to see in Houston. If he was any more slimy you'd have to hose down his office with disinfectant."

"Probably comes with the territory in that business."

"This was different. Son of a bitch is hiding something, for sure. Something just doesn't feel right."

Cort Wesley chuckled. "You being an expert on human behavioral traits."

"This coming from somebody who takes advice from a ghost."

Cort Wesley tipped his bottle toward her. "How's the root beer?"

"Damn fine."

"Then it's good advice." Caitlin watched his face grow somber. "Think I'll head back up to that Indian reservation in the morning. Something doesn't feel right there, either."

She held his stare until a pair of june bugs buzzed between them. "You give Luke the news?"

"Nope. I'd rather he didn't know I had any part in it."

"Why?"

"Because I don't want him thinking the two of us are always going to be there to win all his battles for him."

"You mean fight, not win."

Cort Wesley drained the rest of his Hires. "I've got the same feeling you do."

"That the next battle's right around the next corner." Caitlin felt her phone vibrate and found a voice mail from a call she hadn't noticed. "It's from Jones. I better see what he wants."

"Knock yourself out," Cort Wesley said, tipping his root beer toward her and watching her expression tighten as she listened to the message. "Bad?"

"That's likely an understatement, Cort Wesley. Looks like tomorrow's going to be another interesting day."

25

BALCONES CANYONLANDS, TEXAS

"Drink your tea," Ela said, sipping from her own steaming cup.

Dylan took one sip, and then another, wrinkling his nose at the effort.

"You ever hear of sugar?" He realized he couldn't find his phone. He ruffled the blanket in search of it, coming up with Ela's iPhone 6s instead. "I should've gotten you a different case, so we could tell them apart."

She gave him the smile she'd first flashed upon taking the seat next to him in their Native American studies class at Brown. Dylan hadn't even been sure it was aimed at him, to the point where he looked around to see if there was another guy in the area, and he still hadn't known how to respond when he discovered there wasn't.

What am I, like, in middle school?

That's what it had felt like then, and it didn't feel all that much different now. Sure, he believed in the cause Ela was fighting for on her native land and all. But dropping everything and coming home to Texas with her was all about Ela holding him by a string, making him dance on command.

"Sugaring the tea would spoil the effect." She winked at him, the steam from her cup rising between them and seeming to stain the lantern light.

Dylan took a bigger sip this time, starting to detect a slightly acrid odor to go with a bitter undertaste that left his tongue feeling dry. They were seated in the long-abandoned root cellar beneath Ela's family's ancestral home, once used to store perishables for the long winter, and later appropriated by Ela as her personal hideaway. She'd spent lots of time shoring up and beautifying the fifteen-foot-square chamber as much as she could. Then college had brought new interests and demands on her time, her personal hideaway deteriorating back to its original damp and musty form. The furniture Ela brought down here from storage was rotting, and the planks she'd laid over the earthen walls had warped and puckered. The old-fashioned kerosene lantern they were using had once hung from the ceiling, but the hook that had held it there was gone.

"Peyote?" Dylan asked, the cup still touching his lips.

She flashed that smile again. "Uh-huh."

Dylan wanted to stop drinking the tea, should have stopped, but didn't let himself.

"You're not scared, are you, boy?"

"Do I look scared . . . girl?"

He tried to chuckle, but his mouth was too dry. He managed a smile that seemed to freeze in place, to the point where he had to make his mind pry it free.

"If you only knew," Dylan said, taking sip after sip now, feeling the liquid cool, or maybe not feeling it at all.

"Knew what?"

Dylan didn't want to tell her, to risk spoiling the moment. "Let's just say there's lots of assholes in the world and I seem to have gone up against most of them."

In the now quivering light, Ela's eyes looked like molten lava. "You sound like a Comanche, like my Lost Boys."

"Lost Boys?"

"What I call the young Comanche I practically grew up with. They're all cousins of mine. Even more radical about our land and heritage than me; you can tell, because I don't paint my face."

"Or draw a red X on your chest."

Ela smiled at him playfully. "You sure about that, boy?"

Dylan realized he'd finished his cup. "I didn't know you could make tea out of it," he said, his voice sounding like somebody else's, like he was hearing it from outside his body.

"Only for a few thousand years. Especially in these parts, since the buttons harvested from the roots of West Texas cacti are unusually high in mescaline sulfate."

"So now you're a chemist, as well as an activist."

"You can take the girl out of the school, but not the school out of the girl."

Dylan felt her sliding close to him, nearly tipping the kerosene lantern over as she shifted on the blanket warming them atop the root cellar's cold, flattened ground.

"The Native American Church believes peyote to be crucial to obtaining spiritual guidance, so long as it's ingested in the proper environment."

Dylan looked about dramatically. "A root cellar?"

Ela laughed. Their eyes met and locked, and Dylan could see a light sheen on her flesh, her face seeming to glow in the twinkling lantern light. The world before him was shifting and shaking slightly, though not in the way that left him dizzy. It was more like the effects of the IV anesthesia he'd gotten before a stomach test he'd needed, a few years back.

If anything, Dylan felt more alert, more aware, hyperfocused on his surroundings, with Ela shining as the only light amid the darkness. He couldn't see the lantern anymore; there was only her. And then they were kissing, without Dylan realizing their faces and mouths had come together.

Even though the tea tasted sour, her breath was sweet, reminding him of sunflowers, for some reason. Then he seemed to be with her in a field of them, green and yellow and bright, their hands sweeping about each other. Dylan's arms felt disconnected from his body, like snakes pulling free of his shoulders, acting independently of his own thoughts. It felt like a dream he could control, all of this happening according to his own direction as he stood outside himself and watched it all transpire. He heard a baby crying, and then his mother was somewhere else in the field, picking flowers with his younger brother. Then something was crawling into the jeans his dad hated because they were too skinny to suit his tastes and cost too much, and Dylan realized it hadn't crawled in at all, just morphed into something altogether different, over which he had no more control than he had over his arms or his thoughts.

The lantern tipping over burned his eyes with a splash of light that brought Dylan back to where he was. Except his shirt was off and the wool of the blanket was scratching at him. Or maybe it was Ela scratching at him. Didn't matter, because there was no way this was really happening, no way. It was just a dream or an illusion he'd lost hold of, and soon he'd wake up with his underwear soaked, the way it had happened when he was, like, twelve.

The raw newness of his feelings then was what he felt now, but it was a newness heightened by an awareness, in the recesses of his mind, that he had gone back to that time with all his knowledge and experience retained. Then Ela was wrestling him, pounding him, it seemed, until he realized it wasn't her at all but his own heart, thudding up a storm, his naked rib cage seeming to expand more with each beat, threatening to explode.

And then he did explode.

But not there.

Somewhere else.

Everywhere at once.

He thought he heard Ela gasping, screaming, glimpsed grayish shapes like the Dementors from the Harry Potter movies, slithering through the air, enveloping both of them in their dark shroud.

"Ela!" he cried out.

Or thought he did.

"Ela!"

Didn't she see them closing in? Didn't she know?

Gotta stop, gotta stop, gotta stop . . .

Words spoken or merely formed, it didn't matter anymore, the difference reduced to nothing. Action and thought became indistinguishable from each other, to the point where Dylan could no longer tell which was which. Or what was really happening from what his mind conjured.

The Dementors . . .

Everywhere. And nowhere.

Just like him, just like them—him and Ela.

Together. Separate. Here. Gone.

And then it was happening again, inside him, only different this time. Because the Dementors were gone, replaced by ghostly specters watching him from afar and from up close at the same time. Dylan saw his mother smiling down at him, and he hugged Ela even closer, for reasons he didn't understand.

But then his mother was gone, replaced by a series of spectral images drawn from among the monsters who had visited him in the past. Dylan had learned much too young that there were things that really did go bump in the night, that monsters were real. But they didn't seem real now, making him question the integrity of his own memory and whether these beings were the products of comparable delusions, which attacked him only in his mind.

The faceless thugs who'd nearly beaten him to death just outside the Brown University campus, still faceless now.

The white slavers who'd kidnapped him in Mexico.

The serial killer with hundreds of victims to his credit.

Girls had been part of his crossing paths with all of them. And now they were watching him with Ela, as if to decide which would get another go at him.

You can't. You're dead.

"Don't speak," he thought he heard Ela say, atop him now.

Maybe it didn't matter whether they were dead or not. His father thought he saw ghosts, at least one, so why not Dylan, too? Maybe the lines between the two worlds weren't as well constructed as everyone thought. The right person, at the right time and place, might be capable of bulldozing right through them.

Leave me alone.

"Quiet," Ela was saying, pressing a hand against his mouth.

Dylan realized he couldn't breathe, that she was smothering him with a palm that tasted like the peyote tea, which was driving bile up his throat. He still couldn't breathe, but her hand was gone, and then the spectral images were dissolving around him and the lantern light was fading to a soft blur. Then he saw only darkness, even though his eyes were open.

Dylan awoke in the root cellar, Ela pressed against him, their clothes shed in unkempt piles about the mossy earth. The blanket had bunched up, conforming to their dual shapes and no longer spreading any farther.

He had no idea where his phone was, to check the time, and the next time he opened his eyes Ela was gone, and he was terrified, until he slipped off again. But, the next time, her naked form was still there and his wasn't, making him wonder whether he'd ever been there at all. If what had happened was real, if anything was real . . .

His head pounded like a jackhammer was working between his ears; his mouth and throat were so dry that he couldn't swallow. He tried to open his eyes again, only to realize that they already were open but that there was nothing to see except the empty darkness, broken only by a sliver of light still shed by the fading lantern. The dark scared him, the night scared him, left visions of scurrying through the woods and brush on four legs instead of two, his nails turned to talon-like claws raking at the ground and air. Empty of thought, with the world his to embrace. Grasping at the air and seeking Ela amid the mist-shrouded night alive with the sounds of crickets and night birds. Calling out for Ela, except he had no voice. Hypersensitive to the world around him, every smell, sound, and sight.

Everything magnified until it all washed away in a splash of water that turned to blood, the light appearing from slivers cut out of the world above, just in time to remind him to breathe.

26

BOERNE, TEXAS

Guillermo Paz sat at his priest's bedside, the side rail lowered so he could feed the man his dinner, which was watered-down oatmeal with the texture of drilling mud, to make it easier for him to swallow. Paz was the only one who could get him to eat anything at all, which convinced the colonel that his priest could grasp the meaning of his words, even if he could no longer respond to them.

"I'll tell you, Padre," Paz said, as the old man worked his mouth feebly and then managed a swallow, "I really miss our talks. Remember the first time you heard my confession? I know I threw you for a loop with that one, but you never shied away from telling me the God's honest truth, if you'll pardon my choice of words."

Paz dabbed the spoon into the bowl of soupy oatmeal and eased it forward. His priest opened his mouth a crack and sucked up the meager contents with a slurping sound.

"I know you can't talk to me anymore, Padre, but

you can still listen, and that's almost as important. I got back too late to call tonight's bingo game. I know somebody from the home was there to fill in, but I still feel I let people down. I don't like letting people down."

The old priest finished working that spoonful down his throat and opened his mouth for the next. His once-bright eyes were dull and lifeless, his thinning white hair flattened to his scalp in some places and sticking up askew in others. The room was laced with deodorizing spray to hide the stale scents of bodily waste and dried, scaly skin racked by bedsores. Paz detested injustice of all kinds, but this seemed like the ultimate one, for a man who'd given his life to others to have his own snatched from him this way. Feeding the man was the least he could do, but it always left him wishing he could do more. It had made Paz feel good at first, but now the whole process left him empty and drained. Powerless, too.

"I've got that feeling again, that something bad's coming. I got it in this apartment I raided today that belonged to some pissant who normally wouldn't amount to a speck of dust in the great chain of the universe. Problem is, all that's changed now. Pissants like him have become as dangerous as assassination squads. They're walking nuclear bombs, Padre, able to do a lot more damage with a keyboard or a test tube than men like me could ever do with a rifle. When I killed the man who killed my priest back home in the slums, I did it up close and personal, just him and me. I even used the same knife he did. But those days are gone. Now the worst danger, the biggest threat, comes from people you can't even see, who don't have the *cajones* to do face-to-face what they thrive on from a distance."

Paz watched his priest swallow the latest spoonful and readied another.

"The philosopher Rousseau wrote that 'Man is born free, and he is everywhere in chains.' Now those chains are power cords, and they have the potential to strangle everything good people hold dear. Your favorite philosopher, Aristotle, bucked the system by believing in free will over determinism. But it's the free will of people like that pissant whose apartment I raided that's bringing us all to the edge."

Paz realized his priest's lips were trembling in anticipation of more oatmeal, and he quickly readied the next spoon, scooping too much up for the old man to manage and needing to shake some of it back into the bowl.

"I know what you'd say, if you could still speak, Padre," Paz told him, gently dabbing up the stray oatmeal with a napkin. "You'd tell me that was my job, that my lot in his life is to tighten a noose on the necks of all the pissants before they can do the same to the world. Problem is, there's just too many of them for me, my Texas Ranger, and her outlaw to contend with now."

Paz's words froze there. He was thinking of the apartment he'd raided this morning and the kid who lived there. The spoon froze, too, suspended in the air halfway between Paz and his priest, the excess oatmeal concoction dribbling down to the bedsheet. Paz thought of the cold feeling that had enveloped him as soon as he crashed through the apartment door, a vague sense of discomfort, coupled with a certainty that something very, very bad was coming—a product of this kid now gone missing. The ratty apartment stank of body odor and unwashed clothes. It was infested with ants, thanks to the stray candy wrappers strewn about. But it was the residue of something else that plagued Paz the most.

The kid's thoughts.

They seemed to hang in the air, and now they clung to Paz's consciousness the way the stench had clung to his clothes.

"Yup, there's more pissants than ever looking to do damage. And you know what, Padre?" Paz resumed, starting the spoon toward his priest's waiting mouth again. "I've got this feeling the worst is yet come."

27

SAN ANTONIO, TEXAS

"Love the new digs, Ranger," Jones greeted her, the next morning, when Caitlin reached the back corner of the open first-floor office space of Texas Ranger Company F headquarters. His shiny new cowboy boots were propped up on the still drying varnish coating her desk.

"Glad you approve," she said, twisting the back of his chair around so his feet flopped back to the floor. "Nice boots, by the way."

"Had some business up in Austin, so I picked them up at Allen's, just like you recommended."

"I recommended you buy them a size too small."

"The sales clerk frowned on the notion. He said it would make my feet go numb. Cause a fall maybe."

"A girl can hope."

"Homeland Security is no longer investigating your use of an alleged weapon of mass destruction."

"Should I say thank you?"

"Not to the people whose houses still smell like roadkill. Next time you unleash a stink bomb, you may want to advise people to close their windows."

"I'll keep that in mind. And I appreciate you making this go away."

"Speaking of which . . ."

Jones popped up out of his chair, reaching for something inside his jacket. He looked to be in better shape than the last time Caitlin had seen him. She couldn't say exactly what Jones did with Homeland Security, especially these days, and she doubted that anybody else could, either. He operated in the muck, among the dregs of society plotting to harm the country from the inside. Caitlin doubted he'd ever written a report or detailed the specifics of his operations in any way. He lived in the dark, calling on the likes of Guillermo Paz and the colonel's henchmen to deal with matters, always out of view of the light. When those matters brought him to Texas, which seemed to be every other day, Jones would seek out Caitlin the way he might a former classmate.

She'd first met him when his name was still "Smith" and he was attached to the American embassy in Bahrain. Enough of a relationship had formed for the two of them to remain in contact and to have actually worked together on several more occasions. Sometimes

Jones surprised her, but mostly he could be relied upon to live down to Caitlin's expectations.

This morning, the thin light kept Jones's face cloaked in the shadows, where he was most comfortable. Caitlin tried to remember the color of his eyes but couldn't, as if he'd been trained to never look at anyone long enough for anything to register. He was wearing a sport jacket over a button-down shirt, and pressed trousers, making him seem like a high school teacher, save for the tightly cropped military-style haircut.

Jones finally started to ease his hand from his pocket, withdrawing a heavy, shiny piece of paper folded in two. "You're about to thank me, Ranger," he said.

"For what?"

"Getting you out from behind this desk."

Caitlin glanced at the chair he'd just vacated. "Your message last night said you had something important to show me," she said.

"Actually," Jones corrected, "I said 'vital.' And the voice mail I left said we needed to play a little show-and-tell. I show and you tell, starting with this."

Jones unfolded the picture he was holding and held it so Caitlin could see a tall, gangly young man with a bad case of acne.

"Holy shit," Caitlin said, not believing her eyes.

"Recognize him, I see."

"I spotted him yesterday bird-dogging a protest outside the Comanche Indian reservation near Austin."

Jones shook his head, as if he were having trouble processing what Caitlin had just said. "What time?"

"Early afternoon. You need me to be more specific?"

Jones shook his head again. "I don't believe it."

"What?"

"How you find shit to step in, no matter how well the pile is hidden."

"Did I miss something here?"

"No, I did." Jones looked down at the picture. "On a major terrorist suspect yesterday, because he happened to be in the same place as you. Then again, nothing just *happens* when it comes to Caitlin Strong, does it? You are a genuine force of nature, Ranger."

"Maybe we should start this conversation again."

"So you really don't recognize this kid?"

"Should I?"

Jones held the picture up again. "We lifted this picture off social media." Then he reached into his pocket and came out with a second photo, which he slowly unfolded. "This is a copy of one we found framed atop a bureau in the suspect's apartment. Let's see if it jogs your memory."

"Oh, man," Caitlin said, looking at it.

28

San Antonio, Texas

Caitlin was still shaking her head, moments later, unable to lift her eyes from the shot from ten years ago, of her standing next to a younger version of the kid she'd spotted outside the Comanche reservation yesterday. They had their arms around each other's shoulders.

"Well, I guess that explains why he looked familiar to me," she told Jones, finally raising her eyes.

"Remember his name?"

"Daniel Cross, I believe."

Jones nodded. "Currently age twenty-four, lifelong resident of Austin, and recent frequenter of ISIS-related social media. In fact, you could call him a genuine fanboy, enough of one to hit our radar, with all the pinging he'd been doing."

"You saying he's a convert?"

"Sure. Straight to the terrorism watch list. The bureau's been keeping tabs on a couple of hardcore ISIS homegrown operatives with ties right up to the organization's top. They're the ones who pinged Daniel Cross back."

"Why?"

"Apparently, the kid's a frigging genius, with degrees in molecular and chemical engineering. Most of the time, losers like him who hate the world can't even steady an assault rifle long enough to do any real damage. But what put Daniel Cross on our radar was his brains, not his bullets. And in case you didn't get the message, we've got ISIS seriously on the run. They're desperate, and that's given their midlevel operatives operational freedom to ditch the purity test. Whatever Cross put on the table before the two on the FBI's radar was obviously more than enough to compensate for the fact that he doesn't pray five times a day." Jones stopped there, leaning slightly forward. "That makes this a good time for you to tell me the basis of your association with him."

"I don't think you really want to hear it."

"Try me."

"Cross got himself into a scrape, just before I left the Rangers for a time."

"Yeah, I heard the death rate in Texas dropped precipitously those couple of years."

"Anyway, Jones, I tried to help the kid."

"What kind of scrape was it, exactly?"

Caitlin swallowed hard. "He was planning to blow up his high school." She paused, then continued, "I don't think I've ever seen a worse case of bullying."

"So the kid tries to blow up his school and you give him a shoulder to cry on?"

"It never got to the 'trying' stage, Jones. Cross left a page of some manifesto he was writing in a lavatory stall. Somebody found it and Rangers got the call."

Jones took the picture back from her, wanting to crunch it into a ball so much his hand was shaking. "A kid does something like that today, it's him who gets flushed down the toilet."

"I notice you haven't said anything about the bullies who pushed him to the edge."

"Maybe because they're not the ones who reached out to ISIS, Ranger. And I can't wait to shove my fist down the throat of whoever left out of Daniel Cross's file the fact that he was a bomber."

"He was a juvenile at the time, and last time I checked, nobody's a bomber until they actually blow something up."

"A mere formality, in my line of work."

"In mine, we actually try to help people from time to time, Jones."

"Whether they deserve it or not." Jones's face had reddened, his cheeks seeming to puff with air as he shook his head. "So I guess your experiment in mentoring failed."

"I lost touch with Daniel Cross after my sabbatical from the Rangers."

"So we'll have you to blame if whatever this kid is up to comes to pass. Did you know Cross's real mother was a prostitute who tried to abort him with a coat hanger, after one of her johns raped her?"

"I knew she was a prostitute."

"The kid was born a stain on the entire human race. Fits the classic loser profile, ends up courting favor with anybody who'll give him the time of day on social media."

"But a group like ISIS wouldn't give him the time of day unless he had something to give them, Jones."

"Hence the raid on his apartment yesterday, Ranger. I've got a team working on the contents of his computer as we speak, but so far they've found squat. Don't ask me to explain the details, but the gist of it is he's probably carrying around whatever got ISIS's attention on a thumb drive in his pocket."

"Meaning you've got no idea what."

Jones let the shot picturing Daniel Cross and Caitlin together dangle between them. "I might, if we can figure out what the kid was doing at that Indian reservation."

"So you're drawing a link between ISIS and the Comanche?"

"I'm drawing a link *from* Daniel Cross and the Comanche. You're a jump ahead of me, and I'll leave it to you to fill in the gaps, now that you're personally involved and officially off desk duty."

"I haven't seen the kid in over ten years, Jones."

"And I've been avoiding tall buildings ever since nine eleven. So what's your point?"

Caitlin's phone rang, CORT WESLEY lighting up the caller ID, as if his psychic radar was switched on. "You're not going to believe this, Cort Wesley," she greeted him.

"That's my line. I'm back at the reservation. You better get up here."

"More trouble?"

"You might say that. That construction work foreman I beat up yesterday was found murdered, Ranger, and I think I'm about to be arrested."

29

BALCONES CANYONLANDS, TEXAS

"We didn't call for the Rangers," Travis County sheriff Tom Winkmeister told Caitlin, after she slipped inside the cordoned-off crime scene.

"I'm here, all the same," she said, not even breaking stride.

She'd glimpsed the protesters, milling about before the entrance to the reservation instead of arranged in a neat line, and spotted Dylan and Ela among them, but she didn't stop to greet either.

"Tell you what," Winkmeister said, holding his gaze on Cort Wesley, who was standing on the other side

of the yellow crime scene tape, "if you can view the remains without losing your breakfast, I'll listen to what
you've got to say. But he stays right where he is, right
where I can see him," he continued, pointing toward
Cort Wesley. "On account of the fact that I expect he'll
be in custody before the day is out."

"Find anything here to support that theory yet?"

"You mean besides the fact that he busted the victim up yesterday?"

"And that would be thanks to the victim inciting his
workers to break your police line and attack those Comanche protesting peacefully, right?"

"You implying something, Ranger?"

"No, Sheriff, just stating a fact. I might even go as
far as to say that Cort Wesley Masters saved you a
heap of trouble by preventing an all-out riot."

The sheriff puckered his cheeks and let the air out
of them through his mouth like a balloon deflating.
"Maybe a little dustup would've made those protesters see the error of their ways."

"I was referring to one of them being Cort Wesley's
oldest son. If anything had happened to him, the wrath
of God would be nothing compared to what you'd be
facing. Now, about that body . . ."

The remains were so mangled that they best resembled
a human form after being dumped in a blender. Caitlin could tell from the size of the twisted limbs that
the victim was big, and she thought she spotted a beard
on the parts of his face left recognizable, trying to
match that up to the foreman of the construction crew

she'd glimpsed yesterday. He lay with his limbs askew, one arm detached and the other hanging by sinew, his mouth hung obscenely open as if his lower jaw had been broken away, the bone separated from the rest of his skull.

Caitlin rose to find the sheriff staring at Cort Wesley again.

"You want to tell me what business he's got here, Ranger?"

"Protecting his boy, I imagine."

"Do I need to remind you that he's still our primary suspect?"

"Condition of the remains indicates the murder was committed last night, Sheriff," Caitlin told him, peeling off her latex gloves. "After midnight, for sure."

"So what?"

"So Mr. Masters and I were together from ten o'clock on," she said, leaving it there.

Winkmeister smirked, then snickered. "Then I guess it's a good thing this isn't your case. Truth is, I'm not even sure we're looking for a man, based on the condition of the body. I'm thinking of putting out an APB on stray bears or wolves."

Caitlin gazed back toward the remains, where a swarm of flies thick enough to cloud the air had gathered. "You should know this isn't the first time, Sheriff."

"What isn't?"

"That a body's been found just off the rez, in almost the identical condition. It happened before, around a hundred and forty years ago. My great-great-grandfather's case."

"And here you are, figuring yourself to be following in his footsteps."

Caitlin pocketed her balled-up gloves, noticed Cort Wesley gazing toward the protest line, where trouble seemed to be brewing again. "Only if I'm after the same killer, Sheriff, and it's not Cort Wesley Masters."

"What would you like to explain first, Ranger?" Tepper said, as soon as he answered Caitlin's call. "Why you're not at your desk or where the hell you're calling from?"

"Jones didn't talk to you?" Caitlin asked, as Cort Wesley listened to the conversation from nearby.

"Jones? What's he got to do with this?"

"He's why I'm back at the Comanche reservation. We got a murder on our hands."

"You mean the Travis County sheriff has a murder on his hands."

"I need you to get us assigned lead on the investigation."

There was a pause, followed by a clicking sound Caitlin was certain was Captain Tepper's lighter firing. She pictured him lighting a cigarette, probably holding the receiver to make sure she'd heard him light it.

"Don't smoke on my account, D.W."

"What other account is there? There, you hear me puffing now? How important is this, Ranger?"

"Important enough for you to get Doc Whatley up here," Caitlin said, referring to Bexar County's longtime medical examiner.

"It's not even our case yet."

"It's a Homeland Security matter now, Captain. That means Jones will back us up."

"And how's that exactly?"

"I recognized someone watching the rez yesterday who's linked to ISIS."

"Say that again."

"You heard me."

"I was hoping I heard wrong. ISIS? Frigging ISIS?" Tepper's sigh dissolved into a cough. Now Caitlin could picture him pressing out his Marlboro in a new ashtray, brought in to replace yet another she'd hidden from sight. "Next time I put you behind a desk, Ranger," he resumed, "will you please just stay there?"

30

BALCONES CANYONLANDS, TEXAS

Dylan and Ela stood in the blistering sunlight blazing down on the entrance to the Comanche reservation, their faces shiny with sweat and shirts dappled with spots where it had soaked through in patches. They seemed bent on not letting their discomfort either show or detract from their commitment to stop the construction workers from entering the rez.

But things had clearly changed since the body of the foreman had been found, just off Comanche land. More cops manned the line between the workers and protesters. But there also looked to be a lot more workers on the scene today, their frustration and declining patience evident in beet-red expressions and sweat-blanched shirts, both of which suggested more violence was in the offing.

"You look like hell, son," Cort Wesley said to Dylan.

"I had a long night."

"I spoke to someone in the registrar's office at Brown. She told me the window for reenrolling in school for next semester is five days away. You want to mark that on your calendar or should I?"

Dylan glanced toward the cordoned-off crime scene. "Everyone thinks you killed that guy."

"That what you think?"

"Not for a minute. He looks too good."

"Ripped to shreds?"

"I've seen what you can do to people who piss you off."

"You're wasting your time," Ela said suddenly, her words aimed at Caitlin.

"How exactly are we wasting our time, miss?"

"With that," Ela answered, tilting her gaze toward the crime scene back off the road. "This isn't the kind of killer you can catch."

The confidence with which the young woman said that sent a chill up Caitlin's spine. Again, her tone bordered on smugness, but the look on her face was somber and calm. She was not in the least rattled by what had transpired, and seemingly was not even surprised by it.

"Nature takes care of its own," she continued.

"What was that, Ela?"

"Something my grandfather told us last night."

"You think your grandfather can shed some light on that man's murder?" Caitlin asked her.

"I think he knows this land is watched over and protected by a force you can't possibly imagine. I think he knows man's presence is tolerated only so long as we live by the land's rules. And I don't think he has any interest in talking to you."

"Tell you what, Ela," Caitlin said, turning her tone more conciliatory. "Why don't you go tell your grandfather that the great-great-granddaughter of Steeldust Jack Strong wants to have a talk with him? I've got a feeling he'll welcome the opportunity."

31

BALCONES CANYONLANDS, TEXAS

Dylan and Ela led Caitlin and Cort Wesley through the center of the reservation toward the more rustic outskirts where Ela's grandfather made his home. As was the case on many contemporary Indian reservations, the contrast in the living accommodations was striking: from mansions claiming large parcels of land for themselves, to more modest ranch-style homes, to trailers and dilapidated shacks that looked lifted from old black-and-white pictures, right down to the barren ground from which they'd sprouted.

A handful of cases over the years had taken her to other reservations, all dealing with crimes committed off Native American land, when the Rangers had been called in to assist the efforts of the tribal police. She saw none of those officers in evidence now. Their entire number was gathered closer to the entrance, more to keep watch on the protesters, it seemed, than to protect them. Cort Wesley had said none of the tribal policemen had so much as moved a muscle when the work crew launched its attack yesterday. Hardly surprising, given that they were likely beholden to the elders whose deal with Sam Bob Jackson to sell off mineral rights to the land put them squarely at odds with those for whom that land was sacred.

To that point, Caitlin reasoned, the Comanche reservation sat on some of the most pristine, bucolic land the state of Texas had to offer. She wondered if Stephen Austin and the others behind the deal understood that, during the post–Civil War years when the land was deeded to those Comanche willing to lay down their arms and accept peace with the fledgling state of Texas. The Quahada Comanche under the great chief Quanah Parker, on the other hand, had refused to accept the terms of the 1867 Medicine Lodge Treaty. As a result, the U.S. Army, along with the Rangers, including Caitlin's great-grandfather William Ray Strong, had spent years practically exterminating them in battles that remained shrouded as much in folklore as in fact. Parker himself finally surrendered at Fort Sill, in 1875, a year after Jack Strong's encounter here, and she couldn't help but wonder whether that timing had been more than coincidental.

The fact that this tribe continued to live off the land was well documented and was exemplified by the lush, rolling fields of crops, corn most notably, with plenty of other crops grown in smaller patches. Judging by the tree growth and younger landscaping, she imagined many of the mansion-like homes dotting the reservation had usurped land on which acres of crops had once sprouted.

"You like the homes of the *to'sarre*, Ranger?" Ela asked Caitlin, following her gaze.

"That's what we call the Natives behind the land deal," Dylan elaborated. "It means 'black dog.'"

"We?" Cort Wesley repeated.

The developed portion of the reservation ended abruptly, extending a bit farther into the untouched land where the wildlife refuge took hold. It was on these grounds that Ela's grandfather White Eagle lived, on land unspoiled and unchanged since the time of his ancestors. Sure enough, their trek brought them up to a hump that settled onto a narrow strip of earth perched against a pond fed by a churning waterfall. A man with a hunched back and stooped frame stood in the spotlight of the sun, between matching elm trees, hands clasped behind his back and flowing hair tossed about at the whims of the wind.

He had the look of a man who'd once been tall, now shrunken by the ravages of time and age. He wore trousers stitched out of some kind of hide, moccasins, and a leather vest over a tattered woolen shirt, in spite of the heat. Drawing closer, Caitlin could see that the furrows and wrinkles crisscrossing his face were so thick that the sun turned it into a patchwork road map of dark avenues carved through the light. She let herself imagine that if a man from the nineteenth century really were still alive today, this was what he'd probably look like.

"Caitlin Strong," the old man said, through lips that seemed not to move, his jawline utterly slack.

Caitlin felt Cort Wesley tense just to her right. Something about the old man knowing her name seeming to activate his defenses. She watched Ela advance, approaching White Eagle.

"Grandfather, this is the—"

"I know who she is and what she is," White Eagle said, never taking his eyes off Caitlin. "I feel like it's 1874 again and I'm looking at a different Strong."

"I'm sorry to intrude, sir."

"I'm not a 'sir.' *Sir* is a white man's term. Call me White Eagle, just like your ancestor once did. I'll call you *eckawipe*. Means 'first woman,' since you are the first woman Texas Ranger—at least the first one to truly last and make your name. Come and sit with me."

It seemed to Caitlin that the old man wasn't even acknowledging the presence of the others. Even when they all took short stools set in the cover of a grove of shade trees reflected in the shimmering surface of the still pond, it was as if the two of them were alone. Silence dominated at first, broken only by the regular dappling of the waterfall's currents slapping against the pond waters.

"Do you know why I'm here, White Eagle?" Caitlin finally asked.

"That man was killed off our lands. It's not our problem or our concern."

"I was hoping you could shed some light on other matters."

"They should know he will only be the first," White Eagle continued, ignoring what Caitlin had just said, sounding like he was playing a recording through his mouth. "That if they don't heed this warning, others will die too, just as they did in the time of your great-great-grandfather. You hear my words, Eckawipe?"

"I do, and they sound like a threat."

"Because they are, not from me but from the land itself. From nature."

"Your granddaughter mentioned that."

White Eagle's gaze shifted to Ela, as if noticing her for the first time. "My granddaughter does not speak for me or the land. She has yet to learn that language."

"You're aware of Steeldust Jack Strong's experiences here, then."

"I remember it like it was yesterday, Eckawipe."

Caitlin let the old man's comment stand. "He came to the reservation because of a killing just outside it, too. The victim today was found in virtually the same condition."

"Torn apart, as if by an animal?"

"I was thinking bear."

"So did Jack Strong. But I'll tell you what I told him. No bears roam these parts. No wolves or mountain lions, either. Not then, not now."

"*You* told him," Caitlin repeated. "In 1874. A hundred and forty-two years ago."

"I believe your math is correct," White Eagle told her. "And the white man today who repeats the same mistakes will pay the same price, Ranger. Many more will fall now, just as they fell then."

"Your own tribal leaders made this deal, White Eagle," Caitlin reminded. "Your granddaughter's standing in a protest line facing across the road, when really she should be teaching those kids she came back here for, and watching her back."

"Then the land will protect her as she protects it. That is the sacred bond our people made too many centuries ago to count. Persist in your trespass and you place your own life in jeopardy from forces you can't possibly imagine or understand."

"Why don't you help me understand them?"

White Eagle shook his head. "You're no different from your great-great-grandfather. I'll tell you the same thing I told him: begone and let nature handle its own."

"And what if I can't do that?"

"Then even I won't be able to protect you." The old man's eyes fixed briefly on Cort Wesley before moving to Dylan and holding on him. "Or those you love."

32

RALEIGH, NORTH CAROLINA

"Will the defendant please rise?"

Cray Rawls rose from the table, smoothing the folds of his suit straight as he looked toward the jury, meeting each and every one of the members' gazes with an ominous glare that suggested he might still be able to affect the outcome of the case. He looked at them and smirked, his nostrils still teeming with Candy's cheap perfume from the night before, reminding him of what it felt like to hold all the power, a sensation he clung to while awaiting the verdict.

"Ladies and gentlemen of the jury," the presiding judge continued, "in the first count of the indictment, People of Lynchville, North Carolina, versus Rawls Energy, Petroleum, and Chemical, or REPC, also known as REPCO, how say you?"

"We find the defendant, Cray Rawls, not guilty."

Rawls could hear the murmurs of surprise spreading through the jam-packed courtroom, continuing until the judge rapped his gavel.

"In the second count of the indictment . . ."

Rawls listened intently, but his mind drifted elsewhere. He hadn't been overly concerned about the verdict because the state clearly hadn't met its burden in trying to prove his company was responsible for poisoning the tainted drinking wells. Under his direction, his legal team had opted for a risky strategy of conceding REPCO's coal ash storage ponds had indeed leaked nearly forty thousand tons of toxic ash into a major river basin. Coal ash, containing such toxins as arsenic, lead, mercury, and cadmium, was what was left over when coal was burned to generate electricity.

Even the company's concession that this was among the worst such spills in history still left the burden on the state to prove REPCO had poisoned the class action complainants' well water. Experts called by both sides proved to be a study in contradiction and confusion. Then, Rawls had surprised opposing counsel again by not taking the stand in his own defense. They had elected to name him as a defendant in the suit, so he could face jail time even as his company faced ruin. In doing so, though, they had removed the option of calling him to the stand, relying on an inevitable cross-examination that had proven not so inevitable at all.

"We find the defendant not guilty."

The media was as disappointed by the unexpected

turn as the prosecution. Rawls had denied them the show they were anticipating. One national outlet had nicknamed him the Dark Prince, poking fun at his dark hair and Mediterranean features, marred by scars and pits—the pits had been left by acne, the scars from when a well cap blew on an offshore rig and sent steel bits into his face. When the first wells he invested in struck big, he let his investment ride, like a bettor on a hot streak, building the stake for founding his own company, which would ultimately grow into REPCO.

". . . not guilty."

The media never focused on that, choosing instead to belabor the various rumors and tall tales that had accompanied Cray Rawls on his climb up the corporate ladder. How he had punched out rivals who underbid him, sabotaged the rigs of competitors who encroached on his perceived territory, and burned down an East Hampton country club that had denied him admission. To them, he was no more than Texas trash, even though that experience was mired in a long-forgotten stage of his life.

"In the eleventh count of the indictment . . ."

Cray Rawls wasn't going to let rumors or lawsuits spoil his day, especially not while he was on the verge of something that would catapult him to the forefront of American business moguls. He would be a billionaire many times over, thanks to the greatest scientific discovery ever known to man. He would buy the goddamn East Hampton country club that had denied him admission and make those behind his ridicule and embarrassment kiss his feet if they wanted to stay members.

Literally.

". . . not guilty."

". . . not guilty."

". . . not guilty."

Once he'd been acquitted on the nineteenth and final charge, the jury was dismissed with the thanks of the court and the bailiff offered to have Rawls spirited out of the courthouse via a rear entrance. Rawls declined, thirsting for the whir and click of the cameras, the microphones shoved in his face, and the media outlets begging for interviews.

True to form, his journey down the front steps of the Wake County courthouse was a portrait in sticking it in the face of both overzealous prosecutors and their parade of holier-than-thou "harmed" who had put all their problems at REPCO's doorstep. He'd sent them bottled water by the truckload and had knocked on hundreds of doors himself to check on their well-being. And in return he got the blame for everything from autism to Down syndrome to cancer, even if such maladies had struck before any of REPCO's coal ash had allegedly polluted the groundwater. One woman went so far as to blame him for her chronic obstructive pulmonary disease, breaking down on the stand when his lawyers reminded her, under cross-examination, that exposure to coal ash doesn't cause that.

Having entertained the media's questions just long enough to stick it in her face and the faces of all the others, Rawls climbed into the back of the limousine, and then noticed the man already seated there.

"What are you doing here, Sam Bob?" he asked the minerals broker from Houston.

"Your driver thought it best I wait in the car."

"I'm not talking about the car. I'm talking about here in North Carolina."

Sam Bob Jackson swallowed hard, his heavy breathing pushing his stomach in and out over his belt as if there was something trying to free itself from inside. "We've got a problem, Cray. A big one."

33

AUSTIN, TEXAS

Daniel Cross stood next to Razin Saflin as Ghazi Zurif knocked on the back door of Hoover's Cooking.

"Health inspectors," Zurif said, showing his fake identification to the man who answered.

"Why didn't you use the front door?" the man wondered, adjusting his apron as Cross and Saflin flashed their fake IDs, too.

"It's procedure with surprise inspections," Saflin explained.

"Since we don't want to disturb your customers," Zurif added. "Cause as little disruption as possible."

And there are security cameras in the front of the restaurant, but not here in the back, Daniel Cross thought.

He returned the ID wallet to his jacket, hand closing around the capped syringe filled with ten milliliters of clear liquid in his front pants pocket. Ten milliliters seemed a safe estimate; a bit on the high side, in all probability, but he'd opted for it to make sure the demonstration his ISIS handlers had requested achieved its desired results, and then some. Truth was, everything up until today had been theoretical. Even Cross wasn't sure exactly what to expect, once things got rolling—how many would die, or how fast. He hadn't conducted any tests on humans, for obvious reasons. So, little did the diners about to lunch at Hoover's Cooking realize that they were about to become part of the living fabric of history.

Well, the dying *fabric,* Cross thought, trying not to smile.

"We'd like to start with the kitchen, if you don't mind," he heard Zurif say to the man in the apron.

PART FOUR

The Rangers have done more to suppress lawlessness, to capture criminals, and to prevent Mexican
and Indian raids on the frontier, than any other
agency employed by either the State or national
government.

—Alex Sweet, *Texas Siftings* magazine, 1882

34

"So what is it you're saying, exactly?" Caitlin asked Doc Whatley, Bexar County medical examiner, from the side of the sink in his lab.

Whatley finished washing his hands for the second time and went to work on the third.

"That I'm tired of the days ending too late or starting too early on account of you," he groused.

"I didn't kill that man, never mind tear him apart, Doc."

"No, Ranger, you didn't." Whatley shook his hands free of water, then pulled a long stream of paper towels from the dispenser over the sink. He dried his hands yet again and then rolled the sleeves of his lab coat back down. "And if you came here this afternoon expecting me to tell you what did, I'm afraid you wasted the drive."

Frank Dean Whatley had been the Bexar County medical examiner since Caitlin was in diapers. He'd grown a belly in recent years, which hung out over his thin belt, seeming to force his spine to angle inward at the torso. Whatley's teenage son had been killed by Latino gangbangers when Caitlin was a mere kid herself. Ever since, he'd harbored a virulent hatred for that particular race, from the bag boys at the local H-E-B supermarket to the politicians who professed to be peacemakers. With his wife lost, first in life and then in death, to alcoholism, he'd probably stayed in the job too long. But he had nothing to go home to, no real life outside the office, and he remained exceptionally good at his job.

The body currently covered up on one of the room's steel slabs represented the remains of the victim found just outside the Comanche reservation earlier that day. Whatley had certainly completed at least his preliminary examination quicker than she ever expected, perhaps coaxed by this being a Homeland Security matter, thanks to Jones.

"If you can't tell me what *did* kill the man, Doc," Caitlin ventured, "maybe you can tell me what didn't."

"You notice anything about the wounds?" Whatley asked her.

"I couldn't tell much about them through all the blood and mess."

"Let's take a walk," he said, starting for the door.

In his office, Whatley switched on his computer and positioned the screen so that Caitlin could follow along without standing over his shoulder. He inserted the drive containing the pictures he'd shot of the victim, enlarging one that showed a deep wound that had shredded skin and flesh all the way to the bone.

"Tell me what you see, Ranger."

"Three individual tears, one starting above the other two."

"If this were a bear, there'd be five. If a mountain lion had done this, there'd be four. And in both cases the claw cuts would be symmetrical—more shallow for the bear, and teeth marks clearly evident for the mountain lion."

"What about this case?"

Whatley hesitated, looking as if he had no intention of responding at all. "If I didn't know better," he said finally, "I'd say you were looking at wounds that could only have been made by talons, as opposed to claws. And the depth and width of the wounds are indeed consistent with some kind of raptor."

"As in, what, a bird of prey?"

"If I didn't know better, Ranger, yes."

"But you do know better, right, Doc?"

Whatley turned the monitor more her way. "What I know is that whatever did this would need to be maybe ten to fifteen times the size of the talons of a hawk or osprey. The curvature of the wounds tells me that whatever ripped the victim apart did so while standing on two feet before him."

"So what am I looking for, Doc?"

Whatley's expression crinkled, like someone had balled up his skin. "Something I sure as hell can't identify. Didn't your great-grandfather come up against something like this in his time?"

"It was my great-great-grandfather. And what he went up against turned out to be nothing like this."

35

Jimmy Miller stumbled his way down the street from the saloon, toward the hotel where he shared a room with three men who smelled even worse than he did when they took off their boots. They'd made him drink more than his share of whiskey and couldn't stop laughing when he puked his guts up all over the woman who was supposed to be his first.

He was halfway down the dark street before he realized he had no idea where the hotel actually was, even as his stomach was turning again. He leaned over just as a flood of vomit poured up his throat, splattering his boots and leaving his mouth tasting like cow shit. That's when he saw the match flare on the plank walkway across the street, a cigar coming to life.

"I got me a gun," Jimmy managed, fumbling for his Colt. "Don't you move!"

"I'm not going anywhere, son," Steeldust Jack Strong said from the shadows, puffing away.

"I know who you are," Jimmy said, recognizing the voice, which for some reason made him think of a hot blacksmith's anvil. He managed to get his gun out, but the world before him was teetering too much to hold it steady. "I'll shoot you dead I will, Ranger."

"Good shot, are you?"

"Damn good. You don't want to test me."

"I'm sure I don't, least not sober. Ever kill anybody, son?"

The gun felt like a lead weight in Jimmy's hand. "What if I have?"

"It's a lot harder under these conditions is all I'm saying. The night, the rain and all."

Jimmy looked around him. "It ain't raining."

"And in the time it took you to look, I got my own gun out. Know the difference between us, son?"

"You killed more men than me?"

"I'm sober and you're drunk. Not equal ground for a gunfight; trust me on that."

"I ain't scared of you none!"

"It's not the man you need to be scared of, son, it's his gun." Steeldust Jack stepped down off the plank walkway and tossed his cigar aside. "You got two choices, son: either you take your best shot here and now, or you tell me what I want to know."

Jimmy Miller lowered his Colt just a little. "What is it you want to know?"

"Who you and those other boys are working for. Who sent you onto that Indian land."

The Colt started back up. "Nobody. We was looking for who killed our friend is all."

"Man who got himself mangled, you mean. What was his name again?"

Jimmy searched his drunken mind for the answer. "Can't say."

"Must've been a really good friend, then."

Only then did the kid realize Steeldust Jack had drawn closer to him, close enough to make out his features through the flickering firelight behind the nearest windows.

"Think I'm close enough for you to shoot now, son?

Here's your choices: either start talking or start shooting. There isn't a third, and only the first leaves you alive. Second means I'll be the last thing you'll ever see."

The gun was shaking in Jimmy's hand now, and he promised himself he'd never take another drink, not even one. Not when it left him sick to his stomach and the world too wobbly to shoot.

"He just got in tonight," Jimmy said finally.

"Who?"

"The man we work for. I guess, anyway. I didn't meet him, didn't even see him. Just heard his name."

"And what would that be?"

"Rockafella. Something like that."

Jack Strong was having breakfast in the hotel restaurant when Curly Bill Brocius entered ahead of the men the Ranger recalled from the Comanche reservation, and a few more he didn't. Nine in total, ten including Jimmy Miller, who clung sheepishly behind some of the brutes whose smell reached the Ranger long before their presence.

Steeldust Jack sipped his coffee and went back to work on his plate, which was piled with scrambled eggs, bacon, grits, and biscuits swimming in gravy. He pretended not to notice the presence of the ten gunmen until a well-dressed, mustachioed man who looked younger than his years slid through the makeshift tunnel they formed. He was thinner and shorter than Steeldust Jack had expected of someone with his notoriety and growing power.

The Ranger hitched back the long coat he hadn't shed, to make sure the handle of his Colt was in easy range, never missing a beat with his eggs. He glimpsed John D. Rockefeller coming his way, the gunmen falling into step behind him.

"My associates tell me there was some trouble on an Indian reservation yesterday that's claimed my interest, Ranger."

Steeldust Jack looked up, waited to swallow his mouthful before responding. "Your associates tell you they were the cause of it?"

"On the contrary, they informed me one of their number was found murdered and they were merely trying to ascertain more about his killing."

"They tell you the man's body was found outside the reservation proper and, in the wake of ascertaining this, they trespassed on sovereign land?"

"They didn't have to. I'm well aware of the law." Rockefeller pulled back the chair across from Jack Strong. "You mind if I sit down?"

Steeldust Jack gestured for him to take the chair, snatching a bite of a biscuit and stuffing another forkful of eggs into his mouth.

"I have great respect for your organization and the entire state of Texas," Rockefeller said, pushing his chair back under the table and signaling for a cup of coffee. "And I apologize if any man in my service treated you or the Texas Rangers with any modicum of disrespect."

"Small amount," Jack Strong said, laying his own coffee back down.

"Pardon me?"

"Definition of the word *modicum*. It means 'small amount.'"

"You must be a well-read man."

"I do my share, Mr. Rockefeller. Know a bit about history, too. Like how you used your riches and family name to avoid service in the Civil War."

Rockefeller bristled, not noticing as the barman set a steaming mug of coffee down before him. "My shipping business was the sole means of support for my mother and younger siblings. My joining the army would have doomed it and them."

"Lots of men buried off battlefields were the sole means of support for their families, too. How do you suppose those families are getting by now? But that's not the point, Mr. Rockefeller. The point is you didn't just sit out the war, you profited off it, when shipping down the Mississippi became one of the war's first casualties. All of a sudden, the shipment of Midwestern crops was pushed eastward—through Cleveland, sir, where you just happened to be based. At the same time, there was a load of government contracts for food, clothes, and guns, and I hear told pretty much all of it went through that port up in those parts you pretty much controlled."

Rockefeller pushed back his suit coat and tucked his thumbs in the pockets of his vest, his face framed by the steam rising off his coffee, which made him look as much like a ghost as a man.

"You accusing me of being a good and fortunate businessman, Ranger?" he asked.

Steeldust Jack wiped his mouth with a napkin. "No,

sir. I'm accusing you of getting rich off the blood spilled by other men. You packed your warehouses with salt, clover seed, pork, and other supplies to support the war efforts. Then you created artificial shortages and delays to drive up prices while men starved to death before a bullet could take them."

Unruffled, Rockefeller lifted his mug and sipped his coffee, studying Steeldust Jack through the curtain of steam. "Know what I did with all those profits, Ranger?"

"No, sir, I do not, though I suspect you got richer still."

"I did indeed. As luck would have it, headquartering my operation in Cleveland put me a hundred miles from one of the most revolutionary developments in human history: the discovery of oil in the town of Titusville. A risky venture, for sure, but where else was I going to put all that cash? There've been times in my life where I've been short on money, but I've never been short on vision."

Steeldust Jack still had plenty of food on his plate, but he'd lost his appetite. While looking straight across the table at John D. Rockefeller, he also followed the hands of each and every gunman flirting with their holstered pistols. All but the kid Jimmy Miller, that is.

"And what did that vision show that brought you to Texas, Mr. Rockefeller?"

"Same thing that brought me to Titusville, Ranger: ambition. My company, Standard Oil, has been digging wells wherever we have a notion oil is located. And I'm here to tell you that your state is sitting on an ocean of it." Rockefeller kicked his chair back enough to cross his legs, holding court, steaming coffee cup in hand. "My scouts tell me that Indian reservation has stores of oil so vast that it actually leaks up to the surface when there's enough storm runoff."

"Well, sir, that's all well and good," Steeldust Jack told him. "Except for one little problem."

"What's that, Ranger?"

"You don't own the land, and unless the Comanche tribe in question so permits, you can't so much as touch it."

John D. Rockefeller pushed his chair in as far as it would go. Something changed in his expression. Jack Strong recognized it from the faces of the most violent and dangerous men he'd ever encountered. Rockefeller's skin reddened, the flesh of his face seeming pumped up with air, to the point that it all but swallowed his mustache.

"You and me," Rockefeller said, his voice sounding like the words had scraped over icicles, "we're talking about Indians here. The heathen masses the Texas Rangers have done more to eradicate from these parts than any other force." Rockefeller sat straight up in his chair. "And maybe you're forgetting about the man in my employ who was murdered. You should be arresting the lot of those savages instead of wasting your time here. Because I think your governor, and your legislature, know that what I bring is in the best interests of your state and that riling me isn't in the best interests of anyone."

"I'll keep that in mind, sir."

"You do that, Ranger. You do that," Rockefeller said,

the hesitation in his tone rooted in the uncertainty about whether he'd made his point at all. "Progress stops for no man."

"Neither does a bullet, Mr. Rockefeller."

36

SAN ANTONIO, TEXAS

"John D. Rockefeller?" Whatley asked, shaking his head when Caitlin had finished. "Are you serious, Ranger?"

"I'm surprised you never heard the story."

"Well, I suppose I wouldn't believe half of what I've heard about you, if I didn't know it to be true myself."

"Runs in the family, Doc."

"That's an understatement, if ever I heard one. God's honest truth, I didn't know oil drilling, even in this state, went back that far."

"It did for sure," Caitlin told him, recalling pictures her grandfather had showed her to supplement the tale. Grainy black-and-white photographs from that era featured landscape images of raw wood, angular steel, and legions of grimy, exhausted men staring blankly into the camera. Heavily laden wagons threaded for miles along rutted roadways, hauling pipe and supplies. Other pictures of the early oil fields showed scars, scrapes, roads, trenches, and blast holes in the land, which looked more like the refuse of the Civil War. Right from the start, during those post–Civil War years, the boomtowns filled with men who worked, slept, ate, drank. Then they celebrated, waited for mail, prayed with oil field preachers, and occasionally resorted to crime and violence that it took the Texas Rangers to put a clamp on.

Whatley looked at Caitlin for a time, as if reading her mind. Then he drew in a deep breath and turned his gaze briefly out the window.

"There's something else about that body, Ranger. Two things, actually." He turned his eyes back toward her. "I was involved in a similar case before myself, way back at the beginning of my career. Guess I've done my best to put it out of my mind."

"Why's that, Doc?"

"Because it didn't make any more sense then than this killing does now." He started to take another deep breath but got only halfway through. "How well do you know the city of Weatherford?"

"I know it's near Fort Worth and is the county seat for Parker County. Beyond that, not much."

"They got an old legend up there about something called the Weatherford Monster."

"I've heard about that, too, but chose not to mention it."

"With good reason, I'm sure. I was called to the area back when I was doing my residency in pathology. A young couple had been found murdered, their wounds a decent match for the condition of the body lying on my slab right now. Unprecedented amount of blood and tissue loss, with little even left to identify them as having been human. Initial thinking was animals had gotten to them after they were already dead, but my examination revealed otherwise. They'd decided to camp at the foot of some hills rich with caves, in spite of the warning signs and rumored sightings in the past."

"Sightings?"

"Kind of stuff better fit for supermarket tabloids. The reason I'm telling you this is that these stories all originated with the Native Americans who roamed the area we now call Parker County. A story was passed down through generations, about a fire-breathing bull that walked on its hind legs and ventured out of the hills—especially in winter, when the game grew scarce. I took some footprint impressions from the scene and sent them for analysis, but what was left of them had degraded too much for anybody to take a stab at a proper identification. This morning, I'm kind of embarrassed to say, I looked through my records to see if I could dig those impressions up. But that was back in the Stone Age, before computers ruled the world, so I suppose they're gone forever.

"And I'll tell you something else, Ranger," Whatley resumed, after Caitlin had figured he was done. "There've been other reported sightings across the state, sometimes associated with unexplained disappearances, and always near Indian land."

"Nature takes care of its own," Caitlin muttered, repeating White Eagle's own words, which suddenly seemed oddly appropriate.

"What was that?"

"Nothing, Doc."

"Anyway, Ranger, what I can conjure from memory tells me the conditions those victims were found in pretty much mirrors that of the one found outside that reservation. That's the first thing I wanted to tell you about the body, which I left out of my report."

"What's the second?"

"Something I found in the general area of the re- mains," Whatley said, reaching into his top desk drawer to produce an item tucked into a plastic evidence pouch. "Nobody knows about this yet besides you and me," he continued, handing the pouch across his desk. "I figure since the Rangers are running lead on this, you'd know what to do with it."

Caitlin inspected the object through the plastic, felt her breath seize up in her throat.

"I'm going to assume you recognize that," Whatley was saying.

She traced the outline of the object, as if hoping her eyes had it wrong. A strange buzzing filled her ears, making her wonder if her thoughts were coming so quickly they were spilling out her ears.

"I'll need that back, Ranger," Whatley said.

Caitlin hadn't realized she was still holding it, nor did she remember returning the evidence bag to him, until she watched him stow it back in his drawer.

"For safekeeping," he resumed.

She realized the buzzing she'd heard was coming from her cell phone. She eased it from her pocket, forc- ing her hand steady. "I'm here, Captain."

"Not for long, Ranger. You ever hear of a restau- rant called Hoover's Cooking, up in Austin?"

"I think so."

"Ranger chopper's waiting to take you there right now. I figured I'd give you the word before Jones."

Caitlin felt her phone vibrate again and checked the new incoming call. "That's Jones now, D.W. What's he going to tell me?"

"That a storm even bigger than the gale force of Hurricane Caitlin has made a direct hit on Texas, and that's just for starters."

"Starters?"

"Chopper's waiting, Ranger. You'd best get a move on."

37

HOUSTON, TEXAS

"I'd like to see my son, ma'am," Cort Wesley Masters told Julia De Cantis, principal of the Village School.

He'd driven the whole way here with the air-conditioning blowing as hard as he could take it, still arriving at his son Luke's school with his blood simmering and sweat soaking through his shirt. It was enough to make him feel like dropping into a pool full of ice cubes, though he suspected that wouldn't have cooled him off.

"I thought it best we talk first, Mr. Masters," De Cantis said, chair pushed as far back from her desk as the wall would allow. "To update you on everything we know about the incident."

"The incident that occurred yesterday and I heard about for the first time a few hours ago."

"I was traveling on school business and, unfortunately, my subordinates had the wrong contact info for you. I returned as soon as I was informed, but didn't get back until just a few hours ago myself. I called you as soon as I had an opportunity to get up to speed."

"So let's cut to the chase, ma'am," Cort Wesley said, his neck tight and his head pounding from the frantic drive from the Comanche reservation outside of Austin.

De Cantis rose and, to her credit, came around the desk to take the matching chair next to Cort Wesley's. "We don't believe Luke's in any danger. That's not why I called you here."

"Oh no? Then why did you call me here?"

"Because, Mr. Masters, you are."

Cort Wesley felt his skin crawling as Julia De Cantis told him the story, her words sounding far away and registering only at the edge of his consciousness. The state prep championship soccer team, on which Zach starred but Luke mostly rode the bench, had stopped at a McDonald's on the way back from a 5–0 victory. Luke was all smiles, having played much of the second half. He had registered his first goal of the season on a picture-perfect header off a corner kick, which had shocked his coach and opened the door to more playing time. Just before leaving McDonald's, Luke went to use the men's room, but he still hadn't returned when the coach loaded the team back onto the bus. Zach went to look for him but found the men's room empty and no trace of Luke anywhere in the restaurant or parking lot.

The coach called the police, who arrived in force within minutes, setting up a perimeter around the block and preparing an AMBER Alert on the chance Luke had been kidnapped. They were in the process of interviewing all the players, as well as potential witnesses inside McDonald's, when Luke, still garbed in his Village School warm-up suit, came walking across the street, right through oncoming traffic. He was so dazed and distracted he never saw the city bus that screeched to a stop and missed hitting him by little more than a yard.

"This is where things get cloudy, Mr. Masters," De Cantis said, leaning across her chair to draw closer to him.

"Cloudy," Cort Wesley repeated.

"The police suspected someone tried to abduct your son, but the boy has so far refused to provide any specifics, other than . . ."

"Other than *what*?"

"That he was worried about you. That the men who abducted him threatened you."

"Strange he didn't tell me this himself, as soon as the dust settled."

"For security reasons, the coach and I both felt we should confiscate the cell phones of all the players. Keep a lid on this until we got a handle on things, avoid a panic or overreaction."

"And how you doing with that?"

"Hoping that you can do better."

Cort Wesley rose, his spine and knees cracking audibly. "Then let's go have a talk with Luke."

38

"Thank you, ma'am," Cort Wesley said to Julia De Cantis, when they reached Luke's room. "I can take things from here."

De Cantis had arranged for a uniformed Houston policeman to guard the building entrance and had posted a school security guard outside Luke's door. The guard gave ground, pulling his chair out of the way, and De Cantis backed off as well when Cort Wesley knocked lightly on the door.

"It's me, son. Open up."

The door creaked open a moment later, Luke standing behind it. Cort Wesley hugged him tight and waited for his son to break the embrace, the boy's eyes welling with tears he tried to sniffle away.

"Tell me what happened, son."

They sat down atop Luke's ruffled bed covers as the door behind them closed all the way.

"There were two of them," Luke started, blowing the hair from his face, just as his older brother was prone to doing. "I came out of the men's room and they grabbed me."

"Grabbed you," Cort Wesley repeated.

"Took me out a side exit and pushed me into an SUV just outside the door. Big, with its windows blacked out. One of them drove out of the parking lot before one of the doors was even closed."

"What'd they want, son?"

"You. It was about you."

"How's that exactly?"

Luke blew more air from his mouth, but there was no hair to ruffle this time. "They said for you to stop making trouble, that this was a warning." He swallowed hard. "That you needed to get your son in line and that you'd know what they were talking about."

"Dylan," Cort Wesley figured.

"They didn't mention any names. I think they were hired hands, the kind of thugs like you see in the movies."

"What about an Indian reservation? They mention anything about that?"

"Indian reservation?"

"I'll take that as a no. What else did they say?"

"Not much."

"Give me every word."

Luke swallowed hard. "They said to tell you, next time I wouldn't come back whole."

"Exact words?"

"Pretty close, Dad. One of them had a knife."

"You forget to mention that before?"

"I was focusing on what they said, like you asked."

"I get it."

"When the one said I wouldn't be coming back whole, he poked me with the tip," Luke went on, pointing a finger at his lap. "Here. I think he knew."

"Knew what?"

"That I'm, you know . . .'Cause he said he'd cut mine off so I could be the girl I was."

"He said that?" Cort Wesley managed, trying to

steady the quivers that had started in his hands and then spread tension up his forearms.

"I told him to go fuck himself."

Cort Wesley almost laughed, easing his tension. "You didn't."

"I did. He said he'd rather fuck me."

Cort Wesley felt the tension returning.

"He said he'd done kids like me in prison," Luke continued. "Exact words."

"You never saw either of these guys before?"

"I would've told you if I had."

"What about the SUV? You get a license plate, anything like that?"

Luke frowned and shook his head. "I screwed up there. Too scared to think straight. It was a Cadillac Escalade, I think. Smelled brand new inside, but also like paint."

"Paint?"

"You know, like from an auto body shop, like it had just come out of one or something." Luke's expression changed. "What's this have to do with Dylan, with an Indian reservation?"

"What do you think?"

"A girl?"

"It's always a girl with your brother," Cort Wesley said, immediately regretting he'd put it that way.

"You don't have to do that, Dad."

"Do what?"

"Worry about choosing your words. I'm not fragile. I don't break so easy."

Cort Wesley squeezed his son's shoulder. "Well, that's a relief . . . You really told the guy to go fuck himself?"

"Yup."

"How'd that feel?"

"Fucking great."

Cort Wesley rose from the twin bed, its old springs creaking. He waited until Luke joined him on his feet.

"I think I'll tell the son of a bitch that, once I find him."

"You didn't answer my question," Luke said.

"Which question is that?"

"What this Indian reservation has to do with me getting jacked from a McDonald's."

"Long story. Let's just say your brother's latest girlfriend is a Native American who doesn't take kindly to having her land spoiled by oil drillers."

"That's a new one, anyway."

"It sure is," Cort Wesley said, something clicking in his mind.

Doesn't take kindly to having her land spoiled by oil drillers . . .

And then he realized what it was, something he should have realized as soon as he arrived at the reservation the day before.

"What is it, Dad?" Luke asked him. "You got that look."

Cort Wesley shared a smile with his son, started for the door, then stopped and looked back at him. "The head of your school happened to mention your rooming situation for next year has been resolved."

"Really?" Luke beamed. "How'd you manage that? You didn't have to beat anybody up, did you?"

"No, but that's coming," Cort Wesley told him,

taking out his phone to call Caitlin with the news about what he'd just realized.

Before he could dial, though, he saw a half dozen missed calls from her, and one text that read, *9-1-1*.

39

AUSTIN, TEXAS

"They're expecting me," Caitlin Strong said to one of the two Austin policemen manning the checkpoint at the intersection of Manor Road and Comal Street, beneath a blistering late-afternoon sun that made her squint from the reflection off his sunglasses.

She handed over her ID, realizing that this whole section of the city had been cordoned off, from the LBJ Presidential Library to the north, off of I-35, to where Manor met Alexander Avenue, to the east. She might have used the term *quarantined* instead, except that, according to what Captain Tepper had been able to piece together, authorities were in the process of evacuating the area to a one-square-mile radius. Strangely, a lone cloud had settled over the block beyond, leaving it as an ink splotch of darkness enclosed by blazing sunlight on all sides.

Caitlin watched one of the patrolmen get on his radio with her ID in hand, to make sure she was cleared by higher authorities to proceed. Right now that higher authority was Homeland Security, in the form of none other than her old friend Jones, who, just like a bottle top, kept sticking to her boot and scratching everything it touched. Beyond that, she didn't know much, other than that around twenty people were dead inside Hoover's Cooking, a down-home family restaurant squeezed into the Manor Road Plaza, under that lone cloud.

"You're free to pass, Ranger," the Austin cop told her, handing Caitlin back her ID. "Give the devil our regards."

A second checkpoint had been set up a block down from Manor Road Plaza, close enough for Caitlin to glimpse what looked like plastic sheeting layered over the whole of the building that contained Hoover's Cooking. From her classes at Quantico, Caitlin knew this was the standard procedure when some form of contagion was suspected. In this case, because an active ISIS cell was already being investigated, authorities at Homeland Security were naturally assuming the worst.

What extraordinarily few people, outside of those with specialized training, knew was that Homeland had furnished all cities above a certain size with a bio-hazard kit. The so-called kit was actually the size of a small trailer and normally was parked innocuously in the municipality's impound lot or storage garage, where it would attract little or no attention. The kit contained plastic sheeting like that which Caitlin saw already in place around Hoover's Cooking, along with protective hazmat suits for supplementary local personnel and a long, cylindrical tube, inflated with air, that looked like a portable airport Jetway. It, too, was already in place at Hoover's Cooking, wobbling slightly in the breeze.

A city the size of Austin would have a designated team of police and fire personnel trained as first responders. These people would get the proper protective precautions in place to, at the very least, isolate and contain the damage as much as possible. Minutes mattered a whole lot, seconds almost as much. Even a one-hour delay in enacting the proper procedures could cost tens of thousands of lives, according to Caitlin's instructors at Quantico, and she was of no mind to dispute their estimates at this point.

She parked her Explorer in a makeshift lot of other first responders' vehicles and was waved through to a third checkpoint. This one was erected behind layered strips of hazard tape. Hazmat suits hung from hangers on portable racks inside the kind of tent people rent for backyard parties. Caitlin found Jones, already draped in one, waiting for her at the front flap of the tent, looking truly scared and uncertain for the first time she could ever remember.

"The shit has really hit the fan this time," he greeted her. "Why am I not surprised you're right in the middle of things as usual?"

"Come again, Jones?"

"Your old friend Daniel Cross, Ranger . . . The kid you took under your wing, remember? This is exactly what he promised ISIS he could pull off."

40

"I have decided to be merciful to you today," Hatim Abd al-Aziz, supreme military commander of ISIS, announced to the villagers gathered in the dusty central square, which smelled of goat shit. "I have decided not to repay your disrespect in kind."

He continued walking amid the rows of men, women, and children, even as more villagers who'd been found hiding, and children whose parents had stashed them beneath blankets or within crawl spaces, were herded into the square. Al-Aziz stopped and patted the head of an especially frightened-looking boy.

"They've told you stories about me, child, haven't they? Made up tales of the evil monster who came here once before and killed the men who would not swear allegiance to the caliphate and pledge their faith to Allah. They told you how I cut off their heads and made their families witness the act, how I gouged out the eyes of any who tried to close them.

"Can you believe they would say such things about me, Seyyef?" al-Aziz asked the towering figure who walked in his shadow.

Seyyef gave no reply other than a grunt and a shrug. He wore black combat fatigues that made him seem even larger, but no mask, because he'd been unable to find one large enough to fit over his simian-like skull. His cheekbones were ridged and elongated, beneath a forehead that protruded so much it seemed packed with putty. His face and head were so absurdly large that his eyes looked tiny by comparison, giving the giant a perpetually blank stare that made him appear utterly thoughtless.

"The truth is," al-Aziz continued to the villagers, "I did none of those things. God did them, with me serving merely as His vessel, stripped of my own will in lieu of a higher power's. I live to serve Him. That is where we differ, you and I. I live to serve God, while you would besmirch His name and disrespect His greatness with your blasphemy and disloyalty."

Al-Aziz couldn't tell how many of the villagers grasped his words, but soon they'd all understand the intent that had brought him back here, the example that needed to be set.

"I gave you a chance the last time I came, in spite of all your indiscretions. I warned that if you continued serving as a way station and support center for the forces of the West, I would send all of you to the realms of hell, instead of just your leaders. But even that, I fear, will not be enough to turn you from the darkness to the light we are shining on the new world. What sets the caliphate apart is our belief that there can be no compromise. Conquering the world starts with a single village, for that world can be no stronger than the weakest link, represented by that village and all the others."

He stopped and patted another child's head. She shrank back from his touch, clutching her mother, leaving al-Aziz wishing he could wipe the unclean stink of her off his hand. Around him, the sense of fear and desperation rode the air like a cloud, a fine mist of hopelessness sprayed by the weak willed and weak minded. Somewhere near the back of the dusty square, a young child was shrieking. Others, more children and adults, were choking back sobs or wiping their eyes free of tears.

"Today this village ceases to exist," he resumed, walking on. "Today we burn your homes, your crops, your animals, your possessions. Today we take everything that defines you in the evil you have chosen embrace instead of giving yourself to the one true God. But He is a merciful God and has willed me to treat you in that vein. The last time I came here, I took the heads of twenty men identified as leaders. Today, being merciful and compassionate, I will take none. I will spare your lives and let you remain in your homes."

Al-Aziz paused just long enough to give the villagers of Ras al-Maa a semblance of hope. Then he snatched the gift back from them.

"On one condition," al-Aziz continued. "Each parent must take the life of their oldest child. Refuse, and your entire family dies."

The villagers' hope vanished with the stiff wind that blew through the square, whipping the dust into miniature funnel clouds. The villagers dropped to their knees, begging, pleading, screeching, sobbing. The sounds were so joyous to his ears that al-Aziz could barely contain himself from smiling.

"You pray to a God who does not hear you," he said, his voice rising above their desperate cries. "He does not hear you because He is not here to listen. Only I am here. And when you pray, it should be to me, for the power of the one true God I serve as proxy for."

Al-Aziz stopped again to better enjoy the sounds of his majesty. A teenage boy, brandishing a knife he'd hidden under his shirt, tried to rush him, only to be snatched from the ground by Seyyef and held dangling in the air until the giant crushed the boy's throat and discarded his limp form back to the dusty ground.

"A village must pay for the indiscretions of each part as if he was acting for the whole. Because no one stopped the charge of this one, my terms have changed: each family will take the lives of their *two* oldest children, instead of one. Dishonor me again and it becomes three. We will begin now, one family at a time, so others may watch and heed the lessons of the indiscretions that necessitated me coming back here today. I trust I shall not have to come back a third time."

Seyyef approached and handed al-Aziz the satellite phone he'd left with the giant for safekeeping.

"Yes?" the ISIS commander greeted, listening to the report from Syria, feeling his spirits perk up even more. "And this has been confirmed? . . . No, I'll want to handle it personally. Initiate the travel protocols for my men and I, and alert the proper contacts in the United States to prepare. Where again, exactly? . . . 'Texas,'" al-Aziz repeated, after the voice told him.

41

AUSTIN, TEXAS

Caitlin had suited up in full hazmat gear for drills but never for real, and she was amazed at how different everything felt. The suit was bulkier, hotter. The helmet tended to fog up worse than she recalled, and the portable oxygen supply was heavier. As soon as she stepped outside the command and control tent, the sun, which had chased off that lone dark cloud, felt like it was melting the suit's space-age material into her skin. Approaching the wobbly tube attached to the covered entrance of Hoover's Cooking felt like scuba diving on land, right down to the peculiar buzz she felt in her ear from the air pushing through the tank into her lungs.

"Can you hear me?" she heard Jones ask through her helmet's built-in microphone.

"Loud and clear."

"I've been inside already, Ranger, so I can give you the lay of the land and the chronology, as best as we've been able to reconstruct. Zero hour was right around one hundred and sixty-seven minutes ago and counting. We know that because that's when a regular who'd come in for lunch rushed outside, puking his guts out, after finding what you're about to see."

She looked at him through her mask. His face was absent of smirk and snarl for the first time she could remember.

"Austin authorities pushed the appropriate panic button," Jones continued. "Most of the cavalry's still en route, but they got the containment procedures enacted faster than any drill ever conducted for a city this size, including getting the man who dialed nine-one-one into isolation. I'm starting to love Texas almost as much as I hate it."

"We're real good with disasters, Jones," Caitlin told him, nodding inside her helmet. "Far too much practice, unfortunately."

"Nothing that prepared you for what you're about to see, Ranger. You can count on that."

Passing through the tube en route to the thick plastic sheeting separating Hoover's Cooking from the outside world was like some crazy Disney World ride played out for real. Caitlin half expected mechanical or animated creatures to jump out or launch an attack on her from outside the tube.

"The victims were all eating lunch," she heard Jones say in her helmet. "Various stages of their meals."

"So they didn't die at the same time, in the same moment?" Caitlin asked, her voice echoing in her ears.

"Pretty damn close. Within seconds of each other, as near as we can tell. Suggests something airborne, doesn't it, Ranger?"

"I don't know."

"Despite all that annual training you receive at Quantico?" Jones chided. "Come on."

"It just doesn't feel like a pathogen to me."

"Something else?"

"Something worse," Caitlin told him, not yet sure why.

42

AUSTIN, TEXAS

Caitlin followed Jones through the remainder of the tube, parting the last dangling sheets of heavy plastic to enter the normally down-home confines of Hoover's Cooking. She imagined she could smell eggs frying, bacon cooking, and coffee lifted off BUNN warmers to be poured into the restaurant's bountiful cups. But all that slipped away, along with her breath, when the sight beyond her helmet's faceplate was revealed.

Several of the bodies were lying frozen on the floor, arms extended as if to claw forward along the tile toward the entrance now encased in biohazard plastic. Others sat straight up, only the dead sightlessness of their frozen eyes giving away the fact they weren't waiting for their meals to be served. Still more were facedown on tabletops or booths strewn with spilled liquids and food. A few were slumped in their chairs, their limbs canted at odd angles, as if they had been trying to rise when whatever had happened in here struck them. It was like something out of a Norman Rockwell painting drawn by the devil, amid the pie cases and walls covered with fifteen years of pictures from the history of Hoover's Cooking.

"Welcome to the party, Ranger," Caitlin heard Jones say.

A combination of the suit's confines and the encased building's lack of ventilation left her feeling she was being roasted alive. At Quantico she'd been part of any number of drills to prepare her as a first responder to such calamities, but the props and stage dummies had in no way achieved their goal. The suit's restrictions and independent air supply kept all odors from her, though, for which she was glad.

"Give me your first thoughts," Jones said, alongside her now.

"Spacing of the bodies indicates a time lag that puts airborne transmission more in doubt," Caitlin started, getting used to the echo of her own words inside the helmet. "That means the victims might have ingested whatever killed them, as opposed to breathing it in, making the means of delivery a toxin placed inside something they ate or drank." She raised a glove to swipe away the sweat forming inside her helmet, forgetting the presence of the faceplate for the moment.

"Toxin," Jones repeated. "Quantico must've treated you well, Ranger. Most would say 'contagion.'"

"Contagion implies 'spread from person to person.' There was no spread here. It hit fast and it hit hard."

"Are you ruling out natural causation?"

"That's a new term on me, Jones. But if you're asking if this could've been caused by poisoning through means other than a concentrated attack, I'd say the odds are slim to none."

"You learn to make that kind of judgment in Quantico?"

"You asked me a question and the answer's a matter of common sense. Naturally occurring disasters like this—Legionnaires' disease, methane dumps, toxic sludge—aren't unprecedented, but none of them carry a hundred percent mortality rate."

"So," Jones ventured, his faceplate misting up and then clearing in rhythm with his breaths and his words, "assuming enemy action was in play, what stands out the most in your mind?"

Caitlin walked about the restaurant, careful to step over the victims who had slipped from their chairs or died crawling for the door. To a man and woman, they looked to be in the throes of both pain and panic. She stopped at a table occupied by two boys and two girls wearing school uniforms, backpacks tucked under their chairs, their faces pressed against the tabletop as if they'd been glued there.

"Looks like they were all struck within maybe a thirty-second window," Caitlin theorized, turning away from the kids.

"Makes sense."

"No, it doesn't, Jones. It makes no sense at all. Unless all the victims were sharing a toast or a piece of birthday cake, as it turns out there's no way ingestion could've caused what we're looking at here." She started to turn back toward the table occupied by the facedown kids, then stopped. "What happened to all the other people who ate here before them? How is it they walked out of here to go about their day, none the worse for wear? Goes back to what I was saying before, what was bothering me about the notion of whatever did this being airborne. I assume you've taken air samples."

"Preliminary analysis on-site doesn't show a damn thing, Ranger."

"Because this isn't a disease, Jones. I wouldn't expect the CDC to be much help, either."

"Got a better idea?"

Caitlin looked around the restaurant again, her mind conjuring the smells of the place anew. "Whatever it is hits the anatomy like a sledgehammer, and it's got to be something all the victims would have ingested within seconds of each other, for the timeline to work."

"All well and good, Ranger," Jones said, "only what you're describing doesn't exist, either in or out of nature."

Caitlin met Jones's eyes through the faceplate of his helmet. "You mean it didn't until today."

43

Back at the staging tent, Caitlin couldn't wait to yank off her hazmat suit and dump it into the orange drum stickered with warnings.

"What did the dead have to say, Ranger?" she heard Guillermo Paz ask her. She turned to see him leaning lightly against one of the poles holding the tent up.

"Not enough to be of much good," Caitlin told him.

Shedding the suit hadn't helped her shed from her psyche the residue of what she'd just experienced. One of those ultimate nightmare scenarios you train and prepare for but never for a moment believe will ever happen.

"Aristotle once said that 'death is the most fearful thing,'" Paz noted. "But he was wrong, wasn't he?"

"You tell me, Colonel."

"You already know the answer, best articulated by my friend Heidegger, who believed that anticipation does not passively await death but mobilizes mortality as the condition of free will in the world."

"In other words, by this happening, we're enabled to stop it from happening again."

"I believe that's what Martin Heidegger was getting at, yes."

"You don't seem especially bothered by all that, Colonel."

"Because it defines my purpose, my reason for being."

"Is that Heidegger too?"

He smiled. "No, Ranger; yours truly. But Heidegger was very well acquainted with evil. He didn't just endorse the Nazis with the coming of World War II, he joined them. Became rector of the University of Freiburg, where he did his best to mold young minds to the Nazi cause. The impressionability of young people makes them extremely dangerous when motivated. When I was in Daniel Cross's apartment, I noticed the books on his shelves. He seemed as enamored by the Nazis as Heidegger."

"You think Cross was behind what happened here?"

"Don't you, Ranger?" Paz eased closer to her, forcing Caitlin to turn her gaze even more upward. "People leave residue of themselves behind wherever they go," he said. "Imprints of their actions as plain and recognizable as photographs. It's why my mother almost never left the shack in the Venezuelan slum where I grew up; she couldn't bear to be around the evil and ugliness so many left behind in their wake." The colonel paused, seeming to need a moment to compose himself—a first, in Caitlin's memory. "I recognized Daniel Cross inside that restaurant as soon as I entered. I might as well have been looking him in the face."

Caitlin saw Jones addressing some uniformed officials who'd just arrived, and he approached her as soon as he sent them off.

"The colonel agrees Daniel Cross was behind this," Caitlin told him. "If he's really got something he wants to give to ISIS, we just found it."

"You mean we found what it can do, Ranger."

"Which still doesn't provide even a hint about what he was doing outside that Indian reservation."

Jones massaged his scalp through his high-and-tight haircut. "I can see why Captain Tepper finally hammered your ass to a chair."

"As you can see, the nails didn't hold. You suspected an ISIS plot in Texas, with Daniel Cross a primary part of it. Then he disappears and this happens. But, in between, he shows up to watch the Comanche protest from the peanut gallery. You telling me you don't see a possible connection there?"

The air outside was hot and steamy, but still welcome. Being back in the fresh air left Caitlin grateful for the unseasonably hot sun and the sweat she was now free to wipe from her brow and cheeks with a bandanna lifted from her back pocket. It had been her father's, and her grandfather's before that, but neither had ever come up against anything like this.

Caitlin felt a vibration in the front pocket of her jeans and remembered her cell phone was still tucked there.

"I just got your message," Cort Wesley greeted her. "Please tell me you're not in Austin."

"What do you think?"

"I'm headed there now. Give me a place to meet."

"Not here, Cort Wesley. The Comanche reservation. You and me need to have a talk with Dylan."

She could hear him sigh over the phone. "What's he done now?"

Caitlin recalled the item in the evidence bag Doc

Whatley was keeping tucked in his desk drawer for safekeeping. "Could be nothing."

"And if it isn't, Ranger?"

"I'll explain when I see you, Cort Wesley."

44

HOUSTON, TEXAS

"Jackson Whole Mineral," Cray Rawls said, inside Sam Bob Jackson's office. "You come up with that all on your own?"

"Like it?" Jackson asked him, swabbing the sweat from his forehead with a colored handkerchief.

"About as much as I like the rest of this state, Sam Bob. Somewhere between a colonoscopy and getting my prostate checked. How does anyone even live here?"

"You did, after that couple adopted you. Brought you all the way here from North Carolina."

"Even gave me my own room: a windowless closet in the basement they kept locked to keep me from giving in to the devil's temptation."

"That wasn't in your bio," Jackson noted.

"Neither was the fact I was homeschooled, which in that particular household meant the Bible morning, noon, or night. You ever wonder why I haven't set foot inside a church since?"

Rawls had his back to a set of finished oak bookshelves lined with framed photos of Sam Bob Jackson with Texas celebrities, most wearing cowboy hats. A wide-screen television was tuned to the local news with the sound muted.

"You want to explain to me why you had this high school boy kidnapped?" Rawls asked, while gazing out the window toward the Katy Freeway beyond.

Jackson's reflection in the window glass grew so still even the fatty ripples on his face stopped moving. "There's a lot at stake here. I felt I had to take the initiative, so I used the boy to send a message."

Rawls nodded, hating the ridiculously low temperature in Sam Bob Jackson's office, given the scorching temperature outside. He thought about how the environmentalists were always up his ass and figured they'd have a field day in a building like this, where the temperature left you bleeding icicles, in stark contrast to the blast furnace beyond.

"A message to the boy's father, for sending four of our workers to the hospital." Rawls nodded. "I get that. What I don't get is you taking such a risk without knowing squat about the guy."

Jackson didn't look surprised at all. Instead, he looked at Rawls smugly. "He did a stretch in Huntsville. Worked as an enforcer for the Branca crime family out of New Orleans for a stretch. A thug, that's all."

"Really? He puts four guys in the hospital without suffering a scratch and all you can tell me about him is he used to be mobbed up and did some time?"

Jackson shrugged again. "So what do you want me to do?"

"Your job. What I'm fucking paying you for."

"Hey, I'm the one who found this deal for you, Cray. What's that short for, by the way?"

"What's *what* short for?"

"Cray. Cray*ton* or something?"

"No, Christopher Raymond. One thing I got left my real mother gave me."

Jackson's teeth curled over his lower lip. "That Bible-thumping couple . . . I heard they got killed in a fire and you inherited all they had—enough to get you out of Texas."

"True enough."

"The fire was suspicious," Jackson added, after a pause.

"You should keep that in mind, next time you decide to make a move like this without consulting me.

"It's under control, Cray."

"Is it? I don't think so, given we've still got a full construction crew sitting in the shade on my dime, all because some Comanche are communing with nature. All the more reason to find out more about this guy Masters you decided to pick a fight with."

"No other choice I could see."

"You shouldn't have been looking. You're hired help, my friend. Next time you get it in your mind to make a decision on your own, find a bucket of ice water to stick your head in. This goddamn state's full of two things—oil and bullshit—and I don't have any use for either. The sooner I can get this mess cleaned up, the sooner I can fly the friendly skies the fuck out of this circus you call a state."

Rawls finally turned from the window, and west Houston's Energy Corridor beyond, and focused on the muted wide-screen television, which currently showed a slew of flashing lights and a cordoned neighborhood in Austin.

"Like I was saying . . ." Rawls noted, shaking his head.

45

AUSTIN, TEXAS

"So, what do you think?" Daniel Cross asked the two men in the front seat of the car parked as close as they could get to Hoover's Cooking. "You guys happy? You wanna give me high marks, praise, something like that?"

Zurif and Saflin turned toward him at the same time, startling Cross enough to send his shoulders whiplashing back against the seat rest.

"Praise comes only from Allah," said Zurif. "But you can rest assured you have proven yourself before His eyes."

"And the rest of this holy mission follows in accordance with His will," Saflin added.

Zurif nodded in agreement. "We are nothing when measured against the scope of that. The sooner you realize and accept your place, the more peace you will find basking in Allah's good graces."

"I told you I'm not interested in converting. That's not what this is about."

"Actions speak louder than words," said Saflin. "You are now one of us, a soldier in the army of the one true God, who owes all to Him and His word."

Saflin and Zurif kept talking, but Cross stopped listening to them. Suddenly these two men were no better or different than the bullies and braggarts who'd terrorized him through every year of his schooling. He could almost hear them chanting "Diaper Dan," the way kids in school did sometimes. Nothing had changed, and he felt stupid for deluding himself into believing that it had. Except he was right—it *had* changed, because he was the one with the power now, *him*. He was the one who had injected the contents of the syringe into the jug of cooking oil, the kind cooks slather over their grills. All Saflin and Zurif did was provide the distraction and then plug up the kitchen exhaust fan outside to make sure the oil could do its work.

"Well, let me tell you boys something," he said, suddenly emboldened by the endless stream of law enforcement, fire, and rescue vehicles. Their flashing lights made the street look like the Fourth of July beneath the helicopters battling for space in the sky overhead. "Everybody in that restaurant is dead, every single one. As in one hundred percent, as in I delivered what I promised, as in I'm serving up—no pun intended—the ultimate weapon to you, so your friends in the Middle East can save themselves from the coalition that's been kicking their ass."

"They're your friends, too, now" from Zurif.

"That's what you wanted, isn't it?" from Saflin.

"A little fucking respect would be nice, maybe a thank-you," Daniel Cross said. "Maybe you don't get what you're looking at over there, but it's a microcosm of what you can do to the whole of the goddamn U.S. of A., *thanks to me*. Now, *that's* terror."

Saflin and Zurif looked at each other, their glances furtive and excited at the same time.

"The proper communiqués have been sent," Zurif told him.

"We're expecting a message as to when to expect arrival, any minute," added Saflin.

Cross leaned forward again. "Wait a minute. They're coming *here*? From the Middle East?"

"A top-echelon team under one of the senior commanders. What did you expect?" Zurif asked.

"It's what you wanted, isn't it?" Saflin asked.

Cross couldn't answer either of those questions, because he hadn't thought that far ahead. He was starting to think that maybe, just maybe, this time really was different. He found himself gazing ahead again, not just toward the chaos he'd wrought but also toward the future he was helping to create.

"O say can you see . . ."

He spoke the words instead of singing them, but the effect was the same. Both Saflin and Zurif looked as if they were about to speak, when a uniformed Austin policeman rapped his knuckles against the driver's side window.

46

After doing battle with the Hells Angels earned him a Royal Canadian Mounted Police medal, Pierre Beauchamp had been reassigned from his regular duties to an RCMP task force responsible for coordinating antiterrorist efforts with the Mounties' American counterparts. His heroism in a gunfight that had left all the Angels dead and their marijuana grow house burned to the ground had gotten him laid up for several months with a bullet wound. The medal and his reassignment had preempted his plans to retire, a decision he didn't regret for one moment.

Until today.

A bulletin reached his desk about a potential terrorist attack 1,700 miles away, in Austin, Texas.

Texas, he mused, thinking of the state for the first time since the real hero of that gunfight against the Hells Angels, five years before, had saved his life.

The second bulletin changed "potential" to "suspected," while still offering scant details. Those details arrived an hour later, in a third bulletin that came, encrypted, through the most secure communications channel possible. Beauchamp read it three times, growing colder on each occasion. He put his jacket on before he went in to see the task force commander.

"I understand the severity of the situation," Captain Claude Baston told him. "And we're already in close contact with our counterparts in the United States. What I'm not understanding, Sergeant, is why you need to go there."

"Because this has happened before, Captain," Beauchamp said, thinking of what a trapper named Joe Labelle had found when he stumbled into an Inuit village in Nunavut, around eighty-five years before. "And it happened up here."

47

BALCONES CANYONLANDS, TEXAS

"We getting out?" Caitlin asked from the passenger seat of Cort Wesley's truck.

A late afternoon thunderstorm had sprung up suddenly from the day's heat, leaving rain, swept away by the wipers, pooled in the windshield's corners. Drops dappled the freshly waxed finish on the hood of the truck. A combination of the sun's return and the hot engine pushed steam up into the air, which drifted off in smokelike clouds.

"I'm still trying to get my arms wrapped around all this," he said, hands squeezing the steering wheel, even though the truck was parked, its engine cooling.

Caitlin had just told him about the contents of the evidence pouch Doc Whatley was currently storing in his desk drawer. She had immediately recognized the silver Miraculous Medal that Dylan never took off, because it had belonged to his mother and had her initials—MT, for Maura Torres—on the back. The medal had been recovered not far from the body of the construction foreman, splattered with the man's blood.

"I was already figuring what I'm going to do to those guys who threatened Luke," Cort Wesley continued. "Don't know if my arms are big enough to get around this, too."

"Neither of us thinks for a minute Dylan had anything to do with that construction worker getting murdered."

"Which means somebody's trying to set him up. Any guesses as to who?"

"Something's been bothering me about Ela Nocona from the beginning."

"Yeah, my boy sure can pick 'em, can't he?"

"Must take after his father."

Her quip produced no smile from him. "How long can Doc Whatley keep this under wraps, Ranger?"

"Keep *what* under wraps, Cort Wesley?" Caitlin said, waiting for her words to sink in before resuming. "Everything comes back to whatever's going on inside that reservation."

"Speaking of which . . ." Cort Wesley began, and then explained what had struck him earlier in the day.

What Cort Wesley laid out for her was based on his brief experience working oil rigs, after his father, Boone Masters, had checked into the hospital for the last time.

"The kind of exploratory drilling they do now goes down really deep," he explained. "The deeper you go, the harder the pressure, underground being similar to under water in that respect. And that requires piping reinforced and layered with steel casing, to ensure it maintains its structural integrity once you start pushing all that water, sand, and drilling mud down. In a nutshell, none of the piping these boys got piled in their trucks conforms to that basic principle."

"Makes sense." Caitlin nodded, once he'd finished. "How's that, Ranger?"

"I did some checking into Jackson Whole Mineral, the company that secured the drilling rights for this land. They did that in order to sell off parcels to individual bidders, but it turns out there's only one bidder listed in the Texas Bureau of Land Management records: an outfit called REPCO, out of New York and North Carolina, owned by a man named Cray Rawls, who's as dirty as the coal ash he's got a penchant for dumping in rivers."

"And don't tell me," Cort Wesley added, "none of the words beginning with R, E, P, C, or O have anything to do with oil."

"If they do, it would be a first. The company knows its way around petroleum-based products and all manner of petrochemicals, and chemical products in general, all right, but other than a few limited partnerships, they don't have any track record with oil whatsoever. Company's got a pharmaceutical division, a food processing and preservation division, a waste management division, and they ship a whole bunch of stuff I can't pronounce, with ingredients that would scare the hell out of us, cross-country via freight rail."

"But no oil."

Caitlin shook her head. "No oil."

48

BALCONES CANYONLANDS, TEXAS

Dylan sat in the backseat of the truck, both Cort Wesley and Caitlin looking at him from the front.

"I don't know how my mom's medal got there," he said at last, as if finally finding his voice. "I don't know, okay?"

"No, son, it's not okay," Cort Wesley snapped, the bands of muscle in his neck telling Caitlin it was all he could do to keep from exploding.

"I didn't mean it that way. I—"

"No? What did you mean, exactly?"

"I kind of passed out last night."

"Come again?"

"I was with Ela. I passed out."

"From drinking?"

"No," Dylan said, his mouth barely moving.

"What then?" Cort Wesley asked, dragging the words out of his mouth.

"I think it was peyote."

"Peyote? So you dropped out of college to do a drug known to turn people's minds to mush?"

"I didn't drop out."

"But you did peyote, right?"

Caitlin chimed in when Dylan failed to answer Cort Wesley's question. "Dylan, you said you passed out. Does that mean you don't remember anything?"

"I remember . . . some things."

Caitlin left that part hanging. "I'm saying this because peyote's known to create fugue states. Lost time, where hours can pass and you have no recollection of what happened or what you did."

"I know I didn't kill anybody."

"Well," Cort Wesley said, voice scratchy and raw, "what *did* you do?"

"Describe your clothes," Caitlin told Dylan, before he could answer.

"Huh?"

"When you came to this morning, were your clothes dirty, your boots scuffed up? Any blood anywhere on your person?"

"No to all."

"And when did you notice your mother's medal was missing?"

"Are you interrogating me?"

"I'm asking you," Caitlin told him.

"Later that morning. I figured it must be back at Ela's, but I couldn't find it."

Caitlin felt Cort Wesley look across the seat at her. She wished she could jam a hand down his throat, knowing what was coming.

"Maybe we're talking to the wrong college dropout here."

"What's that mean?" Dylan asked, rocking forward

until his father's gaze pushed him back against the seat again.

"That you've been used, son. That girl twisted you around her finger and you were too busy thinking with what's squeezed into those jeans to realize it. Smarten up, will you? When you going to goddamn learn? I guess never, since getting yourself beaten to within an inch of your life didn't change anything last time."

Dylan reached for the door, forgetting that Cort Wesley had locked them after he closed it behind him.

"How's it feel to be stuck in a small space, son? Because prison's what you'd be looking at right now, if somebody didn't see fit to do Caitlin a big, fat favor. Notice he didn't give her back the medal, though. That means this could turn bad in a real quick hurry, unless we get to the bottom of things before somebody on a different wavelength gets the jump on us."

Dylan eased himself away from the door. "What else you need from me?" he asked, his words aimed between them.

Caitlin didn't hesitate, while remembering her tone again. "Was Ela with you all night?"

He swallowed hard. "I can't say for sure, after a time."

She didn't push things on that front, knowing that the peyote had stolen too much of the boy's memory of last night for him to do her much good at all. Ela could have flown to Mars and back, with Dylan thinking she'd been lying beside him the whole time.

"There is something . . ." he began suddenly.

"Go on," Caitlin urged, when Dylan seemed hesitant again.

"The first time we went to visit Ela's grandfather, I'm pretty sure I saw somebody, or something, in one of those caves that overlooks his property." Dylan looked toward his father. "Can I go now?"

Cort Wesley nodded, and this time Dylan worked the door until the lock popped open. He burst out, nearly tumbling to the ground, before making his way back toward Ela and the cousins she called the Lost Boys.

"That went well," Cort Wesley managed, trailing Dylan with his eyes the whole time.

"Know what I think, Cort Wesley?"

"That we should take a look at those caves ourselves, I'm guessing," he said, his gaze clinging to his son.

PART FIVE

Another tale concerns the noted Texas Rangers. They would wait on the Texas side of the Red River for outlaws and criminals to cross the border into Oklahoma and stop at Brown Springs for water. They would shoot them from across the river, then hurry across and bury them on the spot.

—Robert F. Turpin, *Forgotten Ghost Tales and Legends of the Old West* (Grove, Oklahoma: Bob Turpin Publications, 2013)

49

"As I told you on the phone, Ranger, Mr. Jackson has a very busy day," his assistant/receptionist said the next morning, not bothering to hide her annoyance that Caitlin had showed up even after being told Sam Bob Jackson was unable to see her.

"I know what you said, ma'am, but there's something I'd like to show him it's really in his best interests to see."

With that, Caitlin produced an official-looking tri-fold document and handed it across the desk. The Ranger chopper was still at her disposal, thanks to Jones, and she had left a message on Captain Tepper's voice mail that she was using it to check out a lead, without elaborating further.

"That's a search warrant—blank for now, but I've already got an affidavit filled out to get one written for these premises. Oughta shut the office down for, oh, no more than a day, two at most." She leaned forward in line with the blank document she'd just handed over. "Why don't you go pay a visit to Mr. Jackson, inside his office, and show that to him?"

Caitlin laid her palms on the edge of the desk, a clear message that she wasn't going anywhere until the receptionist complied. Looking more angry than annoyed, the woman shoved her chair backwards and headed down the hall.

"I'm truly sorry, Ranger," Jackson pronounced, accompanying his assistant back to the reception area. "I was tied up. But I do believe I can make some time for you now."

She followed him past the line of smaller offices en route to his spacious one at the end of the hall.

"I'd appreciate you making this fast," he said, squeezing his bulbous frame into his oversize desk chair.

Caitlin took the same chair she had during her first visit. "That depends on how fast you can answer my questions."

"I already told you everything I know about that Indian reservation, the last time you were here."

"Funny you can make that claim, without knowing what I intend to ask you."

Jackson dropped the blank search warrant and it fluttered to his desk, landing in the space between them. "Well, then, by all means, Ranger, ask away."

"How is it you secured mineral rights to that Indian reservation for a company that's never gotten closer to oil than the local gas station?"

Jackson jerked forward in his chair, the leather making a squishing sound, as if he'd just passed wind. "I have no idea what you're talking about."

"You secured the mineral rights on behalf of a man named Cray Rawls and his company REPCO."

"You understand what confidentiality is, Ranger?"

"Quite well, sir."

"Then you must also understand that I'm not at liberty to share any workings of my business arrangements with my clients. Trust is everything in my line of work."

"Is it now, Mr. Jackson?"

"I don't like your tone."

"It's been a difficult few days, sir. Maybe you heard about the incident that took place in Austin yesterday."

Jackson nodded. "And I'm sure you're involved."

"The Rangers are, yes, sir. If my tone offends you, that's why. I'll try to moderate my behavior, and I apologize for any disrespect I've shown you. Let's start with the last time you saw Cray Rawls."

"That's really none of your business, Ranger."

Caitlin ignored his comment. "Because I was hoping you could set up a meeting with him for me, and just wanted to make sure I go through the right channels, to avoid any potential misconceptions."

"How's that?"

"Well, it occurs to me that you may have represented something about that land that's not necessarily accurate."

Sam Bob Jackson's jowls seemed to pucker, the lower of his two chins quivering. "That's a serious allegation, Ranger."

"That's why I called it a possibility and asked you to set up a meeting with Mr. Rawls so we can get things sorted out." Caitlin held Jackson's eyes, not bothering to disguise the intent in hers. "I figured this would be the perfect opportunity, given that he's in Texas right now, according to his office in North Carolina. You flew back here with him from there."

"Well, he's gone."

"His private jet isn't. It's still parked in the same airfield he landed in. You think he'd go back to North Carolina without his plane?"

Jackson swallowed hard. "There's a simple explanation for all this I'm not authorized to share with anyone."

"All the more reason to tell Mr. Rawls I'd like to see him while he's still in town." Caitlin slapped the knees of her jeans and rose slowly. "Tell you what . . . why don't I give you some privacy so you can make that call now?"

50

SAN ANTONIO, TEXAS

"You know what my brother always said about you, Masters?" Miguel Asuna asked Cort Wesley.

Asuna's office was lit too brightly by a big fluorescent fixture that matched the array of lighting in the body shop beyond. It made Cort Wesley want to put on his sunglasses, but he left them in his pocket, to make sure Asuna could see his eyes.

"What?"

"That you had the biggest set of balls he ever saw but he could never get a fix on which way they were swinging, like you enjoyed playing both sides."

Miguel's younger brother, Pablo Asuna, had been the

STRONG COLD DEAD 215

only one still waiting when, after four years, Cort Wesley got out of the Walls prison in Huntsville, thanks to an overturned conviction. Back when Cort Wesley was working for the Branca crime family, Miguel Asuna's body shop had doubled as a chop shop where stolen cars were brought to be disassembled for parts. He'd once heard Asuna boast he could strip a Mercedes in thirty minutes flat.

Miguel Asuna was twice the size of his dead little brother, and by all accounts he was still living and working on the fringe of the law. As a result, his body shop was filled to the brim, every stall and station taken, with not a single license plate to be seen. The shop smelled heavily of oil, tire rubber, and sandblasted steel. But the floor looked polished, shiny. A coat of finish over the concrete showed not a single grease stain or tire mark. For obvious reasons, Asuna kept the bay doors closed and, with the air-conditioning switched off, the whole shop had a sauna-like feel, fed by heat lamps switched on to dry paint faster.

"You mind if we make this fast, amigo?" Asuna resumed.

"Black Cadillac Escalade, almost brand new, that just had some bodywork done. I'd like to know who owns it."

"That's all you've got?"

"You told me to make it fast."

Asuna's eyes flashed and narrowed, as if someone had just shined a bright light into them. "Black Cadillac Escalade," he repeated, something changing in his tone. "You got a reason why I should spare the effort, the favors this'll take?"

"A couple of thugs driving it threatened one of my boys. As in stuck him in the backseat for a little heart-to-heart at knifepoint. They grabbed him out of a Mc-Donald's in Houston, where he was with his high school soccer team."

"Bad *hombres,* that's your point."

"My son just turned sixteen, Miguel. You do the math."

"Tell you what," Asuna said, hooking his thumbs through the empty belt loops of his grease-splattered overalls, "give me a little time. Get yourself a coffee or something, maybe a doughnut."

"I thought you wanted to make this fast."

"A half hour work for you, amigo?"

51

HOUSTON, TEXAS

No one turned toward Caitlin when she entered the Savarese Fight Fit boxing gym on Austin Street, right in the middle of downtown Houston, hardly raising an eye toward a woman with a badge and a gun.

"I'm looking for Cray Rawls," she told a man behind a reception desk, whose ears and nose looked like patchwork quilts of matching scar tissue. "He's expecting me."

He looked up from his magazine, without saying a word, and pointed Caitlin toward a man working a heavy bag.

Rawls's age and grooming left him looking out of

place. He looked like a classic car someone kept meticulously polished to disguise the rust and rot festering just beneath the surface. More fit for a high-end health club than this no-frills boxing gym that smelled of a combination of stale sweat and glove leather, mixed with the processed air circulated by floor fans. She spotted two younger boxers doing interval training on matching treadmills, and two more working with a trainer inside an old-fashioned ring complete with resin-stained canvas discolored in more places than it wasn't.

"I'm Caitlin Strong, Mr. Rawls," Caitlin greeted him.

"Yeah," Rawls said back to her, breathing hard and barely looking up from pounding the bag, "Sam Bob Jackson told me all about you."

"I doubt that, since we only met a few days ago."

Rawls didn't miss a beat with his blows. "You know how many hits I got when I Googled your name?"

"Believe me when I say that tells only a small part of the story," Caitlin told him, grasping the bag on the opposite side to hold it steady.

"Does it now?"

Rawls stopped his pounding, annoyed by the break in his punching rhythm. He tapped his gloves lightly together and looked at Caitlin closer, breathing already steadying.

"Mr. Jackson informs me you had some questions about my operation in the Balcones Canyonlands."

"The Comanche Indian reservation, specifically, sir."

"Because that's only a small part of my work here, you know," Rawls said, punching the bag lightly now.

"What work is that, sir?"

"Oil—what else?"

"I did notice a number of leases that had been taken out under your company, REPCO, but that reservation is the only parcel where you got permits up and running."

"A lot of good that's been doing me. As you're well aware, we've had some issues with protesters."

"I am aware of that, yes, sir."

"Then you'll be happy to know they've been resolved, as of this afternoon."

"Really?"

Rawls started hitting the bag with a precision one-two motion, the smacks of impact sounding to Caitlin like a medicine ball hitting the floor. "Protesters had a list of demands, and we met each and every one of the reasonable ones. We agreed to fund the construction of two new schools on the reservation, in addition to providing both college and secondary school scholarships to deserving students."

"At the Village School, maybe," Caitlin said, something pulling the words up out of her to see how Rawls responded.

One-two . . . One two . . . One-two . . .

"Top-notch college prep academy, right here in Houston," she continued, when he failed to acknowledge her point.

"I'll check with the people I've got handling that end of things for me," Rawls said finally. "Mr. Jackson also mentioned you raised the issue that we aren't actually drilling for oil on that land."

"An anomaly showed up in the construction equipment, which caught a few eyes, yes."

"Another consolation to the tribal elders, Ranger. How much you know about oil drilling?"

"As much as anybody from Texas, I suppose."

"And a lot more than me, I'm guessing, until a few months back. One of the conditions we agreed to, in order to secure the mineral rights, was that we avoid the typical deep-drilling exploratory operation. Picture jabbing a sword in a dark room until you pop a balloon; that's essentially what exploratory drilling is. We know the oil's down there, but not necessarily the best way to reach it. What we agreed to do in the Balcones was to use a pin instead of a sword. Not wise, from a cost, time, or labor perspective, but a lot less intrusive and significantly less destructive to the environment."

"That didn't seem to matter much to those protesters, sir. Guess the point of all your efforts was lost on them."

"Not all, just enough. Those kids schooled themselves on what happened up in North Dakota, on the Fort Berthold reservation, and figured that was what was coming here. A bit overblown, in my mind."

"Only if you call murder, corruption, and causing a few earthquakes overblown, sir. But it wouldn't be the first time that reservation in the Balcones came under fire."

"Oh no?"

"Similar kind of thing happened before. An ancestor of mine was involved back then, going up against a man who, I'm guessing, must've sounded a lot like you."

52

"We don't need your help, Ranger," Isa-tai told Jack Strong, a few hours after Strong had left John D. Rockefeller in his Austin hotel.

"You got it, all the same. On account of the fact that the state of Texas don't need a range war in these parts."

"Leaving dead Comanche in their wake is nothing new for the Texas Rangers."

"Funny, Rockefeller said almost the very same thing to me," Steeldust Jack said, glancing around at the tribe going about its daily chores. "But I don't see any of your Comanche marauding over settlers and ranchers and making war on the plains."

Steeldust Jack noticed a number of Comanche women carrying huge sacks of corn, harvested from the nearby fields, on their backs. One stumbled, lost her balance, and the sack went flying. Ears of corn, wrapped in thick husks, scattered in all directions. Impact with the ground split some of those husks, enough for the Ranger to glimpse moldy spots, as brown and ugly as warts, growing on the kernels.

"I wouldn't eat those, if I were you," he advised Isa-tai, stopping short of helping the Indian girl gather up her spilled sack, since none of the other Comanche did, either.

"But you're not me," said Isa-tai, "and you're not us, either, are you, Ranger?"

Isa-tai followed Jack Strong's lingering gaze to the corn that, at first glance anyway, clearly looked infested by some kind of vegetable rot, or worse.

"A matter of perspective, *taibo,*" the tribe's young medicine man told him, using the less-than-friendly Comanche word for a white man. "You see only the ugliness of the fungus, what happens when rain seeps into the cornstalks and rots the kernels. Our Aztec brothers called it *cuitlacoche,* and we consider it a delicacy."

"It's still a fungus to me," Steeldust Jack said.

"Sometimes our Mother Earth makes ugly what is truly beautiful."

The Ranger took off his hat and put it right back on. "That's all well and good. But the fact is, Rockefeller and his men are coming. I'm just advising you of that fact, along with my intention to hold the sumbitch off, even if I have to arrest or shoot him."

Isa-tai frowned, his smooth complexion furrowing. "I've known you for only a day more than this Rockefeller. And we are fully capable of taking care of ourselves."

"You mean, like you took care of that gunman who trespassed on your land a couple nights back."

Isa-tai's spine stiffened, seeming to make him taller.

"What I didn't have time to tell you yesterday," Steeldust Jack continued, "was that the man had black mud caked inside his boots. Kind you've got all over your land, thanks to the very oil Rockefeller wants to yank out of it. No such mud to be found anywhere else otherwise in these immediate parts. That means the victim was trespassing on this reservation almost for sure. Could be somebody spotted him and followed him off it."

"You *taibo* speak a lot without saying much."

"I'm just trying to do right by you here, Isa-tai. Catching me a murderer is one thing; protecting your land from trespass by outsiders with no call to be on it is another. Right now, John D. Rockefeller is commanding the bulk of my attention when it comes to the latter."

"Then do what you have to do to keep him off our land, Ranger, but once he crosses it, he's our problem."

Steeldust Jack looked about at the Comanche braves who'd gathered during the course of their conversation. "In the meantime," he said, "if you could lend me a few of these boys, I just might be able to stop that from happening."

Jack Strong sat on his horse at the head of the only road big enough to handle the kind of equipment John D. Rockefeller would be toting along to the reservation.

His position in the relative clear, looking down over a pass snaking through the grasslands and trees, allowed Steeldust Jack to spot an endless procession of the biggest wagons he'd ever seen. They were hauling pipes, tubing, drums of water and sand, and the disassembled parts of massive steam engines to power the actual drilling apparatus, which would be erected utilizing the lead wagons' load of lumber. The wagons carrying the heavy steel were outfitted with double-thick wooden wheels, their extra-large cargo beds boasting three sets, with an extra pair riding the center. Lugging these required four horses—and in some cases, unless the Ranger's vision was deceiving him, six horses—instead of two.

John D. Rockefeller led the way himself, on horseback, centered between two groups of the gunmen Jack Strong recognized from the hotel restaurant. He gave no quarter, just held his ground as the convoy ground to a halt on Rockefeller's signal, when they saw the Ranger blocking their way. To Steeldust Jack, it looked like a staged military march. The line of wagons and men was so vast that he could barely see the end.

"I knew I'd be seeing you again, Ranger," Rockefeller said from thirty feet away, his voice booming as if he were giving a speech. "I just didn't think it'd be this soon."

"You're in Texas now, sir. Biggest little state you ever did see."

"Speaking of which, I've got a letter here from Governor Richard Coke himself, granting me permission to drill for oil on Comanche land and—"

"That's all well and good," Steeldust Jack interrupted, "except the actual authority, as far as the treaty goes, is the nation's capital, not Austin. That would be Washington, last time I checked."

"You didn't let me finish, Ranger. I was going to say my men have all been appointed deputy U.S. marshals, under the command of Marshal Brocius here."

"Congratulations, Curly Bill," Jack Strong said, tipping his hat, before stealing a glance at young Jimmy

Miller, the one rider not wearing a big silver badge, since he was too young to be officially deputized.

"So I would ask that you respect the wishes of the governor of your state, and the authority vested in these marshals by the United States government, and stand aside, Ranger."

"Why don't you ride up here and show me that letter first, Mr. Rockefeller."

Steeldust Jack had enjoyed issuing the challenge, and was only half surprised when John D. Rockefeller accepted it. He stretched his mustache straight to both sides, signaled his newly appointed lawmen to hold in place, and then rode forward to Jack Strong's position in the road.

"It does seem to be in order," the Ranger said, handing the letter back to the man, who smelled freshly shaved and barbered, in spite of what must have been an arduous ride from Austin for the convoy. "How much it cost you?"

"I don't think I follow you."

"I believe you do, sir. I was just wondering what you had to promise Governor Coke for him to take a stand against what I know him to believe. I was just wondering the price a man's conscience is going for these days. You cut him in on the deal, give him a percentage of the oil you expect to find, or was it strictly cash?"

Rockefeller sat straight in his saddle, his expression not changing in the least. "Everywhere else in this country, you Texas Rangers are considered a joke."

"Is that a fact?"

"Your time's coming to an end. There's not even going to be a frontier anymore, before you know it. The transcontinental railroad's going to finish it for good, because where there's open land there's opportunity for people like me to make something out of it. Industry's coming, business is coming, the future is coming. Only place you and the Rangers will exist soon will be in a museum."

"But I'm here now, aren't I?"

"And I expect you to do your duty and stand aside, to yield the road, Ranger."

Jack Strong took off his hat in a feigned show of respect. "I will do that for sure, sir," he said, pulling his horse off to the grasslands strewn with all manner of pebbles and rocks. "The road is yours."

He then watched as the procession of horsemen rode on ahead, the wagons following, with the heaviest of the lot bringing up the rear. But the road gave away under the initial phalanx of wagons laden with both men and supplies. Cavities appeared where the bed had been just moments before, the road seeming to splinter and collapse, swallowing whole wagons—or at least half, if only the front or back wheels hit a sweet spot.

To Steeldust Jack, it looked as if the front portion of the convoy was being sucked down into hell itself. Wheels splintered and wagon frames cracked, shedding their contents. Guards both on horseback and manning the wagons drew their sidearms or steadied their shotguns. He knew the fear on their faces from that of Union soldiers caught in a Confederate ambush, the difference being the confusion that blossomed in its stead, with the realization that no ambush was coming. Still, a smattering of shots erupted, flashing through the haze of the dirt cloud rising from the collapsed roadbed, but hitting nothing.

John D. Rockefeller bucked his own horse around to face Jack Strong, but the Texas Ranger was already gone, his horse galloping through the grasslands and kicking up gravel in its wake.

53

HOUSTON, TEXAS

"It was an old trick my great-great-granddad learned in the Civil War," Caitlin said, finishing up the story.

The stale air of the gym seemed to have thickened through the course of her tale, the stink of sweat growing more pronounced in the process. It felt to her as if the air-conditioning had shut down, leaving her roasting inside her cotton shirt.

"Confederate soldiers," Caitlin continued, "would dig and disguise trenches in the road to slow supplies headed to the Northern troops, like guerrilla warfare. It almost worked well enough to tilt things in the South's favor."

"Almost," Cray Rawls repeated.

"Even so, it slowed up Rockefeller's wagons enough to delay him for a while."

"Well, Ranger, nobody's ever compared me to John D. Rockefeller before," Rawls said, lifting the gloves hanging limply by his sides and tapping at the heavy bag in preparation for resuming his pounding of it.

"I wouldn't take it as a compliment, sir."

"I guess it's a matter of perspective again, isn't it?"

"But here's the thing, Mr. Rawls. Back then, nobody had the resources to find out the truth behind John D. Rockefeller's cutthroat business practices or how many lives he left trampled in his wake."

"Is that the comparison you're drawing here?"

"Not exactly, sir."

One-two . . . One two . . . One-two . . .

Back to his punching again, Rawls seemed not to hear her.

"Because I wonder," Caitlin continued anyway, "how much the Comanche tribal elders know about your history in Texas?"

One-two . . . One two . . . One-two . . .

"I wasn't aware I had much of one to speak of, really," Rawls said, as casually as he could manage.

But something had changed in the way he hit the heavy bag. Caitlin could feel the reduced intensity of his blows, which suddenly sounded hollow on impact.

"It's true, isn't it, sir, that following the death of your mother in North Carolina, you were adopted by a couple from Texas?"

Rawls forced himself to continue punching, just going through the motions now.

"For a time," he said.

"Nine years is a long time."

Caitlin realized the man's entire demeanor had changed. His shoulders were sagging and his wrists were bending inward too much on impact. And he was breathing rapidly, mostly through his nose, the smooth and practiced cadence gone.

"What I'm getting at, Mr. Rawls," Caitlin resumed, "is whether you informed the tribal elders you're doing business with about your criminal record in this state."

Rawls stopped punching altogether and held the bag steady with his gloves. "I was a juvenile at the time. Those records are sealed. Are we almost done here?"

"You were charged with rape, and would've been charged as an adult if the charges had stuck. But the woman was a prostitute who never showed up to give her statement. Lucky for you. Along with the fact that the fire marshal never followed through much on the investigation into the fire that killed the couple that adopted you."

"Thank you for not calling them my parents," Rawls said stiffly.

"Religious types, I'm told. Real Bible thumpers."

"Are you finished, Ranger?"

"Just one more question for now. You ever actually get in the ring, Mr. Rawls?"

"What does that have to do with anything?"

"Just this, sir: I've known a lot of great shots on the range, some of the best. Champion target shooters who've never actually been in a gunfight. I never understood why anyone would shoot for sport, any more than I can understand why somebody would learn how to box and never get into the ring for a real bout."

"You didn't let me answer the question."

"Your face gave it away," Caitlin told him, "along with the way you're hitting the bag. Boxers hold back when they're practicing. It's a necessary evil, so they can unleash themselves in the ring. But you aren't holding back anything, like that bag is as close as you'll ever come to a real opponent."

"Maybe you didn't notice my nose."

"I did, sir, along with the lack of even a blotch anywhere else. I'm guessing you did some simple sparring that turned bad. Looks to me like somebody sucker punched you."

"I'm sure there's a point to all this," Rawls said, breathing faster and louder.

"Only that an actual opponent is a whole different thing, either in the ring or in a gunfight. I just thought you should know that. Call it a little friendly advice."

Rawls leaned back against the heavy bag, crossing his arms against his chest. "Did I do or say something to offend you, Ranger?"

"When you first saw me coming over, you looked at me like you knew you'd been caught. Like you'd done something that made you figure me or somebody else was coming, and that maybe you were glad, at least resigned. I've seen that look before, plenty often, and it always makes me wonder what a person's hiding. Because if they're hiding one thing, it's a pretty safe bet they're hiding something more."

Rawls grinned, his brilliantly white teeth glistening in the spill of overhead gym lights. "Did you rehearse that? I mean, it sounds like a speech you've given before."

"I'm not one for giving speeches, sir, but I got roped into speaking at a high school graduation, come spring, at that Houston prep school I mentioned to you."

"Lucky kids."

"We'll see. Anyway, one of them got kidnapped the other day, right out of a McDonald's, if you can believe that."

"Well, this is a pretty dangerous state, Ranger."

Caitlin slapped her hat against her side and then fitted it back in place over her hair. "I was just about to say the same thing to you, sir."

54

San Antonio, Texas

Bobby Roy's Used Cars and Bail Bond Service was located just down South Frio Street from the Bexar County magistrate's building, in a beat-up lot bleeding macadam amid a patchwork pattern of what looked like gravel instead of tar. Cort Wesley parked his truck next to a construction site in the shadow of a John Deere front loader, waiting to make sure the men identified by Miguel Asuna were inside.

The John Deere kept him hidden from sight while not shielding him much from the sun, and Cort Wesley was fine with that. Fine with it roasting him, to further fuel the fury he felt every time he considered a couple of two-bit thugs rousting his son to make their bullying points.

And two-bit thugs, according to Miguel Asuna, was exactly what they were.

"Body shop right here in the city did the work," he had told Cort Wesley, forty minutes after their initial meeting. "The Escalade's registered to Bobby Roy, guy who rips people off on his used cars as much as his bond work. My guess is your boy was worked over by a couple of ex-cons who sell jalopies off his lot, when they're not chasing down bail jumpers for him."

"You're kidding."

Asuna raised his hand theatrically. "God's honest truth, amigo. They're brothers, Terry and K-Bar Boyd."

"K-Bar?"

"What can I say?" Asuna shrugged. "Man fancies himself good with a knife. Word is he gave himself the nickname after shanking a couple guys in prison. God's honest truth, too."

"Tough guy, eh?" Cort Wesley said, thinking of what Luke had told him about a guy with a knife, sticking the tip in Luke's crotch, explaining how he'd had his way with boys before.

"If doing them in the back makes him tough, sure. And I'll tell you something else that's true: I do much better work than the clowns Bobby Roy took that Escalade to. Tell him that, if you see him."

"Oh, I'll see him."

The black Escalade pulled into the lot and slid into a space directly in front of the entrance, two hours into

Cort Wesley's superheated vigil. Luke hadn't been very specific in his descriptions of the Boyd brothers, Terry and K-Bar, but he'd still provided enough for Cort Wesley to recognize them climbing down out of the Escalade. Both wore leather gloves with the fingers cut back, as if they'd bought their toughness on sale at Walmart. Living, breathing caricatures who were plenty good enough to track down desperate bail skips and scare high school kids, which wasn't very good at all. But they were probably armed, and Cort Wesley wanted to find out fast, without making a mess, who'd sent them after Luke.

Unless making that mess better served his cause, Cort Wesley reasoned, his eyes falling on the John Deere front loader again.

The driver from the nearby work crew had been kind enough to leave the key in the starter of the Deere, which handled like a big, angry SUV.

"Hey!" Cort Wesley thought he heard someone yell, as he turned the Deere wheel all the way to the left and swung out into traffic. "Hey!"

He thumped across the eastbound traffic lane and moved into the westbound lane, accompanied by screeching brakes slammed by drivers doing a collective double take at the sight of the massive vehicle ranging across their path like some iron dinosaur.

Cort Wesley hopped the curb into Bobby Roy's used car lot, managing to steer clear of the twin rows of vehicles, which were covered more by dust than by paint. He headed straight for what passed for a showroom.

55

SAN ANTONIO, TEXAS

Cort Wesley barely felt the impact as the big Deere's raised shovel crashed through the showroom glass and plowed T-Bird and Caprice classic convertibles from its path like they were Matchbox cars. A guy he thought he recognized as Bobby Roy flew out of a desk chair, in front of which sat a couple with whom he'd been in the process of closing a deal.

Terry and K-Bar Boyd stumbled out of the back office, struggling to free nine-millimeter pistols from fancy holsters tucked under their sport jackets. But Cort Wesley was out of the cab by then, boots crunching over shattered glass, kicking aside a back bumper that had separated from one of the convertibles on impact. He reached the Boyds just as they finally found purchase on pistols, and he tore the weapons from their grasps in a motion so fluid that both brothers were left absurdly aiming their empty hands at him.

"What the fuck?" one of them managed, before Cort Wesley slammed him in the nose with a ridged palm.

He watched the potential buyers flee through a side door, closely followed by Bobby Roy himself, as Cort Wesley stuck a leg out to trip the second Boyd brother. Then he hoisted both of them up onto a big rectangular planter, which looked decorative compared to the rest of the showroom. He smelled spilled coffee somewhere as he smacked the Boyd brothers' heads together to further make his point. The impact sounded like a golf club thwacking a ball off the tee.

"You K-Bar?" he said to one, producing a dazed headshake. "Then nice to meet you, Terry," he greeted him. "You too, K-Bar," he said to the other. "I'm the guy whose son you pulled out of that McDonald's the other day, in Houston. Sound familiar? You were trying to scare me off. Thought I'd give you boys the opportunity to do it in person."

"Fuck you!" Terry managed in nasally fashion. He was pinching his nose closed in a futile attempt to stanch the blood that Cort Wesley's blow had unleashed.

Cort Wesley let them see him grin, ignoring Terry Boyd's failed show of bravado. "You boys crossed a line here, and the only reason you're not under the big wheels of that John Deere now is I need to know who put you up to it."

The Boyd brothers heard the screech of police sirens picking up cadence in the distance, their expressions flashing hope that their assailant would surely flee. Clearly, they were uneducated on the damage a man like Cort Wesley could do to them in his remaining minute or so.

"You give me a name and you get a pass. Call it your Get Out of Hell for Free card." Cort Wesley glanced at the blood running from Terry's nose, between his fingers, and the lump the size of a baseball that had already formed on K-Bar's skull. "Well, not quite for free, but close enough as things go."

"We ain't gonna give you nothing!" K-Bar ranted,

his words stringing into each other. "You wanna kill us, go right ahead."

His bravado, inspired by the increasingly loud police sirens, was ignored by Cort Wesley, who snatched up a pristine fan belt, once displayed on a partition wall that now had fallen to the Deere. The sign had said something about the belt coming from the Mustang the great Steve McQueen had driven in *Bullitt,* but Cort Wesley had his doubts.

"Okay," he said, wrapping the fan belt around K-Bar's neck and tightening it until K-Bar's breath choked off and his face began to purple.

"What the fuck, man?" Terry Boyd ranted, his voice whiny. "What the fuck?"

Terry's brother was starting to gurgle now, his cheeks so pumped with air they looked as if they were ready to explode.

"A name, Terry. Give me a name."

56

HOUSTON, TEXAS

"What's that pounding sound?" Sam Bob Jackson asked Cray Rawls. "I can hardly hear you."

"That pounding is me smacking a heavy bag, because if I stop now, I might drive back there and pound you instead, you fucking moron."

"Cray, I didn't catch what you just—"

Rawls stopped his punching long enough to adjust the Bluetooth device riding his ear. "Never mind. Nice talk I just had with that cunt of a Texas Ranger you sent my way."

"She wasn't taking no for an answer."

"Your job, while you still have one, is to run interference. That means keep the attention off me."

"She's a determined gal, with a reputation like an Old West gunfighter's."

"A cunt gunfighter?"

"Pistols don't come in genders, Cray."

"And you're scared shitless of her."

"This is the Texas Rangers we're talking about."

Rawls started hitting the bag again. "I'm glad you made that point for me, you fat tub of lard. I did some checking into Cort Wesley Masters. Remember him? The man you tried to scare off after he made that scene at the reservation?"

"I told you—"

"I know what you told me. Now let me tell *you* something. Before Masters did a stretch in Huntsville, before he worked as an enforcer for the Branca crime family, he was Army Special Forces."

"What?"

Through the Bluetooth device, which had loosened up again, Rawls could almost hear the air going out of the fat shit. "That's right, Sam Bob. You picked a fight with a genuine Green Beret. And that's not all, not even close. Would you care to hazard a guess who his girlfriend is?"

"Oh, shit . . ."

"Match made in heaven, wouldn't you say? So your dumb ass has gotten us two for the price of one. You better hope the boatload of cash I had to dump to get those damn Indians to drop their protest alleviates things, because my next step is to drop you down an abandoned oil well. It's sure to be nice and slimy down there, so you'll feel right at home. By the way, that money I had to leave on the table at that reservation? It's coming out of your end."

Rawls heard Sam Bob Jackson gulp down some air. "What does the Ranger know?"

"She's getting close, lard-ass."

"But what we're doing, it's not a crime. Mineral rights we purchased plainly state 'oil and gas reserves, along with anything else of monetary value discovered along the way.' "

"Oh, really? And does that absolve you from kidnapping charges, too, or how about from being an embarrassment to your mother's loins?"

"This coming from the son of a prostitute."

Rawls started hitting the heavy bag so hard his hands throbbed inside his gloves. "I'm going to do you a favor and forget you said that, Sam Bob. What I'm not going to forget is, thanks to you, I've got a Texas Ranger and a Green Beret crawling up my ass. I don't know why I let you fly back here with me on the company Gulfstream. Given it to do all over again, I'd rather you hitchhiked, maybe shed a few pounds on the way."

"Nothing's changed," Jackson said, his words ringing hollowly in Rawls's ears, between smacks to the bag. "You said so yourself."

"You know the biggest yacht in the world's longer than a football field and cost a quarter billion dollars? That's the kind of money I'm talking about. Enough to make your Texas oilmen kiss my ass, as long as you don't cause me any more problems."

Through his earpiece, Rawls heard the tinny click tone of an incoming e-mail or text message on Jackson's end, followed by the return of Jackson's loud breathing.

"What's wrong now, Sam Bob?" Rawls asked.

"Er, we may have another one."

"Masters did *what*?" Rawls asked, pounding the bag so hard he could barely hear Sam Bob Jackson on the other end of his Bluetooth device.

"I just got the call. He busted up a used car showroom, nearly killed the guys who were supposed to put a scare into him."

"These being the ones who kidnapped his son."

"They're headed for the hills as we speak. That's not the problem."

"What is?"

"They told Masters I was the one who hired them to do the deed."

Rawls let his gloves drop to his waist and leaned against the heavy bag to catch his breath. "I guess you can expect a visit too, then. Maybe Masters will take your whole building down this time."

"I thought you should know, Cray, in case this leads back to you."

"Only way that can happen is if you spill the beans. You wouldn't do that, would you, Sam Bob?"

"Of course not. But . . ."

"But what?"

"The Texas Rangers are involved too. Do the math."

Rawls began tapping at the heavy bag. "Why don't you do it for me?"

"Adds up to us both being fucked here. Time to do some damage control, what you do best, Cray."

Rawls started hitting the bag harder again. "The only damage of concern here was done by you, without my permission or knowledge. I'd say it's not time for me to do anything."

Dead air filled the line. Rawls heard nothing but Sam Bob Jackson's heavy breathing, which fell into an awkward cadence that mirrored his own.

"Like you said, I'm the only one who can link you to all this, Cray."

"Is that a threat, Sam Bob?"

"Call it an accommodation."

Rawls started slamming the bag anew with his gloves. "I call it a load of shit. A Texas Ranger who thinks she's Wyatt Earp and an ex-Green Beret with a hair across his ass—they're your problems."

"I messed up the Masters thing, for sure. But you should remember it was the Balcones land deal that poked Caitlin Strong like a stick. And, last time I checked, you were front and center on that one."

"So what would you suggest?"

"Damage control, like I already said. Maybe I didn't go far enough. Maybe you need to go farther."

"Against a Texas Ranger and Rambo? Others who've gone up against these two haven't fared so well, from what I've been told."

"Don't believe everything you hear, Cray."

"I'm glad you said that, Sam Bob, because it gives me call to do what I should've done five minutes ago."

"What's that?"

"This," Rawls said, and clicked off the call on his Bluetooth device.

57

OVER THE ATLANTIC OCEAN

"Hey, mister, you wanna play?"

Hatim Abd al-Aziz turned in his window seat in the big plane's rear section to look at the young boy sitting next to him. The boy had set up an old-fashioned checkers game on his tray table. His parents and older siblings were sleeping abreast of one another, across the aisle in the plane's center seating section.

"I'm not very good," he told the boy.

"How can you be bad at checkers? And don't let me win, either," the boy said, making the first move. "Your turn, mister."

Hatim Abd al-Aziz forced a smile, and then a move. That wasn't his real name, and he'd done his best to strike from his mind and memory the one given him at birth, since that person no longer existed. He'd taken the name Hatim because it meant "determined and decisive," while Abd al-Aziz meant "servant of the powerful." Especially appropriate, because he lived to serve Allah and nothing else. He did as Allah willed, and always had, ever since the time, as a boy, when he'd loosened the lug nuts on the wheels of his soccer team's bus and hid behind a tree to watch what came next. He'd been thrown off the team for fighting and figured that if he didn't get to play, then neither should anyone else. The bus had spun across the road at fifty kilometers per hour, knocking vehicles from its path like the flippers on an old-fashioned pinball machine. Several of his teammates were hurt, but none had been killed.

Which disappointed the young man destined to become Hatim Abd al-Aziz.

"You really are bad," the boy was saying now. "I don't think you're paying attention."

"I have a lot on my mind."

"Work?"

"I love what I do."

The boy cocked his gaze across the aisle, toward the sleeping form of his parents, who were resting against each other under a single blanket. "My dad hates his job."

"That's too bad."

"He makes a lot of money, but he hates it. I hear him talking to my mom sometimes."

"Probably because he doesn't believe in what he does."

"I don't know what that means."

Al-Aziz began paying more attention to the game of checkers. He found himself losing badly. "A man must believe. It's where the love of one's work, one's duty, comes from."

He began studying the board, seeking a strategy to seize the advantage from the boy, who'd already jumped five of his pieces and was marching unchecked across al-Aziz's side.

"I don't know what that means, either."

Al-Aziz's first kill had been when he was just a bit older, a few years after he sabotaged the bus. It was a young woman his own age who refused to wear a veil, calling herself secular. Totally acceptable, as was her promiscuousness, in Western-leaning Turkey, but not to him. So, one night he pretended to give in to her overtures, leaving her in the woods to die after he bashed her skull in with a rock. At that point, it was the greatest moment of al-Aziz's life.

He'd been fifteen at the time, twenty years ago now, when no one had dared to contemplate the existence of the Islamic State to which he'd dedicated his life—first as a soldier, then quickly rising through the ranks as the group formed its hierarchy and system of succession on the fly. His fluency in several languages made him a great asset, and his penchant for violence fueled his even faster rise. Today, many believed that what the world knew as ISIS was on the run, both its numbers and its influence declining. But members of the cadre, like al-Aziz, knew the group was just biding its time, picking its spots, lying in wait for the right moment to make its impact felt in a way that would secure its legacy and service to Allah forever.

And now, that moment had come.

"King me!" the boy pronounced, as al-Aziz realized that winning the game was impossible.

This game, anyway, he thought, as he kinged the boy. Back in Syria, he trained boys of this age to behead men kneeling at their feet. How to handle the heaviness of the sword and turn its weight in their favor. The angle, the aim, the cut—it was all about technique.

"I could teach you how to play better," the boy was telling him, as if he honestly felt bad. "So you could win."

"I could do the same for you." Al-Aziz smiled.

Perplexed, the boy looked at the game board, which showed him far ahead. "But I'm already winning."

"There are other games."

Al-Aziz gazed across the aisle and pictured this boy slicing off the heads of his parents and siblings as they slept. In his experience, that was a great test, revealing a young warrior's true mettle and level of loyalty to the caliphate. He must renounce everything in the past so that he might turn toward the future unencumbered. Al-Aziz genuinely believed he was doing these boys a favor. The process had yielded ISIS some of its finest young warriors.

"Mister . . . ," the kid was saying.

Al-Aziz gazed about the plane. The majority of passengers were sleeping now. He wondered how many heads he could take before anyone stirred. Imagined them cowering before his masked form, his sword splattered with blood, which had splashed the walls and windows of the plane as well.

"Hey, mister."

They wouldn't fight back because they were sheep. In killing them, al-Aziz would be performing a service, ridding the world of their burden. They served nothing and no one, did not understand the vision for the world as expressed by the one true God al-Aziz existed merely to serve. Al-Aziz wouldn't rest until that day had come to pass. The power and efficacy of his beliefs was about to be more righteously rewarded than even the caliphate's supreme leaders had dared to foresee.

"Mister . . ."

They would bring their greatest enemy to its knees, al-Aziz himself now responsible for wielding a sword that could slaughter millions instead of one. A great gift, bestowed by Allah Himself, in recognition of al-Aziz's devotion to the word of the one true God, a devotion that wouldn't cease or even abate until all the nonbelievers were gone. Nine others were accompanying him on this blessed mission, all taking other flights, on other airlines, to different cities, en route to their rendezvous a day later. Nine others, to bring the total to ten, the same number the prophet Muhammad himself had killed when he conquered Mecca. A holy number.

Ten.

"Mister!"

Al-Aziz finally turned back the boy's way.

"It's your move, mister," he said.

Al-Aziz smiled. "Yes, it is."

PART SIX

Cattlemen and ranchers went to war over the practice of stringing barbed wire around plots of land. Bands of armed "nippers" worked at night cutting the barbed wire, causing an estimated $20 million in damage. The Texas Rangers were called in on patrol. Ranger Ira Aten proposed arming the fences with bombs triggered to explode when the fence wire was cut. The idea was nixed. (September 1, 1883)

—Bullock Texas State History Museum,
"The Story of Texas"

58

"I made us a snack," Ela said, clambering down the plank steps, back into the root cellar.

She sat down on the blanket across from Dylan and laid a plate down between them.

"It's corn," she continued, as Dylan peeled the foil off one of the ears, "grown right here on the rez. I cooked it over a fire upstairs."

Dylan finished peeling, noting a grayish-black patch that swelled out from a patch of kernels. "Looks like you burned it."

"Nah," Ela said, working the foil from her own ear of corn, "that's what makes it a delicacy."

Dylan gave the discolored growth a closer look. "Fungus? Mold?"

"Just eat it, dumb-ass. It's a secret my people have kept for centuries, our greatest secret. Now, hand me my phone."

Dylan did, still holding the ear of corn by a section of foil he'd left in place so he wouldn't burn his fingers. Then he noticed that Ela had driven a roasting stick into one of the ends, so he could eat the corn while holding it, instead.

Ela took the phone and slid the cursor from left to right. "I said *my* phone."

"Whoops, sorry."

Dylan gave Ela her iPhone and took his back, watching her fire off a text as he raised the corn toward his mouth.

"It smells like shit."

"But it's good for you, that fungus included."

He ate around the tarry patch anyway. Once they'd both finished, Ela handed Dylan a cup of the tar-colored tea, playing with the zipper of his jeans under the spill of lantern light.

"Stop," he said, giving her back the cup and easing her away from him.

She took the cup and laid it aside, then went back to his zipper.

"I said stop."

"Come on," Ela said, flashing Dylan the smile that melted his insides, "we won. I want to celebrate."

"What'd we win?" Dylan asked her. "You said this was all about maintaining the purity of the land. That we couldn't let them spoil what nature had wrought—your words, Ela. You said this was about the survival of your people. That's a quote, from when you got me to leave school."

She pushed him down, atop the blanket on the uneven floor, straddling his torso, her butt pressed against his crotch. "We were never going to win everything. We won enough."

"You never win with these kinds of people," Dylan insisted. "They only let you think you have. Believe me, I know."

Ela started pressing down on him. Dylan felt his insides flutter. "We're the ones letting them think that they've won," she said.

"What happened to my medal, the one that used to belong to my mother?"

Ela moved her toned butt back and forth. "You're wearing it."

Dylan pulled his shirt back to reveal a pair of chains, but not that one. "It was found near that dead guy's body. How'd it get there?"

He took the tea she'd laid near him and spilled it onto the ground, its pungent aroma and black tar coloring telling him it was even stronger than the last batch of peyote tincture. "I was wearing it when we tripped, Ela."

"We didn't trip."

"No? What would you call it then?"

"Opening our minds to a deeper, higher plane, where our emotions could communicate directly."

"My mother was wearing that medal when she was murdered. My father gave it to me, said she'd want me to have it."

"I'm sorry."

"How'd it get out there?"

"How should I know?"

"Because I was wearing it when we reached that deeper, higher plane. Maybe our emotions communicating directly wasn't such a good idea."

Ela stopped rubbing against him. "You think *I* did this?"

"There's not a lot of other options."

"You don't remember us being together all night?"

"I don't remember much of anything."

"Both of us ended up passed out. You were still passed out when I woke up—early, like I always do."

"With the sun."

"Close enough," Ela said.

Dylan looked up at her, straddling him. He believed her because he wanted to. In that moment, he realized he'd been a fool for walking away from school to accompany Ela on this crusade, which had ended when the oil company agreed to fund a whole bunch of scholarships, provide job training, and, in the meantime, put every unemployed Comanche on the reservation to work laying the pipeline.

"You knew this protest shit wasn't going to work," Dylan said to her. "You knew you and your Lost Boys weren't going to stick it out, from the beginning."

"But we got more than I ever figured out of the deal."

"Why didn't you tell me that?"

"Tell you what?"

"That was the plan all along."

"Because it wasn't."

"So you're telling me you weren't working with the tribal elders on this the whole time?"

Ela swung her legs off Dylan and sat up next to him. She took his hands in hers.

"I'm going to forget you said that. It was my grandfather who told me to back off. After that man was killed," she added. An afterthought.

"With his blood ending up on my medal."

"Back to that again?"

"We never left it."

Ela let go of Dylan's hands. "My grandfather said

there could be no more death. He said the spirits were angry, just like back in 1874, and if we didn't make peace, the same thing would happen now that happened then."

"What happened then?"

She looked away, the spill of the kerosene lantern light catching only one side of her face. "Ask your Texas Ranger."

"I could be arrested, you know. I could end up getting charged."

Ela smiled. "You have friends in high places, boy."

"Caitlin's not going to obstruct justice to protect me forever. Sooner or later, I'll be called to the table." Dylan hesitated. "Maybe you'll be called, too."

"Me?"

"As a witness. My alibi."

"Even though we both passed out." She took his hands again. "Are you sure you were wearing the medal that night? Can you really remember?"

"I wear it all the time, girl."

"But you could have lost it earlier in the day, even the day before. If you wear it all the time, you might think it's still there even when it isn't, right? Doesn't that make more sense than your girlfriend setting you up as a suspect?"

Dylan could feel his insides melting at the way she had referred to herself as his girlfriend.

"Because that would mean I had something to do with the murder," Ela continued. "An accomplice, accessory, or something. Is that what you think?"

"I didn't say that."

"You might as well have."

Dylan pulled Ela in close and kissed her, as hard and as deep as he'd ever kissed anyone.

"That's better," she said, brushing the hair from her face when they finally separated.

"I don't know why I did that."

"Because I was about to, and you sensed it."

Dylan blew the hair from his face and rolled his eyes. "Please."

"Please what? You told me your dad talks to a ghost who steals root beer from him. You told me your Texas Ranger's got some warrior protecting her, who's part witch and has visions of the future. But you don't think you knew I was going to kiss you and kissed me first?"

Dylan let himself smile. "What if I did?"

Ela smiled back. "That's better."

"What?"

"You, back to being you," she said, pulling the shirt up over her head. "And me being me."

59

San Antonio, Texas

"You got something you want to say, Ranger?" Cort Wesley asked Caitlin from behind the wheel of his truck, en route back to the Balcones.

"Just trying to sort things out, that's all."

"You mean the part about Sam Bob Jackson ordering the Boyd brothers to scare me, through Luke?"

"A muff like Jackson doesn't tie his shoes on his

own. That means Cray Rawls is the one we really need to nail for this."

"I haven't met either of them yet."

"Let me save you the trouble, Cort Wesley. Rawls is like any of a thousand rich jerks I've met over the years who think their money and power makes their shit taste like chocolate. I've learned never to put anything past men like that."

They were headed north to the Comanche reservation to check out the caves dug out of the hills overlooking White Eagle's patch of land, where Dylan thought he had spotted somebody lurking about, a few nights back.

Cort Wesley glanced across the seat at her. "And where's Daniel Cross fit on the scale?"

"Come again?"

He gave her a longer look. "You need to stop beating yourself up over this."

"Over what?"

"Not changing the kid's ways. It was ten years ago. You did what you could."

"Well," she admitted, to him and finally to herself, "I should've done more."

"Did Cross actually build a bomb, back then?"

"He would have."

"You don't know that, Ranger."

"But I do now, don't I?"

"Caitlin—"

"No, Cort Wesley, let me finish. I knew he was trouble from the first time I laid eyes on the kid, but I got it in my head I could change him. First I had a little

talk with the kids who'd been bullying him into sub-
mission."

"Oh, boy, here we go . . ."

"I let those boys have it, and their parents too. Visited the wrath of the Texas Rangers upon them to make
my point."

"Did it work?"

Caitlin shrugged. "Well, Daniel Cross never did blow
up the school. But maybe if I focused my energies on
him he wouldn't be planning to blow up the whole
country now, so to speak."

"Of all people," Cort Wesley said, shaking his head.

"Of all people *what*?"

"Of all people, you should know some people are
just born bad. You told me this kid's mother was a
prostitute and that the couple that adopted him wasn't
anything to write home about, either. You ask me,
that's because they would've much preferred to have
returned him, when it became clear they were raising
a monster."

"Daniel Cross wasn't born a monster, Cort Wesley."

"Oh no?"

"He was born with a genius IQ. Forty points less
and maybe he's loading a gun instead of planning to
build a bomb. Adults failed him at every stage of his
life, from his mother all the way to me. And ever since
I realized who he was, from that old picture, I've been
racking my brain, trying to figure what else I could
have done."

"It ever occur to you there was nothing more you
could've done?"

"Nope, not for a minute." Caitlin's phone rang.

"Captain Tepper," she told Cort Wesley before answering it. "I'm off the clock, D.W."

"Not if you're wearing your gun, Ranger, and since you're not asleep, it's a safe assumption you are. Whatever you're doing, stop, and get over to the office five minutes ago to join the party."

"What gives, Captain?"

"If I told you, you wouldn't believe me. But I can't tell you anyway, given this isn't what your friend Jones calls a 'secure line.'"

"He's there too?"

"It's his show, Caitlin, and you definitely want to be here when the curtain goes up."

60

SAN ANTONIO, TEXAS

Caitlin and Cort Wesley entered the conference room of Company F headquarters late. Everyone else was already assembled, including Doc Whatley, an honorary Ranger named Young Roger, and four unidentified faces occupying equal quadrants of a wall-mounted wide-screen.

"I guess we can begin now," said Jones from the head of the table, clearly indicating that Homeland Security was in charge here. "Doctor Whatley, chief medical examiner of Bexar County, has been assigned by Homeland to run point on this until CDC and other authorities are totally up to speed."

Caitlin thought she saw Jones's eyes glimmer when

he said "other authorities." And then his gaze moved to her, holding briefly, as if he could read her thoughts, before continuing.

"We'll get to a review of the particulars of yesterday's incident in Austin shortly. First, I want to cover something goddamn divine Providence has dropped in our laps."

Jones touched a remote, changing the wide-screen view from the four faces to a shot of three men inside a car. Caitlin recognized the occupant in the back as none other than Daniel Cross. She'd never seen the two in the front seat before.

"The man in the driver's seat is Razin Saflin," Jones continued, again seeming to read her mind. "The one seated shotgun is Ghazi Zurif. Both born to first-generation Americans whose parents emigrated from Lebanon and became model American citizens—their children too. Their grandchildren are something else again."

Jones touched another button on the remote and the screen split into two halves; the left displayed a dossier on Saflin, and the right a dossier on Zurif.

"Our intelligence indicates they showed no interest in Middle Eastern or Arab affairs whatsoever for the first twenty-seven years of their lives. That all changed when ISIS hit the ground running. Suddenly, they began making trips to the home country they'd never visited before—three in all. On each occasion they took side trips to Turkey, where our assets in the region lost track of them. Homeland flagged them for scrutiny by the FBI after incidental evidence showed they crossed over into Syria, at least one report further indicating they had direct contact with ISIS leaders. Our boots on the ground here have tried to reach out to them through traditional social media channels, employing the latest code words, but those overtures have been spurned at every turn, making them a lower surveillance priority, particularly when they exhibited no pattern of activity consistent with homegrown terrorist behavior." Jones paused dramatically. "That all changed yesterday."

Jones flipped back to the original grainy picture of Saflin and Zurif, with Daniel Cross centered in the backseat between them.

"This was taken by a local Austin policeman manning a checkpoint a few blocks from Hoover's Cooking. He did nothing more than rap on their window to ask them to move their vehicle. That's it. But his body camera caught what you're seeing now, and our software pinged on their faces."

Which implies that Homeland has access to every security, police, and maybe even traffic camera in the country, Caitlin thought, picturing a computer the size of the Company F building sorting through the billions and billions of bits of data in search of pings like the one displayed on the wide-screen before her.

"The fact that the two of them are pictured in the vicinity of the attack," Jones was saying now, "along with who they're pictured with, there in the backseat, has us operating at DEFCON one in a figurative sense." Jones used the remote to zoom in on Daniel Cross's face, turning it even grainier. "This beauty here used the Deep Web to make overtures to ISIS commanders overseas. From what we've been able to glean, he claimed to have knowledge of a weapon that could help ISIS 'kick the shit out of America.' That's an exact quote, people. We've had eyes on Cross, but until today had never linked him to the likes of Saflin and Zurif. Confession time, folks: two days ago we decided to move in on Cross in preemptive fashion, but my team missed him, by a few hours probably. And now we're left with the conclusion that whatever he promised to provide ISIS has gone operational, which brings us to the particulars as we know them at the moment."

Jones looked toward Doc Whatley.

"Doctor, would you please update us on what you and the consulting experts have managed to determine about the victims in Hoover's Cooking, so far?"

Whatley frowned, looking more tired and worn than usual. The source of his clear displeasure likely lay with those "consulting experts" Jones had mentioned.

"We are proceeding on the assumption that we're dealing with a new and never before identified neurotoxin here," Whatley said finally. "I say 'neurotoxin' based on all indications found on the scene and my initial examination of the victims." He frowned again. "Those bodies have all been removed to an undisclosed location to await further examination by officials from the CDC. But my preliminary findings indicate that all their vital systems shut down at once: respiratory, circulation, digestion, motor reflex, and brain function. They all stopped on a dime, leading to the unavoidable conclusion that a neurotoxin released inside that restaurant is to blame."

"Released how?" a disembodied voice asked, and only then did Caitlin realize that the four faces had re-

turned to their individual quadrants on the wide-
screen.

"Well, something ingested by the victims would be
the most likely means of delivery," Whatley answered.
"But the tests performed so far have shown no trace
whatsoever of any toxin or contaminant in any of the
food recovered from the scene."

"Leaving us with what?" one of the faces projected
on the wide-screen asked.

"I may have an idea on that front," interjected Young
Roger.

61

SAN ANTONIO, TEXAS

"One that explains all the variables and variants in
play here," Young Roger continued.

"Who's speaking, please?" asked another of the disembodied faces.

As Young Roger stated his name, credentials, and
position with the Texas Rangers, Caitlin focused on
what she knew about him from her own experience.
Until this moment, she hadn't even known his last
name. Young Roger was in his early thirties but didn't
look much older than Dylan. Though he was a Ranger,
the title was mostly honorary, provided in recognition
of the technological expertise he brought to the table.
He had helped the Rangers solve a number of Internet-
based crimes, ranging from identity theft to credit card
fraud to the busting of a major pedophile and kiddie

porn ring. He worked out of all six Ranger company offices on a rotating basis.

Young Roger wore his hair too long and was never happier than when he was playing guitar with his band, the Rats, whose independent record label had just released its first CD. Their alternative brand of music wasn't the kind she preferred, but Dylan told her it was pretty good. She still figured Dylan had a crush on a gal bass guitarist named Patty and had dragged Caitlin to a Rats performance when he was home over Christmas, just to show her off to the blue-haired bass player.

"Explain your thinking, please," Jones instructed, once Young Roger's introduction was complete.

"If you assume ingestion as the means of the delivery of the toxin to the victims," he began, "we need to consider the anomaly of the waitstaff and cooks being infected. Even more, there's the apparent speed of the spread."

"Wait," said one of the faces on the wide-screen, "are you suggesting contagion here?"

"Not at all. That's the point. The analyses I've seen all indicate all victims struck down, without visible symptoms, within between twenty and twenty-five seconds. Based on the photographs of the scene I've examined, six of the victims—two tables—hadn't been served any food, or even water, yet. Then there's the additional anomaly of the bodies found closest to the door."

Young Roger waited, as if for a photo displaying just that to appear on the screen, then continued when it didn't.

"They fell facing the inside, not the outside, likely

toward the end of that twenty-to twenty-five-second time frame of effect."

"So, what are you suggesting?" asked the same face that had posed the last question.

"Nothing yet," answered Young Roger, sounding less committal. "At least, nothing for sure. I need to run some more tests, do some more research. Right now, I'm focusing on why the perpetrators plugged up the exterior venting on the kitchen exhaust fan. What was it they didn't want getting out?"

"You're giving Daniel Cross a whole lot of credit, kid," Jones said, jogging the screen back to the hazy, zoomed-in shot of Daniel Cross from the Austin cop's body cam.

"With good reason. Cross has degrees in chemical engineering, organic chemistry, and applied physics. A poster child for just the kind of technical expertise involved in what we're facing here."

"You do know," Jones started, "that the only job he's ever held for longer than six months was as a candy mixer for Susie's Candies during the holidays a few years back, when he was living in Odessa. He profiles as a disaffected loser who tried to find himself on social media, not a mad scientist. Only, this time, he found the helping hand he'd always wanted."

"If I had my way," groused Captain Tepper from the darkened end of the table, sounding as if he were speaking mostly to himself, "I'd take a hammer and a blowtorch to the whole goddamn Internet until we were back in time maybe a generation or two."

"Given that's not quite a realistic possibility," Jones picked up, "FBI and Homeland already have three hundred agents dedicated to nothing other than finding Daniel Cross, along with Saflin and Zurif. Since they showed no aggression toward the patrolman who asked them to move, and complied immediately, we can assume they don't know they've been identified. That gives us an advantage we intend to exploit to its absolute, goddamn fullest," he finished, his eyes back on Caitlin.

"I notice you left out mention of the Comanche Indian reservation from your status report, Jones," Caitlin said to him, off to the side of the room. The wide-screen television had gone dark.

"You think I don't know where the two of you were headed when your captain made the call?"

"You got eyeballs on us?"

"Electronically—you're damn right, Ranger. This country might be under the gravest threat it has ever faced, so I like to know where my people are."

"*Your* people?"

"Anyone worthy of their spit I can count on to save a few million lives," Jones told her. "I imagine that includes you."

"Daniel Cross was at that reservation for a reason," Caitlin told him, checking Cort Wesley's expression for a reaction. "But I'll be damned if I can figure out a connection between what happened in Austin and drilling for oil, or something else, on Comanche tribal land."

Jones aimed his next remarks at Cort Wesley. "We've got security camera footage of a man resembling you driving a stolen front loader through a used car dealership showroom. Maybe there's some connection there. By the way, the footage has mysteriously disappeared."

"There might be a connection to the bigger picture here," Caitlin said, before Cort Wesley could speak at all. "We're looking into it."

"We?"

"You got bigger fish to fry than worrying about what we're following up on our end."

"What were you doing in Houston earlier today, while your boyfriend was laying waste to car dealerships?"

"Interviewing a person of interest."

"In what?"

"I haven't decided yet, Jones. What do you know about Cray Rawls?"

"Absolutely nothing."

"Could you give your files on him a look and see if there's anything worth noting?"

"Still your old subtle self, aren't you?" Jones asked her.

"I'm just getting started, Jones. And while you're at it, see if you can scrounge up the personnel records of a minerals brokerage company called Jackson Whole Mineral."

"Got a whiff of something, Ranger?"

"Just playing a hunch," Caitlin told him.

Jones looked at her, then at Cort Wesley. "Let me tell you one place I don't want you playing: the Comanche Indian reservation."

"You mind repeating that?" Caitlin asked him, her gaze narrowing. "I don't think I heard you right."

"Yes, you did. The two of you are to steer clear of that land. And this is one time you're going to toe the line, Ranger. See, I'm assembling a strike team to go in there like it's the goddamn Little Bighorn, when the time is right."

"That's your plan?"

Jones smirked. "Live with it."

"You'll never find what you're looking for that way."

"The presence of ISIS in-country just took all other options off the table."

Caitlin stood before him, spine stiffening. "Still got one, Jones."

"No, we don't. You're sitting this one out so the big boys can play."

Caitlin shook her head, stopping just short of a smile. "You have someone write lines like that for you, or do you just make it up as you go along?"

Jones jammed a phone toward his ear. "I need to take this, if you don't mind," he said.

Caitlin watched Jones walk away, unsure whether a call had really come in or not, as Cort Wesley drew even with her.

"So what's next, Ranger?"

Caitlin continued watching Jones, who seemed to have forgotten she was even in the room. "My great-great-granddad faced off against John D. Rockefeller on that rez, Cort Wesley."

"How'd that turn out?"

"Not very good for Mr. Rockefeller, as I recall." She finally turned toward him. "So what do you say we finish that drive north and see if we can make history repeat itself?"

62

"Say it, Ranger."

Cort Wesley's words seemed aimed straight ahead, at the windshield, as he threaded his truck along the final stretch to the Comanche reservation. The night was the color of pitch; whatever moon there might have been was hidden behind clouds carrying a storm. Lightning flashed at irregular intervals in the distance, shining a spotlight through the dark. Thunder had begun to rumble as well, too far off to worry about for now.

"Say *what*?"

"What you're thinking."

"Same thing you are, I suspect: that whatever killed those people in that diner somehow involves the rez."

"Through Daniel Cross. As long as you're not blaming yourself for that, too."

She ignored his comment. "Something about all this doesn't wash, starting with what you noticed about the drilling equipment."

"You didn't buy Rawls's story to that effect?"

"Not for a minute. The man's a powder keg ready to explode, with a history that leaves him considerably short of a man-of-the-year nomination. He's been in court almost constantly, dealing with environmental lawsuits over his coal and chemical plants. From what I've read, he could well be the biggest polluter in the country, responsible for poisoning the water, both above and below ground, through much of the Eastern seaboard."

"Lofty accomplishment."

"The man's a sociopath. In other words, he doesn't give a shit."

"And if he found something besides oil on that land?"

"Doesn't make for a connection with Daniel Cross, at least not yet."

Cort Wesley's eyes narrowed to the point where the whites seemed to vanish. "Why don't you let me have a go at him?"

"You mean, the way you had a go at Bobby Roy? Fixing to drive another front loader through a building, Cort Wesley?"

"Actually, Ranger, this time I was thinking about a tank."

Caitlin found no humor in his remark. "You know what happened is going to get back to Sam Bob Jackson."

"That was the point."

"So is the fact that there's something plenty bigger going on here."

"That your way of warning me off paying Jackson a visit?"

"Were you or weren't you just in the same meeting as me, where we learned Daniel Cross is ready to give ISIS a weapon of mass destruction?"

"Yes, ma'am. But it was Sam Bob Jackson who involved my son in all this."

"You are one stubborn son of a bitch, Cort Wesley."

He lapsed into silence, the moments dragging. "I realized something, when I was waiting to see the principal of Luke's school the other day."

"What's that?"

"Red-tailed hawks supposedly returned to Texas with a flourish, after being endangered for a long stretch of time. But I haven't seen a single one in years, and I don't know anybody who has."

"What's your point?"

Cort Wesley looked over at her, across the wide seat. "That I've learned to only believe what I see, and right now I see Sam Bob Jackson and Cray Rawls party to something that's going to get a whole lot of people killed, unless we find out what's really happening on that Indian reservation."

He eased his truck off the road to where it would be concealed by brush while they checked out the caves overlooking the stretch of land White Eagle had claimed for himself. His lights flashed over a huge figure standing by a truck that looked almost as big as the front loader Cort Wesley had driven through Bobby Ray's showroom.

"Is that . . . ?"

"You bet, Cort Wesley."

"Guess I shouldn't be surprised."

"I miss you mentioning that you called him?" Cort Wesley asked, as the two of them approached Guillermo Paz.

"Hello, Colonel," Caitlin greeted him, instead of answering Cort Wesley's question.

"There's something wrong here, Ranger," Paz told

her, standing so still in the night air that he didn't even seem to be breathing. "I can feel it rising off the land. Much blood has been spilled. More is about to be."

"As long as it's not ours," said Cort Wesley.

63

BALCONES CANYONLANDS, TEXAS

Dylan slinked through the woods, looping around through the darkest reaches, where the bramble bushes grew so thick that the edges caught on his jeans and nearly ripped through his shirt.

He had waited until he was sure Ela was asleep before easing her off of him. She had drunk the peyote-laced tea again, after Dylan had dumped his out. She had kissed him once with some of it still in her mouth, Dylan letting that small amount dribble down his throat. Enough to throw his mind for a loop, but nothing like the last time.

Still, the sex they'd had earlier could best be described as an amusement park ride, a roller coaster traveling upside down. It seemed as if air was swirling about, catching them in a harsh wind as they rotated positions in a prism of lights flashing everywhere, turning the single kerosene lantern into a spotlight.

The effects of the peyote wore off when Ela was still squeezing him so tight he thought his ribs might crack. She seemed trapped in some kind of nightmare and kept muttering something in Comanche while clinging to him. Only when she quieted and her breathing returned to normal did Dylan slip out from beneath her and pull his jeans and boots back on.

Even the small bit of peyote he'd ingested had been enough to steal his intentions from him while they made love, but those intentions returned full bore as he eased himself up out of the root cellar into the still air of the humid night. Something was going on here that felt all wrong. Dylan had forced himself to look the other way, until the matter of his Miraculous Medal showing up as evidence in a murder case, covered in blood, made his perspective do a one-eighty. He wanted to believe Ela had nothing to do with setting him up. Even more, he wanted to believe that nothing had happened, during those dark hours of lost time, that really did connect him to the killing.

He had hoped his mind might clear a bit by now, but everything from that night remained shrouded in fog. If anything, his memory had turned to even more of a muddle. All Dylan could find in his grasp was a leftover nightmare of rushing through a field someplace, being chased by vast winged creatures that swooped down on their prey like osprey in the Gulf. Except they were human, at least humanoid, and the wings were attached to their backs with hammocks of tight, dried-out-looking flesh. They had claws for feet, teeth that protruded over their lower lips, and tawny flesh that looked like a combination of burlap and leather.

Dylan half expected the creatures to swoop down on him between the trees as he made his way to White Eagle's land. Ever since Ela had taken him to meet her grandfather, Dylan hadn't been able to get out of his mind the sounds he was sure he had heard coming from inside that shack. He'd taken it for an old-fashioned outhouse at first, but its size and design were more consistent with a storage shed of some kind, built without windows and constructed of logs heavy and thick enough to withstand a hurricane.

Dylan continued along the circuitous route through the brambles and brush to White Eagle's patch of land, set against the sparkling waterfall that drained into the pristine stream. The last thing he wanted was to alert the old man to his presence. The shack-like structure was located close enough to the woods for Dylan to investigate and be gone before White Eagle was any the wiser.

The problem was that the night, coupled with the lingering effects of the slight dose of peyote he'd ingested, had stolen his bearings. The woods were suddenly a deep, dark place swimming with branches that looked like tentacles and tree roots that slithered about the ground like snakes.

Dylan passed it all off as his imagination, until he heard the crackle of a branch crunching underfoot behind him. Then he wasn't so sure anymore.

64

BALCONES CANYONLANDS, TEXAS

At night, Caitlin realized, the waters of the stream dividing the Comanche reservation from the rest of the nature preserve looked green. A slight mist hung over the surface, seeming to vibrate in rhythm with the endless flow of the waterfall draining downward. When those waters had run stronger and deeper, their currents had forged a winding path that now snaked along the hillside.

Guillermo Paz steered ahead of her and Cort Wesley as they drew closer to the mouth of the cave formations, which were dug out of the hillside along the narrow path. "These openings look man-made, used for shelter probably hundreds—even thousands—of years ago," he said, as the three of them readied their flashlights and tested the beams.

True to his impression, the six caves they examined, as they wound their way down the path from the higher reaches of the hillside, were small, with nothing of note in particular. More likely, Caitlin reasoned, Native Americans of old had cleared existing breaches to take advantage of natural shelters, explaining why archaeologists had been uncovering great finds in caves like this for decades. She figured there were probably plenty of similar finds in these as well, likely buried under layers and centuries of earth, stone, and sediment.

The next and most jagged of the cave mouths opened into more of a passageway, which followed the flow of the stream waters, along a trench that wound its way farther underground. The walls glowed in dappled fashion with some sort of phosphorus extract the color of moss. In patches, it looked as if it was growing out of the walls, almost like tumors, or blights, on the landscape by the spill of their flashlight beams.

"I recognize the smell from when we paid that visit to White Eagle," Cort Wesley noted. "Air's full of it. I also smelled it at the rez entrance, strong when the wind was blowing right."

The waters looked greener as they drew deeper into the cave. The widening path was taking them along a winding route that descended so gradually they didn't even realize they were now venturing underground. The greenish water had lost its sheen; it was cloudy and murky toward the top, with patches of a dark, goo-like residue splotching the surface.

"Looks like John D. Rockefeller was right, Ranger," Cort Wesley noted. "That's oil seep, from reserves flowing all the way up from the earth's core, for all we know, dragging some methane with it for good measure."

"What about the deposits on the wall?"

"That, I can't explain," Cort Wesley said, sweeping his gaze about the cave, "and I've never seen anything like it before."

"We're missing something here," Caitlin said suddenly, frustration getting the better of her.

"Like what?"

"Like this, maybe," Paz called from ahead of them.

Caitlin and Cort Wesley caught up to find the colonel pinning a Hershey's bar wrapper to the ground under his boot.

"A candy wrapper?"

Both of them could see his eyes glowing like a cat's.

"A Hershey bar," said Paz. "Daniel Cross's apartment was covered in wrappers just like it."

"They were his favorite when he was a kid, too," Caitlin said, as she tucked the candy wrapper inside the plastic evidence pouch she carried with her at all times. The partially crumpled foil was smeared with melted chocolate, reminding her of how Cross always needed to wipe his mouth with a towel after eating one, ten years ago. She'd forgotten how much time she'd actually devoted to the effort to redeem him, apparently having accomplished absolutely nothing. "So maybe it was Cross that Dylan saw lurking about the night before last, the night before Hoover's Cooking."

"Let me see if I've got this straight," Cort Wesley said, standing a bit back from her and Guillermo Paz. "You're thinking whatever links Cross to ISIS is somewhere in this cave?"

"You got a better explanation for how this got here?" Caitlin asked, holding the clear plastic evidence pouch out for him to see.

"That's assuming it belongs to him. Hershey wouldn't be doing much business in these parts if Daniel Cross was the only one buying their candy bars."

"It's him," Paz said, staring farther into the cave. Its darkness was broken by splotchy pockets of translucence emanating from the green patches that grew out of the walls. "And there's something down there. Straight ahead."

"All I see is a wall, Colonel," said Caitlin, shining her flashlight straight ahead.

Paz started forward warily, his spine stiff. "Sometimes our eyes deceive us, Ranger."

65

There was no one behind him—at least, no one Dylan could see. He thought maybe just the small bit of peyote he'd ingested had had a more pronounced effect on him than he realized. Had he imagined the sound of something being crunched underfoot? Had his drifting mind led him off his intended route, leaving him lost amid thousands of acres of protected deep woods?

Dylan felt fear and panic reaching for him and barely avoided their grasp. He'd started out charting his direction by the stars, but those had quickly vanished under an onslaught of storm clouds that swallowed their twinkling guidance and drew a curtain before the direction in which he was headed. In that moment, this was the last place in the world he wanted to be. His damn father was right; he should be back at school in Providence, Rhode Island, where spring football practice was in full swing, instead of throwing his whole future into jeopardy.

What the hell was I thinking?

He hadn't been, that was the problem. Maybe he was never going to learn to stop acting on impulse and feeling he had to adopt every stray who crossed his path—girls now, instead of lost animals. He had a sour taste in his mouth, which felt as if he'd just chewed some tree bark, and he flirted with the idea of turning around.

But just then he heard the soft spray of the waterfall flowing down over White Eagle's land, and he caught a glimpse of the stream, which glowed emerald green under the moon's return from behind the clouds. The shedlike structure was closer to White Eagle's cabin than Dylan had remembered. But there was no firelight to give away his presence, and no sign of stirring through the cabin's windows.

Dylan emerged from the tree cover, clinging as best he could to the darkest ribbons of the night to help shield his route to the shed. Sure enough, a lock hung from a heavy hasp secured across the shed's frame. Closer inspection revealed that the logs forming the shed had been reinforced crossways, the way similar structures had been erected in World War II Japanese prison camps. Like those, this structure had been built with no spacing at all, no seams visible, even where the sides met and the peaked roof joined up with the shed's frame.

Dylan was trying to figure how to get the door open, but then a slight jostling of the old padlock revealed it wasn't fastened. As quietly as he could manage, Dylan plucked the lock free and eased the door open wide enough to enter, then quickly sealed the door behind him.

He switched on the small flashlight he'd brought along, aware of the rich pine smell, even though the structure was at least decades, if not generations, old. In that moment, Dylan became aware of a second scent, a musty, stale odor, like rancid clothes left sweaty in a gym bag for too long. It was almost enough to make him gag, and he reminded himself to breathe through his mouth. He swept the small flashlight's thin beam about the shed walls, holding it on something that glinted slightly in the spill.

"Holy shit," he heard himself mutter, stuff falling into place faster than he could process it.

He needed to get off this reservation now, needed to call Caitlin and his father. He swung around, feeling for the phone tucked into his pocket.

And saw a face, streaked like a checkerboard, even with his own, as a hand that smelled like rancid mud closed over his mouth.

66

BALCONES CANYONLANDS, TEXAS

"What do you see, Ranger?" Paz asked Caitlin, when they reached the rear of the cave.

Caitlin and Cort Wesley both shined their flashlights across the jagged rock formation. "Rocks."

"So do I. But the rocks I see are more weathered than those forming the other walls. More weathered and also lighter, from exposure to the sun."

Paz eased his shoulder against the wall and began to push.

"In ancient times, the Mayans would build false cave walls, meticulously matched to the faces around them. The Comanche, apparently, were more ambitious."

With that, the wall began to give under Paz's steady thrust, breaking from the seam first in a sliver, then a crack, and finally in a chasm that allowed a noxious odor to flood outward on a surge of chilly air.

"Any idea how old this is?" Caitlin asked, as the opening continued to widen.

"Hard to say," Paz told her, as she and Cort Wesley added their force to the task. "Hinged structures like this date back far longer than history tells us. But the ground clearance and attention to expansion suggests mid- to late nineteenth century."

"Right around the time Jack Strong was working that murder case here on the rez."

Paz led the way inside to the chamber revealed beyond, shining his flashlight ahead of him. The addition of Caitlin's and Cort Wesley's beams revealed the chamber to be about twelve feet square. The continued push of cold air told them that this part of the cave came complete with a venting passage to the outside, likely cut out of the ceiling. They were about to turn their attention there, when Paz's beam illuminated something dangling from the back wall.

"Looks like a manacle," Cort Wesley noted, holding his beam upon it.

Caitlin added her flashlight to reveal a rusted hunk of matching chain alongside it. Two more chains had been driven into the rock face, lower, at around knee level.

"What is this," she heard Cort Wesley say, "some kind of jail cell?"

Paz's beam crossed over four more sets of manacles. "Not likely, outlaw. Indian tribes were known for holding prisoners in chambers dug underground, not camouflaged in caves."

Caitlin pulled on a manacle, rattling the chain

attaching it to the stone face. "What if they weren't prisoners? What if this was about something else entirely?"

"You've got that look, Ranger."

"You can't see me, Cort Wesley."

"I don't have to, to know you've got that look, the one that says you're about to bite into something."

Caitlin released the dangling manacle and it banged against the rock with a slight clang. "That's because—"

She stopped when the chamber seemed to rumble, shift. Caitlin, Cort Wesley, and Paz all shined their flashlights upward, illuminating a dark river that seemed to be flowing overhead.

"Uh-oh," Cort Wesley muttered, in the last moment before the river came raining down upon them.

67

BALCONES CANYONLANDS, TEXAS

One of the figures, painted in alternating strips of black and white, shoved a mouthful of dirt into Dylan's mouth. He recognized the taste immediately, registering it was pure peyote, and refused to swallow. He tried to spit it out, but the figure shoved it farther down his throat. Dylan gagged, coughing some of the clump up but feeling the rest drop down his throat. He retched, struggling to breathe. He realized he was choking, in the last moment before he coughed up a black wad that looked like a fur ball. Then he was being half dragged, half carried from the shed.

"What are you doing? Leave me alone."

Dylan hated the lameness of the words he heard himself utter, listening as if it were someone else's voice. The peyote was already taking effect, the ground beneath him turning pillowy soft. He thought he was sinking in, the world and the night receding before his eyes. Was he even breathing? Had he really coughed up the peyote they'd forced down his throat?

"I'm gonna fucking kill you . . ."

The threat he managed to utter sounded no less lame. Dylan felt moments dominated by a thick haze wrapped around his consciousness, alternating with moments of intense clarity, which he seized upon to size up his situation. Six Comanche, whom he recognized as some of Ela's cousins, the Lost Boys, had painted their entire faces and exposed parts of their bodies in alternating streaks of black and white, their eyes wildly intense as they dragged him off. They were shirtless, and Dylan noticed that sweat had caked up the paint, jumbling the colors together in portions of their upper arms and torso.

"Let me go," he heard himself say again, or maybe for the first time.

Dylan wasn't sure. He knew there was something he desperately needed to tell his dad, tell Caitlin. But now he couldn't remember what it was, and he couldn't remember where his phone was, either.

He closed his eyes, and when he opened them, found he was somewhere else entirely. His boots were sliding across the leaf-dampened ground now, his feet entirely numb. He couldn't feel his arms, either, and when he tried to wiggle his fingers it seemed they weren't

attached to his hands anymore. The sky above had become a vast open mouth framed between the clouds,
lowering to swallow him.

"Make it stop!" he thought he cried out, and then
realized that something that tasted grimy and grubby,
like a sweaty sock, had been stuffed into his mouth.

Dylan heard himself mutter. There was a pressure
building behind his eyes, like a vacuum cleaner was
pulling air from his skull in a constant hiss, which left
him with a fluttery sensation in his ears.

"You have no place here," said the Lost Boy who'd
wedged the dirt-like clump of peyote into Dylan's
mouth. "You should've stuck to your own. Now, you
go to your grave."

Fuck you, Dylan thought, but he couldn't say it.

More time and space had passed than he found himself able to calculate, the world changing entirely in
what felt like the length of a breath. Every time
he blinked, the world seemed to stay dark longer. And
the next time he pried his eyes open, the Lost Boys were
lashing him to a tree with what felt like baling wire.

"Now, it comes for you," the Lost Boy told him.

It, Dylan repeated in his mind.

The tree bark scratched against his flesh, through his
shirt, and each breath exaggerated the bonds of the
wire further. For a few moments, Dylan actually had to
remind himself to breathe. Once, he felt his chin thump
to his chest.

Regaining consciousness after however long he'd
been out, he saw that the Lost Boys were gone, the oily
odor of the paint with which they'd streaked themselves hanging in the stagnant air like a dust cloud.

Dylan heard himself breathing, inside his head. His eyes wanted to close again, but he stopped them, keeping his focus straight ahead until he heard something approaching from behind.

Whatever was coming seemed to glide across the brush and earth, rustling them no more than the wind. Dylan tried to turn his head, but his neck wouldn't budge. Then he realized the footsteps were upon him, in the same moment he heard himself screaming through his gagged mouth.

68

BALCONES CANYONLANDS, TEXAS

The wave of bats descended on them like an unbroken black blanket. Suddenly jittery flashlight beams caught spokes of big eyes and flashing teeth, much bigger than they should have been, in Caitlin's experience. First backpedaling and then turning to dash out of the chamber, she thought this, too, was an illusion, until one of the bats latched onto her hair with claws that felt more like a raptor's. And, as she yanked it off, taking a chunk of her scalp with it, Caitlin saw why.

The bat was massive, huge, its wingspan expanding to more than five feet when it came at her again with teeth bared.

Caitlin was going for her gun when Guillermo Paz swatted the bat out of the air with an arm that looked to her like a baseball bat. He whirled and swept another swooping trio aside, muzzle fire from Cort

Wesley illuminating the darkness, which was broken only by the flashlight that Paz had managed to hold on to. His beam retraced their route through the cave, heading back to the main chamber and the night beyond.

Afraid to stop moving, Caitlin heard light splashes as the downed bats dropped into the underground river, her eyes adjusting enough now for the luminescent glow off the cave walls to reveal the flight of the bats crisscrossing in the air. They were dive-bombing them, the bats' collective squeals becoming deafening, all but drowning out the flutter of their wings, which made it seem as if the entire cave was vibrating.

Back in the main chamber of the cave, Caitlin lent her fire to Cort Wesley's, careful to keep her aim concentrated upward. Instead of spooking the bats, the assault seemed to further enrage them. They renewed their attack, reformed to concentrate from the cave mouth, as if to deny exit to their captives. She had happened upon bats before, but never any this big or violent. Bats were easily spooked, for sure, but they also were shy creatures that normally backed off after making their point.

But this swarm showed no such inclination. The noxious odor she'd detected as soon as Paz had cracked open the secret chamber was clearly bat guano, but even that was different from what she recalled from past experiences. Sharper and more rancid. Maybe it had been creatures like these that had killed John D. Rockefeller's gunman back in 1874 and had done the same to the work foreman just the other night. Or—

Click.

Before Caitlin could finish that thought, the slide of her SIG locked open and the blanket of black, broken only by glowing eyes and flashing teeth, swept toward her anew in dark waves. She thought about taking refuge in the shallow greenish waters of the underground stream, then recalled the goo-like residue collected on the surface and—

Caitlin's thinking froze there. "Cort Wesley, your lighter!"

It was his late father, Boone's, cigarette lighter actually, tucked in a drawer and forgotten until Cort Wesley had learned the truth about his father's nature and his heroism. Now he carried it with him all the time, the last thing he had to remember his father by, a man he'd once done his best to forget.

Caitlin snatched the lighter out of the air when he tossed it, and yanked a can of mace-like repellent from its clasp on her belt. She'd never used it on a suspect, not even once, and she hoped the pressurized contents hadn't degraded over however many years she'd been carrying it.

She popped the top off and pressed down on the tiny nozzle at the same time that she flicked Boone Masters's cigarette lighter, embossed with an eagle, to life. The aerosol stream touched the flame and ignited in a ribbon of fire, stretching a yard forward, aimed downward toward the surface of the water.

Poof!

The flame burst blew upward, climbing for the swarming bats, who fled from its path, their collective squeals turning deafening. In that moment, the bright glow captured their gaping mouths and enraged eyes, extended snouts making them look like monsters lifted from some horror movie. Their wings flapped so hard, as they sought escape from the fiery air, that they actually fanned the flames further. They moved in what looked like a circle, then a figure eight, before speeding out of the cave in a vast, unbroken mass, into the night beyond.

Caitlin found herself sitting on the cave floor with no memory of dropping down. She kicked at the body of one of the bats, felled by a bullet, maintaining the presence of mind to put her plastic evidence gloves back on before reaching for it.

Cort Wesley brushed off his clothes. The battle they'd just fought and the heat of the flames had left a sheen of perspiration over his features. "You want to venture a guess as to what all this is about, Ranger?"

"What Steeldust Jack faced here in 1874, same thing we're facing now, Cort Wesley," Caitlin told him. "Monsters."

PART SEVEN

Prohibition passed in 1918. The Texas oil boom exploded two years later. Rangers spent a lot of time smashing stills, intercepting bootleg liquor from Mexico, and handcuffing criminals to telephone poles when the jails were too full. It was during this time that Ranger Captain Manuel "Lone Wolf" Gonzaullas cemented his legend as a one-man law enforcement agency along the Texas border. In the 1950s, he became an advisor for the TV show *Tales of the Texas Rangers*.

—Bullock Texas State History Museum,
"The Story of Texas"

69

"Is there anyone you ever listen to, Ranger? 'Cause if there is, I'd like to meet them."

Caitlin squeezed her cell phone tighter. "Maybe you didn't hear what I just said, Jones."

"Oh, I heard you just fine, especially the part about you disobeying a direct order from me."

"I don't work for you. I work for the state of Texas."

"Well, last time I checked anyway, Texas was still part of the United States. Maybe you haven't heard of Homeland Security?"

Caitlin spoke with her eyes on Cort Wesley, while rain from a fresh storm dappled the windshield of his truck, where he'd left it, just off the Comanche reservation. "Why don't I just let you know when I've got a better idea of what we're facing here?"

"Hold on, I want to hear more about what you found in that cave."

"Sorry, Jones. I never listen to anybody, remember?"

After dropping off the bat carcass with Doc Whatley at the Bexar County Medical Examiner's office, Caitlin and Cort Wesley continued back to Cort Wesley's home in Shavano Park. They sat on the front porch swing, the night quiet and still around them. Nothing seemed to be moving at all, not even the air.

"Something I didn't tell you about Daniel Cross, Cort Wesley," Caitlin said suddenly. "Ten years ago, he didn't go to court or jail, because of my intervention. Hell, I even made sure the arrest report went away, all on my say-so."

"Let it go, Ranger."

"I really did believe I could save him. I believed he was *worth* saving."

"A bullied kid—you felt bad for him. Don't make it more than it really was."

"But it was more. It was me ten years ago, thinking I had the world right and nobody could tell me different."

"You weren't much more than a kid yourself, then, not much older than Daniel Cross is right now. Stop beating yourself up."

"I want to think I'm different now," Caitlin said, without looking at him. "You want to know why I'm beating myself up? Because I'm afraid I'm *not* different. I'm afraid maybe the nickname 'Hurricane' suits me too well and that the phrase 'strong cold dead' isn't a joke so much as a warning I've been missing for too long."

Cort Wesley said nothing, because there was nothing to say. He felt her nod off against him, and was being careful not to disturb her, when the scent of fresh talcum powder drew his gaze to the side, where the ghost of Leroy Epps was leaning against the porch railing.

"*Wouldn't happen to have another of those root beers in the fridge, would you, bubba?*"

"Sh-h-h," Cort Wesley cautioned, gesturing toward Caitlin.

"*She can't hear me none anyway, so I got no call to lower my voice,*" Leroy told him. "*Man, you got yourself in a real pickle this time, don't you? One boy kidnapped, the other . . . well, let's just say he's seen better days.*"

"What is it you're not telling me, champ?"

"*Don't fret on that for the present, and stop your stewing.*"

"Come again?"

"*You heard me. You done got yourself in save-the-world mode, as like you're the only one who can.*"

"Sometimes, that seems accurate enough."

"*And sometimes it makes you do dumb-ass things, like driving a Caterpillar through a car showroom.*"

"It was a John Deere, champ."

"*I ever tell you about my Vietnam experience, bubba?*"

"I didn't know you went."

"*I didn't, 'cause the army wouldn't have me. There they are, hard up as hell for soldiers, and they wouldn't even consider my enlistment. Guess I had a touch of the sugar already messing with my eyes, and there was something they didn't like about my feet, which didn't stop me from squeezing them into my boxing shoes enough to fight for the middleweight title. Army must've gotten a kick out of that.*"

Cort Wesley glanced down at Caitlin, still nuzzled

against his shoulder. "There a point I'm missing somewhere?"

"Nope, 'cause I haven't gotten to it yet," Leroy told him, picking at his teeth with a branch stem. "Thing about the ring is, it's you, the other guy, and nobody else—'cept the referee, who doesn't count, even when he's fixing the odds against you. You got nobody to rely on but yourself once that bell rings. But for you, bubba, the rounds never stopped. You just keep coming out to answer the bell all by your lonesome, no matter who's in the opposite corner. And the problem is your thinking's always the same. Doesn't matter who you're up against, how big, strong, or quick they might be, you're going in the same way you did with that car showroom."

"These people crossed a line."

"That an explanation or an excuse?" Old Leroy shot him a disparaging glance from the railing, his mottled flesh creasing like the folds in an origami design. "I'd say I know you pretty damn well—better than anyone, save for that Ranger there—and I've seen you playing this game for too long without the mere consideration you might lose. That's another thing about the ring. It should be clear cut, a winner and a loser, but I had the title swiped from me twice, and the only thing that kept my wits together was understanding there wasn't a damn thing I could do about it."

"That what you're trying to tell me, champ?"

Leroy took a few steps from the rail, the porch light framing him like a shroud. "Listen up good here, bubba. All I'm saying is, your own being harmed is surely cause to do hurt, but it's a lot harder to win a *fixed fight. You don't catch yourself, you're playing by their rules, just like I was, those times the belt should have been mine and I ended up holding my own pants up. You getting the point here, bubba?"*

"If you'd known the fights were fixed in advance, would it have made any difference?"

"Not that I can see."

"That's my point, champ. The fight I intend to have tomorrow is something different altogether."

"You're talking about the minerals guy, looks like somebody glued some extra flesh on him?"

"And the man he's working for, who's hiding so much shit, he probably forgot where he put it all. Whatever I do to them won't be enough, champ."

Leroy Epps turned his empty gaze down the street an instant before Cort Wesley spotted the truck coming, slowing as it drew up to his mailbox before pulling into the driveway.

Cort Wesley realized Leroy Epps was gone and Caitlin was starting to stir, her eyes peeling groggily open and fastening on the truck just as the driver's side door snapped open.

"Looks like we got company, Ranger," Cort Wesley said, rising, as Ela Nocona climbed out of the driver's seat of the truck and then dragged Dylan out of the back.

70

SHAVANO PARK, TEXAS

Cort Wesley had carried Dylan upstairs to put him to bed, after a terse explanation from Ela.

"You want to be a bit more specific?" Caitlin said to her, listening to the sounds coming from upstairs.

"He got himself in a scrape with some of my cousins," Ela explained.

"Involving drugs again? Peyote?"

"I think they maybe forced him to take some, yes." Ela eyed the door. "I really should be getting back."

"That would be back to the place where Dylan was assaulted and tied to a tree with baling wire, according to what you've just told me."

"I can't talk to you about this," Ela said, reluctant to meet Caitlin's gaze.

"Well, then, can you talk to me about why his assailants, these cousins of yours, left him out there, what they expected to happen next, exactly?"

Ela continued to avoid Caitlin's gaze. "He was snooping around where he didn't belong. They just wanted to teach him a lesson, maybe scare him a little."

"Does that include forcing him to ingest a dangerous drug?" Caitlin felt her thinking veer, midsentence. "Oh, that's right—you'd already forced him to do pretty much the same thing."

"I didn't force him to do anything."

"And what about that Miraculous Medal of his

that we found near the body of that construction worker?"

"What about it?"

"You think it got up and walked out of wherever the two of you were prior to that time?"

"I think Dylan lost the medal earlier in the day. I can't explain how it ended up where it did."

Caitlin could feel the heat rising behind her cheeks, a dull ache in her teeth from clenching her jaw. "And what do you suppose he was doing in the woods tonight, when he got jumped?"

"I have no idea. He snuck out after I fell asleep."

"You do drugs when you're at school, Ela?"

"Peyote isn't a drug."

"Oh no?"

"Not the way you mean it."

"And how do I mean it? Or let me put it another way: How would you feel if those disabled kids you came back here to teach knew you were using?"

Ela had moved almost imperceptibly toward the door, putting distance between her and Caitlin. "Could you ask Dylan to call me tomorrow, please?"

"I don't believe he'll need me to remind him. And I'd like you to answer my question before you leave. Serious mind-altering drugs weren't in Dylan's vocabulary until last week, as far as I know. Would you like to tell me different?"

"I'm sorry," Ela said, sounding as if she had to pull the words up her throat. "I'm sorry about all this. I don't know what else to say."

"How about that you've decided to tell Dylan to reenroll at Brown, now that the protest is over?"

"That's up to him, not me."

"Maybe I'll see you tomorrow, when I stop by to sort out whatever happened on the rez tonight."

"You've got no authority there, Ranger."

"That didn't stop my great-great-granddad, and it's not about to stop me, either, not anymore. How about I start with those cousins of yours Dylan calls the Lost Boys? On account of the fact that I'm guessing they take their marching orders from you."

Ela shook her head, looking almost bemused as she headed the rest of the way to the door. "Why would I tell them to tie Dylan to a tree in the middle of a peyote trip, only to let him go and bring him home?"

"I don't know, Ela. Why don't you tell me? Why don't you tell me what your grandfather and everyone else on your reservation is hiding? Why don't you tell me why there's a secret chamber in a cave overlooking White Eagle's land that looks like something from a horror movie?"

Ela opened the door and stepped mostly out, leaving only a flicker of herself behind. "I think my cousins took Dylan's phone. Please tell him I'll try to get it back for him."

"I'll be sure to do that. And if you don't—"

But Ela was out the door before Caitlin could finish her thought, slamming it so hard the whole house seemed to rattle.

71

"You have been given a great honor," Hatim Abd al-Aziz, supreme military commander of ISIS, said to Daniel Cross, "joining us in this most holy of missions."

Cross stood before him on the sixtieth-floor Sky Lobby, the observation deck in the JPMorgan Chase Tower. Zurif and Saflin were hanging back but within earshot, near the ISIS commander's hulking bodyguard. Cross's insides had turned to ice as soon as he stepped into the elevator, in anticipation of meeting the man behind so much of the unspeakable carnage that had dominated the news for years now. His breath had seized up in his throat when he reached the Sky Lobby and the bodyguard held Zurif and Saflin back so Cross could proceed alone.

Sunlight framed al-Aziz's shape like a shroud, blinding Cross as he drew closer, further unsettling him. Since going down this path, to once and for all escape the shadow of Diaper Dan, Cross had never once doubted his intentions or his actions, not even for a minute.

Until now.

What have I gotten myself into?

Al-Aziz's presence brought home the reality of what his actions had set off, even more starkly than the demonstration Cross had staged at Hoover's Cooking. He had truly reached the point of no return; no going back now.

"You are not Muslim," al-Aziz said.

Cross hadn't even seen his mouth move, through the blinding sunlight. He drew close enough to al-Aziz to see a freshly trimmed beard darkening his gaunt face. His eyes looked too small for his face, dominated by grayish, languid pupils that seemed to have swallowed all the white. His hair, too, had been neatly coiffed, making him look like a businessman—an investment banker or something like that. He was shorter than Cross had expected, and al-Aziz's frame was only slightly more muscular than his own.

"No," he heard himself say, in a voice that sounded like someone else's. "I'm not Muslim."

"You know what *alhamdulillah* means?"

"Praise to Allah."

"And *ashokrulillah*?"

"Thanks to Allah."

Al-Aziz grinned slightly. "*Alhamdulillah w ashokrulillah*. Praise and thanks to Allah for your presence here. He has delivered you unto me, the nature of your faith irrelevant before the path He has set forth that has brought us together. So you need not be one with our fate, only one with our cause."

"I am," Cross said, forcing the words up through what felt like a dust ball in his throat.

"It is His will that has brought us here and His will that is certain to see this through to a blessed end." Al-Aziz turned and swept his gaze about the whole of the city of Houston, left to right and then back again. "Do you know why we are meeting here?"

Daniel Cross shook his head, following his own reflection in the window glass.

"Stand on a hill of this height back in Iraq or Syria and there is nothing to see but wasteland. Nothing to rule, nothing to ravage and destroy." The ISIS commander continued to stare straight ahead. Below, those pedestrians who were visible looked like creatures smaller than pencil tips, poised against a vast urban landscape. "Looking out over places like this fuels my vision, restores my faith in the great mission and calling to which I've been summoned. I was standing near the top of the Burj Khalifa building in Dubai when our bombs went off in the central train station. I was looking down from Petronas Towers in Kuala Lumpur when I conceived the idea of an attack on that nation's subways. And I will be standing at the top of the International Commerce Centre in Hong Kong when the bombs go off in the city's financial district, as Allah wills."

Al-Aziz turned his gaze back on Daniel Cross. "And now the forces that have laid in wait in this cursed land have assembled the next phase of Allah's grand plan before us. You will tell me everything you know. I will hear it in your words, and then the great reckoning will commence, and you will thank me for making you a party to it."

Al-Aziz's eyes widened as he smiled, freezing Daniel Cross's breath and his insides anew.

"*Mashallah*," said the military commander of ISIS. "As Allah wills."

72

Company F headquarters was already frantic with activity by the time Caitlin arrived the next morning. Captain Tepper looked like a traffic cop, directing Caitlin toward the conference room as soon as he spotted her. She spotted White Eagle seated at one end of the table, flanked on either side by men with graying ponytails and clothes better fit for the nineteenth century.

"Glad you stopped by, Ranger," Tepper said, before they entered. His expression was tight and pained, as if talking was aggravating a toothache. "White Eagle was just getting ready to press charges against you."

"For what, exactly?"

"Criminal trespass, mostly, since Rangers have no authority to operate on the rez—a fact that seems to have slipped your mind. Speaking of which, I just heard from Doc Whatley. That candy wrapper you found in the cave matched the DNA from identical wrappers recovered from Daniel Cross's apartment. He also said he needs to talk to you about the other 'sample' you left with him. That's what he called it."

"Guess the trespassing paid off, then, Captain."

"Not until you tell me what the hell all this has to do with ISIS and those deaths in Austin."

"Maybe White Eagle can tell us," she said, as Tepper finally thrust open the door to the conference room.

Caitlin looked the old man in his milky eyes the whole time introductions were exchanged. She figured the men flanking the old Comanche were tribal elders, chiefs, lawyers, or maybe some combination of all three.

"You mind taking a seat, Ranger?" Captain Tepper said, his words more than just a suggestion.

Caitlin sat down four chairs from White Eagle, unable to keep her eyes off him. His skin looked like the top layer peeling off of sun-ravaged shingles, his eyes encased in flesh so mottled it looked like meat left too long on a grill.

"All right, Chief," Tepper said to White Eagle, "I'm doing you the courtesy of seeing if we can deal with all this like the men we are, before the horse gets too far out of the barn."

"I'm not a chief," White Eagle told him. "Never was. And there's nothing to deal with. Your officer trespassed on Comanche land last night and I want her prosecuted for that to the fullest extent of the law."

"She's not an officer, sir, she's a Texas Ranger."

"My apologies, Captain."

Tepper looked toward Caitlin. "You mind addressing the man's charges?"

"They're false and baseless."

"Beyond that, I mean."

"I was investigating the presence of a person on the reservation, wanted in connection to the potential terrorist attack in Austin two days ago, in my capacity working adjunct for Homeland Security. Specifically, Daniel Cross was spotted in the vicinity the day before that attack. I tracked him to a cave on the river that cuts through the length of the preserve and straddles the rez."

"So you're admitting the trespass," one of the tribal leaders or lawyers said, leaning forward so fast he came half out of his chair.

"Not at all," Caitlin told him. "I've been over the old maps. The start of the river has always been a natural demarcation point that divides reservation land from the nature preserve. As such, the cave where I recovered vital evidence last night is off the reservation. How is that a trespass?"

"So you deny being on White Eagle's property," the man advanced, "disturbing his peace, and entering a storage shed?"

"I do indeed," Caitlin said, thinking of Dylan's misadventure the previous night, which had left him tied to a tree with baling wire. "And I'll tell you something else," she continued, her words aimed at the old man now. "I believe your client, or fellow tribesman at least, is a liar, a con man, an original snake oil salesman for the books. He tells quite a story, about being a century and a half old, how he met my great-great-granddad and all, when his birth certificate, registered with the state of Texas, lists him born in the year 1937. Near as I can tell, he's not even related to his namesake, and he was picked up by Austin police and the county sheriff more than a dozen times for running games on folks off the rez when he was a younger man. Tell me, 'White Eagle,' have I got all that right?"

"You have nothing right," the old man said, the smugness of both his voice and his expression surprising her, "and neither did your great-great-grandfather. He was a fool, just like you are. Sticking his nose where it didn't belong, believing it was to see justice done."

"As I recall, he stood up against John D. Rockefeller on your behalf."

The old man suddenly looked twenty years younger; even the white film seemed to slide off his eyes. "We didn't need his help then and we don't need your help now. And you have things all wrong, then and now, as well."

"How's that, sir? If you've got a story to tell, let's hear it."

73

AUSTIN, TEXAS; 1874

According to Sheriff Abner Denbow, the bodies of the three young braves had been found dragged to death across the rocky ground. The rope burns were still evident on the insides of their wrists, indicating they'd been dragged facedown, which accounted for the unrecognizable condition of their features. Their faces looked like somebody had peeled the flesh off in random patches. One boy was missing a big chunk of his nose, two might have died from blood loss after somebody took a bowie knife to their testicles, and all three had been scalped. No one had known the young braves were missing until their bodies were discovered propped against a tree just outside the reservation, not far from where the body of the gunman had been found. Each was clutching a piece of John D. Rockefeller's letterhead stationery.

Denbow had gotten word about the bodies from a farmer driving his crop-filled wagon down the road. By the time he'd ridden out there the Comanche had started removing the bodies and, having no particular desire to venture onto the reservation himself, Denbow summoned Jack Strong to the scene. Steeldust Jack had been certain he'd be returning to the rez before long, though he hadn't expected it would be this soon, or under these circumstances.

"I'd like to see the bodies," he told Isa-tai, outside his shack on the edge of the Comanche land, which was set against a brook fed by the backflow from a nearby river.

"They aren't your concern, Ranger."

"I'd prefer you let me be the judge of that, all the same."

"Matters are under control," Isa-tai assured him.

"Is that what you call having three boys strung from horses and dragged to death?"

"They were only boys in age. Their spirits have already been reborn many times in our history, and now they will be reborn again."

"What about the need to hold their funerals first, or doesn't that count for anything?"

"Everything is under control," Isa-tai said, as quiet and sure as the first time. "We take care of our own. And when you cross us, you cross nature itself."

"Like you took care of those boys, you mean. Rockefeller's hired guns must've been laying in wait when they ventured out to fish, or hunt maybe. This has got ambush and cold-blooded murder written all over it. Why don't you just cooperate and help me take this John D. Rockefeller down?"

Isa-tai looked into the sun without squinting. Braves, their faces colored with war paint, flanked him on both sides like statues. The only trace of movement was the wind whipping their long, coal-black hair about. Steeldust Jack didn't think they were blinking.

"They'll be back," Steeldust Jack told Isa-tai. "This won't stop 'til Rockefeller gets what he wants. Right now, that's the oil on your land, and he's not about to back off until his pumps are lifting it out of the ground."

"So we should make a deal with him, Ranger? That's what you're saying?"

"I could go to him on your behalf, see if we can come to terms, to be secured by the Texas Rangers. He's a businessman, and a fight like this is bad for business."

Isa-tai held his eyes closed for a long moment, then opened them again, the cadence of his breathing unchanged. "They must've gone fishing before the sun. I heard their screams, felt their pain, in my sleep. I've been feeling it ever since. Only one thing can stop me from feeling it."

"You don't wanna do this, son."

"Do what?"

"Rockefeller isn't a man you cross, unless you got an army backing you up."

"We don't need an army. We have the land."

"What the hell does that mean?'

"He would violate nature. So I will call upon nature to be our army."

"You mean, like you did for that gunman who was found torn apart?"

"Nature takes care of its own, Ranger," Isa-tai droned, the words sounding as flat as memorized stage lines. "And we are its own."

"I might still be able to make this right," Jack Strong told him, " 'fore anybody else gets hurt."

"Ride off, Ranger. You don't want to be here for what's coming next."

Which, Steeldust would later reflect, turned out to be ever so true.

He found John D. Rockefeller again in the Metropolitan Hotel, which he'd pretty much appropriated for his own use, including a back portion where he'd based his offices. Twenty years earlier, a man named George J. Durham had shot William Cleveland to death right outside the entrance, after the younger man had attacked him with a walking stick, in a case later ruled by a judge to be justifiable homicide. Steeldust Jack didn't think it a coincidence that the Northerner had headquartered there, being of the firm belief that places soured by violence tended to attract men with a penchant for it themselves.

Rockefeller greeted his presence with a wide grin, pulling at his mustache, first one side and then the other. "You know what it means to walk into a lion's den, Ranger?"

"Mr. Rockefeller, I spent time in the Civil War getting shot at from as little as five feet away," Jack Strong told him. "Compared to that, a lion's den is a church picnic."

"I don't think that's the case at all," Rockefeller said, sizing up Steeldust Jack as if he were an animal in a cage. "I hear you fancy yourself a hero, a gunfighter. Maybe you are. But did you really think that little stunt of yours would make me pull up stakes and run?"

"Well, I was hoping it might make you come to your senses about sitting down with the Comanche instead of trampling on their sovereign land."

"Negotiate with them, you mean. And what do you expect the result of that would've been?"

"I imagine they would've told you to stuff hot tar up your rear. Which doesn't change the fact it's their land."

"So it is, and so it will stay. But, unless you've forgotten about that letter from the governor, duly authorized by the United States Congress, you know that I have the rights to mine the oil *beneath* their land."

"I don't believe I follow you, sir."

John D. Rockefeller got the look of a gunman who knows he's got his target centered. "The Comanche were deeded that land all right, but they don't control what's beneath it. Call it a technicality."

"I call it bullshit."

"All the same, Ranger, neither you nor anyone else has the authority to stand between me and that oil—or to come in here accusing me of being complicit in the tragic murder of three Indians when the Texas Rangers have killed thousands."

Steeldust Jack took a step closer to Rockefeller, invading his space, unperturbed by the bodyguards who were coming just short of unholstering their pistols.

"So you're telling me you weren't sending a message by leaving a piece of your stationery in the hands of all three Comanche who were found dragged to death?"

"I'm afraid I have no idea what you're talking about."

"Then try this: those Indians may have no claim to what's beneath their land, but once the oil breaks the surface it becomes Indian property, to do with what they please, doesn't it? Maybe you should ask Governor Coke to weigh in on that one."

Rockefeller moved his mouth to the left, the right, and back again. Around him, nondescript men were busy at desks, working ledger books and studying detailed maps. In Jack Strong's mind, they were either tallying up the profits from one venture or looking for the best sites for the next one. Whoever was either inconvenienced or displaced was considered meaningless.

"Progress stands aside for no man, Ranger," he said, his voice scratchy and genuine.

"The victims who got dragged to death were boys, sir. How does that fit into your equation?"

That night, Steeldust Jack set himself up in a chair down the street from the Metropolitan Hotel, off the plank walk and in the cover of a mercantile exchange, so he couldn't be seen. Prior to sitting down with a twelve-gauge shotgun laid across his lap, he'd fastened a lock through an old hasp on a rear door that formed the only other entrance to the building, leaving this as the only access point.

Activity in the area had increased significantly since

John D. Rockefeller's arrival. Each day the noon train seemed to bring more of his security men and sycophants, their dress and demeanor distinguishing them from one another, though their loyalties were the same. That, coupled with Rockefeller having taken over pretty much all of the hotel for his use, indicated he intended to be here for a while, perhaps as a base for his entire Texas operation. This surely accounted for the endless parade of town officials into the Metropolitan to kiss his proverbial ring, and the governor bending over backwards to do his bidding.

For his part, Steeldust Jack's concern lay in what he saw as inevitable retaliation on the part of the Comanche. In times not long past, they would storm the street on horseback, firing at anything that moved, using Winchester lever-action rifles stolen off trains they'd raided or soldiers they'd killed. But he wasn't expecting that here. It didn't seem to fit this particular tribe's style, although Isa-tai's surly and confident manner suggested that the Comanche had no intention of taking this lying down.

Nature takes care of its own, Ranger, and we are its own.

Isa-tai's words made no more sense now than they had when he'd spoken them earlier, but their memory held more than enough portent to keep Steeldust Jack mostly awake and alert through the night. He caught himself snoozing a couple times. Once, he was actually roused by his own snoring, a fact that set him to smiling—just before the gunfire began.

———

It was wild and unfocused, crackling through window glass and thudding squarely into walls bracketed by heavy studs. Steeldust Jack had his shotgun ready as he sprinted down the street, which was wet with mud from a heavy storm that had blackened the sky briefly, back when day still shined. He burst through the doors of the Metropolitan to find men in various stages of dress rushing about, clambering up and down the stairs that led up the whole of the building's four stories. A number of men, the last of the residents not associated with Rockefeller's dealings presumably, blew past him, desperate to escape what seemed like an all-out attack sure to claim its share of bystanders.

More gunfire echoed, a cascade of it that seemed to suck the oxygen out of the air, now rich with the odor of gun smoke, hanging over the second-floor landing like a cloud. Steeldust Jack pushed past men struggling with boots or suspenders, to the third floor, where the first window glass had blown out. Rounding the stairs up there, he recognized Curly Bill Brocius and another gunman from the original group, their pistols aimed at the last three doors down the hall, which from this angle looked to be torn from their hinges.

Jack Strong advanced ahead, paying them no heed, his nose sucking in the thick odor of sulfur and the coppery scent that could only be blood, likely lots of it. Even during the war, in the worst battles in which he'd been embroiled, he'd never smelled it this strong, and the sight of the inside of the first room showed him why.

From what he could tell, a pair of men had been bedded down in matching beds. The scent of their sweat and boot odor was light on the air in comparison to the smell of blood and, this close, their shredded entrails. Because what was left of them was scattered about the twisted bedcovers and the floor, with portions strewn across the walls. It looked and smelled like a slaughterhouse, only the room's darkness sparing him closer consideration. The splashed blood and gore looked black in the glow of the moonlight sifting through the window and the spill of the lanterns coming from the hall.

Nature takes care of its own, Ranger, and we are its own.

Isa-tai's words flashed through his mind again. But this wasn't the work of nature, at least not any nature Steeldust Jack was familiar with.

The other two rooms were the same—two men in one of them, three in another, for a total of seven men slaughtered and mutilated, inside of a minute by all accounts. Steeldust Jack reconstituted the sounds and sights that had roused him in the street, ultimately figuring that the occupants of all three rooms had been struck within seconds of one another.

When his stomach settled, the Ranger made it a point to check the pools of blood for residual footprints, but he found none. Neither did he find any trace whatsoever in the hallway. Bullet holes stitched the walls of all three rooms in jagged designs, indicative of wild shooting absent of aim. A few of those holes, more like chasms dug out of wood, wallpaper, and plaster, looked to be made by shotgun shells, which were unlikely to miss anything they'd been pointed at from so close a distance.

None of it made a damn bit of sense.

Just after Steeldust Jack's cursory inspection of the rooms was complete, John D. Rockefeller came striding down the hall, within a protective circle of gunmen armed to the teeth.

"I didn't want this to go to guns, Ranger," Rockefeller told him, his voice groggy and his gaze uncertain. "I truly didn't. But now that it has . . ."

He let his thought trail off, the intent of his words hanging there between them with more meaning than any he could have spoken.

"I don't know what killed your men, sir," Steeldust Jack told him, "but it wasn't guns."

"Say that again, Ranger?"

"I checked the bodies as best I could," the Ranger explained, his hand still hot from holding the lantern before him. "I know a bullet wound when I see one, and I didn't see one. No, sir, not even close. And I'll tell you something else, Mr. Rockefeller. From what I heard and seen, the men in all three rooms were attacked at pretty much the same time."

"What are you telling me, Ranger?"

"That maybe this time you're up against something you can't beat. Maybe it's time to leave town, and Texas too."

Rockefeller's lips quivered, making his mustache seem like it was fluttering. "I don't scare easy."

"I suppose not. You hired soldiers to fight in your stead in the Civil War," the Ranger continued. "Buying out the Clark brothers positioned you to make your fortune off the backs of men like me, coming home to try and pick up our lives. You have a reputation for destroying your competition and just about anyone who gets in your way. Just ask Charles Pratt and Henry Rogers. The horse that plowed their company over was really your Standard Oil, and I believe you came to Texas intending to employ the same strategy here."

Rockefeller's thin smile glinted in the flickering light. "You been checking up on me, Ranger?"

"Local library got its share of newspapers, for any man willing to look."

"Don't believe everything you read."

Jack Strong watched John D. Rockefeller close the distance between them, until he was close enough to smell the stale aftershave clinging to the man's clothes, mixing with stale sweat.

"You tell those Comanche I won't be scared off, Ranger. You tell them if it's a war they want over their oil, then they've got it."

Steeldust Jack cocked his gaze briefly back toward the blood-soaked rooms. "I believe they're already aware of that, sir."

74

SAN ANTONIO, TEXAS

"I assume all that jibes with your recollection," White Eagle said, upon finishing his tale.

"Close enough. And you know something? It doesn't change a thing. I'm not Steeldust Jack and you're not Isa-tai, no matter what you want to lead people to believe."

"People believe whatever they want. John D. Rockefeller crossed my people back then, just like Cray Rawls has crossed my people today."

"I don't know. It sounds to me like Rawls and Sam Bob Jackson have bought their way onto Comanche land with the promise of scholarships and gainful employment. How'd you make out in that deal, sir?"

White Eagle moved his gaze back to Captain Tepper. "This conversation was a waste of time," he said. "We'll be filing a complaint directly with the Department of Public Safety."

Caitlin looked him right in the eyes, which suddenly appeared clear and sharp. "Whatever you're involved in here isn't going to come to a good end for any of those involved, especially you."

"I'm too old to care about your threats. Nothing much scares me anymore, least of all the Texas Rangers."

"I'd rethink that, if I were you, sir."

D. W. Tepper closed the door to the conference room after White Eagle and the other two men had left.

"Could you refresh my memory as to what century this is? Because you sure talk like the nineteenth never ended at all. Aw hell, forget it. There's someone else here you need to speak to, someone who might actually be able to serve our cause."

"Who's that?"

"A Royal Canadian Mounted Police officer who's got information he says he'll share only with you."

75

Cray Rawls hadn't slept much the night before. It reminded him of the nights he had spent huddled outside his mother's room while the floorboards shook in rhythm with the bed inside. How he'd tucked his arms around his knees, trying to make himself as small as possible, even invisible, to whatever man eventually emerged from inside, smelling salty and something like the odor that hung in the air in his elementary school gymnasium.

Accompanied by his pair of hulking bodyguards, Rawls arrived at the west Houston offices of Jackson Whole Mineral to review plans for the operation about to commence on the Comanche Indian reservation outside of Austin. An auspicious day, indeed, given the stakes and potential profits involved, but all Rawls felt was trepidation and anxiety. A little boy again, huddled against the wall in the cold, fearful of what was to come.

It shouldn't have been that way. Should have been smooth sailing from here, after getting the deal closed with the damn Indians. It was going to cost him additional millions, but who cared? Spending millions to make billions was the price of doing business.

One bodyguard preceded him through the entrance of the office building where Jackson Whole Mineral was headquartered, the other trailed slightly behind. He noticed the security desk was unmanned. This wasn't a surprise, considering the likely cost-cutting efforts, but it further jangled his already jittery nerves. He felt like an old dog sensing a thunderstorm in the offing, looking for a bed to roost under until it passed.

Upstairs, the glass entrance to Jackson Whole Mineral was open and unguarded—contrary to the strict orders he'd given that fat-ass Sam Bob. Rawls stormed down the hall ahead of his bodyguards, canting his shoulders sideways as he entered Jackson's office overlooking the main artery of the west Houston Energy Corridor.

The fat man sat there, sunk into his overstuffed desk chair, his blank expression fixed straight ahead. He seemed reluctant to stop looking at whatever he was staring at.

"What gives, Sam Bob?" Rawls demanded. "I have to wipe your ass for you now?"

He felt a presence behind him, just before a whoosh of air signaled the door blasting closed. Cray Rawls swung around to find a rawboned man glaring at him with an expression forged in steel.

"I'm Cort Wesley Masters, Mr. Rawls. I believe it's time the three of us had a little talk." He stopped when he heard the door easing back open.

"Excuse me," Cort Wesley corrected, as Guillermo Paz entered, dragging the limp frames of Rawls's bodyguards behind him as if they were rag dolls. "I meant the four of us."

76

Cort Wesley had driven straight through the last of the night, once he was sure Dylan was going to be fine. He couldn't bear waiting out the hours while the boy got the drugs and the awful encounter he'd experienced out of his system. He'd be left pacing the floors and punching holes in the walls out of feeling helpless to do anything to those who had tied his son to a tree with baling wire.

He'd arrived in west Houston before the building even opened. No stops. The sky was beginning to brighten without him even noticing. He'd found Paz waiting outside his massive extended-cab pickup, in an area around the side, out of sight of any visible security cameras, his thoughts mirroring Cort Wesley's.

"Hello, outlaw."

"Did Caitlin send you?"

Paz's huge eyes looked like curved saucers wedged into his skull. "I was running a bingo game last night and called the number seventy, under the O. O for *outlaw*—that's what I said, and when I knew."

"You haven't answered my question."

"I believe I did," Paz told him. "Now, are you ready to get to work?"

"Take a seat, Mr. Rawls."

Cort Wesley had thoroughly enjoyed Rawls's and

Sam Bob Jackson's reactions to the sight of Guillermo Paz dropping two men with chiseled frames in heaps on the carpet. Hovering over both, on the chance either of them stirred, in the course of the meeting about to commence. The absence of the additional three guards Rawls had ordered posted no longer needed to be explained.

"Right there," Cort Wesley continued, gesturing toward the chair set before Jackson's desk. "Make yourself comfortable."

Cray Rawls did as he was told. "Who the fuck are you?"

"I think you know."

"If you got business with Mr. Jackson here, that's no concern of mine. You want to get on with it, I'm glad to leave."

Cort Wesley glanced at the two limp frames on either side of Guillermo Paz. "What about them?"

"I couldn't even tell you their names."

"The fact is, I've got business with both of you," Cort Wesley told him. "And, just for the record, it was my son you kidnapped to roust me. Well, consider me rousted."

Rawls glared at Jackson across the desk, then turned back to Cort Wesley. "You put a couple construction workers I was paying in the hospital during this unfortunate protest. In responding to that, Mr. Jackson here overstepped his bounds. If you'd let me make it up to you and your boy, I'd be glad to—"

"What about my oldest son?" Cort Wesley broke in, before Rawls could finish his thought.

"You didn't kidnap him too, did you?" Rawls snapped toward Jackson.

Sam Bob was in the midst of a shrug when Cort Wesley resumed. "My oldest was attacked on the grounds of that Comanche reservation last night."

"Why does that concern me?"

"Because it concerns whatever you're fixing to draw out of the land."

"Oil?"

"Don't play me for a fool, Cray."

"We on a first-name basis now? I still don't even know who you are."

"Yes, you do. I'm sure you had me checked out after your business partner 'overstepped his bounds,' as you call it—though I'd prefer to call it scaring the wits out of a teenage boy."

"He's not my partner."

"Oh no?"

"Barely qualifies as an associate."

"Then we're getting somewhere."

Cray Rawls straightened his shoulders and crossed his legs. "What do I have to do to make this right, Mr. Masters?"

"Ever hear of Homeland Security?"

"Is that a joke?"

"Answer the question."

"Okay," Rawls relented, shaking his head. "I've heard of Homeland Security."

"Right now, you're talking to me," Cort Wesley picked up. "You don't tell me what I want to know, I let the colonel there take over. He works for Homeland. Isn't that right, Colonel?"

Paz nodded, once.

Rawls uncrossed his legs and leaned forward in his chair. "Wait a minute. What am I missing here? What's Homeland Security's interest in all this?"

"You talk to me, Cray, maybe you never need to find out. Let's say that Indian reservation now involves a big, fat national security issue. You keep playing coy here and you might find yourself a resident of Guantanamo with all your assets frozen."

This prospect didn't seem to faze Rawls at all. "I'm not some sand jockey who tried to blow up a plane with his underwear. And I just beat a major class action beef back East."

"Where they let you have lawyers. No such luck when dealing with Homeland, right, Colonel?"

Paz nodded again. Once.

Rawls flashed a smirk that looked only partially forced. "You really think I'm buying this shit? You think a man like me can disappear, no questions asked?"

Cort Wesley took a few steps closer to him, glaring down. "For sure. But you can spare yourself the bother of all that by just telling me what it is you're after on that Comanche land."

Rawls swallowed hard, his eyes flashing like the tiny lights on a computer modem. "You in a position to offer some guarantees, Mr. Masters?"

"Like what?"

"What I'm after on that reservation stays mine."

"How about this?" Cort Wesley spoke down at him. "You get to keep your freedom."

"You got this all wrong, cowboy."

"What'd you call me?"

"Hey, you're from Texas. It was meant as a compliment."

"Sure it was." Cort Wesley crouched just enough to be even with Cray Rawls. "Let's try some simple yes-or-no questions. Is there oil on that land?"

"I wouldn't know."

"So you're after something else."

"I'm telling you, you're way off on this, cowboy."

"Let's go back to yes or no. Are you after something else?"

"Yes."

"On that reservation?"

"Yes."

Cort Wesley stood back up. "Essay question now. Describe for me what it is, exactly."

"Not a weapon."

"I didn't ask you to say what it isn't."

"It can't hurt anyone, only help. And I mean help on a level truly beyond your comprehension."

Cort Wesley turned toward Paz. "You want to have a go at him, Colonel?"

"No, wait!" Rawls pleaded, hands thrust before him, bulging eyes fixed on Guillermo Paz. "It's about how long those Indians have lived through the generations, the contents of their medical records."

"What the hell are you talking about?"

"Potentially the greatest medical find in history."

"What else?"

"Isn't that enough?"

"Depends," Cort Wesley said, crouching down again,

an instant before he heard a ping, followed by something whizzing through the air over him.

The same instant that Sam Bob Jackson's head exploded.

77

SAN ANTONIO, TEXAS

"You're looking good, Ranger," Royal Canadian Mounted Police officer Pierre Beauchamp greeted Caitlin, upstairs in Captain Tepper's office where he'd been waiting for her.

"I wasn't the one who got shot on the last case we worked together, Mountie," Caitlin returned, taking his outstretched hand.

Beauchamp shrugged humbly. "All worked out for the better. Thanks to *us* taking down those Hells Angels, I ended up reassigned to a Joint Terrorism Task Force dealing primarily with border issues."

"Big shot now, eh?" Caitlin asked him, doing her best to mimic a Canadian accent.

"You've been doing pretty well for yourself, too, from what I hear."

"If you count being a pain in just about everybody's ass, I suppose."

"You take down the Hells Angels, you can take down just about anyone."

"They're nothing compared to what we're facing now."

"ISIS, from what I've heard."

STRONG COLD DEAD 321

"You've heard right. And my guess is your coming all the way down here is connected to them. Something my captain said you're only willing to share with me, I'm figuring's, got nothing at all to do with border issues. That because of our history, Mountie?"

"More on account of the fact that I know you'll believe what I've got to say, Ranger."

Beauchamp laid it all out as quickly and succinctly as he could; he was a no-nonsense man, good at making his points. Except for a touch of gray at the temples, he looked exactly as Caitlin remembered him: straitlaced and by the book, from his demeanor to his dress to the way he held himself. His pants were perfectly pressed and his shirt showed nary a wrinkle, to the point that Caitlin figured he must have changed after getting off the plane. He had a boy's plump, rosy cheeks but a gunman's steely-eyed stare that could look both ways and straight ahead at the same time.

Beauchamp closed Captain Tepper's office door before launching into the tale of a Canadian fur trapper named Joe Labelle who, in 1930, happened upon an Inuit village in Nunavut, Canada, where the entire lot of residents had vanished at virtually the same time. Meals had been left uneaten, fires were untended, and big jugs of water, filled at a tributary off the nearby Lake Anjikuni, had been abandoned on the ground and left to freeze.

"For a long time," Beauchamp told her, "it was Canada's version of your lost Roanoke Colony."

"Difference is, that mystery's really never been solved," Caitlin reminded, "while I'm guessing yours was."

"Not to the knowledge of many, Ranger. I knew I had to get my ass on a plane as soon as I read the situation report on what happened at that Austin restaurant. Eighteen dead, was it?"

"Twenty-two, including the staff."

"That Inuit village numbered twice that."

"But they disappeared."

"Turned out, they didn't disappear at all. Turned out, Labelle found what was left of them, after somebody had burned all the bodies." He paused, then continued, "Near as I've been able to tell, the residents of the village were all struck down within minutes of each other."

"Sounds like quite a leap, Mountie."

"Not when you consider the trapper's story, along with the on-scene reports from my predecessors. Just about the entire village was eating, or about to eat, supper at the time. And the fact that the food was still on their plates told the first Mounties on the scene that whatever happened, happened fast. Just like in your restaurant."

"And what did those Mounties say about what killed your villagers?"

"Nothing, because they didn't have a clue, especially given that whatever evidence there might've been had gone up in smoke."

"What about whoever did the burning? Did this trapper Labelle mention anything about them?"

"He didn't. But the Mounties who responded to Labelle's report recovered two still-whole bodies not far from where the rest of the bodies had been burned. One had his throat cut, and the other his wrists. They died sitting back to back. I believe it may have been determined they were brothers."

"One cut the throat of the other, then slit his own wrists," Caitlin concluded. "Makes sense. What doesn't is why they did it, and why they burned the bodies in the first place."

"The tribe was relatively primitive, having lived the same way for centuries. They were also superstitious, beholden to the spirit world for guidance. The brothers might have returned to the village and saw the mass deaths as the work of evil spirits who intended on taking over the bodies of the dead."

"Their only solution being to burn them." Caitlin nodded.

"Exactly. Knowing the whole time they'd have to die too, to stop the spirits in their tracks."

"And this is what that trapper stumbled his way into."

Beauchamp moved to the window and opened the blinds all the way, as Captain Tepper was normally loath to do. He wrinkled his nose at the stale scent of cigarettes that hung in the air like a stubborn cloud, and opened the window all the way, in the hope of vanquishing it.

"Labelle's trapping trails had likely brought him to the village before. He probably knew some of the residents."

"But not what killed them."

"No. The trapper lit out through the cold and snow for civilization and ended up at a ranger station with a telegraph, ranting that whatever killed all the villagers was following him."

"*What,*" Caitlin repeated, "as opposed to *who.*"

"The cold had turned him delirious. He passed out after the wire was sent, and he thought the whole thing had been a bad dream, when he finally woke up."

"What else did the Mounties find when they got to the village, Pierre? You wouldn't be here if there wasn't *something.*"

Something changed in the Mountie's expression. His cheeks paled, and the flatness of his face suddenly seemed to lengthen it. "There was, Ranger, and this is the part only *you* are going to believe."

78

HOUSTON, TEXAS

The echo of the broken glass and hiss of the bullet were still cutting through Cort Wesley's skull when he yanked Cray Rawls off the chair and dragged him to the floor, where Guillermo Paz was already lying, safe from the angle at which the shooter was firing.

"There's a taller building, three hundred yards to the west," Paz noted. "That's where the shot was fired from."

"Three hundred yards," Cort Wesley calculated, running the distance through his mind. "Shooter's no rank amateur."

But that same mind had already moved in another direction altogether, the puzzle pieces starting to link together. Somebody was covering their tracks, somebody who didn't want anyone else to learn what Sam Bob Jackson and Cray Rawls knew: the truth about what was on that Indian reservation.

Not oil.

Something else.

Clear enough.

"I'll move on the building," Paz was saying, "as soon as we're outside."

"Got to get there, first." With that, Cort Wesley pushed closer to Rawls, across the rug, positioning himself right next to the man's ear to make sure Rawls heard what he said. "We're going for the door, into the hall. Don't raise even a hair on your neck. You hear me? Nod if you do."

Rawls managed what passed for a nod, fingers stretching out to pull himself through the nap in the carpet.

Cort Wesley drew his gun; Paz had his in hand already. The sniper would know he'd missed at least one of his primary targets, along with the two men whose presence he couldn't have anticipated. In point of fact, Rawls was only alive now because Cort Wesley had yanked him to the floor ahead of the inevitable second shot, which as a result had never come. That meant a backup team would be left to finish the job. They were either en route to this office now or were lying in wait downstairs.

Pfft, pfft, pfft.

More gunshots showered flecks of glass through freshly bored holes. Those had been fired in desperation. The shooter was hoping to panic his intended victims, make them launch into a desperate rise. Cray

Rawls started to do just that, but Cort Wesley pushed him back down before he got anywhere.

Pfft, pfft, pfft.

Still pulling himself across the carpet, Cort Wesley couldn't chase from his nostrils the scent of blood and gore from Sam Bob Jackson's ruptured skull. Paz was in the hallway by then, reaching back inside to drag Rawls the rest of the way. He kept his gaze fixed toward the office entrance, in case the backup team elected to storm the premises.

The moment his upper body crossed through the door frame, Cort Wesley was thinking origins, and only one possibility came to mind: ISIS.

The two men Homeland had managed to identify from an Austin patrolman's body cam . . . Cort Wesley couldn't remember their names, but clearly their cell had gone active. They wanted whatever was on that land belonging to the Comanche, and they didn't want anyone to know that they were after it.

Back on his feet, finally, out of view of any windows, Cort Wesley jerked Rawls upright and held him against the wall to the side of the door.

"What's on that land, you son of a bitch? What are you hiding?"

Rawls's features had calmed, his eyes suddenly as steely as they were evasive. "Get me out of here and I'll tell you everything you want to know."

Cort Wesley pulled him on again, drawing almost even with Paz, once they reached the reception area.

"No one's coming," the colonel reported, eyes and gun focused on the bank of elevators immediately beyond the office's glass front wall.

"Downstairs, then."

"Dressed as first responders, police or medical."

"How do you know?"

"How do you think, outlaw?" Paz said to him, leaving it there.

"Right," Cort Wesley said, stretching a hand out toward the paneled wall, where it met the glass. "Just what I was thinking."

And with that, he pulled the fire alarm.

79

SAN ANTONIO, TEXAS

"You won't find this village or the tributary off Lake Anjikuni on any map," Pierre Beauchamp continued. "In the spring of 1931 the remains of the village were bulldozed, buried under tons of earth and ice, all trace of anything that had ever been there wiped clean."

Caitlin continued to regard him from the other side of Captain Tepper's desk, the two of them standing and facing each other across it.

"And the villages for maybe fifty square miles were emptied," he continued, "their residents resettled elsewhere, on orders of the government, without explanation. It wasn't hard to cover things up in 1931."

"But what were they covering up, besides old Inuit folklore?"

"We caught the Russians sniffing around the area a few years back."

Caitlin nodded. "I had my own run-in with them not too long ago."

"So I heard. I'd say Texas seems to attract this kind of stuff, but as I recall, you dragged it with you to Canada and got me shot."

"I didn't drag anything with me, Mountie; the Hells Angels were waiting when I got there. Get back to those Russians."

"It was close to being a diplomatic fiasco, and we didn't get a thing out of them before the powers that be arranged for their safe passage home."

"You're kidding."

"Wish I was. That's what put the now missing village and Joe Labelle on my radar." Beauchamp stopped, as if to study Caitlin across the desk, but it was more to steady his thinking. "Something killed those Inuits as they ate, sat, or stood, and I think that same thing is responsible for the victims found in that Austin diner. And, whatever it is, what's left of ISIS has come out of their desert to claim it for themselves."

Caitlin was about to respond, then realized that her silenced phone was buzzing up a storm in her pocket. She yanked it out, saw CORT WESLEY running down the center maybe a dozen times, a single text message grabbing her attention.

"Looks like ISIS isn't coming, Mountie," Caitlin told Beauchamp. "They're already here."

PART EIGHT

Retired Ranger Captain Frank Hamer (who brought down Bonnie and Clyde) wrote a letter to King George V of England offering the services of 49 retired Rangers to help defend England against German invasion. Although FDR vetoed the idea, Germany got wind of the offer and panicked. In a radio address, Third Reich Propaganda Minister Joseph Goebbels assured the German nation that the mighty Texas Rangers were not invading. (September 16, 1939)

—Bullock Texas State History Museum,
"The Story of Texas"

80

Cort Wesley and Paz reached the lobby with Cray Rawls in tow, just as the evacuation of the building was peaking. The fire alarm continued to blare while building security made a concerted but calm effort to evacuate according to plan. There was no panic in evidence anywhere as the two men escorted Cray Rawls, between them, across the floor.

Cort Wesley's gaze was primed for anyone probing or scanning the crowd. They'd likely come in the guise of first responders, so their actions wouldn't particularly stand out. They would look like part of a larger operation connected to the sniper firing from a neighboring building. It was the way such things were done, the way he'd do it.

But there was nothing that set Cort Wesley's defenses screaming—no glimpse of any figures out of place or moving against the grain, no one studying the building occupants as they emerged into the sunlight. That suggested that the sniper had *been* the operation rather than just a part of it. Even the best shooter couldn't be expected to bring down four men from such a distance. That told him that the presence of Cort Wesley and Paz likely had nothing to do with Sam Bob Jackson's brains getting plastered against the walls, with Cray Rawls's sure to have followed, had Cort Wesley not intervened.

Cort Wesley watched Paz moving as if he expected—even hoped for—something to happen. But, with Rawls tucked between them, they exited into the harsh light and thick, still air without encountering any resistance at all. The fact that the building from which the sniper had fired looked down on the back of this building but not the front allowed them to skirt through the milling crowd unhindered and without slowing. Paz's truck was parked closer than Cort Wesley's, so they headed toward its position, a half block down, the sun just beginning to encroach on the shade in which Paz had parked it.

"Deal's a deal," Cort Wesley said to Rawls, when they were in the backseat of Paz's massive truck. "We got you out of there. Now talk, starting with the truth about what you're after on that Indian reservation."

Rawls had his phone pressed against his ear before Cort Wesley even realized he was holding it. "Think I'll just call my lawyer first."

Cort Wesley snapped out a hand, clamping it on the man's wrist. "You might want to rethink that, partner."

Rawls winced from the pain in his wrist, but clung to his cell phone. "I'm not your partner, cowboy. My partner just got his brains splattered back up in that office."

"I thought he was just your associate."

Rawls tried to smirk through the bolts of pain shooting up toward his elbow. "If you're really working with Homeland Security, I'm sure we can work something out, once I get my lawyer on the horn here. Now, take your hand off me."

Instead, Cort Wesley squeezed his hand harder, picturing his fist reducing the man's nose to mincemeat and wiping the smirk from his face.

"You were raised here in Texas, have I got that right, Mr. Rawls?" he asked, his breath heating up as he posed the question.

"What's that got to do with anything?"

"I'm just curious why you left. Heard you may have had a beef with the law."

Rawls stiffened, the smirk wiped from his expression. "You heard wrong."

"Something about hurting a woman."

"People make up stories, Mr. Masters. I've got lots of enemies."

"Then you don't need another, do you?"

"Could we get to the point?"

"I believe I already did," Cort Wesley said. "Reason your partner's brains are painting his office walls is what you found on that Indian reservation. Problem is, somebody else found it too, and we haven't got time for phone calls."

"How do I know you're not intending to steal it? How do I know that sniper wasn't working with you and this isn't all some kind of setup?"

Cort Wesley let go of Rawls's hand and watched it flop into his lap, still holding the smartphone. "Make the call, partner. Tell your lawyer to meet us at the Texas Ranger barracks in San Antonio."

81

Dylan knew the combination to the safe that held his father's guns, because his father had given it to him. It was a kind of ritualistic rite of passage, especially in Texas. Passing down the responsibility of guarding the house when his dad wasn't around. He'd been fourteen at the time, not long after Cort Wesley Masters had moved into the spare bedroom, following the murder of Cort Wesley's girlfriend, and Dylan's mother, Maura Torres.

"So next time you'll be ready," his father had said, after teaching him to shoot on a nearby range.

Cort Wesley Masters wanted his oldest son never to feel helpless again, but Dylan felt helpless now. His memory of what he'd seen in the shed on White Eagle's property had been foggy, a result of being forced to ingest more peyote, but it had been sharpening again in the past few minutes.

Hanging from hooks all over the walls of the shed were things like iron lawn tools, which looked lifted from some cheap horror movie. At first he had mistaken them for work gloves, but then he recognized one tool, fashioned in black steel, as a cultivator—a hoe-like assemblage with two curved prongs set over a third. He touched a fingertip to one of the prongs, then jerked it away when the slight motion was enough to prick his skin. Somebody had sharpened it to a razor's edge. It was nine inches long, with a wooden handle half that size sewn inside a work glove.

At first glance, it might have seemed that the jerry-rigging was intended to make the tool more convenient to use. But a second glance revealed something else entirely: the tool would make a deadly weapon, as would all the other tools dangling from the walls, like the one he recognized as a loop hoe. Impossible to determine how old they were or how long they'd been hanging there. The only clear thing was that they'd been fashioned for one purpose and one purpose only: killing, up close and personal, in the most violent style imaginable.

Like the work foreman whose mutilated body had been found within reach of the Miraculous Medal that had belonged to Dylan's mother. The apparent victim of an attack by an animal bigger and stronger than a bear.

Or by a person, or *persons,* trying to give that impression.

Ela knew all about that, and more—Ela and her Lost Boys. Neither his dad nor Caitlin was answering their phone, and Dylan wasn't about to wait around for them to get home to tell them what he'd finally recalled from last night.

You don't pull a gun unless you intend to use it.

Something else his father had taught him. So, was that what he intended to do now, to head back to the reservation and gun down Ela's cousins, the Lost Boys? Was that just punishment for how they'd humiliated him the night before?

He'd been spared only by Ela's intervention—which made no sense, considering everything else. If she was setting him up, why save him? Why the second thoughts?

It made only slightly more sense than the Lost Boys leaving him tied to that tree with baling wire. They were out to make more than just a point. It was like they were leaving him there *for* something, sacrificing him, the way the ancient Greeks chained virgins to rocks for monsters to have their way with, so the monsters would leave them alone.

Was Ela supposed to finish him, the way she or someone else had gutted the work foreman with something like a cultivator or loop hoe, probably zonked out on peyote at the time?

What do you think you're doing here, exactly?

Whenever Dylan got it into his mind to do something stupid, he'd hear Caitlin's voice in his head. The more cocksure he felt, the more softly it reached him. He heard it now as a whisper, because who was she to talk, anyway? How many bad guys had *she* shot?

The safe snapped open.

From within, Dylan removed a stainless steel Smith & Wesson model M&P9 nine-millimeter with striker fire action, a seventeen-round magazine, and a reasonably compact 4.25-inch barrel. Wedging it into the back of his jeans, however, left his dad's voice humming in his ear instead of Caitlin's: *I warned you about those skinny jeans, son, didn't I?*

Dylan would leave his shirt untucked, bring a jacket along for the ride. Ela had been playing him this whole time. Time to turn the tables. Get to the reservation and get Ela to help him smoke out the assholes who'd tied him to that tree. He couldn't let it go, just couldn't. Beyond that, he didn't have much of a plan.

The doubt set in when he clambered down the stairs and headed for the garage, where the 1996 Chevrolet S-10 pickup that he'd bought with his own money sat mostly unused. He couldn't remember the last time he'd started it up, and he couldn't be sure his dad had been keeping up with things, either. So, with doubt making its presence felt and second thoughts creeping in, Dylan made a deal with himself: If the old truck started, he was heading to the rez. If it didn't, he wasn't.

He hit the garage door opener and welcomed the sunlight, looking forward to feeling it burn into him the whole time he was driving north toward Austin. Maybe.

Dylan climbed behind the wheel, got himself settled in the old seat, worked the key. The engine sputtered, coughed, almost stalled.

Then started.

82

SAN ANTONIO, TEXAS

"Why don't you have a go at this guy?" Caitlin said to Jones, after Cort Wesley had escorted Cray Rawls into a third-floor office that Captain Tepper had emptied out, intended as a replacement for her desk downstairs.

"Am I hearing you right?" Jones asked her, disbelief

crinkling the hard features of his face, which made it look like someone had soldered the skin into place.

"Man's already called his lawyer. I don't believe that matters much to Homeland Security."

"No, Ranger, it doesn't."

"We got maybe twenty minutes before the lawyer gets here."

"He could still make some trouble."

Caitlin looked totally unbothered by the prospect. "Maybe Cort Wesley can do something about that."

"What about you?"

"I got somebody waiting downstairs I need to speak with."

"Now?"

"She might know Cray Rawls better than anyone."

"Who's that?"

"The woman he raped in Texas twenty-five years ago, not long after the house belonging to the couple who adopted him burned down, with them in it."

Jones held Caitlin's stare as he ran that through his mind, his mouth puckering. "You want to tell me what else it is you're holding back?"

Caitlin managed a smile, feeling the vibration of the cell phone in her pocket. "If I told you, I wouldn't be holding it back anymore."

She answered the call in the hallway, recognizing the number in the caller ID as the Bexar County Medical Examiner's office. "What have you got for me, Doc?"

"Where'd you find that bat, exactly?" Frank Whatley asked her.

"I told you, in a cave rimming the outskirts of the Comanche rez, up in the Balcones."

"I know what you told me. I was looking for something else. Like what planet or mad scientist's lab."

"Why?"

"You sitting down, Ranger?"

"What do you think?"

"Then find a chair," Whatley told her, his voice
cracking with fatigue, "because you're going to need
one for what I've got to tell you."

83

SAN ANTONIO, TEXAS

"He was one sick fuck," Brandy Darnell said, seated
next to Caitlin on the old velvet-colored fabric couch
squeezed against the wall in Captain Tepper's office.
"Does that answer your question, Ranger?"

"In part, ma'am. But I understand the police elect-
ing not to charge him wasn't the end of things."

The woman stiffened. "I don't talk about that. I
never talk about that. To anyone," she said, her voice
quieter, the words practically disappearing before they
emerged from her mouth.

Back when she claimed to have been raped by Cray
Rawls, twenty-five years before, she went by Brandy
Wine. Because she had never disputed that she was a
prostitute, the report Brandy filed was never adequately
investigated and, as a result, Rawls was never charged.
By the time a volunteer legal aid group got involved,
Rawls had left the state and returned to his native
North Carolina, where he began building his empire

with the inheritance from the couple who'd adopted him. In almost all such cases, that would have been the end of things. But not so in Brandy's case, Caitlin had discerned.

"How'd you figure it all out?" Brandy continued, when Caitlin remained silent.

"You used your real name when your injuries brought you to the hospital, ma'am. Same hospital records had you returning a couple times for follow-up visits." Caitlin paused long enough to hold the woman's stare. "I noticed you saw a different doctor the last time. It wasn't hard to add things up from there."

Brandy Darnell swallowed so hard that her face looked pained as she gulped the air down. "So what do you want?"

"Phone records from twenty-five years ago show you made a whole bunch of calls to North Carolina."

The woman's expression grew so still and rigid that Caitlin wondered if she was even breathing. "Son of a bitch was always talking about the way he'd grown up, how much I reminded him of his mother, if you can believe that."

"That doesn't sound like a compliment."

"It wasn't, believe me. His mother was a dirty whore too—that was his point. I think he was screwing her more than me, if that makes any sense."

"It makes plenty, ma'am."

"A few times we were together he'd actually cry, before he'd start getting rough."

Caitlin leaned in closer. "So you'd been with him before the night of the rape."

"When the police heard that, they pretty much

showed me the door. Asked me what made that night different, since he was paying for it and all."

"And what'd you tell them?"

Brandy tried to swallow again, but didn't quite finish. "That there wasn't enough money in the world to pay for what he did to me that night. My insides haven't been the same since, if you can believe that."

"I can, ma'am."

Brandy's eyes turned glassy, her gaze going distant. "I don't know . . . Maybe he did me a favor. That was the end for me in that life. I'd outgrown it anyway, ancient by comparison with most of the girls still working the street, at all of twenty-nine."

Caitlin looked at the woman, who was now fifty-four. Her badly colored blond hair was gray at the roots, hanging limp from either a bad perm or too much futile blow-drying. Her face was sunken, pitted with depressions that looked as if someone had taken a chisel to it, and thinking of Cray Rawls made Caitlin wonder if someone had. Brandy Darnell's skin was dry and flaking, almost like she was peeling from a bad sunburn, though that clearly was not the case; she had the palest skin of any Texan Caitlin could remember. Her cheeks were puffed with fat and her eyes were so bled of life that only their occasional blinking told Caitlin the woman was still alive.

"I got pregnant," Brandy said suddenly, confirming what Caitlin had surmised from the information she'd been able to gather. "That bastard left a baby inside me."

"That's why you tried to contact Cray Rawls in North Carolina."

Caitlin wasn't sure whether Brandy Darnell nodded or not. "Tell him I was going to have his kid. I never actually got him on the phone."

"You wanted money?"

"I wanted him to know. I wanted him to know I was going to have the kid just so I could give it up, that he was never going to see it."

When the woman started to shake, Caitlin reached out and squeezed her shoulder, rubbing it gently. Brandy's eyes glowed with life, young and hopeful again for that fleeting moment before the memories came crashing back like a wave, drenching her anew in misery.

"I got one look at the baby before they took it away," Brandy managed, her voice cracking. "I went home the next day, but my parents wouldn't let me in the house. Pretended I wasn't there, no matter how hard I pounded the door. Eventually a neighbor called the cops. They came and found me on the porch. My parents finally opened the door and told the cops they'd never seen me before."

Caitlin looked at the slovenly woman, her misery worn in every gesture.

"Can I tell you something I've never told anyone else?"

Caitlin nodded.

"I tried to get rid of it myself. One time, when I got big, I propped a baseball bat against the floor and . . . and . . ."

Caitlin wrapped an arm around Brandy's bony shoulder and drew her in close. Brandy didn't respond, just remained frozen.

"Bastard who did this never did pay for it," she said, barely above a whisper.

"I know that, Brandy. And I wish I could do something about that, but I can't."

Brandy stiffened and eased herself away. "Then what am I doing here?"

"I thought there might be another way you could help me get the man who hurt you."

"What's that?"

And Caitlin told her.

84

SAN ANTONIO, TEXAS

"I'm going to tell you the same thing I told Blockhead here," Cray Rawls said, referring to Jones, as soon as Caitlin had closed the door behind her. "I got nothing to say until my lawyer arrives."

"That's your choice, sir," Caitlin said, taking the chair next to him. "But it's not one I recommend."

Rawls smirked, shook his head. "Of course you wouldn't."

"To tell you the truth, Mr. Rawls, I'm a bit disappointed. You talk up a good game on the subject of patriotism, but now, when push comes to shove, you run for the hills."

"And how's that exactly, Ranger?"

Caitlin aimed her gaze briefly at Jones. "It's like 'Blockhead' here undoubtedly told you. We're looking at a situation we have strong reason to believe involves

ISIS and the same Comanche Indian reservation you've got a big stake in. And we believe you and ISIS might be after the same thing."

"Oil?"

"You want to lie to my face, Mr. Rawls, go ahead. But please don't play me for a fool. You wouldn't be waiting for your lawyer if this were about oil on that land," Caitlin told him, suppressing a smile over the fact that Cray Rawls's lawyer had been informed by Cort Wesley, downstairs, that his client had been transferred to the FBI's regional office in Houston to await questioning. "We're talking about something else. We're talking about something that, unbeknownst to you, can be or already has been weaponized."

That seemed to stoke Rawls's curiosity. "What do you mean, weaponized?"

Caitlin glanced toward Jones again. "You didn't tell him?"

"It's classified," Jones offered in explanation.

"You can arrest me later," Caitlin said to Jones, then looked back toward Rawls. "You heard about what happened in Austin, at that restaurant two days back?"

Rawls nodded stiffly.

"Well, then, let me tell you something you haven't heard: We've identified suspects connected to that Comanche land through a third party I spotted outside the premises myself. We know said third party was skulking around the reservation proper, and we believe he left with whatever killed those folks eating their lunch at Hoover's Cooking. And we suspect that your construction crew is about to lay the groundwork for pulling whatever it is out of the ground. How am I doing so far?"

"No comment," Rawls said, his smirk not able to hide the sudden wave of doubt and uncertainty that had claimed his features.

"Then allow me to continue. If you don't help us, you'll go down as an accessory to whatever ISIS is planning to do. You'll be aiding and abetting a terrorist organization committed to our destruction, and you would've, unwittingly or otherwise, provided the means for them to stage an attack on the homeland. Anything you want to say now, sir?"

"I didn't provide them with a goddamn thing."

"And who's going to believe you, given your lack of cooperation, Mr. Rawls?"

Caitlin backed off a bit, letting Rawls have his space, to provide a false sense of comfort.

True to form, he seemed to quickly recover his bravado. "Ranger, I know my way around the law well enough to be sure you haven't got anything on me that's actionable. So, you want to try shipping me off to Cuba or some other hellhole, have at it, and bear the wrath of my thousand-dollar-an-hour attorneys—a fate worse than death, believe me."

Caitlin slid her chair in closer to his. "That may be true, sir. But you've got another problem, which I don't think they'll be able to help you out with. Something I don't think you'd want even your high-priced shysters to hear about. Goes back a whole bunch of years, to when you raped that call girl before you fled Texas to return to North Carolina."

"Allegedly," Rawls was quick to point out.

"I've come up against more than my share of men like you, sir," Caitlin continued. "Men who've risen to wealth and power on the backs of others, who feel they have a license to hurt people on account of them being hurt themselves. You're all like characters out of Shakespeare. In your case, I know your own mother was a working girl herself, until she was killed by one of her johns, and growing up that way is surely call for a man to be angry. But that doesn't entitle you to pay the world back for your pain by inflicting it on women just like your mother. I even heard that, a few days back, not far from that Wake County courthouse where your verdict came down, a prostitute claimed she was beaten with a sock full of motel soaps by a man she couldn't identify. Then she disappeared."

"What are you getting at, Ranger?" Rawls asked, the slight distance between them suddenly seeming like a dark chasm.

"It's like I said, sir. I know the life you came from, that brought you to Texas as a boy, and how you saw fit to pay the world back by beating up call girls, starting with Brandy Darnell. That name ring a bell?"

"No."

"That's right," Caitlin remembered, "back then she went by the name Brandy Wine. You fled Texas after you raped her, never responded to any of her letters or messages about leaving her pregnant."

Rawls had grown stiffer than the wooden chair in which he was seated. "She was after money, Ranger. She tell you that? And she didn't even raise the kid herself."

"No, sir. But she tracked him down when he turned

STRONG COLD DEAD 347

eighteen, learned everything she could about him. That's why you're going to cooperate with us, Mr. Rawls. That's why you're going to tell us everything we want to know, without your lawyers present. Save yourself a boatload of money."

Rawls looked genuinely befuddled. "I have no idea what you're talking about."

"Of course you don't, so let me spell it out for you, sir. That suspect I mentioned goes by the name of Daniel Cross. He's a brilliant but troubled kid, and a genius when it comes to chemical engineering. Any of this ringing a bell?"

"No."

"Cross was part of the original analytical team retained by Jackson Whole Mineral," Caitlin explained, a fact that she had discovered during her scrutiny of Sam Bob Jackson's personnel records, provided by Jones. "He spent six months on that land, trying to pinpoint whatever it was you were looking for, but he found something else entirely, which he decided to put to his own use. That's what ISIS will soon have in hand, if they don't already. That's why somebody put a bullet in Sam Bob's head this morning and would've put one in yours, too, if Cort Wesley Masters hadn't been there. They're tying up loose ends, eliminating anybody else who might have knowledge of what's on that land."

"Well, then, by all means thank Mr. Masters for me," Rawls said, his tone laced with enough smarmy sanctimony to turn Caitlin's stomach. "But none of that, in any way, shape, or form, links me directly to this Daniel Cross or makes me somehow culpable for this potential attack ISIS may be about to launch. You have any more shit you want to throw at the wall to see if it sticks, Ranger?"

"Just this: Daniel Cross is your son, Mr. Rawls."

85

San Antonio, Texas

Rawls didn't respond, didn't speak. The air in the cramped office, which was overstuffed with storage boxes, felt thick, the way air outside did when foreshadowing a thunderstorm. Soupy, heavy, moist—all of it seemed to radiate off Cray Rawls, whose expression was that of a man who had just relived the last twenty-five years of his life in slow motion.

Jones dropped a file folder into the man's lap, fanning the still air a bit. "Everything we've got on Daniel Cross. I was going to share it with you for different reasons entirely," he added, eyes straying to Caitlin, "until the Ranger here shocked the shit out of both of us."

Rawls started to open the folder, then stopped. He looked up to find Caitlin staring at him, her face utterly blank.

"I met your boy myself, when he was fourteen," she said, "a gangly, bullied freshman who'd threatened on MySpace to blow up his high school. I couldn't help but feel bad for him, the kid being so smart and all, and being tortured by bullies. I got him out of that scrape, gave him a second chance, thought I could make a difference in his life. But then things took a bad turn for me. I left the Rangers for a time and lost track of him, and for the past few days I've been blaming myself for his involvement in all this. But now that I know he's got your blood pumping through his veins, I guess nothing I did would've mattered, would it, Mr. Rawls? I never had a chance, and neither did he."

Rawls clutched the folder in his lap tighter.

"Here's what's going to happen, sir," Caitlin said, rising from her chair and standing over him. "You're going to tell us everything you know about that land. You're not going to wait for your lawyer, you're not going to pass Go and collect two hundred dollars, you're going to talk. And if you don't, the whole world is going to find out that you fathered a child who's planning a terrorist attack that'll make nine eleven look like a drill. Have I got your attention?"

Rawls looked up at Caitlin in painfully deliberate fashion, as if he had to wait for some puppet master to pull on his strings. "That's blackmail."

"No, sir, it's the truth."

"You don't understand."

Caitlin leaned forward and grasped the arms of Rawls's chair, forcing him to twist himself tight and small, further exaggerating her advantage. "Then make me understand."

"Tens of billions of dollars, hundreds of billions of dollars . . . That's what it's worth."

"What *what's* worth?"

Rawls looked as if bile had just kicked up his throat. "The cure for cancer." He paused, and then continued. "Not just a cure. A vaccine that can stop the disease at the genetic level. The data was anecdotal, but still convincing enough."

"What data?" Caitlin managed to ask, the air seeming to thicken even more, to the point that she wondered if that was thunder she heard in her suddenly throbbing head.

"About this particular tribe of Comanche, dating all the way back to your great-great-grandfather's time. They've got so many other health issues of note—alcoholism, liver failure, malnutrition, breathing problems from smoking, drugs, diabetes, heart disease—that nobody paid attention to the fact that the tribe enjoys a cancer occurrence on the order of a thousand times less than the overall population."

"Keep talking." Caitlin nodded.

"I get this data, the question I ask myself is why."

"What made you look in the first place?"

"The belief that the truest medical miracles can be found in nature."

"Most valuable, you mean."

"That too, yes, Ranger. I admit it. I'm a greedy son of a bitch who looks back on his youth like somebody took a sandblaster to it. What do you think I'm thinking of when I'm hitting the heavy bag, like you saw me doing? I'm thinking about all those nights my mother brought men home. When I hid in the corner, in the dark, until they left. You know what? I can't remember what a single one of them looked like, but they all smelled the same. And that's what I smell when I'm pounding the bag, and I keep pounding until the smell goes away."

"How about all the women you beat up, Mr. Rawls,

like Brandy Darnell? What do they smell like? Having wrong done to you doesn't entitle you to do it to others."

"Don't preach to me, you bi—"

Rawls just managed to stop himself in time.

"I'd rather shoot you, but I won't," Caitlin said. "Better get back to this cure for cancer, before you give me reason to change my mind."

"You going to let her talk to me like that?" Rawls said to Jones.

"Like what?" Jones asked him.

Rawls forced himself to look back at Caitlin. "It's like I said."

"What did you say?"

"No one paid attention to the fact that those damn Indians almost never get cancer. Not just an improbability, a virtual *impossibility*."

"So what'd you do?"

"I asked myself why. I asked myself how. See, the medicinal applications of plant life are hardly new. As I'm sure you're well aware, many valuable drugs of today, like atropine, ephedrine, tubocurarine, digoxin, and reserpine, came into use through the study of indigenous remedies. And chemists continue to use plant-derived drugs such as morphine, Taxol, physostigmine, quinidine, and emetine as prototypes in their attempts to develop more-effective and less-toxic medicinals."

"Something was different on that rez, I'm guessing."

"It sure was, Ranger. Those other examples I mentioned don't necessarily have any effect on the people indigenous to those lands. What's different on the

Comanche land is that the cancer anomaly could only be the result of something the Indians ate or drank."

"Native Americans," Caitlin corrected. "They're called Native Americans."

Rawls pursed his lips and frowned. "Sure. Whatever you say. The point is, these *Native Americans* weren't getting cancer, as a direct result of something they were ingesting."

"The water?" Caitlin asked him, thinking of how they'd found Daniel Cross's candy wrapper near the stream running through the cave overlooking White Eagle's patch of land.

"That was my first thought, too. I spent months having the water tested, over a year, spent millions before I gave up. Figured I had everything wrong, that I was delusional."

"Yeah, greed'll do that to you."

This time Rawls ignored her insult, checking his watch as if wondering what had become of his lawyer—who was currently en route to Houston. "I don't give up so easy, Ranger. Since you're so well acquainted with my background, I assume you know that. The water didn't test magical, but some of the samples didn't test normal, either. Something was definitely going on, likely spurred by cracks deep underground, from fault lines on which the reservation is located. The water was contaminated with something, which I came to believe might be working its magic in other ways."

"The crops," Caitlin realized. "Something the Comanche were growing."

Rawls settled back in his chair. "I've said enough."

"You ever test any of the animals on that rez, sir?"

"Animals?"

"Like the bats that live in the cave formations."

Rawls looked genuinely curious. "Why?"

"Because I did, after a colony of them attacked me. Turns out they're a species of Mexican free-tailed bats, common to the area, known for nesting under the Congress Avenue Bridge in Austin. What's not common is that the ones in that cave were maybe ten times bigger than the ones found under the bridge. And here's the kicker: the average life expectancy for Mexican free-tailed bats is between four and six years, but by all accounts, the one we tested from the rez was at least fifty."

That got Rawls's attention. *"Fifty years?"*

"Could be a hundred. The testing's not finished yet." Caitlin paused again, to let that sink in, before continuing. "So, if you weren't drilling for oil, what exactly are those workmen supposed to do, now that the protesting's over?"

"Whatever's growing on that land is being affected by the chemical composition of the groundwater leaching up from an aquifer we can't reach through normal means. And to properly recreate the conditions, I'm going to need an oil well's worth of that magic water."

"And if you're right, I imagine a barrel of that water will be worth a thousand times more than a barrel of oil."

"Closer to ten thousand times, Ranger."

"So here's where we're at, Mr. Rawls." Caitlin nodded. "Your cat's out of the bag, as far as the government goes. Keep obstructing us and you'll end up a coconspirator with whoever we nail in connection with ISIS. You want to tell him how things go from here, Jones?"

She stepped aside so Jones could take her place, looking down at Cray Rawls, but he took a seat on the edge of the desk instead, showcasing the cowboy boots he figured made him a genuine Texan.

"Who you think you're talking to here, hoss?" he said, the slightest Texas twang evident in his cadence. "I'm Homeland Security, and you won't find a Miranda warning card anywhere on my person. I snap my fingers and—poof!—you disappear. We'll seize your assets, freeze your accounts, turn every employee you've got into a person of interest, to make their lives a living hell, too. See, there's no gray area with Homeland, and we never have to defend ourselves in court. You're in or you're out. So which is it?"

Rawls fixed his gaze back on Caitlin. "If I tell you what you want to know—"

"No deals, Mr. Rawls," she interrupted. "The only thing I can promise you for sure, in return for your cooperation, is not to go public with the fact that your son might be directly aiding and abetting the biggest terrorist attack by far in American history. I can't take anything else off the table."

Rawls shook his head, moved his eyes from Caitlin to Jones and then back again. "When did this stop being the United States of America?"

Jones answered before Caitlin could. "When ISIS decided to use a weapon of mass destruction they found on land you currently control."

"A man like you never gives everything up until his back hits the wall, Mr. Rawls," Caitlin picked up. "That's where you're at right now, and you've got one more chance to come clean about what else you're after on that rez besides water."

Rawls's expression tightened into one familiar to Caitlin from the Houston boxing gym where they'd first met: exhaustion, after he'd punched himself out and could barely raise his arms. "Just one question, Ranger. How much do you know about corn?"

Before he could continue, a knock preceded the office door opening, and Captain Tepper poked his head in.

"We got a lead on these bastards," was all Tepper said.

86

BALCONES CANYONLANDS, TEXAS

Dylan parked his truck off the rez, in a grove set well back from the entrance, near a trail through the woods that Ela had shown him. During the drive north, he'd noticed a tear in the tan cloth upholstery, down the middle of the passenger seat.

That made him think of the day he'd bought his beloved Chevy S-10, after his freshman year at Brown, without telling his dad, and how it had conked out almost as soon as he'd gotten it home. Instead of being pissed, his father had taught him how to change the starter, then the alternator, and finally, the battery.

Never criticizing him for the purchase or preaching something like "What'd you expect for five hundred bucks?"

Dylan had bought the truck because it was the same age as him, and something felt right about that. Having a vehicle under him that had grown up on the same track, with lots of secrets and stories to share. He'd put in a new radio, sound system, tires, shocks, and custom bed liner, and had waxed, polished, and rubbed until the finish looked showroom new and rain fled from the paint before it could even bead up. But he'd never done anything, not a damn thing, about the upholstery, and now there was a tear down the center of the passenger seat, leaving him to wonder what he could and should have done differently.

Kind of like what was bringing him back to the reservation now. He was glad he had the truck to think about during the drive, because it spared him too much further contemplation of what Ela and the Lost Boys were up to. She had been playing him the whole time, ever since they'd first met, in Providence. Had almost surely set him up as a suspect in the murder of that construction foreman.

Then why rescue me, clipping the baling wire with a cutter she just happened to bring along? Why drive all the way to Shavano Park to face my father and Caitlin?

Dylan slid through the woods, past waist-high concrete pillars marking the beginning of Comanche land, his dad's Smith & Wesson nine-millimeter scratching at his skin. His iPhone was probably back in Ela's root cellar, so he'd bought one of those cheap phones at a drugstore on his way up to the rez, just in case he needed it.

His route brought him back to White Eagle's property, where he could finish checking out that shed, or maybe confront the old man about whatever he was really up to. He heard the flutter and then lapping sounds of the waterfall next to White Eagle's home, and he clung to the cover of the trees the rest of the way. Dylan stopped there and pressed out a text, starting with, IT'S DYLAN, since his father wouldn't recognize the throwaway phone's number. He kept it short and sweet, his mind having cleared enough to realize he was in over his head here and needed his dad to dig him out.

No one was in sight when Dylan reached the edge of the clearing—no sign of Ela, White Eagle, or any of the Lost Boys. The door leading into the shed he'd inspected was open, blown by the wind against the frame, where it rattled on impact with the hasp. Walking out into the clearing under cover of night was one thing. Doing it now, with light streaming everywhere, presented an entirely different challenge.

His dad had warned him not to find a false sense of security in a gun, to never do anything with one in his possession that he wouldn't do without one. But Dylan couldn't help but feel emboldened by the steel of the nine-millimeter heating up against his skin. Like a flashlight cutting through the dark, its presence propelled him out into the clearing, where he clung as much as possible to the shadows that shook and trembled in cadence with the wind rustling through the trees that cast them.

He reached the shed and pressed himself against its back side, closest to the woods, safe from being seen by anyone who might be about. When no new sounds came to signal such a presence, Dylan sidestepped around the shed's perimeter to the unlocked door. Peering inside through the crack between door and frame, he saw that the shed appeared to be unchanged from the previous night. Then the wind caught the door and widened the gap just enough to let a shaft of light pour past Dylan.

It illuminated the dark gravel floor. Only, a central square of it looked even darker.

The gravel had been shoveled aside, revealing a hatch that was now propped up to provide access to some secret underground chamber. Impossible to tell how long it had been here, though the scent of freshly dug earth suggested maybe not too long. Maybe.

Perhaps again reassured by the Smith & Wesson, Dylan slid all the way inside the shed, just before the door clanged against the hasp once more. The shaft of light had been reduced to a sliver, but it still was enough for him to see a ladder descending into the darkness, maybe going all the way down to Dante's nine circles of hell, which he knew well from another of his classes at Brown.

Who said football players couldn't be smart?

He'd played lacrosse in high school, too, after squandering years on youth soccer. Sports had always come easy to him, in large part because of a fearless nature on the playing field, which belied his modest size. He took after his mother in that respect, instead of his father. And it was that same nature that led Dylan to position himself in place over the ladder, grasping its top-mounted handles as he lowered his feet several rungs down. If he'd known for sure that the Lost Boys were down there, maybe he would have just closed the hatch and sealed it, trapping them, as apt payback for what they'd done to him the night before. Ela, though, could be down there too, and beyond that, Dylan reminded himself, there was a greater mission here: to get to the bottom of whatever was going on and why it had led her to use him the way she clearly had.

Dylan descended slowly and cautiously, careful to keep his boots from clacking against the wooden rungs. Whatever light he'd been using was pretty much gone at around what looked to be the halfway point. But shortly after that he glimpsed the naked spray of lantern light and thought he caught the faint smell of kerosene in the cooling air.

Just like the kerosene lantern Ela had used to light the root cellar where they'd made love and gotten zonked out of their minds on peyote.

Dylan stepped off the lower rungs of the ladder, onto a cushion of soft, moist dirt pitted with pools of standing water. The lantern-lit, winding tunnel before him didn't look man-made so much as it seemed like an underground extension of the caves that were dug out of the hillside overlooking White Eagle's property. It was like some kind of beehive, combined with a maze that twisted and turned this way and that.

Dylan started to reach for his dad's pistol, then stopped. He hadn't bothered to turn off the ringtone of the ancient-looking flip phone forming a bulge in the front pocket of his jeans, because nobody had the number he'd made himself memorize. He could take it out right now and call his father, or Caitlin, and tell them what he'd uncovered. But something pushed him on instead, gun left tucked in place until he was sure he needed it.

Drawing deeper down the labyrinthine path, he was struck by a rising odor on the air, something rotten and spoiled. Not a carrion or death smell, though, nor a scent resembling excrement of any kind. This was a different smell, foreign and yet vaguely familiar, as if the far reaches of his mind held some notion of it. The stronger and more acrid the stench grew, the less familiar it became, until Dylan began to consider the original thought an illusion.

Only he couldn't, not totally, because he was sure it held some meaning for him, some memory he couldn't quite grasp.

A bit farther along, the path canted upward, toward a smell of freshly dug earth that was strong enough to break the persistent oily, stale stench, at least for a moment. The path seemed to widen where it forked to the left, seeming narrower to the right. Then Dylan realized that the right path actually led to an evenly carved, door-size breach leading to a passageway forged by man and not nature.

The acrid stench seemed to peak, and Dylan saw he'd entered some kind of chamber. But it was too far from the spill of lantern light to discern anything more, until he noticed a matching pair of lanterns on either side of the dug-out entryway and turned one of them up.

A chamber all right—a *storage* chamber, encased by limestone walls.

He spotted what looked like tarpaulins thrown over uneven heaps and piles of *something* that seemed to hold the source of the stink, overpowering in the tight confines. Breathing through his mouth, Dylan peeled back the edge of one of the tarps as unobtrusively as he could, pulling—stupidly maybe—a clump of whatever was concealed beneath it free and up to his nose.

Its powerfully sour scent almost made him retch, and it was all Dylan could do to steady his stomach. He recalled the same scent emanating from the patch of fungus on the mold-riddled ear of corn that he'd made himself eat after Ela had called it a delicacy.

It's a secret my people have kept for centuries, our greatest secret.

Dylan moved deeper into the chamber, into the shaft of light illuminating almost all of it.

And that's when he saw the bodies.

87

DALLAS, TEXAS

"A blessed target," Hatim Abd al-Aziz proclaimed, seated at the picnic table across from Razin Saflin, Ghazi Zurif, and Daniel Cross in Klyde Warren Park. "How many do you think are here now who could be dead tomorrow by the grace of God?"

Al-Aziz said that in a way that sent a chill up Cross's spine, reminding him of how close he'd come to a moment like this a decade ago, of the lives he had wanted to take in his crowded school cafeteria. And that made him wonder whether Caitlin Strong had noticed him the other day outside the Comanche reservation. A decade ago, she'd done her best to convince him he was worth something, but the feeling had only lasted until the other kids started up on him again. Caitlin Strong might have talked him out of pulling a Columbine, but he knew his day was going to come. Now that it finally had, he found himself fearing her disapproval.

Why'd she have to be at that damn reservation?

"I only wish I could be here to see it," al-Aziz continued, smiling so placidly at the prospect that it utterly unnerved Daniel Cross.

Klyde Warren Park was a pristine, tree-lined, eco-friendly stretch of land erected on a mothballed overpass of the eight-lane Woodall Rodgers Freeway. A public and private partnership initiative to combat urban sprawl and create a sprawling green space on the site of a former crumbling concrete blight between Pearl and St. Paul streets, where uptown and downtown Dallas meet. An urban oasis set in the shadows cast by skyscrapers lining the site's east and west peripheries.

The park was normally dominated by a large, open grassy stretch lined with lawn chairs, food vendors, and ice cream trucks, adjoining a botanical garden, walking trails, and an assortment of pavilions. But an old-fashioned traveling carnival had set up shop on the grounds in recent days. The bulk of the rides and attractions—including the House of Horrors, the Buggy Whip, the mini Flume, various kiddie rides, and a family-friendly roller coaster that swept over the expanse of the entire carnival, erected from Pearl Street, across the great lawn crossing Hart Boulevard. Food booths and game attractions forming a makeshift midway rimmed the perimeter on the eastbound side of Woodall Rodgers Freeway, across from the Dallas Museum of Art.

Al-Aziz sat alone on one side of the shaded picnic table, amid the smells of grilled hamburgers, falafel, and various Mexican-style offerings. Saflin, Zurif, and Daniel Cross sat across from him, with a clear view of the botanical garden and the section of the park devoted to children's activities, which today had been usurped by a pair of bounce houses, where lines had begun to form. The carnival was just starting to fill up, locals streaming in to loiter away a few hours during spring break for Texas schools. A local radio station was doing a live remote, and both the Nancy Collins Fisher and Muse Family Performance pavilions offered live performances featuring clowns, mimes, and jugglers.

Cross looked around at the rapidly growing crowd of happy people who had no clue about the fate that ultimately awaited them. Thanks to him.

"I just want to see the world burn," Cross said, to no one in particular. "I want to be the one lighting the match."

Cross glanced back at al-Aziz, who was lowering a cell phone from his ear, grinning anew above his trimmed beard. "This place will be our second target. Houston will be the first."

"Houston?" Cross asked, feeling something quiver in his stomach.

"*Inshallah*," al-Aziz said, bowing his head slightly.

88

Dylan recognized the Lost Boys immediately, the same ones who'd tied him to a tree and left him for dead the night before. He counted seven of them. Their blood was everywhere, whether from bullet or knife wounds, he couldn't be sure.

He tried to make sense of what he was seeing, to put everything together.

Our greatest secret . . .

That greatest secret of the Comanche had been stockpiled down here atop trays sealed in airtight plastic wrapping. Hundreds of pounds of the mold, fungus, or whatever it was, divided into six stacks, squeezed tightly against the walls. Hidden in this secret chamber for who knew how long to do who knew what. Dylan whipped the phone out of his pocket to call his father and started to back out of the chamber.

He turned to find Ela Nocona standing before him, and she collapsed in his arms.

Dylan crumpled under her weight, cushioning Ela the whole way.

"Take it easy," he tried to sooth her.

He was cradling her waist and her head at the same time, the hand nearer her torso feeling warm, wet, and sticky.

With blood.

"They thought I was dead," she managed to say, after swallowing hard.

"Who?"

She shook her head, eyes gaping in fear at the re-kindled memory. "I don't know. They spoke . . ."

"What?"

Ela swallowed hard again. "Arabic, I think. I'm sorry . . ."

"Sh-h-h."

"For what I did."

"You didn't do anything."

"I set you up. Left your medal out near the body of that construction worker, so you'd get hauled in. Get the blame. Turning you into a patsy, following my grandfather's plan."

"It doesn't matter."

"It does, because I stopped it. I stopped Houston, wouldn't let them go through with it, any more than I could let them hurt you."

Dylan looked into Ela's eyes, grasped her terror.

"It wasn't supposed to be this way," she said.

"Sh-h-h," Dylan soothed her again. "I already texted my dad. He's coming. He'll know what to do."

She shook her head. "It's too late. They've got them—the backpacks I took from my cousins. Wired and ready to blow. To make our mark, our point." Ela tried to smile, but failed. "Be badasses."

Dylan looked around the chamber again at those hundreds of pounds of mold, fungus, or whatever—but some must be missing now. Loaded into the backpacks Ela had just mentioned, now in the killers' possession.

Our greatest secret . . .

"You have to go after them," Ela said, her voice strong in that moment, her grip digging into his arm.

"I'm not going anywhere."

Another swallow. "I'll be okay."

"For sure."

Her eyes faded, then came back to life. "My pocket. It's there."

Dylan felt about her jeans, which were darkened by blood, until he found a folded piece of paper, similarly stained around the edges.

"What is this?" he asked, unfolding it to find a schematic of some kind, with a bunch of red Xs at what looked like equidistant points.

"Houston. Our plan. The one I stopped."

"What plan?"

Her eyes faded again, fluttered, closed.

"Ela, what plan?"

She was trying to hold her eyes open, leaving Dylan to picture a bunch of killers who spoke Arabic carrying backpacks filled with some weapon the Comanche had been safeguarding for generations.

"What do the Xs mean?" he asked, regarding the schematic again.

Ela's breathing came in fits and starts, but her eyes suddenly sprang to life. "Targets," was all she said, before her eyes closed again.

Dylan eased her head into his lap, cradling it with one hand while the other hand felt for his cheap flip phone to text his dad again.

PART NINE

A lot of the old-time Rangers were not happy when they had to start reading Miranda warnings to suspects. They thought the world had ended. They couldn't figure out why on earth you would spend months investigating a case and hunting down a suspect, and then once you've got him, the first thing you have to say is "You have the right not to talk to me."

—Ranger Doyle Holdridge, in *Tracking the Texas Rangers: The Twentieth Century,* edited by Bruce A. Glasrud and Harold J. Weiss, Jr. (Denton: University of North Texas Press, 2013)

89

"Footage off a traffic camera shows all three of our targets entering Klyde Warren Park in Dallas less than an hour ago," Tepper explained to Caitlin and Jones, after Cray Rawls had been escorted from the room.

"They wouldn't be there unless it was to meet someone," said Caitlin.

Jones started for the door. "I'm going to move every drone we've got up to the area over that park, see if we can figure out who exactly that is."

"How many drones we talking about exactly?" Caitlin asked him.

"Hopefully enough to avert an ISIS attack on the homeland, Ranger," Jones told her. "Is that good enough for you?"

Jones left the room to work the retasking and make the arrangements to get the team to Dallas. In the meantime, if Zurif, Saflin, and Daniel Cross left Klyde Warren Park before they arrived, the drones would pick them up again immediately.

"I ever tell you I once played the rodeo circuit?" Captain Tepper asked Caitlin, the two of them now alone in the office, which still held the smell of Cray Rawls's cologne.

"No, D.W., definitely not."

"Well, I did. Your dad and granddad got a real hoot out of it, especially old Earl. Once, when I was riding some country festival, he shot his gun into the air just as they were lifting the gate. Turned that bucking bronco into a goddamn stegosaurus, I swear, snorting so hard I could feel his breath. Anyway, I lasted seven point three seconds. Made it my last ride ever. I mention that 'cause that's what all this resembles. Like we're on the back of a bucking bronc, hanging on for dear life."

"But it's happened before, hasn't it? Back when Jack Strong went up against John D. Rockefeller."

"You comparing Standard Oil to ISIS, Ranger?" Tepper asked, a note of sarcasm clear in his voice.

"How was it Standard Oil never made inroads in Texas until years later, D.W.? Something happened back then, on the same Indian reservation we're dealing with now, that scared off one of the most powerful men in American history."

Tepper's eyes widened. "Old Earl never told you that part of the story?"

"Not that I recall. Then again, he often left out the real bloody parts from his bedtime tales."

"Well, Ranger, that certainly qualifies here . . ."

90

"What'd you do to those men?" Jack Strong asked Isa-tai.

"You mean the dead ones in the hotel?"

"I never said nothing about dead men in a hotel."

"Word travels fast, Ranger."

"So does the smell of shit, Chief."

"I've told you, I'm not our chief."

"No, but you're running the show all the same, sure as I'm standing here and sure as you having something to do with some of Rockefeller's men getting torn apart."

"Nature takes care of its own."

"You said that before, Chief."

"Because it's true. Then, now, forever."

"I believe you've told me that, too. So let me tell you something. Whatever you're up to may have chased off other men, but this Rockefeller ain't one of them. He won't stop until he's staked his full claim to the oil on this land, and he'll call up as many men as he needs to do the job."

"Let him."

The same bevy of young braves enclosed Isa-tai, their faces painted up to make them look like criss-crossing checkerboards. Steeldust Jack knew a war party when he saw one, knew that he was looking at an all-out clash between the Comanche and the forces of John D. Rockefeller, which would put to shame the ongoing battles being fought by the Frontier Battalion today.

"How many guns you got on hand?" he asked the young leader, whose coppery skin looked shiny in the sunlight.

"We won't need guns."

"Don't talk that nature dung to me again, son. Wasn't nature that killed those men in the hotel. I don't know what it was, but I know it walked on two legs and came from this here reservation."

Isa-tai backed off, the added distance between them slight but seeming much greater. "Get off our land, Ranger. When our enemies come, the land will deal with them."

Two days later, Steeldust Jack was watching from a nearby cattle pen, leaning up against one of the fence posts, when the train carrying Rockefeller's reinforcements arrived. The Houston and Texas Central had resumed construction on its lines after the Civil War, in 1867. The company built steadily northward, reaching Corsicana in 1871, Dallas in 1872, and the Red River in 1873. At the same time, the company began work on a spur that reached Austin on Christmas Day in 1871, creating boom times for the fledgling state capital.

The gunmen who emerged from that train seemed to form an endless wave, some still dressed in their Confederate uniforms, as if to remind passersby of their lineage and loyalty. They were met by Curly Bill Brocius, along with Rockefeller's personal bodyguards,

culled from Pinkerton's agency of cutthroats and killers. Steeldust Jack wondered whether the country recognized this offshoot of violence spawned by the war's
aftermath—how a side effect of all that blood, bit-
terness, and fighting had been to create a dark under-
belly of law-averse gunfighters who were used to
killing with impunity and not needing to justify their
actions, beyond the uniforms that they'd worn. Maybe
that's why a whole bunch still wore those uniforms,
as if it gave them license to pursue the same violent
predilections that had been spawned by their service
and spurred further by the alienation that followed the
defeat of the South.

He spotted Rockefeller standing a ways back in the
company of more of his Pinkerton's men, checking a
pocket watch he'd pulled from his vest. Steeldust Jack
approached right down the center of the day's light,
making no effort to appear either threatening or
menacing.

"What can I do for you, Ranger?" Rockefeller asked,
under the protective cover of his hired gunmen, as soon
as he spotted Steeldust Jack.

"I was hoping you could hold off your men for a
while, sir. Give me time to see if we can bring all this
to a peaceful conclusion."

"Broker a deal, in other words. What do you have
in mind, given that time is of the essence?"

"I don't have much right now, but I'm working up
a couple of things," Jack Strong lied, hoping to buy
whatever time he could.

"You'll have to be more specific than that."

"Mr. Rockefeller, I'm just trying to avoid any more bloodshed here."

"I appreciate your concern, Ranger, given that the only blood spilled so far belongs to men in my employ."

"Maybe you're forgetting those Indian boys who got dragged to death."

Rockefeller's features tightened, his head canting slightly to the side. "I hope you're not suggesting, again, that was the work of anyone working for me. If you have any evidence or witnesses to the contrary, then let's hear it."

Steeldust Jack regarded the surly smirks cast by the Pinkerton's men. "That reservation has plenty of women and children living on it, sir."

"I'm sorry to hear that. Truly."

The Ranger looked back toward the widening mass of gunmen still spilling off the just-arrived train. "I'm going back to that reservation to have one more go at this, peacefully."

"I'll give you the day, Ranger. We move come tomorrow."

But Jack Strong found the Comanche reservation abandoned when he got there, not a soul in sight. Riding through that land felt like exploring a graveyard. There were no signs of life at all, including livestock. He'd ridden through ghost towns before, and had been witness to the aftermath of massacres at the hands of marauding Indians or Mexican bandits, where the bodies had been buried and the survivors had fled. This felt like neither of those. There was no residue, sense, or smell of death. No hopelessness to be found in tumbleweeds blowing about the abandoned settlement of buildings. The Comanche reservation was just . . . well . . .

Empty. Like the residents had picked up and left. On closer inspection, he saw that even their meager belongings were gone, right down to the wooden utensils and iron pots with which they cooked and ate, the animal hides they used for blankets.

Steeldust Jack inspected the grounds thoroughly, chewing tobacco even though he hated the taste of it and the feeling against his lips, because it kept his mind off whatever had happened here. He wasn't sure whether to suspect foul play, wasn't sure whether to expect anything other than the involvement, somehow, of none other than John D. Rockefeller, who'd lied right to his face, back at the train station, about giving him the rest of the day to continue working toward a peaceful solution.

Just after noon, Jack Strong saw the man himself approaching, riding high in his saddle at the front of an endless procession of wagons bearing his workmen, equipment, and army of hired guns. Steeldust Jack had just become aware of a smell caking the air like a fine mist, an odor that was sweet and acrid at the same time. Overpowering in some of the spots he rode through, barely noticeable in others. He stopped paying the scent any heed at all as he approached Rockefeller.

"Why, howdy there, Ranger," Rockefeller greeted him, doing his best impersonation of a Texas drawl.

"What happened here, Mr. Rockefeller?"

"Why are you asking me?"

"Because I believe you had something to do with this."

"With what?"

"Look around. Tell me what you see."

John D. Rockefeller obliged, in melodramatic fashion. "Nothing at all, my good man."

Steeldust Jack cast his gaze beyond Rockefeller. For as far as he could see, the path was lined with wagons and with men, wielding both Winchesters and shotguns, guarding those wagons. "You and your gunmen have something to do with that?"

Rockefeller almost laughed. "You give me too much credit, Ranger."

"The Comanche turned tail and fled. You expect me to believe they did that on their own?"

"I expect you to believe they must've smartened up. I expect you to believe I had nothing to do with their timely departure, because I didn't. I'm sure you told them what was coming."

Jack Strong let his gaze drift beyond Rockefeller to all his hired guns, a number of which were gathering in a tight mass, weapons showcased in a show of intimidation.

"And now it's here," he said.

"Like I said, Ranger, they must've smartened up. This was inevitable, anyway; both of us know that. If the Comanche refused to stand down and adhere to both Governor Coke and the U.S. Congress's orders, they would've been forcibly removed."

"From their own land, you mean."

John D. Rockefeller gazed around at the emptiness,

the desolation of the abandoned Comanche reservation. Nothing in the air but the sweet and sour smell.

"Smell that, Ranger? It's the smell of oil bubbling to the surface. So much of it I'll use the proceeds to buy this whole goddamn state of yours."

"Texas ain't for sale, Mr. Rockefeller, and neither are the Texas Rangers."

"Don't worry." Rockefeller grinned. "I wasn't interested in buying you anyway."

Steeldust Jack took a seat atop the nearest hillside to watch the procession fan out through the reservation. The activity was centering around a stretch of grasslands where Rockefeller's surveyors and engineers must have pinpointed the biggest of the potential oil strikes. Steeldust Jack watched them work, while sipping water from his canteen and eating the dried beef he'd smoked himself. Ate it all and drank, while trying to determine his next move, only to conclude he didn't have one.

It took much of the rest of the day for Rockefeller's workers to empty the wagons of the digging and drilling equipment they were hauling. A whole bunch of men were already taking to the ground with shovels while Rockefeller's brigade of ex–Civil War gunmen watched over them protectively. Their eyes continued to scan the nearby woods, lands, hillsides, and ridgelines as if expecting to see an attack coming at any moment. But none followed, and by the time light began to bleed out of the day, Jack Strong had pretty much figured none would be.

How wrong he turned out to be.

Somehow Steeldust Jack was certain he felt, actually *felt*, the hot gush of air blowing past his ear an instant before the flames erupted. He wasn't sure where the fire actually started—everywhere at once, it seemed. One minute the dusk air was cool and crisp, and the next it was superheated amid the blinding glow of an inferno that swept across the land like a blanket being draped on a body. It was dark and then it was bright, with seemingly no transition, as if he'd blinked the flames to life between breaths.

The smell he'd detected on the air before blew into him with a force that nearly toppled Jack Strong from his feet. The noxious scent of oil, he realized, now aflame with burned pine, grass, and oak added to the mixture. Steeldust Jack wasn't thinking right then about how the Comanche had managed to light the whole of the oil nearest the ground on fire. Most likely, they'd figured out some way to force it up to the surface, if it wasn't there already, and then let it spread in pools, following the natural grade of the land. But Steeldust Jack wasn't thinking of that.

He was thinking of the screams. Just a few to start with, but increasing by the second as the flame burst fed by the oil captured more and more of Rockefeller's men in its grasp. The worst of the screams came when those who escaped the initial burst realized they were trapped by walls of flames on all sides of them. Jack Strong thought he saw men, some with their clothes flaming, tearing out for the stream that supplied the reservation with its water. And when they got close, a fresh wall of flames spurted upward, yet another trap sprung.

The screams only got worse from there.

And kept coming.

Steeldust Jack thought he'd never lose sleep over anything but memories of the Civil War again, only he was wrong. The awful screaming and stench of burning flesh and hair, pushing through the oil-rich air, was worse than any battle he'd fought in or any carnage he'd seen.

Nature takes care of its own, Isa-tai had told him.

He'd been a fool not to listen, not to realize that damn kid had something deadly up his sleeve—carried out in concert, no doubt, with the tribal elders holding his leash. Steeldust Jack had tried to warn off John D. Rockefeller, but the man wasn't hearing it, convinced that his wealth and power, rising behind the guise of Standard Oil, insulated him from the kind of violent opposition he was hardly averse to dispensing himself. The Comanche likely would have accepted the men killed in the hotel as trade for the three boys dragged to death the day before, but once Rockefeller wouldn't back down, all bets were off.

Jack Strong cursed himself for not recognizing the pungent scent of oil on the air, for not figuring the reservation's abandonment had to have some deadly plan behind it. Now dozens of men were being roasted alive, their plight worsened by the secondary explosions that came when the oily flames found boxes of dynamite loaded onto wagons. Huge curtains of flame exploded both out and up; the hot gush of wind blown into him was comparable to a cannon's backdraft.

Steeldust Jack made himself stay on the hilltop until the echoes of the final screams had faded into the descending night. He'd never get that sound from his ears, or the smell from his nostrils. Nor had he ever felt more helpless. The Indians may have prevailed in this battle, but the war against the likes of John D. Rockefeller was one they were destined to lose.

The flames were still raging when Jack Strong finally walked his horse down the hillside. He wasn't sure if Rockefeller was among the survivors who'd managed to flee. But before he could give the matter more thought, his eyes settled on one of the strangest sights he'd ever seen.

The flames had all spread downwind from the Comanche corn crops, miraculously sparing them. Stalks blew in the smoke-rich air, seeming to dodge the floating embers that disappeared into the fall of night before Steeldust Jack's eyes.

91

San Antonio, Texas

"Opinions vary as to how many of Rockefeller's men died that day," D.W. Tepper finished. "I've heard as many as fifty to as few as a dozen. You won't find any of that written up in any Texas history book, but it's supposed to be the God's honest truth of what happened."

"But you don't think so," said Caitlin.

"In spite of all the money he spread around, I think there were plenty in Austin back then who wanted John D. Rockefeller, and everything he represented, out

STRONG COLD DEAD 381

of the state. He was a Northerner, and I doubt the folks in Austin fancied him any more than the Comanche did. Who knows, maybe they were in it together, since where else did the money come from to help the Indians rebuild the reservation? They reclaimed the land sometime in the next decade, led by a leader who called himself White Eagle."

"You're kidding."

"Wish I was, Ranger."

"If it's not the whole truth, it's something close. All that's missing is the part about what killed those gunmen in the hotel. We found a hidden chamber in that cave just off White Eagle's land that looked like something out of the Inquisition. I think they chained Comanche warriors inside there after pumping them full of peyote and unleashing them to kill. I think they used a version of this neurotoxin ISIS is after to incapacitate their victims first, so they couldn't fight back. Create the illusion it was monsters, not men, who did it. Nature taking care of its own," Caitlin said, repeating the words of both White Eagle and Isa-tai. "Just like that work foreman found torn apart a couple nights ago, and Rockefeller's hired guns in 1874. History repeating itself, the Comanche making the same point now they made back then."

Caitlin stopped short of mentioning Dylan's Miraculous Medal being found in the vicinity of the construction foreman's body, the boy being set up as the killer by the same girl who'd rescued him from the woods last night—a contradiction she still couldn't make sense of.

Caitlin watched Tepper fan a Marlboro from his

pack and then press it back downward when he caught her disapproving stare. "Does this story belong in the fact or fiction section of the library, Ranger?"

"You tell me, D.W., because I believe there's one chapter still missing."

This time, Tepper finished the process of knocking his Marlboro from the pack. He stuck the cigarette in his mouth and raised his lighter, Caitlin's glare stopping him.

"We're about to take on ISIS, Ranger. I believe I'm entitled to a smoke. Now, if you want to know how things finished up for Steeldust Jack Strong and John D. Rockefeller, I need to hear what Cray Rawls told you, first."

"He believes he's found the cure for cancer on that reservation, Captain."

"And what's that got to do with whatever ISIS is after?" Tepper asked her, finally lighting his cigarette.

"I think they're one and the same. What survived the fire back in Steeldust Jack's time? What was it the Comanche needed to preserve?"

"Their corn."

"Not just the corn," Caitlin told him. "Something that was growing on it. Something that lengthened the life span of the Comanche, just like it lengthened the lives of the giant bats that attacked us the other night."

"You can explain how that pertains to ISIS on the way," Jones said, stepping back into the office and leaving the door open behind him. "I've got choppers prepping now. We need to get a move on."

"Choppers, *plural*?"

"Looks like we're going to war up in Dallas," Jones said, turning all his focus on Caitlin. "Speaking of which, where's your boyfriend?"

Tepper dropped the cigarette to the floor and crushed it with his boot. "I must've forgot to mention that apparently he's left the building with Elvis. Your friend King Kong says he got a text message and tore off."

"A text message from who?"

"I'll give you two guesses, Ranger."

92

BALCONES CANYONLANDS, TEXAS

Dylan was still alive.

That was something, anyway, Cort Wesley figured. He clutched his cell phone in his grasp as he drove, to make sure he'd feel the buzz of his son's next text message coming through. He hadn't recognized the phone number, then saw DYLAN in the first text and knew his son must be using a burner phone and, against everything that made any sense at all, had returned to the Comanche reservation where he could easily have died the night before.

HURRY! the next message had pleaded, after explaining where he was, and that's what Cort Wesley had been doing ever since, driving into the sun until it burned his eyes. For some reason, he didn't put on his sunglasses or lower the visor, maybe to make it so he couldn't see things clearly, since, when it came to Dylan, he might as well be seeing nothing.

"*Well, bubba,*" Leroy Epps started, from the passenger seat.

"I don't want to hear it, champ."

"*You ain't even got a notion of what I was gonna say.*"

"Whatever it is, I don't want to hear it."

"*Never had kids of my own,*" the ghost said, settling back in the seat. "*Never going to now, circumstances being what they is.*" Epps regarded Cort Wesley closer. "*That makes yours as close as I'm gonna come, but I'm in no particular rush to see one of them on my side instead of yours.*"

"That makes two of us."

For some reason, he had the sense that Dylan had uncovered whatever Daniel Cross had found on the Comanche reservation while working for Sam Bob Jackson, whatever it was he'd used to kill two dozen people in an Austin diner and now intended to hand over to ISIS.

It was a beautiful day, the afternoon heat beginning to build outside his truck, just making its presence felt inside the cab. Cort Wesley realized he was sweating up a storm and that he'd neglected to turn on the air-conditioning after closing the truck's windows. He slid them open again, needing to feel the real air and hear the sounds of the outside.

"*'Bout time, bubba,*" the ghost of Leroy Epps told him. "*I didn't think I could sweat no more, but at two hundred degrees, I guess anything's possible.*"

"Why don't you hitch a ride with somebody else, then?"

"And miss out on such wonderful company and conversation? You out of your mind?"

"I'm talking to a goddamn ghost."

Cort Wesley could have sworn he heard the leather crackle as old Leroy leaned back in his seat and stuck his right hand out the window. *"Your boy's always one to finish what he starts, bubba."*

"The problem being, champ, maybe this is the time it finishes him instead."

93

DALLAS, TEXAS

Jones had arranged for a pair of Black Hawk UH-60 helicopters out of Martindale, a Texas Army National Guard airfield in eastern San Antonio, ten miles from Texas Ranger Company F headquarters. Guillermo Paz's seven men, along with their weapons, were squeezed into the trailing Black Hawk, while Jones's chopper was running in the lead.

Caitlin had never ridden in a Black Hawk before, but her unhinged nerves settled a few minutes after takeoff. Across from her, Young Roger looked much the worse for wear, doing his best to compose himself with deep breath after deep breath. Guillermo Paz sat on the other side of her, with Royal Canadian Mounted Police officer Pierre Beauchamp seated next to Young

Roger. Captain Tepper was along for the ride, too, just as Cort Wesley should have been, if he weren't off somewhere else, not answering her calls.

Dylan . . .

Caitlin didn't need Cort Wesley to call to tell her that much. The boy had an uncanny nose for trouble, but this time he may have finally found a Goliath he couldn't drop with a slingshot. Something was going on for sure on that Indian reservation, and Dylan was right in the middle of all of it. Apple of his father's eye, sticking that nose of his where it didn't belong.

"We got twenty-seven minutes until we land at the Grand Prairie base on Mountain Creek Lake, Ranger," Tepper said over his headset, which was just loud enough to be heard over the engine and rotor sounds. "That's how long you got to tell us less fortunate souls what you figured out."

"Comes down to fungus, Captain."

"Fungus?"

"Corn fungus, specifically," Caitlin told them all, recalling Cray Rawls's revelations and ready to gauge Young Roger's milk-white face for a reaction. "Also known by its Aztec name of *cuitlacoche.* Looks like a gray, stone-shaped growth when the corn's picked, and turns into a gunky, tar-like mush when cooked."

"Did I pass out from exhaustion, or did you just call a fungus the weapon of mass destruction that ISIS is after?" Tepper groused, shaking his head.

Young Roger answered him before Caitlin had the chance. "Mexican farmers also call it *el oro negro,* or black gold."

"Thanks, son, I truly appreciate the agricultural perspective here."

But Young Roger wasn't finished yet. "The fungus grows inside corn husks. *Cuitlacoche* flourishes when droplets of rain seep into a stalk of corn and the kernels begin to rot. The fungus can grow over, or side by side with, the kernels themselves."

"So just how," Jones chimed in, "do we go from there to a genuine weapon of mass destruction?"

"I'd be guessing, without an actual specimen to analyze."

"So guess, son."

"A catalyst." Young Roger shrugged, as if he wasn't totally convinced himself. "Something that altered the genetic structure of the fungus to create a mutation that can be weaponized."

"Forget *can be*," Jones said. "Try *has been* and *will be*."

"Not if we can help it," Caitlin reminded him.

"Figure of speech, Ranger."

"And you're forgetting something, Jones, the wild card in all this: Cray Rawls wasn't after what created that fungus because it's a weapon; he was after it in the belief he'd found the cure for cancer."

"So how can something be deadly and medicinal at the same time?" Jones wondered.

"Because plenty of the most effective drug therapies are, at their core, toxic," Young Roger told him. "And the likelihood is that the Comanche developed a natural immunity and resistance to the toxic effects of this particular *cuitlacoche*. While this strain might kill anyone exposed to it in concentrated forms, like the people in that Austin diner, it extended the lives of these Comanche to a dramatically quantitative degree and basically eliminated cancer from their existence."

"So Native peoples have been eating this shit since the time of the Aztecs." Jones nodded. "Only, not all of them lived forever and, last time I checked, they never created a weapon of mass destruction. One of you want to try telling me what's different here?"

"I believe I may have an idea," said Pierre Beauchamp of the Royal Canadian Mounted Police.

94

BALCONES CANYONLANDS, TEXAS

Dylan stroked Ela's hair, continuing to say anything that came to his mind, in the hope she'd open her eyes again. When she didn't, he just kept stroking, speaking, and hoping.

He wished he'd never taken that damn Native American studies class, wished he'd never met her or got involved in all this.

What was I thinking?

He wasn't. Again. Dropping out of school, temporarily or not, to take part in an adventure for a greater cause that had turned out to be a crock of shit. He was only here because he was part of a grand scheme that Ela had ultimately abandoned. But for some reason that didn't bother him, beyond the fact that he'd let himself be played for a fool.

Again.

It was like he had "Sucker for Love" tattooed across his forehead. Was it really that obvious?

Dylan was a prisoner of his emotions, just as Ela was of her beliefs. In both cases, their vision had ended up skewed; they had seen what they wanted to be before them, instead of what was really there.

"We're going to stop this," he heard himself saying. "No one else is going to get hurt."

He had no idea how the shit piled in that limestone storage chamber worked, only that it had to be the source of whatever Ela and the Lost Boys had really been up to—whatever the schematic, kind of a map, of some area of Houston was really about.

Dylan . . .

He heard his father's voice in his head, wanted to tell Cort Wesley that he had been right all along and that Dylan only wished he could do it all over again.

"Dylan."

This time the voice was accompanied by a gentle but strong grasp of his shoulder. He looked up to see Cort Wesley Masters leaning over him, eyeing Ela sadly.

"She's dead, son."

"I . . . think I knew that."

Dylan retrieved the schematic, map, or whatever it was from the ground and extended it upward.

"What's this?" his father asked him.

"You tell me, Dad," he said, feeling the tears welling in his eyes. "But whatever it is, it's not good."

95

DALLAS, TEXAS

"Rawls pretty much confirmed my thinking when he finally came clean about the fact he's there for water and not oil," Pierre Beauchamp continued, inside the Black Hawk cabin, as they streaked through the sky toward Dallas. "That Inuit village where the residents all died was located on a volcanic plain, directly over a fault line, accounting for high acid levels from time to time in the river they drew their water from. Before I came down here, I did some checking and learned there's a similarly ancient volcanic plane located in the general area beneath that Indian reservation as well."

Probably right in the area of White Eagle's patch of land, Caitlin thought, as Young Roger leaned forward.

"So you figure some portion of the aquifer feeding the reservation its water has levels of acidity comparable to this river," he presumed.

Beauchamp nodded. "Corn wasn't a staple of the Inuit diet; fish was. So, yes, I think the fish was contaminated with the very same toxin that killed all those people in that Austin diner. And since that area has been abandoned ever since, we have no way of knowing how often the toxicity has returned."

"But like you said," started Caitlin, "fish was as much a part of the Inuit diet as corn is for the Comanche on that reservation. But I'm guessing only a small portion of the *cuitlacoche* is affected when the contaminated water leaches upward. And that's the portion that can be weaponized."

"All well and good," Jones noted. "But in case we're forgetting, those folks in Hoover's Cooking weren't killed by accidental leaching. They were murdered, and in case you didn't read the report, no trace of any such toxin was found in the remains of their food—either what was left on their plates or inside their stomachs."

"That's because it was gone," Caitlin interjected.

"Ranger," said Captain Tepper, holding his box of Marlboro reds in his lap, "if I weren't strapped into this damn thing, I'd come over there and shake some sense into you."

"Hear me out on this, Captain. It's the only thing that makes any sense, the only explanation for how the waitstaff in Hoover's was killed too, even though they didn't eat or drink anything during the same period."

"Christ on a crutch. So what killed them?"

"Smell," Young Roger answered, before Caitlin could. "The neurotoxin entered the body through the nasal cavity, just like it did to those Inuit in 1930." He paused to let that sink in, then went on. "More specifically, through the paranasal sinuses. I'd recommend the CDC teams on the ground now perform detailed examinations of those sinuses in the remains of the victims, along with the throat, larynx, and primary nasal passages, in search of any abnormalities in the form of lesions or even the slightest tissue damage. I expect they'll find enough—at least something that proves we're looking at a weapon spread through smell."

Caitlin turned back toward Tepper. "Go back to the days Jack Strong got himself involved with the same reservation, D.W. All those men who got torn apart in those hotel rooms were already dead, or totally incapacitated, when they were attacked. That's how it all happened so fast; that's why they never even screamed. The Comanche were trying to scare John D. Rockefeller off by perpetuating the myth of a monster spawned by nature, some otherworldly force rising when necessary to protect them. But that monster was no more than warriors turned into violent killing machines after ingesting a particularly potent strain of peyote. That's what those manacles I found in the cave were for, to keep the warriors restrained until the effects of the drug finally wore off."

"You're saying they brought their mythical killer back when the need arose," said Jones, "only this time thanks to Cray Rawls instead of John D. Rockefeller."

"I believe so, yes. And I asked Young Roger here to look into the possibility of smell as a weapon, even before I had any inkling about this corn fungus. This ringing any bells with you, Jones? Because the military's had a program in it for decades."

"Sure," Jones cut in, "under nonlethal weapons development. Last time I checked, though, what we're facing here is pretty damn lethal."

"On that subject," began Young Roger, "in 2007, a fireball hurtled out of the sky and blasted a forty-foot crater in Peru. The crater filled with boiling liquid and a noxious gas poured out that sent dozens of people to the hospital. Some of them suffered temporary paralysis and nerve damage. It was determined that whatever leaked out of that crater affected their nervous systems. Sound familiar?"

"Any of them die, kid?"

"Not a one," Young Roger told Jones. "But you ever hear of an Israeli company called Odortec?"

Jones stiffened. "That's classified."

"Not here, it's not," said Tepper. "Keep talking, son."

"Odortec has been specializing in scent-based weapons of the *nonlethal* variety for law enforcement for years. Word is they've expanded their horizons considerably as of late."

"Word from where?" Jones challenged.

"The Deep Web. Would you like me to cite the specifics?" Young Roger asked him.

"Homeland's connected to this company . . . have I got that right, Jones?" Caitlin challenged.

"I'm taking the Fifth," he said, still glaring at Young Roger.

"The fact that the toxin disappears when the smell does makes it close to the perfect weapon," Young Roger said, addressing all of them. "No trace elements, no residue, minimal collateral damage, and no way to trace anything to potential perpetrators."

"I imagine that would make aroma the perfect means of delivery," Caitlin ventured. "Right, Jones? An untraceable weapon of mass destruction."

"You said it," Jones conceded. "I didn't."

"You might as well have," Caitlin told him. "Man oh man, where does it stop?"

"It doesn't, Ranger. You want to talk to me about new avenues in lethal weapons development, fine, let's have that conversation. Right now, people scream when we use drones; they scream when we launch raids; they scream when we take out a wedding party to take out a dozen militants who'd cut the heads off their own children."

"Something I'm trying to get straight here," Captain Tepper said, his words aimed squarely at Young Roger. "These two incidents, the one up in Canada a long way back and now the one down here at Hoover's—it wasn't *eating* the food that did the deed; it was *smelling* it?"

"That's right."

"But in both cases the food had to be cooked . . . have I got that right, son?"

"As rain, Captain. An aquifer on that reservation created a super-deadly strain of corn fungus, but not until heat was added to the equation. Kind of like a final catalyst."

"Any kind of heat?"

"I suppose. Why?"

"Because," Caitlin answered, before Tepper could, her gaze fixed on Jones, "what would happen, exactly, if somebody blew up a whole bunch of that toxic *cuitlacoche*?"

96

BALCONES CANYONLANDS, TEXAS

Cort Wesley studied the bloodied piece of paper that Ela had given Dylan.

"Ten red Xs," Dylan said, following his eyes, standing over Ela Nocona's body, which was now covered with an extra tarpaulin. "I think it's a map. I think they're bombs."

"Safe assumption." Cort Wesley nodded, without looking up.

"Ela said something about backpacks. She stopped her cousins from using whatever was inside them, but then the killers showed up. She said they spoke Arabic."

"Arabic," Cort Wesley repeated, drawing out the syllables.

"You have any idea what that's a map of . . . where in Houston?"

Cort Wesley folded it back up. "I think I do, son. Now let's see if we can get there in time."

Cort Wesley climbed the ladder back into the shed first, lending Dylan a hand the final stretch of the way.

"You need to call Caitlin, Dad."

"That's the plan."

Cort Wesley opened the shed door all the way, revealing what looked like a wizened corpse standing before them, holding an ancient double-barreled shotgun.

"This is as far you go," said White Eagle.

97

DALLAS, TEXAS

Both Black Hawks landed at the Grand Prairie Armed Forces Reserve Complex on Mountain Creek Lake in southwest Dallas, a fifteen-minute drive from Klyde Warren Park.

"We got drones up and active over the target zone," Jones reported, eyes fixed on a tablet, after they piled into a pair of massive SUVs.

"What about intelligence as to who Cross and company might be meeting there?" Caitlin asked him.

"We're running every picture of every person who entered the country flying international in the past forty-eight hours. Problem we're facing is that plenty of these ISIS fighters aren't in any databases, and if the mother ship in Syria did send a team here, you can bet it would consist of those not on our radar."

"What about running a cross-match on all known leaders?"

"Those deployments at Quantico have served you well, Ranger."

"Just answer the question, Jones."

"Nothing, so far, from our facial recognition software. We get a hit out of Klyde Warren Park, it'll trigger an alarm you'll hear from coast to coast."

"Is that supposed to make me breathe easier?"

Jones looked up from his tablet. "Right now, we're not just the front line on this, we're the only line. Washington only wants to know what it wants to know. No Black Hawks were requisitioned out of Martindale. We never landed at Grand Prairie, and the SUVS we're riding in don't have tags that match up with any existing registration. For all intents and purposes, we're not here now and whatever ends up going down in Klyde Warren Park will lead absolutely nowhere."

"Just the way you like it, Jones."

"Not a question of like; it's a question of need. If we show up and find Zurif, Saflin, and a geek with the secrets of the universe, it's going to get messy. We show up and find ISIS making a field trip, it's going to get even messier. Right up your alley," Jones said, just as his tablet made a pinging sound. He zoomed in on what the drones circling overhead had locked onto below, in Klyde Warren Park. "Looks like we've got a firm location."

He angled the tablet screen so Caitlin could see the frozen image of three figures seated at a picnic table, all immediately recognizable.

"What about the fourth guy?" she asked Jones.

PART TEN

Charlie Miller was one of the first Rangers to see the value of the Colt 1911 pistol as a peace officer's weapon. However, Miller had a severe dislike for the grip safety on the pistol. His solution was to tie the grip safety down with a length of rawhide. He also carried his pistol with a round in the chamber and the hammer on half cock (a practice that is definitely not recommended). To make matters even more interesting, Miller disdained the use of a holster and generally just carried the .45 auto shoved down in the front of his pants. In later years, his big belly pretty well made this a concealed-carry technique.

—Sheriff Jim Wilson, "Texas Ranger Tales"
http://sheriffjimwilson.com/2011/10/14/texas
-ranger-tales

98

The SUVs were able to make spaces for themselves in a rear corner of a parking lot on the northbound Woodall Rodgers Freeway access road, normally reserved for the park's Savor restaurant. They had no staging area per se and had to rely on the cover of the SUVs for their final weapons check and prep.

"What'd you tell the Dallas cops?" Caitlin asked Jones.

"What they need to know: nothing."

"Come again?"

"You want to run the risk of them doing something stupid?"

"We could use the backup if this goes bad, Jones. To help with the evacuation, if nothing else."

"I'll take that under advisement," he said, and turned away.

The logistics necessitated that Paz and his men use only light weaponry, including submachine guns tucked under light jackets that fell just below their waists. Even without flak jackets, which Guillermo Paz never allowed his men to wear, that was sure to draw some attention to them. A necessary trade-off, and one that

Jones was willing to accept, given that their targets were stationary and confined.

Both the sprawl and the clutter bred by the carnival would work in their favor, offering additional camouflage for Paz's men. Jones never questioned Paz on how he handled such matters, just pointed the big man in a direction and let him off his leash.

"I hope you're reading this right," Caitlin said to him.

"Just keep your nose out of it, Ranger."

"Be glad to, Jones, after you tell me why they're meeting where thousands of people can see them?"

"Good question. Got an answer?"

"Only that maybe it was the fourth man's idea," Caitlin ventured, an instant before Jones's iPad began chiming.

Daniel Cross had laid it all out for Hatim Abd al-Aziz. How he could make the weapon work in either an open or a confined space. How much it would take, and how long to handle the logistics. The ISIS commander drank his words in, almost giddy at the prospects and enamored by the supply his men would soon be returning to the Indian reservation to collect.

Al-Aziz seemed to bow his head slightly. "You said you were not a Muslim."

"I'm not."

"Perhaps not in this life. But in another you were a soldier of God, likely fighting by my side then as you are now. Perhaps then, too, you bestowed a great gift upon our movement, to enable us to realize God's will.

Tell me how it will happen. Tell me the instruments by which His plan will be realized."

"Extreme temperatures, like when the stuff is cooked, release the aroma. That aroma indicates the neurotoxin has been activated. If you can smell it, you're dead."

"Extreme temperatures," al-Aziz repeated. "That would, of course, include percussion, yes? I speak of spreading this toxin over a wider expanse through the use of explosives."

"For sure," said Cross, nodding enthusiastically, "if the results of the testing I've done is any indication. One thing to keep in mind is that the effects last only as long, and reach as far, as the aroma. Once the smell dissipates, it's over."

"But if such a blast were detonated over a city as crowded as, say, this place?" the ISIS commander wondered, spinning his gaze about Klyde Warren Park.

"You'd have close to a one hundred percent mortality rate," Daniel Cross told him, imagining just that, on these premises in the coming days.

"One hundred percent."

"No survivors. None whatsoever."

"*Bismillah*," al-Aziz said, closing his eyes. "In the name of Allah."

The park had continued to fill up around them, only narrow gaps left between the various rides, booths, and attractions of the carnival stretched across the rolling, flat lawn. The result was to compress the crowd tighter and tighter.

If such a blast were detonated over a city . . .

Cross imagined it happening here, instead. Thousands dead, literally within seconds. Falling as they stood.

Wow, was all he could think.

99

"You really going to shoot us, Chief?" Cort Wesley asked White Eagle, buying the time he needed to ease Dylan all the way behind him. "Go ahead. We'll say hello to your granddaughter, or whatever she is, for you."

Doubt crossed White Eagle's expression, not fitting him right.

"She's dead down there," Cort Wesley continued. "Her cousins, too. Killed by human monsters I intend to hunt down, if you'll stand aside and get out of my way."

The old man remained rigidly planted in place, but his expression wavered, its confidence gone.

"You don't think I could take that gun away from you or shoot you dead right now? But I'm not going to do that, because it would be too easy. You put your crazy thoughts inside that girl's head and never bothered to rein her in when she went too far."

The shotgun began trembling in White Eagle's grasp.

"You goaded her and those boys into pretending this was still the nineteenth century. You got them killed, old man. I don't care if you're a hundred and fifty years old or a thousand. You're a self-centered asshole who didn't take care of the people who needed him."

"Where is she?" White Eagle stammered.

"Just inside the chamber where you stored your killing concoction those dead kids were going to unleash on Houston, until Ela stopped them. But she couldn't stop ISIS, so get out of my way and let me do it."

The shotgun barrel dropped toward the ground, as if suddenly weighed down. Cort Wesley started to advance, but White Eagle latched a bony grip onto his arm, holding him briefly in place. White Eagle's expression crinkled into a patchwork quilt of hatred and disgust, segmented by the way the sunlight framed it.

"Nothing else has worked," the old man insisted. "For almost two centuries, nothing else has worked. The defilers and spoilers of the land must be shown the error of their ways. They would build and build and build, until our way of life is gone. I stopped Rockefeller then. I'll stop these men now."

Cort Wesley shrugged off his grasp. "Yeah, keep telling yourself that."

He started on again, angling Dylan before him in case White Eagle had a mind to use the shotgun.

"Ela's map, that part of Houston," the boy said. "You recognize it, right, Dad?"

"Yes, son, I believe I do."

100

"Stand down! Stand down!" Jones ordered Paz and his men, who'd moved into flanking positions around the picnic table. "We've identified the fourth bogey! Repeat, we have ID on the fourth bogey!"

Caitlin and Jones had accessed the park off Olive Street and had appropriated an information kiosk next to Moody Plaza to set up a command center. Captain Tepper and Pierre Beauchamp, meanwhile, had hung back, near the exit closest to the picnic table in question, off Pearl Street and not far from the St. Paul DART station. If any of the targets fled, the thinking went, it would be in that direction.

Caitlin gazed at the flashing red box enclosing the fourth man at the picnic table. "Friend of yours?"

"The fucking Antichrist has joined the party. Head of ISIS's military operations. As in top dog. As in Hatim Abd al-Aziz, beheader in chief."

Caitlin hitched her light windbreaker back to expose her SIG Sauer. "Man like that wouldn't have come alone."

"Tell me something I don't know, Ranger. Colonel Paz, do you read me?" Jones said into his throat mic.

"We've identified six men already," Paz reported into their ears, "all heavily armed. My men are moving on them now. And I know this al-Aziz. He's an ethnic Chechen, raised in Turkey, who trained with my secret police in Venezuela. As brutal as they come, and always travels in the company of a man known only as Seyyef."

"The name never crossed my desk," Jones said.

"It's not a name so much as a title: *seyyef* means 'executioner' in Arabic. There's an old Arab folktale about a giant, shunned by a village, who gets revenge by blocking the sun from their crops. He was called Seyyef, too, for starving the villagers to death."

"A giant," Jones repeated. "You got eyes on him, Colonel?"

"I will. My men are in position and ready," Paz reported.

Homeland Security's private army, reserved for situations just like this.

"What's the certainty you've marked all the fighters al-Aziz brought with him?"

"In this crowd, not certain at all. Six seems light. I'd expect two or three more. Somewhere."

"What about Seyyef?"

"I'm still looking."

"A man that big shouldn't be too hard to find."

"Are you sure I'm not standing right behind you now?" Paz wondered.

Jones spun to find only Caitlin standing there.

"Something on your mind, Ranger?"

For some reason, she couldn't stop thinking about Daniel Cross. Viewing him, seated at that picnic table, she was seeing the same frightened, gangly boy she'd met in an Austin jail over a decade before. She'd promised him she'd stand by him, always stick around, and then had gone away. Now fate had brought them back together, though Cross was on the verge of doing far more damage this time, unless she could stop him.

Caitlin spied a banner strung between two posts hammered into the ground just off the carnival's makeshift midway. "How about we take the battle to them, Jones?"

"Tell me more about this holy weapon," Al-Aziz said to Daniel Cross, his marble-like eyes seeming to flash. "The Indians have used it themselves?"

"According to legend, yes."

"Legend," al-Aziz echoed. "Then how is it this weapon has been kept secret for so long?"

"First of all, the *cuitlacoche* that's grown on the reservation is consumed there. And the Comanche have built up a natural resistance to its deadly effects, after making it a staple of their diet for so many centuries. Secondly, I've determined that the deadly strain of the fungus is limited to a relatively small patch of wild-growing corn in a remote corner of the reservation. I figure that's because the water feeding that area leaches out of a truly ancient aquifer, with just the right acid and alkaline balance to turn that particular strain of fungus deadly."

Al-Aziz leaned back, scratched at his freshly trimmed beard, and then crossed his arms. "And how many, here and elsewhere, could we kill with the amount of this fungus you can harvest off the Comanche land, before the authorities and this Texas Ranger catch on?"

"Not enough. But the fungus isn't the real weapon here; the water that produces it, the way it interacts with *cuitlacoche,* is," Cross told him, thinking of the still pond he'd found inside a cave just off the reservation. "With that water, I can figure out how to synthesize as much of the weapon as you need, a potentially unlimited supply."

Daniel Cross cast his gaze beyond al-Aziz, toward the now jam-packed crowd. Barely any foot of space on the former overpass was unoccupied for more than a second. Kids dragged their parents toward the rides, which spun in elegantly graceful motion, in stark contrast to the way the world really worked. Nearby, water splashed into the air from the mini flume ride, where cackling children rode faux motorized logs about a sweeping course. Cars clanked past them on the roller coaster that wound its way over the entire length of the carnival.

"It would take time, but I could do it," Cross heard himself tell al-Aziz, hating all the smiles more than anything else.

Smiles that disappeared when the first gunshots rang out.

101

KLYDE WARREN PARK, DALLAS, TEXAS

Except it wasn't gunfire at all but fireworks Caitlin had purchased at a nearby stand, which was already selling them in anticipation of the coming Fourth of July.

FIREWORKS! TWO FOR ONE SALE! read the banner she'd spotted.

She'd lit four packs aflame within seconds of each other, tossing them in that many different directions in the immediate area of the picnic table where the ISIS commander was seated with Daniel Cross and the kid's homegrown handlers. At first, all she could feel was a collective ripple in the crowd, as the press of startled carnival patrons reacted instinctively, before almost settling back down, once the truth became clear.

And then the ISIS fighters appeared, bursting out from everywhere at once, it seemed.

The crowd packed along the midway saw the gunmen first, the assault rifles sweeping about behind hateful, determined glares, fingers ready on triggers, waiting for their targets to appear, initially believing the firecrackers had been real gunfire. The chronology tightened, unfolding in still shots instead of video, starting with the recognition that it had been merely fireworks that had drawn them out, not gunshots.

The gunmen froze, eyes shifting but holding.

The carnival patrons froze, too, for the length of a breath, maybe two. Then they began to run, scattering in all directions at once, a swarm quickly filling what little space remained between the rides that swept and soared about the landscape, packed with children and families.

Leaving the ISIS fighters alone, holding their ground.

Exposed for Guillermo Paz's men to fire upon.

Al-Aziz had his own pistol out by then, aimed across the table at Zurif and Saflin, who had already lurched to their feet, backing off.

"You betrayed me . . ."

"No!"

"And now you pay the price for your treachery before Him!"

With that, al-Aziz shot them both in the face as Daniel Cross watched, realizing only then that he'd risen to his feet, too, and that urine was running down his leg. Al-Aziz swung toward him, pistol leading.

"We will kill them," the ISIS commander sneered hatefully. "We will kill all of them! *Allahu a'lam . . .* Allah knows best!"

Al-Aziz grabbed Cross by the arm and dragged him into the panicked throngs, as actual gunfire burst from everywhere at once.

The familiar scent of gun smoke filled the air as Caitlin shoved her way against the grain of the crowd, in al-Aziz's and Daniel Cross's wake. Every time she drew reasonably close, another surge from the crowd forced her back. The jostling was uneven, unpredictable, thrown to the whims of the gunfight that had erupted between Paz's troops and the ISIS gunmen.

The clang and echoing racket of fire made for a constant din in the air, like soft thunder rumbling from one clap seamlessly into another. The panicked cries and screams drowned it out in splotches, the whole scene backed by the melodic hum of the local radio station's greatest hits medley playing over a set of freestanding loudspeakers, which toppled to the ground under the panicked flight. Divergent streams of patrons fled the park in all directions, in the shadow of the skyscrapers enclosing it, darting into traffic running east and west, which had almost immediately ground to a complete snarl punctuated by screeching brakes and honking horns.

Caitlin lost track of al-Aziz and Daniel Cross and focused her efforts on the nearest ISIS gunman instead. He was firing a shaved-down Kalashnikov with one hand, using a teenage girl as a human shield with the other, to ward off Paz's men. More than one bystander had fallen to his fire, when Caitlin mounted one picnic table and then leaped onto another, which brought her over and behind him. The ISIS gunman was twisting his weapon on her when she fired twice, one bullet taking him high in the shoulder and the second obliterating the right side of his jaw.

That was enough for his hostage to tear free of his grasp. The man still had the presence of mind to swing in the direction of a pair of Paz's soldiers, who pulverized him with twin automatic bursts. Fired from opposing directions, the bullets had the bizarre effect of holding the ISIS gunman upright until both stopped firing and he crumpled in a heap.

Caitlin had moved on by that point, focusing her efforts on shepherding as many of the panicked to safety in the adjoining streets as she could, amid the traffic clog. The windshields of numerous vehicles had been struck by stray gunfire, which continued to clack away in a constant cacophony, courtesy of a close-in firefight like nothing she'd ever witnessed before. Paz's men swept and swerved about the crowd, paying little heed to the collective safety of bystanders, whose presence didn't seem to fully register with them. They were killers, plain and simple, chosen by the colonel for their prowess and their willingness to utilize it.

Caitlin added her help and fire to bystanders, pulling the wounded to safety, as far out of harm's way as she could. Amid it all, in insane counterpoint, the rides continued to twirl and spin, on three- to five-minute looped cycles that swept riders about, through, and above the carnage and panic, as more people rushed to flee Klyde Warren Park.

"Go, go, go!" she instructed, herding panicked patrons along, ready the whole time with her SIG Sauer.

An ISIS fighter, wounded by fire from Paz's troops, snapped a fresh magazine into his Kalashnikov and started to sweep it forward. Caitlin poured bullets from her SIG into him, punching him backwards until he flopped over a trash container and took it down with him to the grass. Gunfire continued to sound, a bit more sporadically now, as she turned her attention back to protecting the crowd.

And spotted al-Aziz dragging Daniel Cross with him toward the botanical garden and the nearest exit, which spilled out not far from Captain Tepper's and Beauchamp's position.

"You read me, Captain?" she said into her hand mic.

"Got ourselves a genuine shit storm out here."

"It might be about to get heavier. Al-Aziz is headed your way with Daniel Cross in tow."

"Jesus H., Ranger. Where's Lee Harvey Oswald when you need him? The Mountie and I will be ready."

Caitlin lit out after al-Aziz, stopping just short of the boarding point for the roller coaster, pistol steadied, with al-Aziz square in her sights. She was about to fire, when a huge shape obscured her vision of everything ahead, seeming to block out the whole world, in the last moment before she was launched airborne.

102

HOUSTON, TEXAS

Dylan could only shake his head when Cort Wesley finished explaining Ela's map. "Pedestrian tunnels? Beneath Houston? How could I never have heard of them?"

"Because you never had call to use them, son," Cort Wesley told him. "Twenty feet below street level, spanning six miles over maybe a hundred city blocks. Whole bunch of access points from buildings and off the streets. A subterranean world all onto itself."

Dylan looked down at the map lying on his lap, as Cort Wesley sped down an access ramp to Route 290 that would connect up with the 610 into Houston. "Then these ten red X's . . ."

"Major chokepoints at what's got to be one of the most congested areas during rush hour, all centered around the Downtown loop where lots of the retail establishments are concentrated."

"Let me have your phone."

"Jesus," Dylan said, jogging through the app he'd just downloaded for Houston's underground tunnels on

Cort Wesley's smart phone, "there's like two hundred stores. They got everything down there."

"Including people, lots of them. In a confined space where that shit can spread at will."

Dylan was trying to compare a schematic featured on the app to the red X's on Ela's map. "You're right. They're all in one central area, along the tunnels converging on this food court here. Shit, you wouldn't believe how many Starbucks are down there." He shook his head. "Near as I can tell each of the X's is located near one of the entrances."

"Chokepoints," Cort Wesley repeated, "like I said."

"Each between fifty and a hundred yards apart, all centered around this part they call the Downtown Loop."

"Highly congested for sure and accessible via the McKinney Garage where the terrorists can all park." Cort Wesley checked his truck's dashboard clock. "Give me my phone back. I need to try Caitlin again."

Cort Wesley had never driven faster, the miles to Houston along U.S. 290 East dragging on forever. Caitlin wasn't answering her phone, Jones wasn't answering his phone, nobody was answering their phone. And he didn't know if he was going to reach Houston in time for it to matter. His navigation screen had read 166 miles at the outset of the trip, and they had covered the bulk of those already, slipping from one lane into another, then veering sharply across traffic when space allowed, the whole time holding his breath against the possibility of congestion or an accident snarling traffic. He was ever so glad, in that moment, that he'd let Dylan and Luke talk him into buying the more expensive truck model, which included the sport package.

"I'm sorry, son," he said, breaking the silence that had settled between them.

"For what?"

"For Ela."

"She'd tried to stop them, Dad. She changed her mind."

"I know."

"I was holding her when she died. It brought me back to when Mom died. I never wanted to feel that way again."

Cort Wesley swallowed hard. "You said it yourself, son. It was different this time."

The boy twisted toward him, tugging against the bonds of his shoulder harness. "Sure it was. Because you were right all along. I let myself be duped. I didn't see it coming 'cause all I saw was Ela. I feel like an idiot. I feel like it's my fault."

"How's that?"

"I should've known I was getting played. I should have played her instead."

"You mean, like, show her the error of her ways?"

"Something like that. At least get her to change her mind, get her to realize she had things wrong."

Cort Wesley took a deep breath that dissolved into a sigh. "I believe you did that, son."

"I don't know if I can ever go back to school now, not after this."

"Not a decision you need to make today."

Dylan turned back toward the windshield, board-stiff in his seat. "We're gonna kill them, right? These ISIS fighters who killed Ela. Just tell me we're gonna get some payback here."

Cort Wesley's expression fixed as flat as the windshield glass. "Count on it."

103

Klyde Warren Park, Dallas, Texas

Caitlin's grandfather always talked about vision, when it came to gunfighters. Not that they could see better so much as they could see more. Like, three things at once: left, right, and center.

Caitlin's center was dominated by the huge, looming shape of al-Aziz's chief henchman, Seyyef, his head like an anvil atop his shoulders.

To her right, the whirling shape of Guillermo Paz barreled forward against the grain of fleeing families, a path seeming to open for him down a center his charge created.

To her left, al-Aziz was pushing his way through the mass of people fleeing the park on the Pearl Street side, dragging Daniel Cross with him.

Center and right merged as Paz slammed into Seyyef in a collision akin to a pair of semis in a head-on, the two huge forms hurtling backwards. The collective force pitched them up and over the lead car of the roller coaster, which had just discharged the last of its riders.

Dazed, Caitlin fought to reclaim her footing, feeling instantly woozy when she did, the world all out of kilter. She leaned against a stanchion, holding on to a rope divider for balance, vision clearing all the way to reveal Jones yanking Daniel Cross from al-Aziz's grasp, the kid surging away toward the exit beyond the botanical garden.

The two men struggled amid a brief rainbow of muzzle flashes. Jones staggered now, still pushing on as al-Aziz retreated, charging in the opposite direction, to the east, clinging to the tree line.

Caitlin steadied herself against the stanchion, turning back to see the twin hulking shapes of Paz and Seyyef in hand-to-hand struggle. Their search for any advantage they could muster generated enough force to send the gravity-fed coaster rolling down the track, where it banked into the initial climb and then picked up speed as it crested, into the first dip.

Caitlin's head was on fire. Her teeth were chattering. She realized she'd dropped her pistol and she stooped to retrieve it, her mind clawing at the memory of al-Aziz sprinting across the park, likely toward the exit that spilled out on Harwood Street.

Caitlin caught sight of Jones sinking to his knees, bleeding from everywhere at once it seemed, but still with the presence of mind to wave her on, after Hatim Abd al-Aziz.

She lit out in his wake, bettering her angle just in time to cut off his route to Harwood Street, unleashing a torrent of fire. He spun to return it, and his shots went wild as he veered back into the cover of the amusement park and the attraction set off in the very rear, on the grass in front of one of the performance pavilions: the Chamber of Horrors.

Guillermo Paz had known men as big as Seyyef, and as strong, but never one who was both, and Seyyef had a litheness and agility that belied his bulk and brutish appearance. Paz could tell from the first blow he landed that the man used pain, probably liked pain, was impervious to strikes powerful enough to shatter bone. He'd heard boxers were like that, so used to being struck that taking the blow becomes second nature.

The modest roller coaster was into its second rise before Paz realized they were moving, adjusting his footing and balance to make that motion work for him. Claiming the high ground that a moment before had been the low ground. The move seemed to confuse Seyyef, who nonetheless absorbed a brutal flurry of strikes that shattered his jaw and right cheek. One eye was closed now, the other bulging with rage and the sense of battling an opponent equal to him.

True to his name, Seyyef was an executioner who knew how to kill.

Paz was a soldier, a killer too, but one who knew combat. The advantage had turned clearly his way, until Seyyef projected all of his vast bulk forward, whether by fortune or by design, just as the coaster dropped into a fresh dip, giving the high ground back to him. And before Paz knew it, he was bent over the front of the car, Seyyef jamming his face down toward the track.

Caitlin followed al-Aziz through the lingering chaos to the Chamber of Horrors, laggardly at first, forcing the light-headedness from her consciousness and summoning whatever it took to gather herself and beat back the pounding that felt like a knife poking around inside her skull.

She fired when al-Aziz neared the flat-roofed modular building, but her shots flew wildly askew. He spun and returned her fire with his own, just before disappearing into the structure.

Caitlin stayed on his tail, charging toward the same double doors al-Aziz had used, into a black void. Suddenly she was a little girl again, struck by the memory of her father forcing her to board a similar ride with him when she was a kid.

I'm too scared!

That's why you have to do this, little girl.

Her father had dragged her on and lifted her into the lead car, next to him. She was still crying when the car crashed through a pair of double doors painted to look like the devil's mouth.

Now Caitlin found herself charging through a set of double doors made up to look like . . . the devil's mouth. The warped wood and fading colors made Satan's teeth seem chipped.

Because this was the very same Chamber of Horrors, the same ride that had terrified her as a child, around thirty years ago. Time circled about, catching up, and Caitlin half expected to see her father in the next car as dangling skeletons dropped down before her.

———

Paz's face was jammed close enough to the track to smell the grease lubricant. He was helpless to do anything but force his neck and shoulder muscles up against Seyyef's desperately determined thrust downward. Paz, who had once pushed a man's face against a churning fan belt, wondered if this was payback for that. His entire life experience was on rewind, seeming to go only as far back as the first time he'd met the gaze of his Texas Ranger, Caitlin Strong. Wanting the glare that looked back at him to be his. To feel what she did, behind those steely eyes that had changed his life even as he was trying to take hers.

Paz felt the heat of the tracks, imagined the sparks generated by the friction flying upward when his skin met steel. And then he saw Caitlin Strong's eyes in his mind. It was enough to launch him backwards, feeling the sinews tearing in his neck muscles as he twisted around. Facing Seyyef, the brute's breath blowing a stench like roadkill into him, Paz smashed his ridged knuckles into a neck wrapped in layers of muscle. Felt them crunch into the softer cartilage, and the cartilage giving way in their path.

Coming apart, shattering. The man's breath bottlenecking in his throat, his face reddening, only forty-five seconds to a minute at most before he lost consciousness. Paz felt his balance waver as the coaster dropped into its final dip, sweeping round the perimeter of Klyde Warren Park, over Olive Street, in the same moment that Seyyef sank his hands into Paz's throat.

The past and present swirled together, merging, and Caitlin was a little girl, terrified of the dark once again. Monsters jumping out at her everywhere, even though she was on foot instead of huddled against her father in the lead car. Same monsters then as now, with some tweaking and touch-up. The ride had seemed so big and long then, so short and confined now, the real monster she sought lost to her somewhere in the darkness.

A shot rang out and a squiggly, slimy, insect-like thing dropped from the ceiling, severed from its guide wire. The only light came from the face of a clown with red bulbs for eyes, the constant din of laughter emanating from its mouth forming the only sound breaking the silence, except for the stray echoes of al-Aziz's gunshot, which left her hugging the floor.

She felt something cool, smelled something sweet, watched a faux ground mist formed of some dry ice concoction waft over a tombstone-rich fake ground, ghostlike beings lurching out of coffins rising from open graves. Caitlin almost shot two of them, then crawled on with the SIG Sauer extended before her, into the thickest reaches of the mist. Like she'd just dropped out of sight.

Then the graveyard was gone and she found herself in the tight, twisting confines of what looked like a cave, with snapping teeth attached to alien heads shooting out at her, one after the other, triggered by proximity sensors.

You have to do this, little girl.

Why, Daddy? Why?

Because fear ain't got no place in your life. I don't

*ever want you to be scared of anything, not a single
thing.*

And it had worked. After that first ride through
this very Chamber of Horrors, Caitlin was never scared
of anything again. Frightened maybe, but never scared.
And only in later years, when the truth that she had
suppressed the memory of witnessing her mother's
murder was revealed, did she realize why: because after that, whether she remembered it or not, her father
had known he had to make her confront her fears to
the point of becoming inoculated against them.

Caitlin found herself in a fake, fog-drenched bog.
She remembered how creatures sprang up through
trapdoors in the floor. Banshees or something, she
thought, all dressed in shapeless black rags. She found
herself shooting them as they burst upward, figuring
al-Aziz might be among them.

More gunshots rang out from beyond the bog section of the Chamber of Horrors, and Caitlin fired back
in their general direction, no worries about hitting innocent bystanders. Her memory of this place sharpened, time rewinding inside her throbbing head, which
felt stuffed with cotton. It was like she was six years
old again, wishing only that the ride would end. And it
would, soon. Just one more section to traverse before
she spilled out a set of double exit doors that matched
the entrance.

Caitlin raced that way, more of al-Aziz's bullets pinging the darkness, past and present melting together.

Guillermo Paz felt the blood bubbling in his brain, his breath all backed up and his lungs ready to burst, the slowly dying Seyyef squeezing the life out of him as well. Paz realized their car was roaring toward the gravity-fed ride's end, back at the children's park, barreling along into the final straightaway, where the attendant would brake the line of attached cars to a stop.

Except there was no attendant present anymore.

Which meant nobody was present to slow the cars' pace, meaning a violent collision with a standing set of identical cars currently occupying the rearmost section of the track. Meaning . . .

Feeling his thoughts beginning to slow, Paz worked his hands up between him and Seyyef, under the massive shape that seemed to be crushing his chest. He found a place deep inside himself where a reserve of strength had been building, from the time when he was a boy in his native Venezuela and a priest had died in his arms to the day a glimpse of his Texas Ranger's eyes had changed his life forever. Then Paz was hoisting Seyyef from him, the man's massive shape seeming to float before coming back down on the track, an instant before the two sets of cars rammed together.

Seyyef was crushed between them, his bones sounding like wood snapping when they broke, and Paz felt himself launched upward, breathing in the warm air as he went flying.

The final section of the Chamber of Horrors featured a swerving obstacle course through various monsters lunging for the cars as they passed. Caitlin drew close

STRONG COLD DEAD · 425

enough to them to smell the fake fur and what she now realized was foam, rubber, and latex. She wasn't dizzy anymore, but her footing still didn't feel steady and she didn't trust her aim.

She knew al-Aziz would use the lunging, lurching creatures for cover, would launch himself on her from behind them, with whatever bullets he had left.

Caitlin pushed herself the final stretch of the way, through the slog of her thoughts, which felt rich with slurry, time moving in jumps instead of a smooth sweep of a second hand. Almost to the final stretch of the Chamber of Horrors, the mechanical monsters that had haunted her youth poised to pounce from the shadows.

Caitlin almost tripped on a knee-high boulder made of papier-mâché. An idea struck her and she shoved it along, propelling it like a soccer ball to follow the general line of the track the cars rode along. Triggered into action, the monsters lunged out, one after another, claws and talons stretching over the reach of the rails.

A shape trailed them, removed from the camouflage they provided, a shape that merged with their collective menace as Caitlin opened up with her SIG. She fired until the slide locked open, her ears burning from the percussion inside the close quarters.

A mixture of fur, rubber, and plastic fluttered through the air, which was rich with the scent of glue instead of blood. Her bullets had tumbled the monsters of her youth from their perches, left them in a heap on the floor.

Along with a monster from her present.

Hatim Abd al-Aziz, supreme military commander

of ISIS, lay on his back with his eyes open and glazed, amid the marble spheres loosed from the heads of the stitched-together skulls, which weren't nearly as terrifying as she recalled, after all.

Caitlin made sure he was dead and sank to her knees, conscious suddenly of a buzzing in her jeans pocket. She remembered she'd silenced her phone, and she drew it out to find a call coming in from Cort Wesley.

Daniel Cross hit St. Paul Street, following the flow of the crowd before him and looping around to head toward the entrance to the DART station, which was clearly visible across the Woodall Rodgers Freeway. His breath was already heaving, and his legs felt like deadweights. People were shoving their way past him like he wasn't even there. He turned back to check for possible pursuit, someone with a gun following him from the park.

So he never saw the old, scuffed boot that tripped him up. His face hit the pavement with a thud, scattering a bunch of people fleeing the park. Then he felt his head jerked up by the hair until he was facing an old man who looked like somebody had sucked the life from his face with a vacuum cleaner.

"Bet that hurt, son, didn't it?" said Captain D. W. Tepper, crouching to slap a pair of handcuffs in place as Pierre Beauchamp of the Royal Canadian Mounted Police watched, gun drawn, for anyone else who might be coming.

104

"Where the hell you been, Ranger?" Cort Wesley said, Caitlin finally answering her phone when he pulled into the McKinney Garage in downtown Houston and squeezed into a space meant for a compact car on the second level.

"You wouldn't believe me if I told you, Cort Wesley."

"Yeah? Well, you need to get the team to Houston."

"Houston?" she asked, the world seeming to be angled sharply to one side. "I'm all the way up in Dallas. Al-Aziz is dead. We got this licked."

"No we don't. Not even close."

"No way we're gonna get there in time, Cort Wesley," Caitlin told him, after he'd quickly sketched out what they were facing. "No way."

"Then tell me what I'm dealing with," he said, bypassing the elevator for the stairwell that descended into the swirling length of tunnels that ran beneath the city. "Tell me about this shit that ISIS is going to blow up."

"Did you say *blow up*?"

"I did."

"Then, as bad as you thought things were," Caitlin said, thinking of what she now knew about the weapon bred from waters deep beneath the Comanche reservation, "they just got a whole lot worse . . ."

Caitlin's head was throbbing even more by the time she finished explaining to Cort Wesley what he was up against—a mutant strain of corn fungus turned into a weapon of mass destruction.

"The Comanche have hundreds of pounds of the stuff stored away, Ranger," he said, when she'd finished.

"Did you say *hundreds*?"

"Close, anyway. I saw it for myself. Minus maybe ten backpacks' worth that's currently in the hands of ISIS. Enough to kill a whole lot of people in the tunnels beneath Houston. Confined space, poor ventilation . . . A smell could last a good long while, at least 'til everyone down there's dead."

"How'd they put something like that together so fast?"

"They didn't; Ela and her cousins did. It's their plan, their backpacks. And they're all dead now, Ela included."

"Dylan?" Caitlin posed fearfully.

"With me, though I wouldn't say safe and sound, exactly."

Caitlin was running it all through her mind: how Dylan had been set up; where the Lost Boys fit into the picture; the mixed-up motivations of Ela Nocona, no doubt influenced by her grandfather, who was still fighting the wars of the nineteenth century; ISIS showing up on the Comanche Indian reservation, thanks to Daniel Cross.

"Ranger?"

"I'm here, Cort Wesley."

"Any thoughts?"

"What time is it?"

"Closing on five o'clock."

"Rush hour," Caitlin told him, the words echoing painfully in her head. "That's when the ISIS fighters will set off these bombs. There'll be thousands of people down there then, tens of thousands. What about turning the Houston police into the cavalry?"

"Only if you want to guarantee that ISIS sets the bombs off at the first sight of cops supervising a mass evacuation."

Caitlin tried to do some calculations in her head, but it was like drawing on a blackboard without chalk, so she started for the Chamber of Horrors exit instead, the world gone all wobbly again. "I can round up Jones, Paz, and whoever else I can rope in. Get back to our Black Hawks."

"Black Hawks or not, there's no way you can get here in time. Leave this up to me."

"Against, what, maybe ten ISIS fighters?"

"I've got Dylan with me."

"He's still just a kid, Cort Wesley."

Cort Wesley glanced at his oldest son, remembered him looking up from the body of Ela Nocona.

She's dead, son.

I think I knew that.

"But he's got this coming to him. And I can hardly

hear what you're saying. Where the hell are you, Ranger?"

Caitlin realized her speech was slurred. "A Chamber of Horrors, at a carnival."

"No, really."

105

HOUSTON, TEXAS

The tunnels felt like an airport concourse to Cort Wesley, this section of the Downtown Loop crammed with shops and stores layered amid winding stretches of tiled walls, with lighting perched on either side of the ceilings forming a ribbon of brightness stretching as far ahead as he could see. The pedestrian thoroughfares featured backlit signage tracing the entire sprawling, checkerboard length of the tunnels. Symbols and signs clearly denoted where an observer was standing in relation to where he might want to go. The immediate neighborhood above was highlighted as a yellow outline traced over royal-blue markings. Ideal refuge from the heat, bad weather, and cluttered streets above.

It wasn't nearly as crowded as Cort Wesley had feared, but rush hour hadn't officially started yet. That thought made him wonder whether the deadly aroma concentrated down here might leak out to the streets above and claim victims there as well. The mere possibility was too awful to even contemplate.

"Jesus," Dylan said, scratching at his scalp. "How far did you say this goes?"

"A hundred city blocks, give or take a few, this section maybe the most congested of all."

"Oh, that makes me feel a lot better." Now Dylan still had his father's Smith & Wesson. It was the first time he'd actually carried a gun, and the possibility that he was going to need to use it was suddenly very real. "So here we are. What's the plan, Dad?"

From his pocket, Cort Wesley took Ela's blood-stained map that featured ten red Xs designating those choke points along the Downtown Loop handling the spill of pedestrians from Houston's most congested business area. Soon to be packed with mothers and fathers heading home to their families, having no idea what awaited them. He figured all the bombs would be triggered together. And, given the fluctuating signal strength down here, the ISIS fighters would likely remain close to wherever they'd planted their respective backpacks, right up until the last moment. Dial the triggering number and then dash up the nearest exit stairs before the deadly aroma began to spread. Or hold their positions until the last moments before Zero Hour on the chance plans changed at the last minute.

"So what do we do?" Dylan said, gazing at the map. "Divide them up or something?"

Cort Wesley shook his head. "Sorry, son."

"About what?"

"Caitlin's right."

"About *what*?"

"I'd like you to sit this one out."

Dylan's eyes widened. "You said I had this coming to me. I heard you."

"I know, and you do. This is just the way it has to be."

"Because you say so."

"Because I say so. Wait for me at the food court down that way," Cort Wesley said, pointing east. "Things go bad, get your ass out of there. And hold your breath."

106

HOUSTON, TEXAS

Cort Wesley moved toward the closest X on Ela's map covering the Downtown Loop, pondering exactly how the ISIS fighters, and the young Comanche before them, intended to pull this off, as he weaved his way past a collection of retail stores, the names of which blurred into each other. There were covered concrete planters every few hundred feet or so, ornately concealing trash receptacles within. He quickly checked a few out and found them surprisingly free of refuse and thus perfect to plant the deadly bioweapon. Wouldn't even need much explosive to ignite the blasts and spread a mist in all directions, carrying the deadly aroma and rising and clinging to the walls and ceiling within such a confined space. Doubtful it would even dissipate, in that scenario, until everyone within its reach was dead.

Cort Wesley reached the first concrete planter marked with an X on the map Ela had given Dylan. He held back, inspecting the area for the right face, the right bent of eyes, a still figure among all the moving ones.

He found a young man he first took to be a girl,

thanks to hair clubbed back in a ponytail. The kid was pretending to push a broom, which he'd probably lifted from some maintenance closet. Cort Wesley headed in the kid's general direction, appearing to look past him.

Cort Wesley's eyes held there a moment too long, and the terrorist's eyes met his, thoughts and intentions freezing as the kid reached into his pocket. Maybe for a phone, maybe for a detonator, maybe for a weapon.

Cort Wesley wasn't about to wait any longer to find out. Before the kid's hand had cleared his pocket, Cort Wesley was on him, slamming the kid's head backwards until his skull cracked against one of the location markers. The glass lining it shattered, the impact strong enough to knock off all the interior lighting. The kid hung frozen there for an instant while Cort Wesley backed off as if nothing had happened. Then the kid slumped downward, leaving a wake of blood and glass above him.

Cort Wesley pretended to rush to his aid, perfect cover to check the kid's pockets for a phone, something he would use to communicate and perhaps to set off the explosives. His hand closed around a smart phone and pulled it out. The home screen was dominated by a timer, just ticking down below the twenty-minute mark.

Cort Wesley clicked off the timer, watching it reset and freeze at 00:00. He hoped that meant this particular batch of the deadly *cuitlacoche* had been deactivated, hoped he could get to the rest of the terrorists before those twenty minutes clicked down, hoped ISIS didn't have a backup plan in the form of a single operative who could trigger all the explosives at once.

Giving no further thought to the first man he'd downed, Cort Wesley moved on to the next red X on his map.

Dylan reached the food court, the tunnel widening to the size of a city block with restaurants crammed on both sides. He spotted a Wendy's, a Whataburger, a Salata, a Subway, and Beck's Prime, along with barbecue and sushi places he'd never heard of. Several jutted out at strange angles to conform to the spherical shape of this section of the tunnels. A collection of tables, benches, and thick plants lined the concourse before them. He figured the plants must be fake, given the soft, refractive hue of the lighting that made it seem somebody had turned the dimmer switch too far down. Various food smells flooded his nostrils, making him realize that the long, runway-like tunnel he'd taken here smelled of nothing at all, except for an industrial solvent in one patch where a slick spot and caution cones indicated a recent cleanup. He kept checking his watch as five o'clock approached, hoping to spot his father coming, as opposed to mass hysteria breaking out, in the upcoming minutes.

His dad had figured he'd be safe here, but that was wrong; he wouldn't be safe *anywhere*—no one would. Those days were gone, especially for him, as long as he kept putting himself in situations like this. Ela Nocona wasn't the first girl who'd manipulated him, but she had to be the last. Dylan promised himself that much, kind of a trade for him and his father getting out of this alive, along with everyone else currently occupying the tunnels of the Downtown Loop.

What was I thinking?

Walking away from school without a plan, missing spring football practice . . . for what exactly?

What was I thinking?

The more times Dylan asked himself that, the further he got from an answer. So he kept walking about the retail area, trying to sort it all out in his mind while he waited for his father.

Then Dylan spotted a bearded figure with a backpack slung over his shoulder, meandering around a concrete trash receptacle out in the open between a takeout sushi establishment and a Starbucks.

Cort Wesley had left four downed ISIS fighters in his wake, their cell phone timers now deactivated. The second fighter had been even easier to spot than the first, their eyes meeting briefly before Cort Wesley pounced, shoving him through a nearby stairwell door, where he launched a series of blows that dropped the kid in a heap. The few witnesses about kept their distance, and Cort Wesley didn't care whether they called the cops, response time being what it was. He'd be long gone from this area before anyone in uniform showed up.

A third fighter was huddled in a shadowy corner, and the fourth was close enough to a men's room to force him through the door and smash his head against a wall with enough force to drive fracture lines through the tile.

That man's timer had ticked below the five-minute

mark, leaving him that long to reach the remaining six terrorists.

"Hey, you!" a voice blared, when Cort Wesley emerged from the men's room. "Stop right there!"

A beat cop assigned to the tunnels, Cort Wesley saw; no, two of them. Both coming his way, giving chase when he ran.

Dylan approached the bearded man, pretending to be checking his cell phone, although never really taking his eyes off the man's backpack. At that point he was unsure of his own intentions, was still unsure when the man unslung the backpack from his shoulder and brought it around before him.

The man seemed ready to deposit the backpack in the nearest concrete trash container, when Dylan pounced. Dylan slammed into the guy as if he were a tackling dummy back at the football practice Dylan should've been attending right now. The impact drove both of them into a logjam of pedestrian traffic, Dylan using his shoulder to ram the man against the concrete wall.

He could feel the guy's bones crackle, seeming to recede and bounce back. The man's air escaped him in a thick whoosh as his backpack went flying. Hit the ground and scattered college textbooks in all directions.

The man's terrified eyes met Dylan's as he struggled for breath. Dylan backed off, hands in the air.

"Sorry, man. Sorry."

Plenty of people watching him, trying to ascertain

what had just happened, though keeping their distance. Among them, Dylan spotted a kid about his age silhouetted against the glow off a Wendy's sign, clutching a backpack before him as if it were a baby.

Getting away from the cops in the tunnels was easy; Cort Wesley ducked into a stairwell that led up into a big office tower and let them slip right past him The problem was the last terrorist he'd taken out, slammed into a bathroom wall, had seen Cort Wesley coming in time to backpedal for that door. Plenty of time to trigger his explosives, but he hadn't.

Because he couldn't.

Because there must be a single trigger man, the others remaining in place until the very last possible moment to ensure the bomb-laden backpacks they'd hidden remained undetected. Or maybe their intention was to all die down here, become martyrs to their cause.

Then his cell phone rang and he realized he'd neglected to silence it.

"We've got clearance to land in Sam Houston Park, Cort Wesley," Caitlin informed him over a helicopter's engine and rotor sounds.

"How long?"

"We'll be on the ground in five."

"Not soon enough. I'm in the tunnels. This is going down now."

"Dylan with you?" she asked, after a pause.

"Somewhere."

"Then get out of there, both of you."

"You know I can't do that, Ranger," he said, and ended the call.

Then he spun through the door back into the tunnels, heading for the location of the next red X on the map.

Dylan had his father's Smith & Wesson nine-millimeter drawn, steadied on the kid cradling his backpack, before he could rethink the action.

"Drop it!" Dylan said to him, the gun held in a trembling hand by his hip now. "Drop it now!"

The kid looked at him as people backed off, the bustling food court gone eerily quiet. It felt as if they were the only two people there, centered amid the benches and tables, the leaves of a pair of big plants shifting, as if brushed by the breeze.

"He's got a bomb!" Dylan yelled to all of them. "Everybody, run!" All his focus trained back on the kid now, imagining what his father or Caitlin would do or say, as a flood of commuters stampeded from the retail area. "Drop it! You hear me? Drop the backpack or I'll drop you!"

Much to Dylan's surprise, the kid before him let the backpack fall and raised his hands in the air. He was surprised, because it couldn't be this easy.

And it wasn't.

Because the kid was holding something black and flat in his hand. A smartphone.

The trigger. Why else would he be down here, so far away from the others standing in the shadow of an exit?

Shoot him! Dylan heard in his head.

But could he shoot a kid no older than him, no older than Ela? And could he really be sure—like, a hundred percent?

That thought formed just as the kid was maneuvering the phone in his grasp, getting his thumb into position. A single tap of a key was all it would take to trigger the explosives.

Dylan fired the Smith & Wesson, and kept firing. Not at the kid but above him. Into the big-ass sprinkler head, cream-colored to render it all but indistinguishable from the ceiling dotted with recessed fixtures spilling dim light downward. The sprinkler featured a closed head, with water in the pipe held back by a fusible link that would be triggered at maybe 150 or so degrees.

The bullets ruptured the head and punctured the link, releasing a steady stream of water directly over the kid maneuvering the phone in his hand. It slipped from his grasp and clacked to the floor, the kid lurching to retrieve it, when Dylan launched himself into motion.

He crashed into the kid, tackling him to the floor and preventing him from reaching the phone. A nearby table toppled over, spilling food to the polished floor. Dylan felt the air forced out of the kid, his whole sternum rattling on impact. He was still groping and flailing for the phone, Dylan watching big red letters counting down below the one-minute mark. He jammed his left elbow under the kid's chin to hold him in place and stretched his own right hand for the phone.

49, 48, 47 . . .

Almost there, the kid flailing at him, thrashing with his legs to no avail. Dylan grazed the phone casing with one finger, then another, feeling for the screen.

37, 36, 35 . . .

The kid was biting his other hand now, sinking his teeth in deep. Dylan gutted through the pain, kept stretching his fingers outward, aiming for the PAUSE button on the screen.

30, 29, 28 . . .

The kid kept biting. Dylan kept stretching, jerking himself sideways as the kid bit down harder. His index finger was over the glass now and lowering, finding PAUSE. Watching the screen freeze at *22* after he touched it with his finger. Then he managed to get the whole phone in his grasp and slammed it again and again into the floor, spitting pieces of glass and metal in all directions until the thing was barely recognizable as a phone at all.

Dylan stayed on top of the kid, pinning him, until a pair of cops yanked him off. As two more Houston officers stood with guns drawn, one of those cops pressed Dylan down right next to the kid and started to slap the handcuffs on.

The kid wasn't much older than him—the home-grown version, for sure, who'd probably spent the past few years waging make-believe war on shooting ranges and meeting in dark, dingy basements with the windows blacked out. Dylan met his hate-filled eyes, returning a glare the kid probably practiced in the mirror.

"That was for Ela," Dylan managed, with half his face still pressed hard against the tile, "you piece of shit."

EPILOGUE

The Rangers were here before there was a Texas, and we have survived all that time. Now, we didn't survive because we were good at riding horses. We didn't survive because we can hunt or camp out on the prairie. We survived by being able to change with the times. When Texas needed Indian fighters, we were Indian fighters. When Texas needed border war fighters, we were that. When Texas needed someone to quell oil boom riots, we did that. When Texas needed detectives, we became that. When DNA became the mainstay of law enforcement work, we got good at that. We've had to change, and there have been some growing pains along the way. We have tripped and stumbled, and we've had times that were not our finest hours. But by and large we've had more successes than we've had misses. And we're going to keep changing and evolving so we're still here a hundred years from now.

—Ranger Matt Cawthon, in *Tracking the Texas Rangers: The Twentieth Century,* edited by Bruce A. Glasrud and Harold J. Weiss, Jr. (Denton: University of North Texas Press, 2013)

"I'm really proud to be addressing you today," Caitlin said to the students and families gathered on the football field of the Village School, which was adorned with the Vikings logo and the school color, navy blue. "I'd like to talk to you about a lot of things, but mostly I'd like to talk about bravery."

She focused on Dylan, Cort Wesley, and Luke, who were seated in the front row with the other dignitaries at the graduation ceremony. Beyond them was a sea of gowns, caps, and tassels, soon to be flipped from one side to the other before the caps were launched airborne. The warm air smelled fresh and clean, almost like incense. The scent of hope, Caitlin thought to herself, in stark contrast to skunk oil or, worse, the deadly *cuitlacoche* that had come ever so close to killing thousands, just a few miles away, beneath downtown Houston.

"There's a boy who goes to this school who's about the bravest person I know, because he's not afraid to be who he is. Folks like to think that gets easier as you get older, but it's really not true. It only seems that way because, by then, most have given up trying. The difference between someone special and someone ordinary is that the one who's special never gives up, no matter the odds. And the young man I'm talking about had the odds stacked against him, and it's a credit to you folks out there that he's been accepted here for who he is and has found a home."

Cheers and applause interrupted her remarks. Caitlin was glad for that and, even more, for Luke's smile. She had no speech, just a few notes scribbled on some composition paper torn from a pad she'd bought at a drug store, the fringe fluttering atop the podium before her on the stage. She wore the clothes she always wore, because she figured that's what people expected from her and would feel most comfortable with. Jeans and a light-blue shirt, Texas Ranger badge pinned to her chest, holstered SIG Sauer clipped to her belt.

As the applause started to die down, she focused on Dylan and Cort Wesley, who were still clapping the hardest of anyone.

"I haven't decided if I'm going back to school," Dylan had told Caitlin and Cort Wesley the week before, out of nowhere, while they sat on the front porch. "I'm going to need some more time."

"Doesn't seem like a difficult decision to me," Cort Wesley said.

"I've got some stuff I need to sort out, Dad."

"Like what?"

"Stuff. I'm tired of getting involved with people who change me."

"Ela?" Caitlin said to him.

"I go back there, she's all I'll think of. What's the point?"

Cort Wesley remained restrained. "Getting past it, son."

"That's easy for you—for both of you—isn't it? But I'm not like that. I want to be, but I'm not." Dylan swept the hair from his face and swallowed hard. "Why do you figure she changed her mind?"

"Because somebody finally changed her," Caitlin told him.

"Texas is full of brave folks, now and in the past," Caitlin resumed, after checking her notes, finally used to the garbled feedback of her own voice from the speakers. "I'm the fifth in my family to become a Texas Ranger. The first was named Steeldust Jack Strong, and he fought for anyone who was in the right, out of a sense of duty. The Comanche, for example, against none other than John D. Rockefeller. He witnessed the Comanche burn their own land to deny it to Standard Oil. Most figure that was the end of the story, but it wasn't. Rockefeller had a hatred for Texas that knew no bounds, and he saw his opportunity to get his revenge, once the first oil boom hit, with that strike in Corsicana in 1894. Figured he could move in and pretty much buy up the state. Turned out he didn't know Texas and he didn't know Texans, especially one named Steeldust Jack Strong."

New York; 1895

John D. Rockefeller was almost always the first one into Standard Oil headquarters on 26 Broadway, where it had moved from Cleveland a decade before. He liked nothing better than to see the sunrise from his office window. But, on this morning, he entered to see his chair already occupied by a grizzled, unshaven man smoking one of his cigars.

"'Morning, Mr. Rockefeller," Jack Strong greeted him, lifting his boots up atop the man's desk. "I hope you don't mind me making myself comfortable while I was waiting for you."

"How'd you get in here?"

"Why, I took the train, of course. My first time out of Texas since the Civil War."

Recognition flashed in Rockefeller's eyes, along with the loathing stirred by the memories of their previous encounters. "Then you've never seen a Northern jail."

"No, sir, I have not. Just like you've never seen the inside of a Texas jail—or any cell, for that matter. I don't do much rangering no more. Figure it's better left to younger folk like my own son, William Ray, who made this here trip with me, on account of he didn't want to miss the fun."

"There's laws against carrying guns in New York, Ranger."

Steeldust Jack lowered his boots from the desk, the effort clearly paining him, the years having treated his bad leg unkindly. "That's fine, 'cause I didn't bring one. Did bring this, though," he said, sliding a set of trifold pages from his pants pocket.

Rockefeller took the document in hand tentatively, almost as if he expected it to burn his fingers. "What's this?"

"A writ signed by Texas governor Jim Hogg, serving notice of suspension of Standard Oil's business licenses in the State of Texas, subject to investigation for violations of the Sherman Antitrust statutes."

"You have any idea what you just said, Ranger?"

"Not really, but it sounded mighty official, didn't it? It's the truth, too."

Rockefeller gave the writ a quick read. "None of this makes any sense."

"And we'll look forward to you proving that in a Texas court of law."

Rockefeller tore the writ in two. "This will never stand up."

"You can fight it all the way to the Supreme Court, but you'll have to go through Texas to do that—definitely something you may want to think twice about. You don't have a lot of friends where I come from. I've heard told workmen you've fired and small businessmen you've ruined use your picture for target practice." Steeldust Jack pushed himself to his feet, using the desk for support. "I'm here today to tell you that the moment your train comes to a stop in Austin, all the men you wronged, white and Indian, will be waiting. Sounds like a one-way trip to me."

"You and the goddamn Texas Rangers are nothing more than historical artifacts, no different than dinosaur bones. You just don't know it yet."

"You're the one who'll soon be history, Mr. Rockefeller. I'm making it my mission to let the country know what kind of man you really are. A bully and a braggart who never waged a fight when he didn't have his hired guns backing him up. You know what's good for you, you'll start keeping a lower profile, given I heard there's a price on your head," Steeldust Jack said, fitting his hat back on and hobbling for the door.

"You come here to collect it, Ranger?"

"No, sir. I'm the one who put up the cash."

———

"John D. Rockefeller retired from Standard Oil the following year," Caitlin finished, "and, according to legend, never set foot in the state of Texas again."

Caitlin trained her gaze on Cort Wesley, Luke, and Dylan again. She noticed Captain Tepper standing in the back, not far from Jones and Guillermo Paz. She'd been a guest caller last week at a bingo game in the retirement community where Paz volunteered, and it was hard to say whether she felt any more gratified by this honor than by that one.

"But I guess I'm supposed to talk about the future," Caitlin told the one hundred forty graduating seniors of the Village School and their families, along with hundreds more underclassmen and other invited guests. "The truth is, there was a time when I didn't think about it a whole lot. Then some people came into my life who changed all that in me, and plenty more. All of you are going on to college—every single one, I'm told—and plenty of you are going to some of the very best ones, and from there to great careers. I hope you find yourself loving what you do as much as I do, but it won't matter where you go if you don't have the right people with you when you get there, 'cause that's really what it's all about."

The cheers and applause were much louder this time. Caitlin nodded toward Cort Wesley and the boys as it died down.

"There's mostly good in the world, but there's bad, too. John D. Rockefeller didn't set out to do bad, but he did plenty here in Texas, until Jack Strong stood up

STRONG COLD DEAD 449

against him. Men like Steeldust Jack keep the bad
down. They stand their ground against those fixed on
doing harm to others. They do the right thing. I'm here
talking to you today because people think I'm a hero,
but I'm really not. The real heroes are that boy I mentioned earlier, who isn't ashamed of who he is, and his
older brother, who's seen what true evil looks like,
more times than I can count, and never let the sight
change who he is. I hope you never see that sight, but
I suspect you will. Don't let it change you, because
that's how the bad wins and the good loses. You might
not beat it, but don't let it beat you, either."

She let her gaze drift over the crowd again, refreshed
and recharged by the energy and hope radiating from
these young people who, for this day anyway, were in
complete ownership of their lives.

"Because, the thing is, evil exists. It's real and it's out
there," she said, thinking of ISIS, both homegrown
elements and otherwise.

The remainder of the deadly strain of the corn fungus, the *cuitlacoche,* had been removed from the underground storage chamber, and a thorough search of the
reservation land had turned up no additional hidden
reserves. Jones had told Caitlin those reserves would be
"dispatched appropriately"—his phrase, spoken with a
smirk. As far as the water responsible for turning the
corn fungus into a deadly toxin, seismic specialists were
in the process of devising a strategy to seal the underground reserves as much as five miles down, render
them inaccessible to the likes of both Daniel Cross and
Cray Rawls. The opening to the cave with the still pond,
found by Daniel Cross, had been sealed, and serious

thought was being given to temporarily evacuating the entire population of the reservation.

New evidence, meanwhile, had mysteriously surfaced in cases involving Cray Rawls and his consortium of energy companies, leading a number of investigations to be reopened. That would ensure that the bulk of his time over the ensuing years would be spent in court or fretting over the eventual loss of the empire he'd built with his inheritance from the couple who had been roasted to death as payment for adopting him.

And he wasn't alone.

Jones had let Caitlin see Daniel Cross alone before he was placed in total isolation, save for his lawyers. She sat on the other side of a thick glass partition inside ADX Florence, the ultra–maximum security prison in Fremont County, Colorado, where Cross was being held, while two armed guards fixed manacles onto his arms and legs.

"I guess you remember me," he said, voice weak and almost shy.

"Yes, Daniel. I do."

"I don't suppose I should thank you for coming."

"Actually, I wanted to apologize."

His gaze narrowed, as if trying to gauge her intentions. "It wasn't your fault. You're not to blame."

"Yes, I am," Caitlin told him. "I'm to blame for not letting you do some time in juvie. Maybe if you'd spent the rest of your teen years there, we wouldn't be looking at each other right now. So, yes, I'm to blame for thinking a second chance would steer you clear of trouble."

"I'll bet you wish you could take it back," he said, looking identical in that moment to the fourteen-year-old boy, handcuffed to an interrogation table in an Austin jail, whom she'd met ten years before. Only this time, Caitlin felt no sympathy.

"I guess I do," she told Daniel Cross. "I needed to come here just to see how I got things so wrong. And looking at you through this glass makes me think of somebody else, somebody a little younger than you, who believes he can save anybody too. Now I realize I should be listening to the same advice I gave him—that some people aren't worth the bother; the key is the ability to tell which is which."

Cross's expression grew cold and flat. "Know what? I wish I had built that bomb. I wish I had blown up that school and killed all the assholes. Tell me the world wouldn't have been a better place with all of them in hell."

Caitlin rose, having had enough. "Only if you got there first, Daniel."

"I can't tell you exactly what evil is," she continued, meeting Dylan's gaze down in the front row, "only that I know it when I see it, just like you need to do. Because evil is at its best when it's hiding among us, in places we least expect, in the hearts of people we expected better from. If I had one piece of advice to give you today, it would probably be to never disappoint anyone, least of all yourself. I think one of the things that sets evil people apart is that, while they hate a whole bunch of folks, mostly they hate themselves.

"I'm looking out over you today and I want to believe none of you will become like that, except the truth is I really can't say for sure—nobody can. What I can say for sure today is that fate is yours to control, and nobody else's. So I want you to remember this moment, remember this day. Keep it frozen in your mind so you never lose track of the way you feel right now. Because the day you stop feeling that way is the day you may find yourself becoming somebody you don't want to be."

Caitlin had stopped checking her notes, was veering entirely from her intended remarks. Her mind waxed whimsically, applying the lessons she'd learned in her own life, with no way to gauge whether she was striking a chord with the graduating seniors of the Village School at all.

As her speech neared its close, Caitlin thought she caught a fleeting glimpse of her father and grandfather standing along the back of the seated graduates, where shadows and light merged. But today Earl and Jim Strong had been joined by William Ray and Steeldust Jack, their shadowy silhouettes lost to the wind before Caitlin could wave their way. She knew she didn't have to, because they'd been there with her yesterday and would be there again tomorrow. Texas Rangers for life and beyond.

"I hope you all learn lots of times what it feels like to win. And I hope, just as much, you learn how to lose," Caitlin said, letting her gaze wander over the crowd, where a soaring red-tailed hawk dipped and darted about, having reclaimed the sky. "'Cause nobody wins all the time, but the thing is, that doesn't stop us from trying."

AUTHOR'S NOTE

So I'm reading the *New York Times,* back on December 29, 2014, when I come across the front-page headline reading, "Where Oil, Corruption and Bodies Surface." Turns out the article was about the Fort Berthold Indian Reservation in North Dakota. Being a thriller writer, though, I asked myself what if it were an Indian reservation in Texas? And what if it turns out not to be oil at the root of the evil at all, but something else?

At that point, I had no idea what that "something" was. I had a vague notion that one party would be after the secret for its potentially miraculous medicinal qualities, while somebody else would be after it for its potential as a weapon of mass destruction. And for the bad guys, how about ISIS coming to Texas to be taken on by Caitlin Strong and company?

Maybe a third into the book, I still didn't know what had actually been discovered on my fictional Texas Indian reservation. (The Comanche reservation depicted in this book exists only in my imagination.) Then my brilliant agent, Natalia Aponte, mentioned this substance called *cuitlacoche,* a corn fungus that's been turned into a kind of delicacy by Native Americans as well as ancient Indian tribes going all the way back to the Aztecs. In that moment, *boom!* I knew I had my book, grounded in just enough reality to make it credible, especially after my research confirmed the existence of so-called aroma bombs.

I took my share of technological liberties here, as I did with John D. Rockefeller. I believe I've portrayed him accurately and also credibly, except for the fact that his early years of oil exploration in building Standard Oil didn't include Texas. But, as I've quoted before from the brilliant film *The Man Who Shot Liberty Valence,* "When the legend becomes fact, print the legend." And incorporating actual personalities into the historical subplots my Caitlin Strong books are known for is, well, a blast. Just a whole lot of fun.

And that's what these books are supposed to be—a whole lot of fun. Both for me to write and you to read. If this is your first visit to the world of Caitlin Strong, the good news is you've got some catching up to do. Either way, rest assured that Caitlin will be back, around the same time next year, in *Strong to the Bone* (tentative title). Just don't ask me what it's about yet, because I have no idea, other than to say we're both going to have a whole lot of fun with it again. A sacred promise from writer to reader.

So be well until then, and keep reading!

Providence, Rhode Island; January 6, 2016

Read on for a preview of

STRONG
TO THE
BONE

Jon Land

•

Available in December
from Tom Doherty Associates

A FORGE HARDCOVER

I

AUSTIN, TEXAS

"What the hell?"

Caitlin Strong and Cort Wesley Masters had just emerged from Esther's Follies on East Sixth Street, when they saw the stream of people hurrying down the road, gazes universally cocked back behind them. Sirens blared off in the distance and a steady chorus of honking horns seemed to be coming from an adjoining block just past the street affectionately known as "Dirty Sixth," Austin's version of Bourbon Street in New Orleans.

"Couldn't tell you," Cort Wesley said, even as he sized up the scene. "But I got a feeling we're gonna know before much longer."

Caitlin was in town to speak at a national law enforcement conference focusing on homegrown terrorism, and both her sessions at the Austin Convention Center had been jam-packed. She felt kind of guilty her presentations had lacked the audiovisual touches many of the others had featured. But the audiences hadn't seemed to mind, filling a sectioned-off ballroom to the gills to hear of her direct experiences, in contrast to theoretical dissertations by experts. Audiences were comprised of cops a lot like her, looking to bring something back home they could actually use. She'd focused to a great extent on her most recent battle with ISIS right here in Texas, and an al-Qaeda cell a few years before that, stressing how much things had changed in the interim and how much more they were likely to.

Cort Wesley had driven up from San Antonio to meet her for a rare night out that had begun with dinner at Ancho's inside the Omni Hotel and then a stop at Antone's nightclub to see the Rats, a band headed by a Texas Ranger tech expert known as Young Roger. From there, they'd walked to Esther's Follies to take in the famed Texas-centric improv show there, a first for both of them that was every bit as funny and entertaining as advertised, even with a gun-toting woman both Caitlin and Cort Wesley realized was based on her.

Fortunately, no one else in the audience made that connection and they managed to slip out ahead of the rest of the crowd. Once outside, though, they were greeted by a flood of pedestrians pouring up the street from an area of congestion a few blocks down, just past Eighth Street.

"What you figure, Ranger?"

"That maybe we better go have ourselves a look."

2

Caitlin practically collided with a young man holding a wad of napkins against his bleeding nose at the intersection with East Seventh Street.

"What's going on?" she asked him, pulling back her blazer to show her Texas Ranger badge.

The young man looked from it back to her, swallowing some blood and hacking it up onto the street. "University of Texas graduation party took over all of Stubb's Barbecue," he said, pointing in the restaurant's direction. "Guess you could say it got out of hand. Bunch of fraternities going at it." He looked at the badge pinned to her chest again. "Are you really a Texas Ranger?"

"You need to get to an emergency room," Caitlin told him, and pressed on with Cort Wesley by her side.

"Kid was no older than Dylan," he noted, mentioning his oldest son who was still on a yearlong leave from Brown University.

"How many fraternities does the University of Texas at Austin have anyway, Cort Wesley?"

"A whole bunch."

"Yeah." She nodded, continuing on toward the swell of bodies and flashing lights. "It sure looks that way."

Stubb's was well known for its barbecue offerings and, just as much, its status as a concert venue. The interior was modest in size, as Caitlin recalled, two floors with the bottom level normally reserved for private parties and the upstairs generally packed with patrons both old and new. The rear of the main building, and several adjoining ones, featured a flattened dirt lot fronted by several performance stages where upward of two thousand people could enjoy live music in the company of three sprawling outdoor bars.

That meant this graduation party gone bad may have featured at least a comparable number of students and probably even more, many of whom remained in the street, milling about as altercations continued to flare, while first responders struggled futilely to disperse the crowd. Young men and women still swigging bottles of beer, while pushing and shoving each other. The sound of glass breaking rose over the loudening din of the approaching sirens, the whole scene glowing amid the colors splashed from the revolving lights of the Austin police cars already on the scene.

A fire engine leading a rescue wagon screeched to a halt just ahead of Cort Wesley and Caitlin, at the intersection with Seventh Street, beyond which had become impassable.

"Dylan could even be here, for all I know," Cort Wesley said, picking up his earlier train of thought.

"He doesn't go to UT."

"But there's girls and trouble, two things he excels at the most."

This as fights continued breaking out one after another, splinters of violence on the verge of erupting into an all-out brawl going on under the spill of the LED streetlights rising over Stubb's.

Caitlin pictured swirling lines of already drunk patrons being refused admittance due to capacity issues. Standing in line full of alcohol on a steamy night, expectations of a celebratory evening dashed, was a recipe for just what she was viewing now. In her mind, she saw fights breaking out between rival UT fraternities mostly in the outdoor performance area, before spilling out into the street, fueled by simmering tempers now on high heat.

"You see any good we can be here?" Cort Wesley asked her.

Caitlin was about to say no, when she spotted an anxious Austin patrol cop doing his best to break up fights that had spread as far as Seventh Street. She and Cort Wesley sifted through the crowd and made their way toward him, Caitlin advancing alone when they drew close.

"Anything I can do to help?" she said, reading the Austin policeman's name tag, "Officer Hilton?"

Hilton leaned up against an ornate light pole that looked like gnarled wrought iron for support. He was breathing hard, his face scraped and bruised. He noted the Texas Ranger badge and seemed to match her face to whatever media reports he'd remembered her from.

"Not unless you got enough Moses in you to part the Red Sea out there, Ranger."

"What brought you boys out here? Detail work?" Caitlin asked, trying to account for his presence on scene so quickly, ahead of the sirens screaming through the night.

Hilton shook his head. "An anonymous nine-one-one call about a sexual assault taking place inside the club, the downstairs lounge."

"And you didn't go inside?"

Hilton turned his gaze on the street, his breathing picking up again. "Through *that*? My partner tried and ended up getting his skull cracked open by a bottle. I damn near got killed fighting to reach him. Managed to get him in the back of our squad car and called for a rescue," he said, casting his gaze toward the fire engine and ambulance that were going nowhere. "Think maybe I better carry him to the hospital myself."

"What about the girl?"

"What girl?"

"Sexual assault victim inside the club."

Hilton frowned. "Most of them turn out to be false alarms anyway."

"Do they now?"

Caitlin's tone left him sneering at her. "Look, Ranger, you want to shoot up the street to get inside that shithole, be my guest. I'm not leaving my partner."

"Thanks for giving me permission," she said, and steered back for Cort Wesley.

"That looked like it went well," he noted, pushing a frat boy who'd ventured too close out of the way, after stripping the empty beer bottle he was holding by the neck from his grasp.

"Sexual assault victim might still be inside, Cort Wesley."

"Shit."

"Yeah."

"Got any ideas, Ranger?"

Caitlin eyed the fire engine stranded where East Seventh Street met Red River Avenue. "Just one."

3

AUSTIN, TEXAS

Four firemen were gathered behind the truck in a tight cluster, speaking with the two paramedics from the rescue wagon.

"I'm a Texas Ranger," Caitlin announced, approaching them with jacket peeled back to reveal her badge, "and I'm commandeering your truck."

"You're *what*?" one of the fireman managed. "No, absolutely not!"

The siren began blaring and lights started flashing, courtesy of Cort Wesley who'd climbed up behind the wheel.

"Sorry," Caitlin said, raising her voice above the din, "can't hear you!"

The crowd that filled the street in front of Stubb's Barbecue saw and heard the fire truck coming and began pelting it with bottles, as it edged forward through the congested street that smelled of sweat and beer. What looked like steam hung in the stagnant air overhead, either an illusion or the actual product of so many superheated bodies congealed in such tight quarters. The sound of glass breaking crackled through Caitlin's ears, as bottle after bottle smashed against the truck's frame.

The crowd clustered tighter around the fire engine, cutting off Cort Wesley's way backward or on toward Stubb's. The students, their fervor and aggression bred by alcohol, never noticed Caitlin's presence atop the truck until she finally figured out the workings of the truck's deck gun and squeezed the nozzle.

The force of the water bursting out of the barrel nearly knocked her backward off the truck. But she managed to right and then reposition herself, as she doused the tight cluster of students between the truck and the restaurant entrance with the gun's powerful stream.

A wave of people tried to fight the flow and ended up getting blown off their feet, thrown into other students who then scrambled to avoid the fire engine's surge forward ahead of its deafening horn. Caitlin continued to clear a path for Cort Wesley, sweeping the deck gun in light motions from side to side, the five-hundred-gallon tank still plenty full when the club entrance drew within clear view.

She felt the fire engine's front wheels mount the sidewalk and twist heavily to the right. The front fender grazed the building and took out a plate glass window the rioting had somehow spared. Caitlin saw a gap in the crowd open all the way to the entrance and leaped down from the truck to take advantage of it, before it closed up again.

She purposely didn't draw her gun and entered

Stubb's to the sight of bloodied bouncers and staff herding the last of the patrons out of the restaurant. Outside, the steady blare of sirens told her the Austin police had arrived in force. Little they could do to disperse a crowd this large and unruly in rapid fashion, though, much less reach the entrance to lend their efforts to Caitlin's in locating the sexual assault victim.

She threaded her way through the ground floor of Stubb's to the stairs leading down to the private lounge area. The air felt like it was being blasted out of a steam oven, roiled with coagulated body heat untouched by the restaurant's air-conditioning that left Caitlin with the sense she was descending to hell.

Reaching the windowless sublevel floor, she swept her eyes about and thought she heard a whimpering come from a nest of couches, where a male figure hovered over the frame of a woman, lying half on and half off a sectional couch.

"Sir, put your hands in the air and turn around slowly!" Caitlin ordered, drawing her SIG-Sauer nine-millimeter pistol. "Don't make me tell you twice!"

He started to turn, without raising his hands, and Caitlin fired when she glimpsed something shiny in his grasp. Impact to the shoulder twisted the man around and spilled him over the sectional couch, Caitlin holding her SIG at the ready as she approached his victim.

She heard the whimpering again, making her think more of the sound a dog makes, and followed it toward a tight cluster of connected couch sections, their cushions all stained wet and smelling thickly of beer. Drawing closer while still keeping a sharp eye on the man she'd shot, Caitlin spotted a big smart phone lying just out of his grasp, recognizing it as the object she'd wrongly taken for a gun. Then Caitlin spied a young woman of college age pinned between a pair of couch sections, covering her exposed breasts with her arms, her torn blouse hanging off her and jeans unbuttoned and unzipped just short of her hips.

Drawing closer, Caitlin saw the young woman's assailant, the man she'd just shot, in all likelihood must've yanked them down so violently that he'd split the zipper and torn off the snap or button.

"Ma'am?" she called softly.

The young woman tightened herself into a ball and retreated deeper into the darkness between the couch sections, not seeming to hear her.

"Ma'am," Caitlin said louder, hovering over the coed while continuing to check on the man she'd shot, his eyes drifting in and out of consciousness, his shirt wet with blood in the shoulder area from the gunshot wound.

Caitlin only wished it was her own attacker lying there, from all those years before when she'd been a coed herself at the Lone Star College campus in the Houston suburb of Kingwood. Some memories suppressed easily, others were like a toothache that came and went. That one was more like a cavity that had been filled, forgotten until the filling broke off and raw nerve pain flared.

Caitlin pushed the couch sections aside and knelt by the young woman, pistol tucked low by her hip so as not to frighten her further.

"I'm a Texas Ranger, ma'am," she said, in as soothing a voice as she could manage. "I need to get you out of here, and I need you to help me. I need to know if you can walk."

The young woman finally looked at her, nodded. Her left cheek was swollen badly and one of her arms hung limply from its socket. Caitlin looked back at the downed form of the man she'd already shot once, half hoping he gave her a reason to shoot him again.

"What's your name? Mine's Caitlin."

"Kelly Ann," the young woman said, her voice dry and cracking.

Caitlin helped her to her feet. "Well, Kelly Ann, I know things feel real bad right now, but trust me when I tell you this is as bad as they're going to get."

Kelly Ann's features perked up slightly, her eyes flashing back to life. She tried to take a deep breath, but stopped halfway though.

Caitlin held her around the shoulders in one arm, SIG clutched in her free hand while her eyes stayed peeled on the downed man's stirring form. "I'm going to stay with you the whole way until we get you some help," she promised.

The building suddenly felt like a Fun House Hall of Mirrors. Everything distorted, perspective and sense of place lost. Even the stairs climbing back to the ground floor felt different, only the musty smell of sweat mixed with stale perfume and body spray telling her they were the same.

Caitlin wanted to tell Kelly Ann it would be all right, that it would get better, that it would all go away in time. But that would be a lie, so she said nothing at all. Almost to the door, she gazed toward a loose assemblage of frat boys wearing hoodies displaying their letters as they chugged from liquor bottles stripped from the shelves behind the main bar on the first floor. How different were they from the one who'd hurt her, hurt Kelly Ann?

Caitlin wanted to shoot the bottles out of their hands, but kept leading Kelly Ann on instead, out into the night and the vapor spray from the deck gun now being wielded by Cort Wesley to keep their route clear.

" 'Bout time!" he shouted down, scampering across the truck's top to retake his place behind the wheel.

Caitlin was already inside the cab, Kelly Ann clinging tightly to her.

"Where to, Ranger?"

"Seton Medical Center, Cort Wesley."

Before he got going, Caitlin noticed Officer Hilton and several other Austin cops pushing their way through the crowd toward the entrance to Stubb's.

"Don't worry, Officer, I got the victim out safe and sound," she yelled down to him, only half-sarcastically. "But I left a man with a bullet in his shoulder down there for you to take care of."

"Come again?"

"I'd hurry, if I were you. He's losing blood."